THE BIG PICTURE

THE BIG PICTURE

PICTURE

Douglas Kennedy

HYPERION

New York

Excerpt from *The Decisive Moment* reprinted with the
permission of Simon & Schuster from *The Decisive Moment*
by Henri Cartier-Bresson (New York: Simon & Schuster, 1952).

Library of Congress Cataloging-in-Publication Data

Kennedy, Douglas, 1955–
The big picture / Douglas Kennedy. — 1st ed.
p.   cm.
ISBN 0-7868-6298-X
I.   Title.
PR6061.E5956B54   1997
813'.54—dc21   96–44446
                                                    CIP

Designed by Helene Berinsky

FIRST EDITION

10 9 8 7 6 5 4 3 2 1

For Amelia Kennedy,
and for Grace and Max

Beware lest you lose the substance by grasping at the shadow.

—AESOP

PART ONE

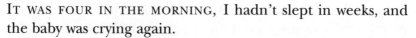

IT WAS FOUR IN THE MORNING, I hadn't slept in weeks, and the baby was crying again.

The baby didn't wake me because I'd been staring at the ceiling for hours when he started bawling. But I was so shell-shocked from lack of proper rest that I couldn't move from the bed. For several numbing minutes, I just lay there, rigid, as Josh pushed his five-month-old lungs to new extremes.

Eventually, his repetitive shrieks prodded my wife, Beth, into a dazed, half-awake state. Nudging me with her elbow, she spoke to me for the first time in two days.

"You deal with him." Then she rolled over and covered her head with a pillow.

I did as ordered, my movements mechanical, tentative. I sat up. I put my feet on the floor. I reached over for the striped bathrobe that had been flung on a bedside chair. I put it on over my matching striped pajamas, tying it tightly around my waist. I walked to the door and opened it. My day had begun—though, in reality, it had never really ended.

The nursery was opposite our door. Up until last week, Josh had been sleeping in our room. But unlike our other son—four-year-old Adam, who started sleeping through the night after he passed the eight-week mark—this kid was a serious insomniac. He refused to collapse for more than two hours at a stretch, and when he woke, his shrill squawks let it be known that he was requesting our full, undivided attention. We'd tried just about everything to knock him out for eight hours straight—keeping him awake until late in the evening, stoking him up with two bottles of formula to ward off postmidnight hunger, doping him with the maximum safe dosage of baby aspirin. Nothing worked. So that's when we decided to move him to the nursery, thinking that he might sleep better if he was on his own. Not a chance. Three hours was now the maximum respite from his howls.

Twenty weeks into his little life, Beth and I had yet to experience a night of unbroken sleep. Recently I'd been trying to convince myself that our jangled nerves, our mutual exhaustion, was the main source of the disharmony between us—a disharmony that turned rather nasty two nights ago, when Beth let fly with some pent-up venom and called me a totally compromised man. Naturally I wasn't going to take invective like that on the chin, so I counterpunched and told her she was a suburban shrew.

Forty-eight hours after that exchange, she still wasn't talking to me. Just like last month, when she gave me the silent treatment for an entire weekend after an argument over our American Express bill. Or two months before that, when she was riding the postnatal roller-coaster and accused me of being the most self-absorbed guy in recorded history.

So it wasn't just Baby Josh's cries that were keeping me awake at night. It was lots of other minor things. Like this house. I now hated this house.

Not that there is anything specifically hateful about my house. On the contrary, it is the sort of suburban American classic that many a citizen would be proud to own—a two-story white clapboard New England colonial, with dark green shutters, four bedrooms, eat-in kitchen, basement family room, a half-acre backyard, and a separate, detached, two-car garage. Asking price: $485,000 . . . but this corner of Connecticut really took a beating during the recession, so we snagged it for $413,000 in 1991. At the time, several colleagues at work told me I had made a "killer deal." But when I was signing the contract with Beth, all I could think was: We really are the architects of our own incarceration.

Like every other room in the house, Josh's nursery is all stripped pine and Early Americana. He sleeps in a mahogany colonial crib, circa 1782. He gets his diapers changed on top of a pine chest of drawers from an old York, Maine, inn. When he gets older, he'll be able to sit in a tiny rocking chair that once housed the backside of little Nathaniel Hawthorne, and play with a set of ancient rag dolls, which, no doubt, kept Harriet Beecher Stowe company while she was writing *Uncle Tom's Cabin*.

How do I know all this bullshit history about my kid's furniture? Beth, of course. Two years after we moved here from the city, she got rid of all that functional, reductionist stuff we once acquired at Pottery Barn and announced: We're Going Colonial. But, to Beth, this didn't mean driving off to the nearest Ethan Allen showroom and buying some leatherette Williamsburg wing chairs. Instead, everything in our new home was going to be 100 percent Guaranteed Federalist. And for months she went on an authenticity binge—scouring every antiques shop from here to New London in search of original Shaker bedsteads, genuine Boston Whaler footlockers, a pew from a Providence meeting house. Every item also had to come equipped with its own little historical pedigree. According to Beth, Thomas Jefferson screwed one of his mistresses on our French divan. And the three genuine New England samplers hanging in our bathroom were all hand-stitched by Daniel Webster's stepsister . . . or was it his blind niece? (I lose track of these things.)

It became an obsession with her, this authentic furniture kick. An expensive obsession, which completely soaked up my $79,000 Christmas bonus that year. Still, I let her have her antiques binge because it kept her preoccupied at a time when she was trying to come to terms with a big disappointment. And, for a while, buying up every old curio she fancied did help to quell her frustration. But eventually she grew weary of auction rooms and the manic hunt for a matching set of original Audubon prints. The house was fully furnished. It was a collector's triumph. When friends came over, she could spend hours discoursing on the origins of a 1789 porcelain shaving mug, once owned by a naval commodore in East Sandwich, Massachusetts. Though Beth never said anything to me, I knew that she secretly despised what she had created, that she realized it was a diversionary tactic designed to deflect her attention from certain uncomfortable truths. Like me, she too now hated this house . . . and all that it implied.

Josh had gone ballistic by the time I reached his crib—that volcanic moment when a baby's yelps for attention turn into one long inconsolable howl. When Adam was this age, soothing his cries was a three-step cinch: reinsert pacifier in mouth, give cuddle, remove pacifier and insert warm bottle. But Josh is a hard sell when it comes to accepting parental comfort. He likes to cry—and he certainly doesn't buy the pacifier/cuddle/bottle routine. You also have to walk him around for an hour. You must keep him constantly amused by singing. If you dare to rest your voice for a moment, he will screech again. If you sit down in a chair, the wails will automatically resume. He is a dedicated sleep terrorist—and he refuses to give in unless you meet all his demands.

I combed the floor for the pacifier that he had flung away. When I found it (under the chest of drawers), I sterilized it by popping it between my lips and then shoved it back into his mouth. I picked him up from the depths of the crib, slung him across my shoulder, and started in on an off-key rendition of "Twinkle Twinkle Little Star." Immediately, he spit out the pacifier and returned to wailing mode. Halfway down the stairs, the pacifier hit the floor again. And when he saw the bottle of formula waiting by the microwave in the kitchen, he really did some ear damage during the very long twenty seconds that it took to heat it.

Adam was a real designer baby, the sort of dead-cute charmer you'd see in some touchy-feely diaper commercial. But Josh is a lump. A little bruiser. With an oversized head, and a boxer's nose, and the disposition of a pit bull. Naturally I love him . . . but I'm not sure if I like him yet. He makes me anxious—and not just because he cries all the time and seems less than happy to have been brought into the world. I guess it also has something to do with the fact that—like the house itself—he represents yet another domestic manacle. A friend of mine put it very succinctly: When you have your first child, you still believe that you have room to maneuver, that you haven't dug yourself so deeply into an overmortgaged life. But when the second kid arrives, you are now a serious family man. You have piled yourself high with obligations. And you know that never again will you be a free agent, adrift in the world at large.

Of course, I have another theory about why Josh cries so much: He's simply reacting to the enmity between his parents. Kids sense these things. Even at five months, they've got ferociously acute antennae. And Adam is very much aware that his parents haven't been getting along. Whenever Beth and I have a nasty exchange—or give each other an extended dose of the silent treatment—I can discern his fear, the way his big gray eyes plead with us to like each other again. It guts me, seeing his little-boy concern, his silent appeal for stability, because it also brings me back to a time thirty-four years ago when I was Adam's age, and I too watched helplessly as my parents pulled each other apart.

As soon as Josh saw me retrieve the heated formula from the microwave, his hands began to flap until I turned it over to him. Then I pulled out a kitchen chair and sat down, cradling him against me while he slurped away. There were at least five minutes of quiet ahead while he finished the bottle. So, with my one free hand, I reached out and hit the remote control for the little nine-inch television tucked away on a countertop. I never believed I would end up living in a house with a television in the kitchen, but Beth insisted that it was handy for cooking programs, so I didn't argue the issue (even though I felt like pointing out that the Sony Corporation wasn't exactly up and running at the time of the Revolutionary War). Like

the other three sets in the house, this one is wired for cable, so
I immediately flipped it over to McNews, a.k.a. CNN.

As the screen flickered to life, I immediately saw something that made me flinch. Not something, actually . . . *someone.* Her name was Kate Brymer—CNN's current star war
correspondent. At that moment she was dressed in designer
fatigues and a flak jacket, reporting from some bombed-out
hospital in Sarajevo. Behind her a team of doctors was ampu-
tating a soldier's leg. They were so short of medical supplies
that they were operating without anesthetic. You could hear
the poor bastard's shrieks over the somber, yet impassioned,
commentary that had become Kate's trademark. I noticed
that her bobbed chestnut hair was looking well coiffed for
someone in a war zone. Then again, she always had a thing
about her hair. When we lived together at college, she used to
brush it incessantly. Just as she would always turn up for
classes dressed to kill, and armed with the sort of intelligent
yet easily fieldable questions that would play to the vanity of a
male professor, allowing him to shine. Even back then, she
was a shrewd political operator. And she understood that—
as a woman with big ambitions—flirtation would be a necessary, if distasteful, weapon in her quest for importance. I
remember her lying in bed one wet Sunday afternoon, browsing through a stack of borrowed library books by Martha
Gellhorn, Oriana Fallaci, Frances FitzGerald—to her mind,
the three great women war correspondents of the past forty
years.

"I'll write a memoir like this one day," she said, her voice so
matter-of-fact, so certain about her professional destiny. Then
she held up a collection of battlefield photos by the great
Robert Capa, adding, "And you'll be this guy."

Josh suddenly flung the bottle to the floor—his way of letting me know that he'd had enough to drink. Within seconds,
the crying game started, developing quickly into the sort of
high lamentation that threatened to wake Adam and Beth. So
I tossed him back over my shoulder, opened the door next to
the fridge, and walked down five steps to the basement.

The basement had become my haven, my island of retreat, filled with lots of gadgetry. "A place for all your toys," as Beth once put it.

It's not a big area, around 16 feet by 12 feet, with two small rooms off the main area, but I think I've managed to use the space shrewdly. It's also the one corner of the house that Beth hasn't managed to Martha Washingtonize: paneled in bleached Finnish wood, with a neutral gray-fleck carpet on the floor and recessed lighting in the ceiling. As you come down the stairs, you immediately see my exercise area—a NordicTrack cross-country ski machine, a StairMaster, and a set of free weights. I try to do a forty-minute workout every morning—ten minutes on the NordicTrack, ten on the StairMaster, the final twenty pumping iron—to keep my body trim at a constant 175 pounds. My doctor tells me it is the perfect weight for a five foot eleven nonsmoking thirty-eight-year-old with a normal 5.2 cholesterol level, and he always compliments me on my ability to stay lean. But perhaps the real reason I'm so fit is because any time I ever feel like punching a wall with my fist, I just come down here and drain the rage with bench presses.

Or I play music. I own over 1,200 compact discs, all stored in a seven-foot-high revolving carousel of solid American cherry. It was custom-built for me by a cabinetmaker in a little Connecticut town called West Cornwall. It cost $1,830, but anyone who's ever seen it has always admired its Shaker simplicity. Just as they've also admired my hi-fi equipment. I go to a serious audiophile outfit on West 45th Street in Manhattan, which sells only high-end British components—the best in the world, if you know what small brands to buy. And I've put together a pretty formidable system for just under $5,000—a pair of Mission 753 speakers, an Arcam Delta CD transport and Black Box DAC, and a truly stunning Cyrus 3 amplifier that combines diamond-hard clarity with an impressive soundstage.

My disc collection is largely based on recommendations from the *Penguin Guide to Classical Music*. I *am* serious about music—and I try to listen to an entire work (or an act of an opera) while exercising. Unfortunately, anything over forty or so minutes doesn't fit into my program, so I have to do without long-winded neurotics like Mahler or Bruckner during my morning workout. But I do like to blare their symphonies at night, when I bury myself in the one place where I am truly content—my darkroom.

It used to be the laundry room, but one of the first things we did after moving in was to transfer the washer and dryer to a pantry off the kitchen. Then the carpenter and plumber got to work. All existing cabinets and fixtures were torn out. A pair of professional stainless steel sinks was installed. The one existing window was bricked up. The walls were replastered and painted light gray, then a sleek unit of customized steel-gray cabinets and work tops was built into one wall. And I dropped $2,300 on a real indulgence: the latest light-trap revolving door, a cylinder within a cylinder that is guaranteed to create the perfect darkroom blackout.

Following the advice of a photojournalist guy I know at *Newsweek,* I also invested in top-range reproduction equipment: a Beseler 45mx enlarger; a Kindermann film dryer; a mechanized Kodak tray rocker. I only use top Ilford-brand laboratory chemicals; I only print on Galleria bromide paper (the paper of choice of all the leading American photographers). And like most serious photographers, I favor two top-grade monochrome films: Kodak Tri-X and Ilford HP4.

Opposite this work area is a large floor-to-ceiling locker. It's fire resistant. It's waterproof. It has roll-down aluminum shutters secured by two pick-proof locks. Maybe all this sounds a little overcautious—but if you have a camera and lens collection that has been valued at over $45,000, you cannot afford to take any chances.

I started collecting cameras in 1962. I was six years old, visiting my maternal grandparents at their retirement condo in Ft. Lauderdale. I picked up an old Brownie that was left on a side table, looked through the viewfinder, and was captivated. Here was a whole new way of seeing things. It was like squinting through a peephole. You didn't have to look at everything that was going on around you—you could narrow your vision down to one single image. But most pleasing to my six-year-old sensibility was the discovery that you could hide behind the lens, using it as a barrier between you and the rest of the world. And for the remainder of our stay—during which my parents squabbled, my grandparents squabbled, and then each couple turned on the other—I spent much of the time glued to the viewfinder of that Brownie. In fact, any time I was around an adult I'd shove the camera in front of my face, refusing to lower it even when spoken to. My father was not amused. When we were seated at the dinner table one night, and I tried to eat a shrimp cocktail while still keeping the Brownie at eye level, his patience cracked. He snatched the camera from me. My grandfather Morris thought his son-in-law was being unduly harsh, and came to my defense.

"Let Benny have his fun."

"His name is not Benny," my father said, a hint of old Yalie contempt in his voice. "It's *Benjamin.*"

My grandfather refused to rise to this WASPy bait.

"Betcha the kid's gonna be a photographer when he grows up," he said.

"Only if he wants to starve," my father said.

That was the first (and mildest) of many confrontations I would have with my father on the subject of cameras and photography. But at the end of that brief, shrill visit to Ft. Lauderdale, my grandfather made a point of handing me the Brownie at the airport, telling me it was a going-away gift to his favorite Benny.

I still have that Brownie. It's stored on the top shelf of my cabinet, next to my first Instamatic (Christmas, 1967), my first Nikkormat (my fourteenth birthday), my first Nikon (high school graduation), my first Leica (college graduation, 1978— a present from my mother six months before an embolism snuffed out her life at the age of fifty-one).

On the three lower shelves are the cameras I have collected since then. There are a few rare museum pieces (a Pentax Spotmatic, an original Eastman Kodak box camera, and a first edition Kodak Retina). And then there is my working gear: an original SpeedGraphic for gritty journalistic shots, a new Leica M9 (with a $5,000 Leica 300 Sumicaron lens), a LeicaFlex, a Hasselblad 500 CM, and a solid-cherry DeoDorf that I only use for very special landscape or portraiture work.

One wall of the basement is filled with a selection of my landscapes—rather moody Ansel Adams–style vistas of the Connecticut coast under low, threatening clouds, or white clapboard barns against a blackened sky. Another wall is all portraits—very Bill Brandt kind of stuff of Beth and the kids in a variety of domestic poses, using only available light and an open aperture to give them a grainy, naturalistic tone. And the final wall is what I like to call my Diane Arbus phase: a man with no legs and an eye patch begging in front of Bloomingdale's; an elderly West Indian woman wearing a surgical mask and clutching a walker on Central Park West; a drunk on the Bowery (with a cankerous sore on one cheek), pulling out a discarded, half-eaten Big Mac from a garbage can.

Beth really hates these freak-show images ("They're too show-offy, too intentionally sick"). She also doesn't much care for the gritty family portraits ("You make us look like we live in Appalachia"). But she does approve of the landscapes, always telling me that I have a real eye for the dark side of pastoral New England. Adam, on the other hand, loves my collection of urban sickos. Every time he visits me down here while I'm working, he climbs onto the gray studio couch beneath them, points to the Bowery dipso, giggles with delight, and says, "Yucky man! . . . Yucky man!" (He's my kind of critic.) And Baby Josh? He notices nothing. He just cries.

He was certainly crying that morning. Ever since I'd brought him down from the kitchen, he hadn't let up. Twenty minutes into this predawn outburst and I must have done at least forty laps on the basement floor. I had also depleted my repertoire of baby songs—to the point where I was repeating "Twinkle Twinkle" for the fourth time. Eventually a wave of exhaustion hit me and I had to sit down, bouncing Josh on my knee in an attempt to make him believe he was still moving. For a moment or two, he did fall silent and my eyes wandered, focusing briefly on a blank patch of wall near my stereo equipment. I've always reserved that bit for my war photos—the big Bob Capa action shots that Kate Brymer said I would take one day. But I've never been anywhere near a war zone, a front line . . . and I now knew that I never would.

End of brief respite—Josh was roaring again. Maybe his diaper was the problem. I laid him down on the couch, undid the snaps at the bottom of his onesie, and peered into his Pampers. A full load. Never a pretty sight, but especially grim with no sleep.

So it was back upstairs to the nursery. I deposited Josh on the plastic changing mat that covers the top of his pine chest of drawers. Josh suffers from incurable diaper rash (since birth, his backside has been a constant red, always festering), so, for him, being changed is like a trip through the chamber of horrors. As soon as he felt that plastic mat under him, he began to twist and shout—his movements so violent that I had to hold him down with one hand while I again undid the snaps and struggled to free his legs from the feet of his onesie. When this was finally achieved (after considerable effort), I pulled back the lower part of his suit, ripped off the plastic fasteners on his Pampers, and stared straight into a diaper from hell: gooey diarrhea that covered Josh's bottom and stomach so completely I couldn't see his belly button. I shut my eyes in disgust—but not for long, as Josh started thrashing his legs, slamming them into the dirty diaper. Now the stuff was smeared across his feet and embedded between his toes.

"Ah, Christ," I muttered and turned away from him for a moment to grab a handful of baby wipes from the windowsill where they were stored.

But in the three seconds that my steadying hand was off his chest, the unthinkable happened: Josh writhed around so wildly that he managed to dislodge himself from the changing mat. When I turned back from the window, I saw that he was about to roll right off this four-foot-high chest of drawers.

I roared his name and dove toward him just as he toppled off the edge. Somehow I managed to get myself under him as he fell, my head crashing into the bottom drawer as he landed on top of me. He screamed in shock. And then the nursery door flew open and Beth was bearing down on me, yelling:

"Goddamnit! I told you I told you I told you . . ."

I managed to say, "He's all right . . . he's not hurt," before Beth snatched Josh from me. As she picked him up his diaper fell off, landing directly on my stomach. But I didn't care that my robe was now smeared with diarrhea, as I was more preoccupied with the big new bump on my head, and with Beth's unforgiving voice.

"You never listen, do you?"

"It was an accident, that's all," I said.

"Don't leave him on top of the mat . . . *never* let him go . . ."

"It was just a *second,* that's all . . ."

"But I told you over and over . . ."

"All right, all right. I was—"

"Wrong."

"Fine." I was on my feet. As I stood up, the soiled diaper slid off me and, with a soft *plop,* landed facedown on the rug (an original hand-loomed 1775 rug from a Philadelphia boarding-house where John Adams once stayed). Beth stared at the mess on me, the mess on the historic $1,500 rug, the mess now smeared across her own dressing gown from still hysterical Josh.

"Terrific," she muttered, her voice weary, defeated. "Just terrific."

"I'm sorry," I said.

"You always are."

"Beth . . ."

"Just go, Ben. Go get a shower. Go to work. I'll deal with this. As usual."

"Right—I'm out of here." I beat a fast retreat from the room. But as I entered the hallway, I saw Adam standing by his door. His favorite stuffed toy (a smiling koala bear) was clutched against him, and his eyes were so wide, so anxious, that I knew our shouting had awakened him.

I knelt down and kissed his blonde head, saying, "It's okay now. Go back to sleep."

He didn't seemed convinced.

"Why are you fighting?"

"We're just tired, Adam. That's all." I didn't sound too convincing either.

He pointed to my splattered robe and pajamas, wrinkling his nose as the smell hit him.

"Yucky man, yucky man."

I managed a small smile.

"Yeah, real yucky man. You go back to bed now?"

"I go to Mommy," he said and ran into the nursery.

"Don't tell me you're up too," Beth said as he entered.

I returned to the bedroom, stripped off everything, put on a pair of gym shorts, a T-shirt, and my Nikes, then headed downstairs, dropping my soiled clothes in the washing machine before withdrawing to the basement. I spun the disc cabinet until I found the Bs, then traced my finger along a dozen or so discs before pulling out a recording of Bach's *English Suites* played by Glenn Gould. It was a morning for headphones, so I popped on the Sennenheims ("World-class sound"—*Stereo-Review*), turned up the volume, and then tried to get the necessary momentum going on the StairMaster. But I found myself unable to move, my fingers clutching the hand grips so hard I thought I'd rupture my knuckles.

Eventually I forced myself into action, my legs building up a steady rhythm. Soon I was climbing upward at a rate of three miles per hour; my neck was beaded with the first hints of sweat. My stride accelerated. I pushed down harder, willing myself on as if in a race. Higher and higher I climbed—the equivalent of twenty stories, according to the machine's digital readout—my tempo now manic as I edged into overdrive. I could hear the rapid thuds of my heart, felt it strain to keep pace with my frantic movements. The Bach played on, but I was now oblivious to it, listening only to the booming timpani in my chest. And for a few brief moments, my head emptied. No rage, no domestic despair. I was free of all obligations, all ties that bind. And I was anywhere but here.

Until, out of the corner of my eye, I saw Adam climbing

down the stairs, dragging a big brown leather satchel behind him. My briefcase. When he reached the bottom, he gave me one of his huge smiles and started carting the bag around in two hands, mouthing something as he marched about. I whipped off the headphones. And over my rapid panting I heard him say:

"Wawyer wike Daddy . . . Wawyer wike Daddy . . . Wawyer wike Daddy."

I felt my eyes water. No kid, you really don't want to be a lawyer like Daddy.

2

IT IS A SEVEN-MINUTE WALK from our house to the train, and though it was only six-thirty in the morning, I counted ten other early risers marching purposefully toward the station. As I joined them—pulling up the collar of my Burberry against the autumn chill—I remembered (as I do every morning) the sales pitch of the real-estate broker who showed us the house. He wore a blue blazer and Black Watch check trousers and deck shoes; he was in his fifties and his name was Gordy.

"At the end of the day," Gordy said, "you're not just buying a great house, you're also buying a great commute."

Our road is called Constitution Crescent. There are twenty-four houses—eleven clapboard colonials, seven Cape Codders, four split-level ranches, and two redbrick Monticellos. Each house has a half-acre front lawn and a driveway. There are children's swings and slides in front of most of these houses; the rest have mini-playgrounds or pools in their backyards. The favored car on the road is the Volvo station wagon (with the Ford Explorer coming a close second). There are also a handful of sports cars: a Porsche 911, owned by Chuck Bailey (a creative director at some big Madison Avenue ad agency); a battered MG that belongs to a local (and not very good) photographer named Gary Summers;

and a Mazda Miata that sits in my driveway, next to the Volvo that Beth and the kids use.

At the end of Constitution Crescent there is a clapboard Episcopalian church. In front of it is a large old New England town sign with gold-leaf lettering:

NEW CROYDON, EST. 1763

I turned left at the church, walked on past the post office, three antiques shops, and a deli that sells thirty-two brands of mustard, and then reached New Croydon's central drag: Adams Avenue. A terrace of single-story white-shingle shops, a modern bank, a fire station, a big redbrick high school with a massive Stars and Stripes dangling from its flagpole. A real suburban small town with all the usual cozy attributes that realtors like Gordy incorporate into their sales pitch:

"You're talking low taxes, virtually no crime, forty-seven minutes to Grand Central, great public schools, five minutes to the beach, and the fact that, unlike the city, 450k buys you a lot of house up here."

Making a right on Adams Avenue, I cut across the parking lot shared by Colonial Dry Cleaners and New Croydon Fine Wines and Liquor, and started climbing the steps to the bridge that spans the railway tracks. The 6:47 was due in three minutes, and as I hurried toward the southbound platform I saw that it was already black with suits. There must have been eighty of us waiting for that dawn express, all dressed in subdued corporate colors: dark shades of gray and blue, frequently bisected by pinstripes. Almost all the women wore white blouses and skirts that touched the knee. There was only one guy in a double-breasted Italian number (pearl gray with pearl buttons—he must run some family hauling business); the rest of us played it conservative in single-breasted suits.

"Never show up here again in anything double-breasted," my mentor, Jack Mayle, told me shortly after I joined the firm. "They make a lawyer appear shifty—and our clients don't associate Lawrence, Cameron and Thomas with shiftiness. Loud shirts are also out; stick to plain white or light blue and simple, striped ties. Remember, if you eventually want to make partner, you'll have to look the part."

So I did as instructed, and shelved the $1,100 Armani masterpiece I'd bought on an expensive whim after I landed this job. Then I spent an afternoon in Brooks Brothers buying several versions of the prescribed outfit. No doubt, every other guy on this platform had also dropped some serious cash at Brooks, because anyone who can afford to live in New Croydon also has to play the corporate game. And playing that game means wearing the uniform they demand.

Ever since I made junior partner, I haven't bothered taking early trains as I no longer need to demonstrate my go-gettingness by being at my desk by 7:30. But I certainly wasn't going to wait around at home today for either the 8:08 or the 8:38 (my usual trains) because Beth made it very clear that she wouldn't entertain any of my attempts to broker a détente between us.

When I came downstairs after my postexercise shower, she was sitting in the kitchen feeding Josh and Adam, while *Today in New York* hummed away in the background. She glanced at me as I entered, then quickly shifted her gaze back to the baby. She had changed into a pair of leggings and a bulky black sweatshirt that didn't disguise her newfound leanness. Beth was never fleshy, but when I first met her seven years ago, she did look like the captain of some hard-drinking field hockey team: an exuberant, big-boned blond who could talk books and football all night, and liked to guzzle beer. She also had the most mischievous of laughs, especially in bed—a place, back then, where we happily spent a considerable amount of time. Now, at thirty-five, she had become aerobically gaunt, as thin and lanky as an Olympic sprinter. Her cheekbones had become sharply defined, she had no waist, and her once long hair was now cut short in that chic mannish style favored by French movie actresses. I still found her enticing, and at suburban soirées she still turned heads, especially when decked out in a slinky black Donna Karan dress that accentuated her angular allure. But most of the time, the tough-girl ebullience had been replaced by all-purpose world-weariness. There were dark, permanent crescent moons beneath her eyes. Her nerves seemed constantly frayed. And she had gone off me in such a big way that she hadn't let me come near her since Josh was born, always fobbing me off with excuses like "I'm just not ready yet."

I walked over to where she was sitting, put my hand on her shoulder, and tried to plant a kiss on her head. But as soon as I touched her, she flinched, shrugging me off.

"Jesus, Beth . . ."

She ignored me, spoon-feeding Josh some orange goo from a Heinz baby-food jar.

"I don't get this," I said. "I just don't get this."

"Don't you?" she said, not looking up at me.

"No, I don't."

"That's too bad."

"What the fuck is that supposed to mean?"

"Work it out."

"Why are you doing this?"

"I'm doing *nothing.*"

"Cold-shouldering me for months, treating me like some useless asshole . . . that's *nothing?*"

"I'm not going to talk about this now."

"You always say that, always avoid the goddamn . . ."

"Not now." Her tone was dangerous.

Silence. Adam stared into his bowl of Cheerios, stirring them listlessly with his spoon. I stood there like a helpless idiot, realizing there was nothing to do but leave. So I kissed my two sons good-bye and picked up my briefcase.

"I might have a meeting at five-thirty," I said.

"Doesn't matter, Fiona's working late tonight," she said, mentioning the Irish nanny who looked after Adam and Josh.

"Right," I said. "Call you later."

"I'll be out," she said.

"Anything interesting going on today?" I asked absently.

"No."

I opened the back door. "See you," I said. She didn't look up or respond.

As I bought *The New York Times* and this month's *Vanity Fair* from the station shop, I felt a little drop of acid hit my stomach. I winced. More bile trickled down, scorching my gut. I bit my lip, shut my eyes. It didn't staunch the pain. When the train rolled into the station, I staggered on board, almost doubled over. Falling into the first available seat, I pulled open my attaché case, dug out a bottle of Maalox from beneath a half-dozen legal briefs, shook it frantically, and downed a good third of it in one long slurp. Then I looked around, wondering if any of my fellow passengers were staring at me, filing me away under "ulcerated" or "stressed out." But everyone was preoccupied with their laptops, their pressing paperwork, their mobile phones. This was the 6:47, after all, domain of the workaholic junior executive, still chasing a partnership or a vice presidency, still willing to give fourteen-hour days in pursuit of that quest. And the atmosphere within this car was so supercharged with nervy ambition and self-absorption that, even if I had been puffing on a crack pipe, it would have been a source of little interest to anyone around me . . . though I'm sure somebody would have eventually told me that smoking was prohibited on this train.

I prefer liquid Maalox to its tablet form, as it instantly douses my stomach fires. And in the five minutes that it took the train to rumble to its next stop—the village of Riverside—the agony abated. But I knew that, before the day was out, I'd be reaching for that Maalox bottle again and again.

First Riverside, then Cos Cob, then Greenwich, followed by Port Chester, Rye, Harrison, Mamaroneck, Larchmont, New Rochelle, Pelham, Mount Vernon, 125th Street, and, finally, Grand Central Station. After three years, I know every stretch of this commute, every minor detail. Like the yacht with a pink hull and a torn mainsail that is always bobbing in the middle of Riverside Harbor. Or the chipped toilet door on the Port Chester platform that says LEMEN (the first four letters having long vanished). Or the ruminative graffiti on a pillar at 125th Street: "White Men Can't Jump . . . But They Sure Can Fuck You Up Good."

Riverside, Cos Cob, Greenwich, Port Chester, Rye, Harrison, Mamaroneck, Larchmont, New Rochelle, Pelham, Mount Vernon, 125th Street, Grand Central. My morning litany. Similar to the one my late father sang every weekday morning for thirty-five years. Only whereas I travel Metro North, his beat was the old Hudson River Line that coasted through the upscale heart of Westchester County.

He too had a good commute. His brokerage firm was on Madison and Forty-eighth: a fast ten-minute walk from Grand Central. When I was eleven he once brought me to his office during a school holiday. Dressed like a midget executive in a blue blazer and gray flannels, using my school satchel as a makeshift briefcase, I accompanied him on the 8:12 into the city. On the train, he introduced me to his commuting cronies: men who all seemed to call each other by their last names ("Hey, Cole . . . Morning, Mullin . . . How's it playing, Swabe?"). They indulged me, asking my dad if I was that new whiz-kid broker he'd been telling them about; demanding my opinion on such crucial matters of the day as whether the Mets would trade their star pitcher, Tom Seaver, did I prefer Rowan or Martin, would George Romney win the Republican nomination for president next year? At his office, I met his secretary, a matronly woman with bad teeth named Muriel. I was shown the company boardroom, the executive dining room, and the executive suite where my father had one of four offices. It was a dark, plush world of big mahogany desks and overstuffed leather armchairs. Just like the India Club, where my father took me for lunch. It was down in the financial district, right near the Stock Exchange. The atmosphere was very Bostonian, very old Yankee: lots of wood paneling, and heavy oil portraits of nineteenth-century burghers, and venerable models of bygone naval vessels. The dining room was high-vaulted and formal. The waiters wore starched white livery. And all around us was a landscape of pinstripes and horn-rimmed glasses and polished black wingtips: Wall Street at lunch.

"You'll be a member here one day," my father said. And I remember thinking at the time: looking down the viewfinder of a camera was fun, but wearing a suit and having a big office and eating every day at the India Club really must be the pinnacle of adulthood.

Eight years later, I vowed never to set foot in the India Club again. It was the summer of '75; I had just finished my freshman year at Bowdoin College and had landed a vacation job as a junior salesman at one of the big camera shops that line West Thirty-second Street. My father was appalled. Not only had I turned down his offer to "start learning the bond business" as a trainee runner on the floor of the Exchange, but I was working in a shop for $70 a week. He also couldn't stand the fact that I was living away from home at a crash pad on Avenue B, where I was shacked up with a Wellesley dropout from Scarsdale named Shelley who described herself as "a macramé artist."

After a few weeks of hippy-dippy bliss—during which I answered all of my father's increasingly annoyed calls in an advanced doped-out state—he summoned me to lunch. When I said, "Lunch, like, is a hassle," he told me that if I didn't show up at the India Club on Thursday at one, I could forget about going back to my fancy New England college in the fall, as he wouldn't be paying the tuition.

A real hard-ass negotiator, my dad, and I had no choice but to make an appearance. I even put on a suit for the occasion— a 1940s gangster-style pinstripe suit I picked up in some secondhand shop in the East Village. And I had Shelley braid my shoulder-length hair into a ponytail.

"You are a disgrace, an embarrassment," my father said as soon as I sat down at his table.

I gave him a stoned smile and said something Gertrude Steinish along the lines of: "What I am I am what I am."

"You're coming home."

"No way."

"I'll expect you to meet me at Grand Central tonight in time for the 6:10. If you're not there, you can find the $9,000 for Bowdoin next year."

I made the train. I went home. I kept my summer job at the camera shop, but commuted in every morning on the 8:06

with my father. I got rid of the gangster suit and had my hair trimmed to just over my collar. I tried to see Shelley on the weekends, but in less than fourteen days my place in her bed was taken by a glass-eating performance artist named Troy. And for the next two summers I did as my dad demanded and worked for his firm as a runner on the floor of the Exchange.

I capitulated, gave in, wimped out. Why? Because it was easier that way. And safer. I mean, what would I have done if he had cut off my funds? Continued working in the camera shop? Tried getting a start as a photographer? Perhaps—but that would have meant going against the huge investment that had been made in me: the private day school in Ossining, the expensive summer camps, the tennis lessons, the four years at Andover, my acceptance at an elite New England college like Bowdoin. When you've been raised and educated in such a select East Coast realm, you don't suddenly throw it all away to sell Nikons on West Thirty-second Street. Not unless you want to be considered a total loser—someone who was offered all the breaks imaginable, but still couldn't achieve.

Achieve. That most American of verbs. As in, "You've been given the most privileged upbringing imaginable—now you achieve." To my father, to just about everybody I ever went to school with, it meant one thing: making serious money. Six-figure money. The sort of money that you can most readily obtain by climbing the corporate ladder or embedding yourself in one of the safer professions. But though I did take the pre-law courses that my father suggested (in addition to photography classes), I always told myself that when I finished college and was no longer economically beholden to him, I would finally kiss his "achieving" world good-bye.

"Don't let him intimidate you," Kate Brymer always told me.

Kate Brymer. As the train pulled out of Harrison, I found myself flicking through the glossy pages of *Vanity Fair.* I skipped a story about some pretty-boy actor who'd finally found "his spiritual center and his star power." I skimmed a "murder among the rich and moronic" tale of an airhead heiress turned serial killer who strangled six tennis pros in Palm Springs. Then I turned the page, and there she was.

It was just a one-page feature in their "Vanities" section, much of it taken up by an Annie Leibovitz portrait of Kate. She was standing in front of some Bosnian killing field, a few fresh corpses reddening the snowy landscape. As always, she was wearing stylish fatigues and stared at the camera with her now predictable Mother-Courage-Dressed-by-Armani look. The article read:

IN THE REAL LINE OF FIRE:
CNN'S KATE BRYMER BRINGS GUTSY CHIC TO BOSNIA

"What's the secret to being a good war correspondent?" asks CNN's Kate Brymer. "Two things: boundless compassion . . . and knowing when to duck."

A little bit of classic New England patricianism doesn't hurt either. And this flak-pack beauty from Newport, Rhode Island, certainly calls to mind another thoroughbred Kate (Hepburn, that is) when it comes to chiseled cheekbones and true grit in testing situations.

"She's the most dazzling television war correspondent in years," says CNN supremo Ted Turner, who has twice invited Brymer to vacation with him and his wife, Jane Fonda, at their Montana ranch. But Brymer—who has been romantically linked with such cerebral hunks as ABC anchor Peter Jennings and French film director Luc Besson—rarely gets well-earned respites from the world's hot spots. Having first made her name with a series of hard-hitting reports from the mean streets of Belfast, she's also dodged sniper fire in Algiers, and is now gunning for a Peabody Award for her flinty, yet deeply felt, reports from war-ravaged Bosnia.

"My job is to bear witness to the worst in human behavior," she says on a crackly phone line from the capital, Sarajevo. "But the challenge for me is to fight off the temptations of cynicism that come with seeing too much carnage. You can't just observe a war, you have to feel it too. And so, I am always reality-checking my capacity for empathy; always making certain that I am in sorrowful harmony with Joe Bosnian as the world he knows is destroyed around him . . ."

Jesus fucking Christ. Talk about Pulitzer Prize–winning bullshit. "Reality-checking my capacity for empathy? . . . sorrowful harmony." You cannot be serious, Kate.

She was always clever on the self-promotion front, always knew which buttons to push to move her career forward. Do I sound envious? I *am* envious of Kate. Always was. Especially after we left Bowdoin in the summer of '78 and (much to the consternation of my father) moved to Paris. We were going to play the romantic expatriate game for a while—and though my father refused to support me while I tried to get established over there as a photographer, Kate had the sort of sizable trust fund that enabled us to rent a cozy little studio apartment in the Marais. Within a fortnight of arriving in the city, she also had a job working as a gofer in the local office of *Newsweek*. After three months, her French was almost fluent and she was taken on as a production assistant at the Paris bureau of CBS News. Eight weeks later, she arrived home one evening and announced that our relationship was history; she was moving in with her boss, the CBS bureau chief.

I was stunned. I was shattered. I begged her to stay, to give us another shot. She was packed and gone by morning. Within two months, so was I—on a one-way ticket back to the States. I couldn't afford to keep the apartment, let alone continue living on in Paris. I was broke, having struck out on the job front. I'd knocked on the door of every newspaper and press agency in town, but bar selling a couple of cafe photos (for a nothing 1,000 francs) to a crappy little tourist magazine, I simply couldn't find work.

"These shots aren't bad, but they're nothing special," the photo editor of the *International Herald Tribune* told me after I showed him my portfolio. "And I hate to say this, but I must get around six guys like you coming in here every week—just arrived from the States, all thinking they're going to make a living here from their cameras. But there's just not enough work to go around, and the competition's kind of rigorous."

When I landed back in New York, every picture editor I met told me the same thing: my photos were "all right," but being just "all right" wouldn't get me far in the Big Apple.

It was a miserable time. Still reeling from the abrupt way Kate had kicked me in the teeth, still not on speaking terms with my dad, I ended up crashing in the cramped Morningside Heights apartment of a friend who was doing graduate work at Columbia. While I desperately hunted for some sort of start in the photographic game, I kept myself fed by working part-time as a salesman at Willoughby's Cameras on West Thirty-second Street. And then my mother died. And panic set in. I was a failure. A no-hoper. Opening up magazines like *GQ* and *Esquire* and *Rolling Stone* only underscored my status as a failure, for their glossy pages were filled with guys my own age who were already big-deal success stories. And I began to convince myself that I would never make it as a photographer; that I would end up fossilizing behind the counter of Willoughby's—a seedy, middle-aged clerk with terminal dandruff, reduced to validating his worth by telling customers, "You know, Avedon buys his Tri-X from me."

Panic, of course, has its own crazy momentum. Once you're in its grasp, you refuse to survey your position with a calm, detached eye. Instead, you surrender to the melodramatic. Your situation is hopeless. There is No Way Out. You must find a solution *now*. And you end up making decisions. Very wrong decisions. Decisions that alter everything. Decisions that you come to loathe.

Achieve, achieve, achieve. I now look back on those few months of mid-twenties angst and wonder: Why didn't I go easy on myself and have a little more confidence in my photographic abilities? I should have told myself that, at least, looking down a viewfinder was something I enjoyed; that it was a craft that took time to master, and therefore I shouldn't be in such a mad rush to get to the next rung of the professional ladder.

But when you've been schooled in the achieving ethic, you think that if you don't move upward at the speed you believe you deserve, you must be doing something wrong. Or you mustn't really be cut out for this line of endeavor.

I fell victim to this delusion. I allowed the failure alarm bells to drown out every rational thought in my head.

Four months after I started work at Willoughby's, my father paid me a surprise visit, showing up unannounced around lunchtime. We'd been in nominal contact since my mother's death, and as soon as he saw me in my salesman uniform (a cheap blue jacket emblazoned with the name of the store), he had to work hard at containing his disdain.

"Here to buy a camera?" I asked him.

"Here to buy you lunch," he said.

We retreated to a little coffee shop on Sixth and Thirty-second.

"Not the India Club today, Dad? Or would the jacket embarrass you too much?"

"Always the smart-ass," he said.

"So the jacket *does* embarrass you . . ."

"You really don't like me, do you?" he replied.

"Maybe that's because you've never particularly liked me."

"Stop talking nonsense . . ."

"It's not nonsense. It's fact."

"You're my only child. I've never hated you . . ."

"But you think I'm a disappointment. A professional disappointment."

"If you're happy doing what you do, then I'm happy for you."

I looked at him carefully. "You don't mean that," I said.

He laughed a bronchial laugh. "You're right," he said, "I don't. In fact, I think you're wasting time up here. Valuable time. But you're twenty-three now, and I'm not going to tell you how to run your life. So if this is what you want, I won't say a word against it. I just want to establish contact again."

Silence. We ordered.

"But . . . I will tell you this. There will come a point, maybe five years from now, when you'll wake up one day and rue the fact that you have no money; when you're finally tired of slumming it and want to live well for a change, but can't afford to do so. Whereas if you had something like a law degree behind you, you'd not only be able to live the way you want, but use your free time to concentrate on the sort of photography that really interests you. And you could also afford the best equipment, maybe even set up your own dark-room . . ."

"Forget it."

"All right, all right, I'll say no more. But remember this: Money is freedom, Ben. The more you have, the bigger your options. And if you ever decide to go back to school—get a law degree or an MBA—I'll pay for it, and pick up your living expenses as well. You won't have to worry about supporting yourself for three whole years."

"You can really afford that?"

"Easily. And you know it."

I did know it, but I still refused to consider his Faustian bargain . . . for at least a month. It was early August. I'd just had four job applications rejected from assorted newspapers (even the picture editor of the Portland, Maine, *Press-Herald* turned me down, saying I needed more photographic experience), and the new manager of Willoughby's didn't like my patrician face and had demoted me from the Nikon/Pentax department to the film desk. One Sunday afternoon, a tall, angular man in his sixties wandered in and asked for a half-dozen rolls of Tri-X. When I rang up the purchase, he handed over his Amex card, and that's when I saw the name: RICHARD AVEDON.

"*The* Richard Avedon?" I asked, sounding far too starstruck.

"Maybe," he said, a little bored.

"God . . . Richard Avedon," I said, making an imprint of his credit card. "You know, I am just the biggest fan of your Texas drifters photographs. Really amazing stuff. Like, I've been trying out a lot of the same contrast techniques—that white-on-black shading you do so brilliantly—in a sequence I'm shooting right now in Times Square. Drifters, pimps, hookers, general lowlife. And, like, I'm not trying to give them the same sort of urban contextualization like Arbus, but really adopt your 'the-face-is-the-landscape' separation of subject from vista. But what I was going to ask was—"

Avedon interrupted my manic monologue.

"We finished here?" he asked.

I felt as if I had taken a left to the jaw. "Sorry," I croaked and handed him the credit-card slip for his signature. He scribbled his name, picked up his film, and left, shaking his head with weary amusement toward the leggy blond waiting for him at an adjoining counter.

"What was he going on about?" I heard her ask him.

"Just some no-hope camera geek," he said.

A few days later I signed up to take a review course for the LSATs. I took them in early January and—much to my amazement—scored high. 695 high. Good enough to get me accepted at three of the top law schools in the country: NYU, Berkeley, and Virginia. I was jubilant. After all the rejections I had been receiving at nowhere newspapers around the country, I finally felt like a winner again, the class act I was supposed to be. And I convinced myself I had done the right thing. Especially since—for the first time in my life—I had actually made my father happy. So happy that, after I told him that I had decided to enter NYU Law that autumn, he sent me a check for $5,000, accompanied by a two-line note:

> I am so proud of you.
> Go have some fun before buckling down.

So I cashed the check, quit my job at Willoughby's, and hit the road. I roamed the Pacific Northwest for a couple of months in a battered Toyota, a camera on the seat beside me, a joint always in my mouth, Little Feat blaring away on the tape player. And at the end of that indolent road movie of a summer, I sped back to New York, sold my car, put my camera on a shelf, and began my study of the law. The year after I passed my bar exam—and was already comfortably positioned in a major Wall Street firm—my father died. A massive coronary after a massive lunch at the India Club. The attending doctor later told me he collapsed as he was collecting his coat from the club's hatcheck girl. He was dead before he hit the floor.

Money is freedom, Ben. Sure it is, Dad. Until you buckle down. And find yourself singing a daily morning litany that goes: Riverside, Cos Cob, Greenwich, Port Chester, Rye, Harrison, Mamaroneck, Larchmont, New Rochelle, Pelham, Mount Vernon . . .

"125th Street, One-Two-Five Street. Grand Central, next stop."

The conductor's voice jolted me awake. I had slept through the suburbs. And for a few befogged moments, I wasn't exactly sure where I was. Or how I'd ended up on this commuter express. Surrounded by suits. Wearing a suit. This can't be right. I must have made a big mistake. I am the wrong man on the wrong train.

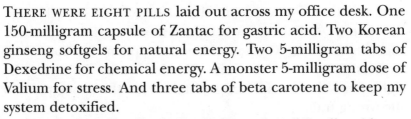

3

THERE WERE EIGHT PILLS laid out across my office desk. One 150-milligram capsule of Zantac for gastric acid. Two Korean ginseng softgels for natural energy. Two 5-milligram tabs of Dexedrine for chemical energy. A monster 5-milligram dose of Valium for stress. And three tabs of beta carotene to keep my system detoxified.

"It's the big jolt of beta that really gets me," Estelle said, eyeing my morning pharmaceutical intake.

"Keeps me clean and pure," I said with a smile.

"You mean, like a Diet Coke after two Big Macs and a large fries?"

"Have you seen my Maalox?"

She handed me the bottle from the office fridge. "If I was your stomach, I'd consider industrial action."

"It already has," I said, scooping up the pills, popping them all into my mouth, and washing them down with a Maalox chaser.

"Now I suppose you want your morning coffee?" she asked.

"No decaf this time, Estelle."

"Caffeine on top of all those pep pills? *Pu-leaze* . . ."

"I can easily handle it . . ."

"Everyone here's worried, Mr. Bradford. Everyone sees how beat you look . . ."

"A hint of fatigue is no bad thing. Makes people think you just might be working. But decaf, Estelle . . . Decaf is a dismissable offense."

Estelle pursed her lips. "You'd be lost without me."

"I know."

"Milk and one sugar?"

"Please. And the Berkowitz file, while you're at it."

"It's already on your desk. You might want to look at article five, subdivision A of the will. There was a violation of the rule against perpetuities because the trust never ended."

"Didn't it end on the death of the beneficiary's wife?" I asked.

"Well, according to a New York County surrogate's court ruling concerning fertile octogenarians, the trust would not have ended—so it could still violate the rule."

I looked up at Estelle and smiled.

"Well spotted," I said.

"All part of the service."

"You're the one who should really be sitting behind this desk."

"Don't want to be drinking Maalox for breakfast," she said. "Don't need the *tsuris*." She opened the door to her outer office. "Anything else, Mr. Bradford?"

"My wife . . . would you get her on the phone, please?"

A quick glance at her watch. I could tell what she was thinking, and what she would tell her coffee-klatch colleagues come lunchtime: "Calling his wife fifteen minutes after he reaches the office . . . and it's, like, the eighth time in two weeks . . . and, I mean, *gevalt*, if you saw how the poor guy looks . . . I tell ya, it's *tsuris*. And *tsuris* always ends in tears."

But being the consummate legal secretary that she is, Estelle said nothing except: "I'll buzz you when I reach her."

Estelle. Forty-seven years old, divorced, with a retarded teenage son, built like a Buick, comes equipped with a voice that sounds like a three-car pileup in Secaucus, New Jersey. If she'd been working in any of the sexier divisions of Lawrence, Cameron and Thomas she would've been sacked by now because her girth, her foghorn vowels, and her Filene's Basement dress sense wouldn't be in keeping with the bullshit dynamism of mergers and acquisitions or litigation. But when she joined the firm twenty-five years ago, she fortunately found her way into the decidedly unsexy world of trusts and estates. And now, she really should be running this division—because nobody in Lawrence, Cameron and Thomas knows more than she does when it comes to the labyrinthine complexities of inheritance law. She has a microchip mind—once she has digested and processed even the most obscure morsel of information, she can call it up at random years later. Ask her about an obscure loophole in some trusteeship ruling and she can quote chapter and verse from an appellate court decision eleven years ago in Glens Falls, New York, that completely changed the nature of the law. Tell her about a "power of appointment" problem you're having with an executor and she'll remember a similar case the firm handled in 1972. And she is probably the world's leading expert on the rule of perpetuities—a law which states that a trust can last no longer than "lives in being" at the time of the creation of the trust, plus twenty-one years. A law that only makes sense to a T&E lawyer.

"T&E." Trusts and estates. We're the folks who are here to remind you that, alas, you can't take it with you. So, with an eye toward your inevitable demise, we will help you plan how to disburse all your accumulated temporal booty. What's more, we will maximize the accrued wealth of your estate through the creation of assorted trusts, cannily constructed to minimize "negative Internal Revenue impacting" (i.e., "killer taxes"). We can, if directed, offer refuge for your capital in assorted tax shelters. We can devise rigidly governed trusts to ensure that your prodigal son will not blow his inheritance on blow. We can easily exclude said son from any share in your estate by setting up a series of contingencies—legally binding clauses in your will that can even block his mother/your widow from subsidizing his profligate habits. And, of course, we will make certain your last will and testament is so rock solid and uncontestable that your beneficiaries will never come into contact with the dreaded rule of perpetuities.

Of course, Lawrence, Cameron and Thomas will not represent you unless your net worth is more than $2 million. We're a small department, T&E. One senior partner (Jack Mayle), one junior partner *(moi)*, three associates, five secretaries. And since T&E is considered a lucrative, but decidedly nerdish branch of the law, we're tucked away at the back of corporate headquarters, with only one corner office to our name.

The offices of Lawrence, Cameron and Thomas are located on the eighteenth and nineteenth floors of 120 Broadway in lower Manhattan. It's one of those Roaring Twenties testaments to boom capitalism, the skyscraper equivalent of a Wurlitzer organ. Legend has it that, after the Crash of '29, more than a dozen brokers flew out of its windows—and those lucky enough to have had an office on the southwestern corner of the building got a terrific view of lower Manhattan as they made their final tumble to the street. Hello, God; good-bye, Mammon. Splat.

Today, people in my firm still consider a corner office to be a big deal. Only full partners are allocated them—but since there are just eight corner offices, many of our senior lawyers spend years fretting about when they'll finally get that two-window executive suite they know they deserve. Just as the associates working on the eighteenth floor fret about whether they'll make partner and move up to the nineteenth floor. And the summer associates fret about becoming associates. And the paralegals fret about their lack of professional progress (due to their lack of a law degree). And the legal secretaries fret about their low wage structure.

There is a lot of fretting at Lawrence, Cameron and Thomas. But, for most of us, there is also a lot of money—which makes the fretting worthwhile. Personally speaking, I don't fret about the position of my office (nineteenth floor, eastern side of the building, nice view of the Brooklyn Bridge, adjoining bathroom, and directly next to the corner suite occupied by Jack Mayle). And I certainly don't fret about the cash they throw at me—around $315,000 a year (depending on profit-sharing participation and bonuses), making me a certified resident of high-tax-bracket heaven. The perks of the job are also fantastic: the free Blue Cross/Blue Shield family health plan; the free membership at the Downtown Athletic Club; the free use of the serviced company apartment at Battery Park City; the interest-free auto loans; the free late-night limousine service to anywhere within a fifty-mile radius of our office (New Croydon just manages to qualify); the company restaurant account with Lutèce and The Four Seasons and 21 . . .

In fact, I can't complain about anything to do with Lawrence, Cameron and Thomas. Except the work. I really fret a lot about the work. Because it bores me. Bores me stupid.

Of course, I knew that T&E was Dullsville when I joined the firm in September 1983. This was the mid-eighties, after all, and as the avaricious juices of the boom years began to flow, every bright young schmuck out of law school wanted to land a place in a Wall Street firm like Lawrence, Cameron and Thomas, because, with junk bond and merger fever gripping corporate America, the Street was the place to be in those days. I mean, I toyed with the idea of maybe signing up with some politically correct firm and spending my first couple of years as a lawyer defending illegal Salvadoran immigrants. But my dad convinced me to first do a stint with a major New York firm.

"Even if you decide to become Mahatma Gandhi later on," he said, "four or five years in some big white-shoe outfit will give you some very necessary street cred. Because it will mean that you have done time as an asshole, and you're not just some righteous do-gooder with no knowledge of the establishment."

So, yet again, I developed a master plan in my head. I'd stay five years max with a big firm, live cheaply, save like an idiot, and then—while still in my early thirties—switch over into a more subversive sector of the law. I saw myself fighting for Indian land rights, or becoming the sort of valiant advocate who represents impoverished fetal drug victims with eight fingers on one hand. And, of course, with all the money I squirreled away from my years as a Wall Street attorney, I'd still be able to devote a sizable amount of my time to photography. Hell, America was brimming with famous lawyer-novelists. Why couldn't I be the first famous lawyer-photographer?

So I interviewed with a half-dozen major Wall Street firms—and I'm sure the fact that Prescott Lawrence was at Yale with my dad helped land me the job at Lawrence, Cameron and Thomas.

Like all new associates, I spent my first year being rotated among departments—a chance for the partners to size up the new talent and see where they might fit into the corporate scheme of things. There's no criminal law division at Lawrence, Cameron; no pro bono sector where the partners soothe their consciences by handling death row cases free of charge. The firm is unapologetically mercenary. And during the height of Reaganomics, every first-year associate scrambled to make a serious impression in the firm's heavyweight divisions—litigation, corporate law, and tax—where you were representing some of the nation's most notorious robber barons.

I did time in each of these departments, but discovered that they were filled with guys with names like Ames and Brad who delighted in gutting "the opposition" and sticking knives into each other. Of course, this breed dominates so much of American corporate life. They've been educated in a "play-to-win" philosophy, and they love using the language of the gridiron when it comes to negotiating even the most negligible contract.

"We want you to play the tough linebacker here . . . We don't like field goals in this department, only touchdowns . . . I'm quarterbacking this deal, understand? . . ."

Group hysteria and free-floating paranoia were the order of the day in all of these departments, and even when there was no need for freneticism or aggression, someone would concoct a crisis (or an enemy) to keep the belligerence level high. After months of dismal football metaphors spoken by guys who worked very hard at being professional shits, I realized that to survive the cutthroat theatrics of a sexy legal division, you had to buy into their gladiatorial belief that "business is war."

But since I simply looked upon the law as a means by which to subsidize my future photographic career, I decided to seek out the quietest niche imaginable in Lawrence, Cameron and Thomas—a niche into which I could disappear, make serious money, yet avoid all the little Napoleons running every other branch of the firm. And when I met Jack Mayle, I knew I had found my mentor, my rabbi—a guy who had also decided, years earlier, that T&E offered secure shelter from the infighting that makes up 60 percent of corporate life.

"If you've got a taste for the internecine—if you're one of those prep school Apaches who wants to collect scalps—then I've got no use for you here," he said during our first interview. "There's no glamour in T&E, no jizz. This is Nebbish Town, *capisce?* Our motto is: 'Let the goys have the coronaries.'"

"But Mr. Mayle," I said, "I'm a goy."

He threaded his liver-spotted fingers together and cracked his knuckles loudly.

"This has crossed my mind," he said with a hint of rabbinical mischief in his voice. "But at least you're a *quiet* goy."

Jack Mayle wore elevator shoes. Check that: Jack Mayle wore Gucci elevator shoes. His fine gray hair was always well oiled and combed straight back. He bought handmade suits from Dunhill. He wore a pearl tiepin and a black cashmere overcoat in winter. He looked like George Raft—a diminutive dandy who decided that dressing well was the best defense against his five-foot-four stature and the fact that he was the only Jewish senior partner in a deeply WASP firm.

"I know they call me 'the Bookkeeper' behind my back," he once told me, "but I also know that *they* know I'm the biggest rainmaker in the firm. I bring in more business than any of those Episcopalian schmucks in litigation. And if there's one thing I understand about Protestants, it's this: Give 'em bang for their buck and they'll pretend that they consider you their equal."

Jack liked to play up this self-appointed role of the Hebraic outsider, marooned in a Gaza strip of *goyische* Wall Streeters. And I think one of the reasons he quickly took to me was that he sensed (and approved of) my outsider status within the firm. As I later found out (from Estelle, of course), he'd done a postcollege stint as a would-be abstract painter in the boho wonderland of fifties Greenwich Village—before bowing to the inevitable family pressure and winning a scholarship to Brooklyn Law. So, watching me backseat my photographic ambitions to play the corporate game must have triggered some strong protective instinct in him—because within two weeks of my arrival at T&E, he let it be known around the firm that, after twenty-four years at Lawrence, Cameron, he had finally found his successor, his *boychik*.

"You play your cards right, I'll get you a junior partnership in five years," he told me when my temporary two-month stint at T&E was finished. "Just think—total career security by the time you're thirty-three. And, believe me, you'll be able to buy a lot of cameras with the cash you'll be taking home."

Another Faustian bargain dangled in front of me. *Partnership?* According to my master plan, I was only going to do a four-year stint as an associate at Lawrence, Cameron, and then find the sort of right-on practice in Berkeley or Ann Arbor where I would become a prize-winning photographer who also led legal onslaughts against the white-slave-trade wing of the Christian Coalition. But *partnership?* At the premature age of thirty-three? That would have totally amazed the old man. All right, T&E wasn't exactly a thrill a minute, but I started convincing myself that the minutiae of legal work—the fine-tuning of codicils, the intricacies of beneficiary rights—suited my nature. I mean, if I loved the minute technicalities involved in printing a photograph, surely I could come to enjoy the detailed craftsmanship of will writing. Couldn't I?

The phone buzzed on my desk. I hit the speaker button and got a nasally blast of Estelle.

"Your wife doesn't answer, Mr. Bradford."

"Try again in a half hour."

"Mr. Mayle was wondering if you had a minute . . ."

"Tell him I'll drop by in fifteen. Finishing up a few adjustments to the Berkowitz document . . ."

These adjustments took all of five minutes. A little tightening up of the language regarding income payments from the residuary trust and I ensured that no rogue member of the Berkowitz clan—heirs to the biggest Lincoln Continental dealership in Huntington, Long Island—would ever be able to claim a share of the estate unless listed as a proper beneficiary in the will. Then I picked up the phone, hit the first button on my speed dialer, and was connected with my home number. It answered.

"*¿Hola? ¿Quién es?*"

Shit. Perdita, our fully legal (believe me, I checked her green card) Guatemalan housekeeper.

"*Hola, Perdita,*" I said. "*¿Dónde está señora Bradford?*"

"*Ha salido. Para todo el día.*"

"*¿Te ha dado un número de teléfono donde está?*"

"*No, señor.*"

"*¿Y los niños?*"

"*Han salido con Fiona.*"

Out all day. No telephone contact number. And the kids were off with the nanny. I bit my lower lip. That was the third weekday in a row she had been out of the house by nine in the morning. I know, because on each of those mornings I had tried to reach her from the office, hoping somehow to broker a cease-fire between us.

Anything interesting on for today?

No.

I flipped open my address book and dialed the number of Wendy Waggoner, a local cookbook writer (I'm sure you've read *Wendy's Waistline Wonders: The Ultimate Foodie Diet*), and the only forty-year-old woman I know who still wore plaid skirts with big safety pins. Married to a real jerk named Lewis—Yale '76, big noise in the bond department at Bear Stearns, who once told me that, bar his secretary, he couldn't remember the last time he'd had a conversation with anyone who earned less than $200,000 a year. Exactly the kind of people I'd cross three state lines to avoid—but Beth enjoyed rubbing shoulders with a minor celeb like Wendy, and played tennis with her one morning a week. Maybe this was that morning.

"*Hola. Residencia de Waggoner.*"

Another Latin American maid. I think all of New Croydon acquires their domestic help from the South-of-the-Border Employment Agency.

"Is Wendy there?" I asked, suddenly tired of bilingual calls to Connecticut.

"Señora Waggoner is in city today. Message?"

"No, *gracias*," I said and hung up. No need to make Wendy wonder why I was phoning her on a weekday morning in search of my wife. No need to turn us into a talking point at her weekly lunch party: "I hear the Bradfords aren't too lovey-dovey these days."

The Bradfords. Jesus.

The phone buzzed. Estelle again.

"Mr. Mayle was wondering . . ."

"I'm on my way," I said.

His office was next to mine. A senior-partner suite. Massive presidential desk. Overstuffed armchairs. A mahogany conference table. Bad Federalist art. I knocked twice and entered. He was sitting in his vast leather desk chair, looking more dwarfed than usual.

"Nice suit," he said, eyeing the charcoal pinstriped number I was wearing. "Brooks?"

"Hugo Boss."

"Letting the Krauts outfit you, eh?"

"You could send me to your tailor."

"Oh no," he said. "I'm the only guy 'round here who's allowed to dress like Nathan Detroit. I want you to stay nice and Ivy League for our country-club clients."

"Like the Berkowitzes?"

"Mr. Berkowitz thinks the sun shines out of your *tukkus*."

"Yeah, right."

"I mean it. I bring a *goniff* like Lee Berkowitz into a firm like this, and then a well-mannered WASP like you treats him with deference . . . I tell you, he now thinks he's Nelson Rockefeller. And I know he'd give you a big discount on a new Eldorado . . . not that you'd ever be seen driving something so Scarsdale in that white-bread town you live in."

"We have Jews in New Croydon," I said, keeping up the banter.

"Yeah . . . as hired help. So how are the Berkowitz papers shaping?"

"Just a few niggling details about patrimonial linkage, and two potentially contestable points regarding residuary trust payments. Piece of cake."

"Wish I could say the same for the Dexter estate . . ." Jack said.

"The recently deceased Deke Dexter of Dexter Copper and Cable?"

"The very schmuck. And a very active schmuck too, from what I can gather—as there are three very aggrieved Chilean women, ranging in ages from fifty-four down to twenty-two, who all claim they bore Mr. Dexter children over the past two decades."

"Why this thing for Chilean women?"

"Biggest copper producer in the world, Chile. And no half-assed banana republic, believe me, because I've got this shyster Santiago lawyer on to me twice a day, threatening to exhume Dexter and do a DNA match between the three Chilean kids and their dead daddy. Wish to Christ Dexter had done the smart thing and specified cremation in his will; then I could've told this Santiago ambulance chaser to roll over and play dead. But the greaseball is a shrewd cookie—knows his U.S. probate law backward."

"How much he looking to score?"

"Ten mil a kid."

"You tell him to get a life?"

"Natch. I've offered 500k a kid, end of story. I think we'll get into bed around 1.1 per dependent."

"Mrs. Dexter must be thrilled to learn she's three mil and change down."

"That golddigger came out posttax with forty-seven mil in principal. So she can well afford the three-three hit—especially as she doesn't want the hassle of an exhumation, which will guarantee *National Enquirer* publicity. You should see this broad—Dexter's fifth wife, and she's had so many face jobs there's a knot at the back of the neck where all the flesh is gathered."

"Well, it sounds like a lot more laughs than the Berkowitz documents," I said.

"Has its moments. Passes the time."

He smiled a weary, cheerless smile. A smile I didn't like.

"Sit down, Ben," he said.

I did as ordered. His speakerphone buzzed. Hildy—Jack's secretary—came on:

"Excuse me for interrupting, Mr. Mayle, but Dr. Frobisher's office called . . ."

Jack cut her off in midsentence. "Tell them I'm not here. Anything else?"

"Mr. Bradford, Estelle wanted you to know that she tried your wife again, but—"

Now it was my turn to interrupt. "That's fine, Hildy. Thank Estelle for me."

Jack killed the speaker button and looked at me carefully.

"Everything okay on the home front?"

"Fine, Jack. Just fine."

"Liar."

"That obvious?"

"You look like hell, Ben."

"Nothing twenty straight hours of sleep won't cure. But you . . . you look the business, Jack."

"No, I do not," he said.

"Hell, yeah," I said, trying to keep him off the subject of my home life. "Like a guy who's just spent two weeks in Palm Springs with a showgirl."

"Now you are talking crap," he said.

"Sorry," I said, taken aback by his irritated tone.

He gazed blankly at his desk blotter for what seemed like minutes. Finally, he spoke.

"I'm dying, Ben."

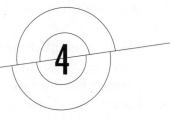

THE CAB WAS GRIDLOCKED on Thirty-first between Sixth and Seventh. I was not amused—especially as I had instructed the driver (Benoit Namphy, license number 48B92) to go west on Twenty-third and then north up Eighth. But the guy could only cope with about ten words of English, and wasn't listening to me anyway, as he had the radio tuned to some Haitian emigré station, blasting out the Port-au-Prince top twenty in between phone-in voodoo requests. I became irritated. Very irritated.

"I told you to avoid this street," I said.

"Wha', mon?" was his reply.

"Avoid this street."

"No can avoid it. We here."

"Don't you listen to customers? Don't they teach you that at cab school?"

"Easy, mon. We get there."

"I don't want to just *get there*," I said. "I want to get there *fast*." I was yelling.

He flashed me a stoned smile. "You having bad day?"

That was it. "Fuck you fuck you fuck you," I shouted as I threw open the door, tossed five bucks through the driver's window, and stalked off down Thirty-first Street, muttering to myself like one of those guys you see selling pencils in front of

Bloomingdale's. After twenty yards, I stopped and leaned against a phone box, trying to calm down.

I'm dying, Ben.

Inoperable stomach cancer. He'd found out two weeks ago, but the tough little bastard hadn't told anyone, not even his wife.

"They say eight months, a year max. You should see the plumber they've got looking after me. Dr. Horace Frobisher. A dead ringer for Raymond Massey, walks around like he's God the Father. Know how he broke it to me? 'I'd start getting my affairs in order if I were you.' Sounded just like a fucking lawyer."

He wanted the "news" kept quiet within the firm. "I'm not submitting to chemo or radical surgery or any other last-ditch bullshit they want to try on me. If it's terminal, it's terminal— so I'll take their painkillers and keep going to the office until . . ."

He broke off, tightened his lips, and stared out his window at the frantic pedestrian parade on Wall Street—everyone looking so purposeful, everyone so preoccupied with getting somewhere.

"You know what's hardest about all this?" he said quietly. "It's realizing that you've lived your life *not* thinking about this moment. Pretending that, somehow, you'll never have to face up to the biggest moment of them all—when you finally know that there is no future possibility for change, for exploring other options, for even dreaming about another life. When you can't even retreat into your fantasy about doing it all differently . . . because you've run out of road."

Then he turned around. Staring me straight in the eyes, he said, "You're going to be the new senior partner, Ben."

I flinched. An involuntary movement, but Jack saw it. And said nothing. Because he knew. He knew exactly what this meant for me. A half mil a year minimum, plenty of corporate prestige . . . and the death of my other life. That unrealized life behind a viewfinder. A life that—like Jack's stint long ago in some MacDougal Street garret—becomes the stuff of daydream. Sometimes bittersweet, sometimes (on bad days) anguished, yet one that never leaves you in peace because you know that you've embraced the securer option. And security, as you discover, is its own form of hell.

"Hey, *you.*"

I found myself staring through the glass of the telephone booth at a slob around forty, his hairy belly protruding below a T-shirt dappled with food stains. He tapped a quarter against the glass to get my attention.

"You," he said. "You need a place to lean, go use a wall."

My fingers tightened into fists.

"What was that, asshole?" I said.

"Asshole? You're the asshole, jerkoff."

An adrenaline charge of rage hit me, a rage so pure and undistilled I felt light-headed, exhilarated, fearless. And ready to tear this fat fuck apart. He must have sensed how dangerous I'd suddenly become because he grew white with apprehension as I informed him in a quiet, temperate voice, "If you are not out of that phone booth by the time I count to three, I will kill you. And I'm not just talking about roughing you up. I am talking about breaking your neck."

His eyes were now two big ovals of fear. I could almost hear him sweating.

"Hey, lookit, like, I'm sorry, okay?" he said. "Like, y'know, I'm having a bad day too."

"I am not having a bad day," I said. "I am having a terrible day. But killing you just might cheer me up. One . . . two . . ."

He was out of the phone booth and charging down Thirty-first Street, his fleshy body shaking like Jell-O. I fell into the booth and grabbed the phone receiver. It trembled in my hand.

This fucking city. It would turn anyone feral. You're lucky the slob didn't have a Saturday night special on him. *Plugged for leaning against a phone booth.* The perfect New York end to a perfect day.

It took a minute or so before I stopped shaking. You've got to get some sleep, *hombre.* Get a little *perspective.* Before you go ballistic.

I dug my AT&T card out of my wallet and phoned home. It rang four times, then I heard my upbeat voice on the answering machine:

"Hi there. You've reached Ben and Beth Bradford. We can't come to the phone right now . . ."

Ben and Beth Bradford. I always told her that if we ever got married, she should keep her own name.

"I'll live with you forever," she said one drunken evening in January of 1988 when we were killing a second bottle of wine down at the Odeon, "but we're never getting married."

"But if we did . . ."

"No way," she said with a boozy giggle.

"Okay. Understood. But just, say, *hypothetically,* in a dumb middle-class moment, we decided to, uh, formalize things between us . . ."

"Then I'd take your name."

"That's kind of old-fashioned of you," I said.

"Nah," Beth said, "just being practical. I mean, Beth Bradford would look a lot better on a dust jacket than Beth Schnitzler. But . . ."

She gave me one of her big, mischievous "I-want-to-undress-you-with-my-teeth" smiles.

" . . . we are *not* getting married."

1988. We'd been living together for just a few months, and with my salary on the rise, we could well afford the $2,000-a-month rent on a loft-style apartment in Soho. The decision to live downtown was a deliberate one. After all, though both of us were working in straight jobs, we didn't consider ourselves yuppie scum, so the idea of renting a place somewhere as white bread as the Upper East Side or Murray Hill was anathema to artists-in-waiting like us.

Artists-in-waiting. That's what Beth dubbed us. Of course, there was always a touch of archness in her voice when she used that phrase. But, honestly, there was a time when we both believed it was only a matter of a year or two before we liberated ourselves from the wage-slave world. And every weekday morning, before heading off to *Cosmo,* Beth would get up at six and work three hours on the novel that she hoped would make her literary name. She refused to let me see the work in progress—refused to even tell me the title—until one Saturday afternoon in March of '89, she handed me the 438-page manuscript and said:

"It's called *The Playpen of Ambition*."

It was Beth's second novel. Her first, *Beyond Ossining*, was never published. Beth wrote it just after she graduated from Wellesley, where she was the editor of the college literary magazine and had won a handful of creative writing prizes. She was also awarded a postgraduate fellowship to some literary retreat in Scotland—and that's where she wrote most of *Beyond Ossining*, a bildungsroman (Beth's word, not mine) about a young, gawky girl attempting to conform to the suburban ethos of Westchester County while coping with her mother's agonizing death from breast cancer. And when Mama eventually expires, the girl escapes to an elite New England women's college whereupon she loses her heart to an Amherst shit, but still discovers her "muse" as a painter. It was, give or take a few obvious details, the large-print edition of Beth's life, written in a style that could best be described as sensitive-girl lyricism ("That autumn, under a salmon sky, my mother began to sew a quilt in our backyard" . . . that kind of thing).

When Beth came back from Scotland, *Beyond Ossining* found its way into the hands of fifteen New York agents, none of whom deigned to take it on (the general consensus being that three other first novels had been published that year which also happened to be lyrical accounts of childhoods in John Cheever country, overshadowed by dying mothers). Though naturally disappointed, Beth didn't let this setback throw her. Instead, she landed a day job as an assistant fiction editor at *Cosmopolitan* to pay the rent while writing her second novel.

"Know what I do for a living?" she told me when we first met at a mutual friend's wedding. "I read five to seven unsolicited stories every day, all of which are about depressed, lonely women looking for their G spot."

I laughed—and was immediately smitten. She was smart and funny and very determined. Determined to make it as a novelist. Determined to avoid the suburban snare into which her mother had fallen. Around three weeks after we'd started seeing each other, she finally opened up about her mother's death, telling me:

"You know, she was a massively disappointed woman. When she was my age, she was a real highflier in public relations. An account executive at one of the big New York firms. But as soon as she married my dad and got pregnant with me—bang, that was it. Off to Ossining and a life of PTA meetings and coffee mornings and dinner on the table when my dad arrived home on the 7:06. She was a great mom. But, Christ, how she quietly hated the narrow life she'd accepted, like just about every other woman of her generation. And I'm sure that her cancer was, in part, triggered by her deep, nagging sense of being a stay-at-home 'little woman,' dependent on a man she'd grown to dislike."

I reached out and took her hand.

"Don't worry," I said, "that will never happen to you."

Her voice was as cold as steel. "I know it won't," she said.

At the *Cosmo* literary department, Beth worked for two chic dykes named Laurie and Gretel. "The sisterhood," as she called them, but so encouraging when it came to Beth's literary prospects that they secured her an agent to represent her new book.

The Playpen of Ambition was another bildungsroman: a young, gawky girl from Westchester County—still scarred by her mother's premature death from breast cancer—moves to the Big City determined to become A Great Painter. But, in an attempt to make ends meet, she takes a job in the art department of a glossy magazine, gets promoted to the art directorship, falls in love with a young dermatologist, and by the end of the novel finds herself torn between the temptations of domesticity and the "inner voice" of her muse.

In the five months after she finished it, twenty-two publishers rejected *The Playpen of Ambition*—but, oh, God, how tantalizingly close she came with three of them. In fact, one editor at Atheneum told Beth he wanted to publish it, but lost his job two weeks later during some corporate bloodbath (and his asshole cost-accountant successor just didn't think it had "commercial legs"). This time, Beth's disappointment was acute—but everyone (her agent, the sisterhood, myself) did their best to keep her spirits buoyed, telling her the usual triumph-over-adversity tales about the usual Famous Writers who'd had five manuscripts rejected before they'd finally broken through.

"You *will* get published," I told her a few months after the final rejection letter rolled in. "Just keep at it."

"Climb ev'ry mountain, forge ev'ry stream," she sang grimly, then added: ". . . and while you're at it, darling, keep your chin *down* when you vomit."

Beth was keeping her chin down a lot that autumn, as she was suffering from a commonplace condition known as morning sickness. She contracted this ailment after we came back one evening from our local Italian joint on Prince Street. Heavily Chiantified, we started pulling each other's clothes off as soon as we were inside our apartment door, and didn't stop to worry about little details like the insertion of Beth's diaphragm. Ah, drunken passion. Ah, morning-after recriminations.

"That was so totally fucking dumb," Beth said as we nursed our hangovers over brunch at the Odeon the next afternoon. "Especially as it was bang in the middle of my cycle."

"Don't worry about it," I said. "My guys probably can't swim upstream."

"A kid's the last thing we need now."

"It ain't gonna happen, toots."

But, of course, it did.

"You want to keep it?" she asked the night we got the news.

"Of course," I said, but that was something of a half-truth. The idea of fatherhood—and all its incumbent responsibilities—terrified me. But I was desperate to keep Beth. Despite her insistence that we'd never marry, throughout the two years we'd already lived together I had proposed the idea at least a half-dozen times—and had been repeatedly turned down, Beth always sweetly telling me that, though she was in this for the long haul, the state of matrimony was far too "bourgeois" for artists-in-waiting like us. Looking back on it now, something in me must have feared her strong sense of personal autonomy. I knew that she loved me and wanted to be with me—but that wasn't enough. Call it male insecurity, but I had to make certain that she couldn't walk away from me with ease. And so, upon discovering that we were now parents-in-waiting, I somehow convinced myself that a child would firmly, *permanently* cement us together.

I also knew that, for all her "right to choose" beliefs, Beth could never bring herself to terminate the pregnancy. She was over thirty now, the clock was ticking, and her novels weren't making it into print. Of course she raised all sorts of fears about becoming a facsimile of her mother, but I gently assuaged them. We would keep on living in the city. She would keep on working. A full-time nanny would be hired to look after the child. She could still get up at six every morning to put in a few hours on her new novel before heading off to *Cosmo*. Life, I assured her, would go on as before.

"It never works that way," she said.

"It can. It will. And after we're married . . ."

"I knew this was coming."

"We might as well. I mean, we're as good as . . ."

"You never give up, do you?"

"Who would ever want to give up on you?" I said.

"Flattery will get you—"

"Everywhere," I said, pulling her toward me. I kissed her deeply. Then she took my face in her hands and looked at me carefully.

"Are we going to regret this?" she asked.

"You know we won't."

"So much for our artist-in-waiting fantasy."

"We'll get there."

"Maybe . . . but if I ever, *ever* suggest moving to the 'burbs, shoot me."

I didn't remind her of that comment thirteen months later when she called my office one afternoon in a state of shock.

"You've got to get home *now*," she said, sounding totally panicked. My heart stopped. Adam was just four months old. Crib death, meningitis, infant encephalitis . . .

"Tell me . . ." I finally said.

"Vomit," she sobbed. "He's covered in vomit. Some asshole's vomit . . ."

The asshole in question was a homeless guy who was camped out in an alley opposite our apartment on King Street. Beth—home early that day from *Cosmo*—was heading out with Adam for a walk. Suddenly, this bum veered into her path, looking like Moses on Thunderbird, his navel-length white beard caked with snot.

"Cute mama, cute fuckin' baby. Give a guy a dollar, huh? Jus' one little—"

But he didn't get to finish that sentence, as he suddenly turned green and blew lunch all over Adam. Beth screamed, Adam screamed, the drunk was apprehended by two cops in a patrol car, and later that afternoon Adam's pediatrician charged his two hyperanxious parents $200 to assure them that their son could not contract HIV, hepatitis A, B, C, or bubonic plague from this baptism of lowlife vomit. Ten days later, while we were out walking with Adam in Washington Square Park, the wheels of his stroller crunched loudly as they ran over two empty crack vials—and the next weekend I suggested we house-hunt in Connecticut.

"I can't believe we're doing this," Beth said after I made an offer on the house on Constitution Crescent.

"Nor can I. But, hey, we'll both be in the city every day, right? And New Croydon is a great town for kids. I mean, as you said yourself, you don't want to raise your son in Calcutta."

"I know what I said. I know *all* the arguments."

"Lookit, if we can't stand it, we'll sell and move back to town."

"We'll never move back," she said bleakly.

The Picket Fence—Beth's third novel—was started a few months after we set up house in New Croydon. My junior partnership had come through and, brimming with arrogant largesse, I made a dumb, but well-intentioned, mistake: I convinced Beth to give up her job and devote herself full-time to writing.

"You're only making twenty-seven thousand a year, which we certainly don't need anymore," I said. "We've now got the space for you to have a proper study, Adam's with the nanny all day, you've always talked about how hard it is to juggle fiction and a day job . . . so what are you waiting for?"

She hemmed and hawed for a while, worried about being home all day, worried about cutting herself off from metropolitan life, worried about failing yet again. But I kept up the gentle, yet firm, persuasion. Why? Possibly because I wanted one of us *not* to be an artist-in-waiting. Or maybe I got a curious macho buzz from the idea of subsidizing my wife the writer. Or perhaps I needed her to sit at home and fail. Failure loves company, after all.

The Picket Fence took Beth nearly two years to write. The gawky adolescent, perma-scarred from her mother's early death, is now even more of a highflier in the New York magazine world. But then, in a drastic volte face, she marries the dermatologist of her dreams, moves with him to an idealized clapboard Connecticut town where she's determined to rediscover her muse as a painter, but gets pregnant, becomes torn between maternal joy and lack of professional fulfillment, goes through a major marital crisis, and . . .

Watch this space for volume four of the Beth Bradford saga.

Only volume four never materialized, because *The Picket Fence* never found a publisher. Her agent liked it, the sisterhood liked it, even I liked it (as I always secretly thought that the two previous volumes were far too precious and self-satisfied). It went out to twenty-four publishers. By the time the final rejection letter arrived, Beth was pregnant with Josh and—feeling even more trapped by domestic routine—she started to withdraw from me.

Her agent, Melanie, said, "I just don't get it. You're my unluckiest client. Maybe you should try to write something different, something not so specifically predicated on your own life."

I said, "You know, Melanie's right. You should try a different genre. Something completely new."

Beth said, "There will be no more novels." And when I tried to argue her out of such defeatist talk, she told me to shut up.

So Beth stopped going into her study and turned her attention to Colonial American furnishings. Josh was born, he refused to sleep, Beth refused to have sex with me and also refused to talk about why she refused to have sex with me. She kept buying eighteenth-century bric-a-brac, I kept buying darkroom equipment, we kept dodging the issue of why our marriage had become so stalled, deadlocked, paralyzed. But we both silently understood why. Because she blamed me for turning her into her mother—a talented, independent woman slowly atrophying in commuter land.

I suggested counseling. She laughed. I suggested a trial separation. She shrugged and said, "If that's what you want." I said it was *not* what I wanted. "Then stay," she said. I said we needed to talk about our problems. "What problems?" she said. I said that we didn't talk anymore. "We're talking now," she said. I said, yes we are talking now, but not about our problems. "What problems?" she said. "The fact that you blame me for everything," I said. "You wanted to get married," she said. "You wanted to move here. You wanted me to give up my job and write full-time. Why talk about 'our problems' when you got exactly what you wanted." I said that I didn't exactly force her to do anything. "True," she said, "you simply used every persuasive trick they taught you in law school." That's not fair, I said. "Don't you dare talk to me about 'fair,'" she said in a voice shaking with anger. "There is nothing *fair* about this situation." I said, "At least let's try to talk through—" She cut me off. "There is nothing to talk about. *We* have no problems." And then she left the room, and I knew I had lost her.

"You renting that phone booth or what?"

I snapped out of my reverie and found myself under inspection by a little dumpling of a woman around sixty, carrying a battered Henri Bendel bag stuffed with old newspapers.

"Sorry," I said, leaving the booth.

"You should be," she shouted after me.

But I am, I felt like shouting back at her. *I am so sorry for so much.*

I dashed across Seventh Avenue, dodging garment guys and their movable racks of clothes, turned north for two blocks, then headed west on Thirty-third. He knew I was coming (I had phoned earlier from the office). And as I approached their front door, Ted held it open for me.

"Mr. Bradford," he said with a smile.

Ted was the manager of Upton Cameras, purveyors of high-end photographic equipment. A guy my age with thinning hair who, winter or summer, always wore short-sleeved shirts. Ted was super-friendly and courteous toward me because I was Ted's best customer. Over the past two years, I had spent around $20,000 in his shop. That's why Ted liked me so much. That's why Ted held open the door for me, and said:

"Well, it's here."

It was the new Canon EOS-1N top-of-the-line pro camera. An amazing piece of equipment: five-point autofocus with multiple metering patterns for optimum results, not to mention a blindingly fast motor drive that could shoot ten frames per second. Just the sort of camera you'd want for covering a fast-moving news story. Or a high-speed sporting event, like the Indy 500. After reading a laudatory review in *Popular Photography,* I ordered it. I had no real use for this camera, and knew it would spend most of its time on the shelf next to my other cameras. But I still wanted it—because, after all, it had the best motor drive of any camera on the market today. And I really must remain au courant with the latest in cutting-edge equipment. I am still an artist-in-waiting, after all, albeit one who can afford to drop $2,499 plus tax on a Japanese toy.

Ted had the camera unpackaged for me on a display counter. It looked sensational: a rugged yet sleek body (solid aluminum-alloy die-cast chassis) in a matte black finish. It also had wonderful ergonomics, as the hand grip was perfectly contoured, while the body had a nicely weighted solidity. And the L Series Ultrasonic lens that I had ordered offered no-nonsense, whistle-clean sharpness—the perfect perspective for news work.

"Try the shutter release," Ted said.

I depressed the black button. It was like pulling the trigger on a submachine gun—a ferocious *rat-tat-tat-tat* as the motor drive revved into action.

"Covers an entire thirty-six-frame roll in less than four seconds," Ted said. "Which is about as fast as it gets. But what I think you're going to find most satisfying about the EOS-1N is its advanced multipoint control system, and its choice of five metering patterns."

"You think I should consider an auto-zoom flash to go with it?"

"Funny you should mention that," Ted said. "Ordered one just in case you might be considering it . . ."

"Mind reader."

"Just thinking about the complaint you made about the last Speed-lite you bought—how it wasn't compatible with an 85-millimeter medium telephoto. Well, this new Canon 540-EZ not only has a focal length ranging from 24-millimeter wide-angle to 105-millimeter telephoto, but if you use its built-in wide panel, you can also cover the angle of an ultrawide 18-millimeter lens, making it perfect for landscape work in diminished light."

"How much will it set me back?"

"It lists for $334, but I'll give you the standard 20 percent professional discount, and will also throw in an optional transistor pack as part of the bargain."

"Sold," I said.

The standard 20 percent professional discount. Ted was one shrewd salesman. In the three years since I'd first discovered

Upton Cameras, he'd never once asked me what I did for a living (even though my clothes and the money I was able to throw around made it pretty obvious that I was pure Wall Street). Instead, he always treated me as a fellow pro, and kept our conversations firmly grounded within the lingua franca of high-end photographic equipment. But I often wondered if he saw me as a spoiled rich suit who bought whatever overpriced gear he fancied; gear that even real photographic heavyweights wouldn't own because it was so nouveau riche. And did he also notice the twitch of guilt and misgiving that crossed my face when I handed over my Amex platinum card to pay for all these absurd toys?

"That's going to work out, with tax, to $2,947," Ted said as the credit card machine whirred to life and a voucher sprouted out.

"Fine," I said hoarsely, noticing that my palms were sweating while I signed on the dotted line. Almost three thousand bucks for a camera I didn't need. I didn't know whether to feel despair or the punch-drunk elation of a man who had just squandered the family fortune. Only, of course, I'd squandered nothing. Three grand was small change to me.

"Mind if I use your phone?" I asked. Ted handed me a cordless. I dug out my AT&T card. "No need," Ted said. Punching in my home number, I waited. One ring. Two rings. Three . . .

"Hi there. You've reached Ben and Beth . . ."

I hit the disconnect button, then punched in my office number. "Any messages?" I asked Estelle when she answered. A few business calls, nothing urgent. "And my wife?" A slight pause from Estelle, then: "Sorry, Mr. Bradford." I bit my lip distractedly, then handed the phone back to Ted. He acted as if he'd been oblivious to that phone call, and to the uneasiness in my voice.

"I think you'll really be pleased with the results you get from the EOS-1N," Ted said, unwrapping a new Tenba Venture Pak (the best camera bag in the world, if you believe their advertising—well, I did have three already). He packed it with my new camera and assorted accessories.

"Uh . . . I didn't buy that bag," I said.

"Let's just say it's on the house."

"Thanks, Ted."

"No, thank *you,* Mr. Bradford, as always. And you know we're always here if you need us."

We're always here if you need us. Retail therapy. But walking east down Thirty-third, I didn't feel that buzz of therapeutic bliss. Just anxiety. Especially as I saw Wendy Waggoner walking directly toward me.

"Well, hey there, Ben Bradford."

No plaid skirts today. Instead, she was power-dressed to kill in a black Armani suit and a white silk T-shirt. Her blonde hair was stylishly cropped, Audrey Hepburn style. She had the sort of perfect bone structure that hinted at patrician breeding and high maintenance. She was accompanied by some super-tall trendy, draped in Versace, with oval designer specs and a gray ponytail. He eyed my Burberry raincoat and Upton Cameras shopping bag with wry contempt. Wendy air-kissed my cheeks.

"Ben, meet Jordan Longfellow, my editor. Ben's a neighbor in New Croydon."

"Sort of neighbor," I said (well, she and her godawful husband did live a mile away from us).

"You're a bit uptown, aren't you?" she said. "Shopping?"

"Some camera stuff," I said.

She turned to the trendy. "Ben's a photographer who just happens to be a lawyer too. You publish lawyers, don't you, Jordan?"

A flash of his teeth. "Some of my best writers are lawyers," he said. "You a writer, Ben?"

"He writes wills," Wendy said.

I wanted to garrote her. Instead I managed a thin smile. Jordan glanced at his watch.

"Must fly, Ben," Wendy said. "Big editorial meeting on the new book. You and Beth coming to the Hartleys' on Saturday?"

In the taxi back down to the office, I felt like punching out a window. *Ben's a photographer who just happens to*

be a lawyer. Bitch. *Big editorial meeting on the new book.* And the
Pulitzer Prize for 1995 goes to Wendy fucking Hemingway for
365 Ways to Cook Meat Loaf.

I finally stopped seething around five, when, after three
action-packed hours analyzing a residuary trust arrangement,
Estelle buzzed me.

"Your wife on line two, Mr. Bradford."

An adrenaline rush of nerves. Try to sound nice and
relaxed and upbeat.

"Hey there," I said.

"Getting you at a bad time?" she asked, sounding surpris-
ingly pleasant.

"Not at all."

"It's just . . . the kids and I have been invited to Jane
Seagrave's for dinner . . ."

"No problem. I was thinking about working late, maybe
catching the 7:48."

"I'll have something ready for you, if you like . . ."

Hang on, we're actually talking civilly . . .

"A Bud will do," I said.

A laugh from Beth Bradford. This *was* promising.

"Good day?" she asked.

Thank you, Jesus! It was the first time in two weeks that she
had thrown a pleasantry in my direction. I decided to say nothing about Jack.

"Pretty average. Estelle got busted for dealing coke.
Otherwise . . ."

Another laugh from Beth Bradford. Peace had finally
been declared.

"How 'bout you?" I asked. "What did you get up to?"

"Not much. Nice lunch with Wendy in Greenwich."

"Wendy Waggoner?" I said.

"The one and only," Beth said with a giggle.

I tried to sound calm. "And how was Wendy?"

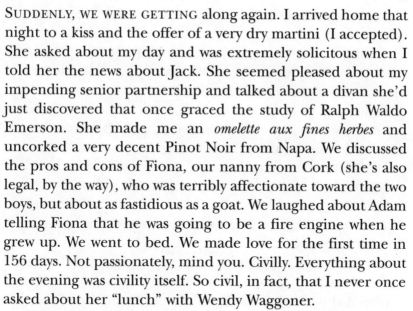

SUDDENLY, WE WERE GETTING along again. I arrived home that night to a kiss and the offer of a very dry martini (I accepted). She asked about my day and was extremely solicitous when I told her the news about Jack. She seemed pleased about my impending senior partnership and talked about a divan she'd just discovered that once graced the study of Ralph Waldo Emerson. She made me an *omelette aux fines herbes* and uncorked a very decent Pinot Noir from Napa. We discussed the pros and cons of Fiona, our nanny from Cork (she's also legal, by the way), who was terribly affectionate toward the two boys, but about as fastidious as a goat. We laughed about Adam telling Fiona that he was going to be a fire engine when he grew up. We went to bed. We made love for the first time in 156 days. Not passionately, mind you. Civilly. Everything about the evening was civility itself. So civil, in fact, that I never once asked about her "lunch" with Wendy Waggoner.

An uninterrupted night's sleep (miracle of miracles!). A kiss in the morning when she got up. The offer of French toast for breakfast (I declined on the grounds of high carbohy-drates). More civil chat over our muesli and fresh mangoes. Pleasant early-morning quality time with the boys. An upbeat reminder of our weekend schedule ("I want to hit Gap Kids in Greenwich . . . the Hartleys' party starts at seven, Fiona's coming in to baby-sit . . . it might be fun to take the boys to Mystic Seaport on Sunday . . . there's a special on wild Nova Scotia salmon at DeMarco's. I thought that would go well with a fantastic New Zealand white I've just discovered . . ."). A kiss on the lips as I walked out the door.

I should have felt relief. Delight that—after months of domestic frost—a thaw was finally in progress. And Christ, how much I wanted to believe that Beth had suddenly decided the enmity between us was poisonous, that I was worth liking again.

But. But. But. I knew this sudden turnaround was no Pauline conversion. No happy result from some "Can-this-marriage-be-saved?" soul-searching. *I knew* . . .

"Anything up for today?" I asked just before leaving the house.

For a nanosecond, she averted her eyes. That's when I really knew.

"I might tootle on up to the Colonial Barn," she said, mentioning an antiques dealer in Westport who probably looked upon Beth as the source of his entire GNP. "Steve has that divan in stock I was telling you about. But there's a lot of interest in it, coming from Emerson's study and all that, so he can only hold it for me until the end of today."

"How much?" I asked.

She looked away from me again. "Fourteen-fifty."

"Buy it," I said.

"Darling . . ." she said sweetly and touched her lips to mine. "You're too good."

So good, in fact, that as soon as I reached the office, I called Directory Assistance for Westport, Connecticut, and obtained the number for the Colonial Barn. I phoned, but got a recorded message, telling me to call back after they opened at ten. An hour went by, during which I tried to concentrate on work—specifically, objections filed by the disgruntled stepdaughter of some big-deal Merrill Lynch stockbroker who suffered a massive coronary occlusion while playing squash at the New York Athletic Club with his cardiologist brother-in-law.

". . . given that the decedent's stipulations regarding spousal beneficiaries did not allow principal to be paid to such spouses . . ."

I tossed the document aside. $315,000 a year for reading riveting shit like this. I walked over to the liquor cabinet ("Always have a little booze in your office," Jack once advised me, "just in case a client needs a steadying shot after getting bad news"). I pulled out a bottle of Black Bush, poured myself three fingers, threw it back. Then I went into my bathroom, rinsed the glass thoroughly, brushed my teeth, and gargled twice with Listerine. Booze on the breath at ten in the morning does not play well in the sober corporate culture of today. And by the time the whiskey kicked in (ninety seconds), it was also time to call Westport.

"The Colonial Barn, good morning. Steve here."

The voice was New England preppy, with a touch of Fire Island. I lowered my voice an octave or two and Anglicized my vowels.

"Morning," I said crisply. "Perhaps you could help me . . ."

"I'll most certainly do my best."

"The thing is, I'm trying to find a divan for my study. Something mid-nineteenth century, preferably American to Victorian."

"Well, you are in great luck, sir. I have just obtained the most fabulous divan. Boston handmade, 1853. Solid teak with carved feet. Original brass-sprung upholstery in the most gorgeous tawny floral print."

"Sounds splendid . . ."

"Oh, but you haven't heard the real selling point. This divan is something of a historical coup. Because—and I have full documentation to prove this—it once belonged to Ralph Waldo Emerson."

"*The* Ralph Waldo Emerson? Transcendentalism and all that?"

"The very one, sir. In fact, the divan was in his study at his home in Concord."

"My, my," I said. "That is impressive."

"A true collector's item, sir. *Serious* Americana. And, if I say so myself, a fabulous investment."

"What would we be talking about . . ."

"Twenty-two hundred. But I must warn you that one of my very best customers has expressed an interest in buying it . . ."

For fourteen-fifty, or so she said. Who's the liar here?

"You mean, it's reserved?" I asked.

"Well . . . not exactly. But she is *very* interested. And she is a *very* serious collector."

"So, if I didn't come in today, it would be gone?"

A pause as the little shit did some fast scheming.

"Well . . . I don't think she'll be in today. In fact, I know she won't . . . because she told me that the earliest she could come back to Westport was next Wednesday."

Bingo. I felt the whiskey somersault around my stomach.

"So," the little shit continued, "if you were to come before then, and were willing to exceed her price . . . say, twenty-three hundred . . . well, I think I'd have to let you have it, wouldn't I?"

"I'll think about it." I hung up. And then buzzed Estelle to tell her "no calls." And went back to the liquor cabinet. And threw down another finger of Black Bush, followed by a Listerine and Maalox chaser.

Anything up for today?

One lie raises your suspicions. Two lies verify them. And there was only one thing she could be hiding from me, only one activity that would suddenly have made her act so cordial toward me again.

But . . . *who?* Who was the son of a bitch? My brain sped, Rolodex style, through friends, acquaintances. No logical suspect came to mind because the culprit had to be someone who didn't commute into the city every day, who was therefore available to see Beth during office hours. And since every guy we knew in New Croydon and environs was a suit with a big job in Manhattan, it meant . . .

Another Rolodex flip through all the work-at-home guys we knew in the area. Bill Purcell, freelance writer extraordinaire? A man who actually bragged about his exclusive contributor's contract with *Reader's Digest?* Not a chance—he was a geek deluxe, with a nightmare wife named Eva who treated him like a schnauzer on a short lead. Gary Summers—that would-be photographer who lived near us on Constitution Crescent? Shaggy-haired with a wispy beard and a smirk so charged with self-satisfaction it could light up Alaska. Beth loathed him. "That guy has just enough of a trust fund to ruin him," she once said. Strike him off the list. Peter Pearson—a fiftysomething corporate burnout who now played the Forex market all day on the Internet? Only if she wanted to sleep with her daddy.

And that was the entire list of self-employed men I could think of. Maybe someone she met in a local shop? Steve in the Colonial Barn? Wrong sexual orientation. Tony the fishmonger? Some rough-trade delivery boy from the local Safeway?

Who, damnit. *Who?*

I hit the memory button on my phone. One ring, two rings . . .

"Hi there. You've reached Ben and Beth . . ."

I slammed the phone back in its cradle. She was probably fucking him right now. Digging her fingernails into his back, tongue down his throat, legs wrapped around his hairy ass . . .

Stop, stop, stop. Think. Clearly. Maybe it's just a flirtation. Maybe she was merely tempted yesterday. Maybe she suddenly realized that casual, down-and-dirty sex without the emotional import of conjugal love was not just transgressible, but spiritually vacuous (Forget it, Father). Or maybe, when faced with the possibility of adulterous behavior, she thought of her smiling husband and adorable sons and could not bear to risk . . .

Yeah, right.

I hit the speed dialer again.

"Hi there. You've . . ."

This time, the receiver was flung at the phone, sending it airborne. As soon as it crashed loudly, it buzzed.

"You all right in there?" Estelle asked over the intercom.

"That's my business, Estelle," I snapped.

"Yes, sir." She sounded hurt. "Sorry to disturb you, but I

just heard from Hildy that Mr. Mayle had to rush off to the doctor . . ."

"Was he in bad shape?"

"Not great, Mr. Bradford. Not great." From her tone, it was clear—in spite of his decision not to tell her as yet—that she'd figured out Jack's prognosis. Estelle always figured out everything. "He asked if you'd deal with his eleven o'clock. Mrs. Bowles."

"Oh, great."

"Thought you'd be pleased."

"Have the fire extinguisher handy, just in case things get too hot."

"I will, Mr. Bradford. And if the phone you've just thrown is damaged, I can call maintenance."

"Thank you, Estelle."

In she walked at eleven. Mrs. Deborah Butt Bowles. The original poor little rich girl. A forty-five-year-old, thrice-divorced would-be theater producer who'd spent most of her adult life running through the $5 million in trust her deeply unpleasant daddy (he'd made a killing as a slumlord) had been stupid enough to leave her. And, at least four times a year, she'd beat her way to our door, pleading poverty, debts, and the fact that the $250,000 in annual income she received from the trust just wasn't enough to sustain her in the fast lane. Worse yet, she was one of those individuals who remade her image every six months. In the late eighties, she was Ms. Power Dresser in black Armani and linebacker shoulder pads. Then she went through a Chanel lady-who-lunches phase while she was briefly married to some dubious Cypriot diamond merchant. When she was trying to get a half-dozen hopeless off-off-Broadway productions off the ground, she started dressing like Mrs. Stanislavsky (as outfitted by the Gap). And now . . .

"Hello, Lawyer," she said, waltzing into my office.

"Mrs. Bowles," I said, rising to my feet and trying not to appear too bemused by her crew-cut dyed-blonde hair, her tight white T-shirt, her black leather jacket, her matching black leather pants, and an unlit Gitanes protruding from her lip. Very Berlin.

"You're looking well," I said, motioning her to sit down.

"You gonna call security if I smoke?" she said, cracking open a Zippo.

"I'll keep them at bay."

She lit up. "Where's Jack?"

"Mr. Mayle is otherwise engaged, I'm afraid. An urgent last-minute appointment outside the office."

"Someone more important than me, you mean."

"All of our clients are of equal importance, Mrs. Bowles."

"Cut the crap, Lawyer. I know neither of you guys can stand me."

Give the lady a cigar for perceptiveness. But I remained lawyerly. "You are a most valued client, Mrs. Bowles. As your late father was before you. Now, how may I be of assistance?"

"You know exactly why I'm here."

"A cash-flow problem, perhaps?"

"Well done, Sherlock."

"You know the terms of the trust, Mrs. Bowles," I said, glancing down at the bulging file on my desk. "Four quarterly payments, no more, no less—and the principal is, I'm afraid, frozen in perpetuity. Untouchable."

"Of course I know the terms, Lawyer. I'm an expert in the fucking terms. But Amex is threatening to sue my ass, ditto Bloomingdale's, ditto MasterCard. And if I don't come up with six months' maintenance, the board at 175 East Seventy-fourth Street will force me to sell the apartment."

"You have spoken with the bank, I presume?"

"Do you think I'd drag my ass down to Wall Street if the bank had said yes?"

I glanced back down at the file. "This is, of course, not the first time that you have run into such difficulties . . ."

"Thanks for reminding me."

". . . and you did default on the last two bridging loans you took out with the bank."

"They were eventually cleared."

"Yes, but only after writs were served against you, Mrs. Bowles. What I'm trying to say is . . ."

"I'm a financial fuckup. A spoiled little rich bitch who can't look after her money. It's written all over your Ivy League face."

"I didn't go to the Ivy League, Mrs. Bowles. And I'm not making any judgments about your . . . uh . . . fiscal responsibility or lack thereof. I am simply trying to point out to you that, given the . . . uh . . . difficult relationship you have had with your bank in the past, bridging finance in this instance might be difficult to come by."

"I bet you're the kind of guy who has never spent a reckless penny in his life. I bet you're oh-so-cautious, oh-so-correct about money."

Twenty-nine hundred yesterday for a camera I didn't need? Fourteen-fifty (or was it really twenty-two hundred?) for the only existing Ralph Waldo Emerson divan on the planet? Lady, the only reason I'm not in as deep financial shit as you is because I don't have your predilection for nose candy.

"I enjoy shopping, like any patriotic American," I said. "But . . ."

"You do it cautiously," she said, yanking up her left leg tightly against her ass. "Bet you fuck around cautiously as well."

"Mrs. Bowles . . ."

"Or maybe you're so cautious that you've never fucked around at all."

Wrong again, sweetheart. One one-night stand. Out of town. Very discreet (rule number one of sensible infidelity: stick to married professionals). Very condomized. And yeah— once the buzzy glow of the clandestine faded away—I did feel guilty as hell about the encounter. I am not good at being louche . . . but it happens. So if Beth has had a one-night stand, I will forgive her. Just.

"I love my wife, Mrs. Bowles," I said mildly.

"I bet you do," she said with a snort.

"But your bankers don't love you—which means that, to

avoid fiscal embarrassment, I presume you require our assistance. Or am I presuming wrong, Mrs. Bowles?"

My cool tone of voice got the message across: If you want me to toss you a life preserver, cut the personal crap. She sat up straight again and played contrite.

"Whatever you can do . . ."

I mentioned the name of a small bank the firm dealt with on a regular basis. They would require some sort of guarantee ("Your apartment, for example . . ."), but probably could be convinced to offer her some sort of bridge financing until her next quarterly trust payment came through.

"What this means," I said, "is that you must attempt to live frugally for the next three months. And I must warn you —if you do default on this loan, Lawrence, Cameron and Thomas may find it difficult to recommend you to other financial institutions should you find yourself in future difficulties."

"How long till I find out whether or not I have to peddle my ass on the street?"

"I will call the bank as soon as we are finished. They should have a decision by this afternoon."

I stood up, indicating our meeting was over.

"This is where I'm supposed to say thanks, isn't it?" she said.

"That is entirely up to you, Mrs. Bowles."

She headed toward the door, then turned and regarded me with a sneer.

"You know something . . . I bet your nice little wife looks at you every night and thinks to herself: 'What a lucky little gal I am.' "

I felt my right hand tighten into a fist. Immediately, I hid it behind my back.

"Good day, Mrs. Bowles. My secretary will call as soon as we have an answer."

She turned on her heel and left. I made a grab for the phone but stopped myself.

No. Don't throw it again. And don't reach for the Black Bush. It's just a bad day, that's all. A very, very bad day.

I sat down at my desk. When I calmed down, I hit the inter-com button on my phone.

"Estelle . . . ?"

"You survive the meeting, Mr. Bradford?"

"A piece of cake. However, when Mrs. Bowles calls back, will you inform her that the bank turned her loan down . . . but that I am looking into other possibilities. And if she's anxious to talk with me, tell her I've gone away on business and will be unable to speak with her until the middle of next week."

"And if she asks to speak with Mr. Mayle . . . ?"

"Don't trouble Jack with this matter. He has enough to cope with right now."

"Anything else, Mr. Bradford?"

"My wife . . ."

Three minutes later she was back on the intercom with the reply I expected: "Sorry, Mr. Bradford. No answer . . ."

I suddenly decided to leave the office. I grabbed my brief-case and my Burberry and headed out the door. Estelle looked up in surprise.

"I'm feeling lousy," I said. "Decided to call it a day."

"You need a doctor or something?" Her voice was con-cerned.

"Just bed. Touch of stomach flu or something. Twenty-four hours and I'll be fine. Nothing major's pending, is there?"

"Nothing that can't wait until Monday."

"Good. And if my wife calls . . ."

Estelle looked at me expectantly.

". . . just tell her I'm out. I want to surprise her at home."

I could see Estelle struggling hard not to raise her eye-brows. "Anything you say, Mr. Bradford. Could I call you a car to Grand Central?"

"Faster to grab a cab downstairs," I said.

"Feel better, Mr. Bradford." She knew that I was lying.

"I'll try, Estelle. Enjoy the weekend."

The 12:46 from Grand Central was deserted. So too was the station platform at New Croydon. I walked quickly down Adams Avenue, feeling curiously out of place. Because, at one-thirty on a weekday afternoon, it was hard to find a man between the ages of twenty-five and fifty on the streets of New Croydon, as the town became the domain of highly educated women, who, like Beth, had probably once sat on the floor of some dorm at Smith, Wheaton, or Wellesley, passing the hash pipe, drinking cheap Almaden, and vowing never to become stay-at-home wives in a tidy 'burb like this one.

And yet, here they all were, dressed in their Brooks Brothers Shetlands and their Lands End khakis, clean limbed, the teeth still white, the hair still lustrous (and still held in place by a black silk headband), their thirty-year-old faces still unlined with the disappointments that their children and husbands would inevitably inflict upon them. Did they, like me, often wake at the wrong hours of the night to wonder how they had managed to paint themselves into such upmarket inertia? Or did they simply accept New Croydon as their cozy destiny? Recognizing that, in the great scheme of things, they had little to complain about, that this was as good as it gets.

As I turned into Constitution Crescent, I could hear my heart pummel my chest. What if she was there with the guy? *In our bed.* What if . . .

I started to break into a canter, but immediately forced myself back into a walk. You don't run down Constitution Crescent in a suit unless you want to inflate your standings in the gossip league. *Saw Ben Bradford home very early from the office the other day, charging down the road, looking pretty consumed about something. Guess he's finally figured it out . . .*

I reached my front door. I took a very deep breath. I silently inserted the key in the lock and turned it as quietly as possible. Opening the door, I crept inside, slowly shutting it behind me. It closed with hardly a sound. I dumped my Burberry, sat down on a little 1768 Providence guest-house footstool, and took off my heavy black wingtips. Then, holding my shoes in one hand, I crept up the stairs and down the corridor, my eyes focused on the door at the end of the hall. Our bedroom door. When I reached it, my hand shook as I touched the knob. One last nervous intake of breath as I flung the door open, falling in after it.

Nothing. Nothing except our perfectly made bed with its perfectly made colonial patchwork quilt, matching bolsters, and Beth's collection of 1784 Philadelphia rag dolls. I have always hated those fucking dolls—and I think the feeling was mutual, as they stared back at me with silent disapproval.

I sat down on the edge of the bed, tried to collect myself, tried to hear something discernible, telltale, amid the silence: coital groans, perhaps, or the panicked sounds of frantic dressing. Nothing. Still not convinced, I crept from room to room. An empty house. Finally, the basement. A closed door. One, two . . .

It flew open. All clear. Nothing but my toys.

I felt no relief. *Where could she be?* His place, obviously. But where did he live? How had they met? What were they doing right now?

Fear kicked in. A helpless fear, as I knew I could do nothing except sit here and await her return.

I pulled off my jacket, sent it flying across the room. Ditto my suit trousers. And my white shirt and tie. And my dark black socks. A thousand bucks' worth of clothing balled up on the floor. Then, reaching into a chest of drawers near the exercise gear, I pulled out a pair of sweat shorts and a T-shirt, found my Nikes, and spun the CD rack in search of something loud, vast, overpowering. Bingo: Mahler, The Sixth Symphony. The Bernstein recording with the Vienna Philharmonic. Heavy on the emotional fortissimo, but knockout on that Mahlerian sense of impending doom, of life being a misadventure that you somehow must get through. I popped on the headphones, climbed onto the NordicTrack, hit the remote for the CD player. Dark, thundering chords from the double basses. The sarcastic snarl of trumpets. The high-pitched squeal of the violins as they kicked in with the main opening theme. Just as I began to build up a sweat, a hand touched my shoulder and made me jump.

"What are you doing here?" Beth looked startled (and a little troubled) to find me home so early.

I pulled off the headphones. "Felt sick, came home," I answered, panting.

She studied me skeptically. "Sick? *Really?*"

"Stomach bug sort of thing. Hit me bad at the office."

"Then what are you doing working out?"

"It was gone by the time I was on the train."

That sounded so lame. She glanced at her feet and saw my crumpled Brooks Brothers suit.

"You certainly were in a hell of a hurry to get on that machine."

"Still pissed off about Jack's news, that's all," I lied. "Guess I took it out on the suit."

"I just had this dry-cleaned for you," she said, picking it up. "Kind of a waste of twelve dollars."

"Cleaning it again won't break the bank," I said mildly. "So tell me . . . you do it?"

"Do what?" She looked alarmed.

"Get Emerson's divan."

"Oh, *that*." Her relief was tangible. "I decided to give it a miss. Just too expensive."

"We could've afforded twenty-two."

"Fourteen-fifty."

Whoops. "Well, we definitely could've handled fourteen-fifty," I said. "You shouldn't have let money stop you."

"I'm just trying to be a little sensible."

Beth, sensible with money? And the sun revolves around the earth.

"So you never made it to Westport, then?" I said, trying to sound as disinterested as possible.

"I didn't feel like the drive, so I ended up in Stamford, knocking around the mall."

"Get anything nice?"

"Nah, just browsed . . ."

Bullshit. Beth never went to a mall and just browsed. Now it was her turn to look ill at ease, to wonder if I knew she was lying.

"But I did pick up that salmon I ordered," she said. "And

a bottle of that amazing New Zealand Sauvignon Blanc. Cloudy Bay, it's called."

"Where'd you hear about it?"

"Herb at the liquor store was giving it raves."

"Herb usually knows what he's talking about," I said. "Can't wait."

An awkward silence broken by the sound of the front door opening, and Josh bawling, and Fiona saying, "Now hang on there, you," and Adam yelling at her, "I watch *Sesame Street!*"

"Hey, big guy!" I shouted up the stairs.

"Daddy!" Adam shouted back, his voice filled with little-boy excitement. As he bounded down the stairs, I crouched down to let him throw himself into my arms, then lifted him up.

"You bring me a present?" he asked.

Beth and I exchanged an amused smile. Adam was always in the market for a present.

"I brought you me," I said.

"No presents?"

I laughed. "Maybe a present tomorrow."

"I want a present *now*," he whined.

"How 'bout McDonald's now?"

Beth didn't like this. "No, Ben . . ."

"It won't kill him."

"He's eating too much junk as it is."

"I'll make sure he orders the Chicken McNuggets. Full of protein."

"I really wish you'd think before . . ."

"Leave it," I said, my tone suddenly curt. Beth was about to counterpunch, but thought better of it.

"Do what you like. You always do." And she turned and headed up the stairs.

"McDonald's?" I asked Adam again.

"I want French fries," he said with a smile.

Upstairs, Fiona was feeding Josh mashed carrots. They covered his face. She was a breezy, large girl who always looked like an unmade bed and always wore jeans. We'd gotten along just fine ever since I came home one night to find her in flagrante delicto on the living-room floor with some tattooed biker from the wrong side of Stamford. The fact that I didn't fire her—or threaten to get her green card revoked—made me her eternal friend. And also meant that she was my domestic ally—something Beth knew and hated.

"How's the monster doing?" I asked.

"Brutal. Six big poos already today."

"Better you than me."

"You're home early, Mr. Bradford."

"Decided to start the weekend early."

"Must've surprised Mrs. Bradford so."

What did she mean by that?

"She wasn't here," I said.

" 'Course she wasn't," Fiona said, trying to force another spoonful of orange muck into Josh's mouth. "It's her tennis day, isn't it now?"

I'd forgotten that. The weekly game with Wendy Waggoner. Canceled. Why didn't Beth mention that? And why was Fiona mentioning it now? Was she trying to tell me something?

"Daddy," Adam whined, "I want McDonald's."

"My master calls," I said, grabbing a suede baseball jacket off a nearby hook. "Have a good weekend, Fiona."

She looked up at me. "Take care, Mr. Bradford."

Was that a warning? Before I could find out, she turned her attention back to Josh. I leaned down to kiss him. As soon as my lips touched his forehead, he began to scream.

We took the Volvo. En route, Adam began to sing his favorite song of the week—"The Bare Necessities"—from his favorite video of the week, Disney's *The Jungle Book*. And I couldn't help but smile as his little four-year-old voice chirped away.

At McDonald's, he was an absolute delight, quietly working his way through his Chicken McNuggets and French fries, concentrating all his attention on the business of eating but glancing up at me occasionally with a big smile and saying "Delish-ous" (this week's new word). I glanced back and wondered how Beth and I had managed to create such a beautiful kid, and whether, ten years from now, when he was a pimply, sullen adolescent, he'd hate us for ruining his life. Terrible images flashed across my brain: Adam as a doped-out grunge, scoring crack from New Croydon High's main dealer. Getting into some older kid's car with five equally doped-out friends. The car roaring off into the night. The druggy driver putting pedal to the metal as they hit Interstate 95. The speedometer touching 80. The driver suddenly falling asleep at the wheel. The vehicle careening out of control as it headed toward the central divider. Adam screaming . . .

"Daddy!"

Adam was holding up his empty bag of French fries.

"More."

"You've had enough," I said.

"Daddy, more!" There was a hint of belligerence to his voice.

"How about a present?"

"Present, yeah!"

That solved the French fries issue. As we drove back toward Adams Avenue, I kept glancing in the rearview mirror at Adam, strapped into his booster seat, staring, wide-eyed, at the suburban lawns of New Croydon, still an adorable, adoring four-year-old, still secure in the cocoon of early childhood. I shouldn't fear for him, I told myself. But I still did. Perhaps because I feared for myself. Feared for the vulnerability I often felt whenever I was with Adam, that "If anything ever happens to you I won't be able to cope" fear that haunts every parent. It's what no one will ever tell you about having kids—just how dependent you become on them. Just how naked and vulnerable they make you. Because you've never loved anyone so unconditionally.

At Talley's Toys, I let Adam choose two new coaches to go with his Thomas the Tank Engine train set. Then we walked down the street and made a stop at "Daddy's toy shop"—New Croydon Fine Wines and Liquors. Herb—the bald old-timer who'd been running the store since the Eisenhower era—was behind the counter.

"Hey, little guy," he said to Adam.

Adam held up his two new acquisitions. "Annie and Clarabelle!" he announced.

"And a happy Annie and Clarabelle to you too," Herb replied. "How you doing, Mr. Bradford?"

"It's Friday, Herb. That's how I'm doing."

"I hear ya. What can I get you?"

"Bottle of Bombay Sapphire. A liter."

Herb turned around, grabbed a bottle of that very overpriced gin, and set it down in front of me.

"Anything else?"

"Vermouth."

"Martini night, huh?"

"Martini *weekend*."

"Then it's got to be Noilly Prat."

"Fine. And how about a bottle of Cloudy Bay Sauvignon Blanc while you're at it."

"Cloudy *what?*"

"Cloudy Bay. New Zealand wine. Been getting rave reviews. You do stock it, don't you?"

"Sorry, Mr. Bradford. Never heard of it. But if you want a great California Sauvignon Blanc . . ."

"I really was interested in that New Zealand stuff."

"You got a minute, I'll make a quick call to my wholesaler."

Adam was tugging at my arm, trying to pull me toward the door.

"That's okay," I said.

"Just take a sec." He picked up the phone. So I played a makeshift game with Adam—How many bottles of cheap Gallo wine can you count?—until Herb finished his call.

"Right," he said. "Cloudy Bay is available in the States, but only through special order. And only two cases maximum per individual customer, as it's in great demand and in very short supply. My guy in the city says it's about the best Sauvignon Blanc in the world—but if you want it, you're gonna have to pay for it. $18.99 a bottle."

Special order. Beth was fucking a rich oenologist.

"I'll think about it," I said.

Back home, Beth was surprised to see me walk in with the liter of Bombay Sapphire.

"We've already got gin," she said.

"Yeah, Gilbey's. Fine drowned with tonic, crap for a good martini."

"You buy it at Herb's?" she asked casually.

I felt like saying: "Yeah, and I also discovered that he has never stocked Cloudy Bay." But instead, I lied.

"Nah, got it at the package shop up on the Post Road."

I saw her eyes flicker down to the little shopping bag that Adam had clutched in his hands: Talley's Toys. Located right near Herb's shop. Dumb, Bradford, dumb. Now she knew I was lying. But she said nothing because she was probably wondering whether I knew she was lying too.

"I think I could use a martini," Beth said.

We drank one, put the kids to bed, then drank a second. Both straight up. Both extra-dry. Perfect mental novocaine. So perfect that we actually had another rather cheery evening. The salmon—baked in a very subtle garlic-butter sauce—was first rate. And the Cloudy Bay . . . well, it was sublime. So transcendentally good (especially after two martinis) that I temporarily stopped obsessing about who might have supplied it to Beth, and instead made her laugh. Especially when I got going on my encounter earlier that day with Mrs. Deborah Butt Bowles and her new incarnation as a butch Marlene Dietrich. Maybe it was nervousness, maybe it was all the drink, or maybe I was actually being amusing—whatever the reason, Beth became convulsed with laughter during this story. Which, of course, pleased me hugely. I liked seeing her laugh. Liked seeing her enjoy my company again. And hoped that this was a sign that, perhaps, nothing was happening—that I was letting my midlife paranoias invent these fantasies about another guy, with (it has to be said) excellent taste in esoteric kiwi wines.

"Beth . . ." I said when she finally calmed down.

"Yeah?"

I covered her hand with mine. "This is nice."

I felt her stiffen.

"Yes," she said. "It is."

"We should do this more often."

"You mean, get drunk?"

"I mean, get along."

She pulled her hand away.

"Don't spoil . . ."

"I'm not trying to spoil anything. It's just, we haven't been getting along for months . . ."

". . . but we are *now*," she said.

"Yeah, now, tonight, after a lot of booze . . ."

". . . and last night too," she added.

"Twice in six months. Big deal." I *was* drunk.

"You don't want to get along, you want to fight, is that it?"

"Of course I don't—"

"Then, *stop*. Drop it."

"You don't understand what I'm trying to say here—"

"I think I do. And I wish you—"

"I just want us to put our problems behind us and—"

"What do you think I've been trying to do for the last twenty-four hours?"

"But you refuse to discuss—"

"There is nothing to discuss—"

"There is *everything* to discuss—"

"Ben, why can't you just shut up and let—"

"Don't tell me to shut up."

"I will if you're acting like an asshole."

"Fuck you."

"That's it. I'm going to bed."

"Go to bed, go to bed," I taunted. "Walk away, refuse to talk, that's just your style. Never face up to—"

But I didn't get to finish that sentence, as she slammed the dining-room door behind her.

So much for our cease-fire.

I staggered into the sitting room, collapsed on the sofa, hit the remote, stared mindlessly at CNN, cursed myself for being such a twerp, nodded off, and awoke around one-thirty to find myself watching Kate Brymer—looking as battle-stylish as ever—reporting from some razed Bosnian town.

". . . scenes of devastation and human suffering, the like of which even the most jaded of correspondents couldn't help but . . ."

Kate. Damn you. Out there. In the midst of it.

I made my way to bed. Pulled off my clothes. Slid in next to Beth, who was dead to the world. I snuggled up against her naked back, kissed the nape of her neck, and let my tongue drift down to the top of her left shoulder blade until . . .

It stumbled across something jagged, rough. Something my tongue certainly hadn't encountered last night when it traveled this same route. I rubbed it with my index finger. Scabby to the touch. I tried to peer at it, but the room was too dark. So I reached over to my bedside table and felt around until I found one of those little book lights that allow you to read in bed without giving your partner grounds for divorce. Flicking it on, I focused its narrow beam on Beth's back.

And there it was: a short, but very discernible scratch, located right between her left shoulder blade and her spine. Still red, still fresh. New today.

6

THE NEXT MORNING Beth wouldn't speak to me. Even after I apologized—many times—she still refused to grant me a pardon for last night's outburst. I am always apologizing to Beth. Even when I know I'm right, I'm still the one who always makes amends. I can't stand her annoyed silences. And I'll always eat copious amounts of humble pie if it means a little peace between us.

"Look, it was the booze talking," I said as I shakily poured myself a cup of coffee in the kitchen.

Beth, tidying away breakfast dishes, said nothing.

"I was just trying to talk about stuff that's been worrying me."

She cut me off. "When you've finished that coffee, get Adam ready. I want to be in Greenwich before parking's impossible."

And she walked out the door.

How 'bout that goddamn scratch on your back? I felt like shouting after her. But I held back, just as, late last night, I also stopped myself from waking Beth up to ask a few questions about who'd been clawing her. Given her current state of exasperation toward me, it was probably the worst moment imaginable to confront her about being involved with another man. Best to keep that ace in the hole until the right moment.

As it was Saturday, we engaged in that most American of weekend activities: We went shopping—in that elegant economic fortress called Greenwich. Natural habitat of the WASP. Impossible on less that $250,000 a year. And, ergo, free of aspiring middle-class mobs. Especially on Saturdays.

We found parking at the top of Greenwich Avenue, a mile-long downward-sloping boulevard that housed just about every upscale retail outlet imaginable. With Beth pushing Josh in his stroller, and Adam's hand clutched in mine, we headed down-hill, the silence between Beth and myself broken only by Adam's entreaties.

"You buy me Thomas the Tank Engine trains." It was a statement, not a question.

"Say *please*, Adam," I said.

"You buy me Thomas the Tank Engine trains. *Please*." It was still a statement, and I couldn't help but smile.

"If you're good."

"And only after we've gone to Gap Kids," Beth said.

"No Gap Kids, no Gap Kids," Adam whined.

"Then no Thomas the Tank Engine," I said. The threat worked. When we reached Gap Kids, Adam patiently tried on the duffle coat ($65) that Beth had chosen for him. And the sweatshirt ($22), and the cotton turtleneck ($16), and the corduroy pants ($28) that she also felt would bolster up his autumn wardrobe. But when we moved on to Baby Gap, Adam kicked up while Beth dropped another $70 on assorted items for Josh.

"I want Thomas *now*," Adam whined again.

"We'll get Thomas in a few minutes," Beth said.

"I want—"

"Just be a little patient—"

"Now, now, *now*." Adam shook the stroller so hard that Josh began to cry. Beth slapped Adam hard, on the hand.

"Bad boy, bad boy," she said sharply. Adam screamed "Daddy" and threw himself into my arms.

"It's okay, it's okay," I whispered into his ear while stroking his head.

"Don't take his side," Beth said.

"Easy, Beth . . ."

"He has to know when he's naughty and—"

"Right, right, right."

Adam had another crying fit in my arms.

"Tell you what," I said, "I'll meet you at Banana Republic in fifteen minutes. Let him calm down a bit."

"Whatever," Beth said and pushed Josh off toward another corner of the store.

Outside on the street, Adam finally stopped bawling.

"Mommy hates me," he whimpered.

"Don't be silly," I said. "She just doesn't like it when you're naughty. And I don't either."

"Sorry, Daddy."

I kissed his head. "Good boy."

"Thomas the Tank Engine. *Please.*"

So we went to a toy shop and bought him his fifth miniature train ($14). Then we walked down to a bookstore, where Adam chose a copy of *Curious George Rides a Bike* ($8.99), and I finally picked up Richard Avedon's *Evidence* ($75)—that amazing retrospective of his portraits over the past fifty years. When we reached Banana Republic, Beth was trying on a short tan suede jacket. She looked very fetching. I nudged Adam toward her. Shyly, he approached and tugged her sleeve.

"Mommy . . . sorry."

She gave him a smile, a kiss.

"And I'm sorry I hit you. Just be a little patient, okay?"

"You look great in that," I said.

"It's too expensive," she said.

"How much?"

"Three twenty-five."

"Do it."

"Darling . . ."

"I mean, you're not getting the divan, right?"

"Well . . ."

"It's just money."

She studied herself in the mirror again, then spun around and kissed me lightly on the lips.

"You have your moments," she said. "Thank you."

Marital crisis averted—for this morning, anyway. One big happy family yet again. And all it took was $623.99 plus tax. Definitely our heaviest Saturday shop of the year. Still, it *is* cheaper than therapy.

Outside Banana Republic, I suggested lunch at a local child-friendly restaurant at the bottom of the avenue.

"I want McDonald's," Adam said.

"Not today, sunshine," Beth said.

"I want French fries."

"You can get them at the restaurant," I said and immediately regretted it as Beth shook her head, exasperated.

"Ben, do you want him to turn into a French fry? Or Barney?"

"Give the guy a break," an approaching voice said. "French fries never killed anyone under forty."

We both looked up. It was Gary Summers. Our neighbor, the would-be photographer.

"Hey, people."

His long dirty-blonde hair was tied in a ponytail. His stubble seemed even more designer than usual. And his famous smirk was as wide as a 70-millimeter screen. But it was his clothes that really got me. They were so . . . *downtown*. Black denim shirt buttoned at the neck. Black baggy trousers held up by black leather suspenders. Black lace-up boots. RayBan shades. Standard operating gear for Wooster Street, but attention-seeking amid the Ralph Lauren suburbanites of Greenwich Avenue. Then again, the only reason Gary lived among us was because he could never cut it downtown. I knew that he'd tried to make it as a photographer in New York, but had never gotten anywhere. And after his elderly parents died, he (as the only child) retreated to the family home in New Croydon and lived off the modest inheritance he'd been left (not more than 30k a year, my professional T&E judgment told me, because Gary's old man had never risen above the upper-middle echelon at IBM, which meant that, even with judicious planning, his estate couldn't have been bigger than

600k maximum, carefully parceled out in bonds, life insurance, and a solid chunk of Big Blue stock).

Just enough of a trust fund to ruin him. Beth's famous assessment of Gary—and one shared by just about everyone else in New Croydon. But though he was widely considered something of a loser, he still talked a great game—always going on about forthcoming big magazine assignments (which never materialized); always saying that it was just a matter of time before he sold and moved to LA; always regarding us suits and our pert, button-nosed wives with smirky contempt.

I loathed him.

"Hi, Gary," I said tonelessly.

"Morning," Beth added and then crouched down to deal with some Josh problem. She didn't think much of Gary either.

"Doing a little consuming, huh?" He took in all our shopping bags, especially noticing the oversized one from Bell's Books. "What's the book?"

"Avedon's *Evidence*," I said.

"Good choice. Those roadside drifters—how he manages to shoot them with just a neutral white backdrop, yet still evoke that vast *nothingness* of the American badlands. Pretty amazing stuff, huh?"

"Yes. Pretty amazing."

"You know, when I saw Richard last week . . ."

I tried to exchange a knowing glance with Beth, but she was busy wiping accumulated snot from Josh's nose.

"Richard who?" I said.

"*Avedon*, that's who."

"Friend of yours?"

"More of an acquaintance. Met him at a party Leibovitz was throwing."

"*Annie* Leibovitz?" I asked.

"The one and only."

"Friend of yours too?"

"Yeah, Annie and I've known each other for years. And she told me that, if she and Sontag don't go back to Sarajevo for *Vanity Fair*, she's going to recommend that Graydon send me."

Sontag. Graydon . . . Gary Summers—whose last photographic exhibition was held in that well-known gallery, Restaurant Grappa on Adams Street in New Croydon—grips the attention of America's resident intellectual, not to mention the editor of *Vanity Fair.* Sure.

"So what did *Richard* say to you then?" I asked.

"Daddy!" Adam pulled my hand. "I want French fries."

"We should go," Beth added.

"Still taking pics?" Gary asked.

"When I have the time."

"Buy anything new and groovy recently?"

"A Canon EOS-1N," I said.

"Hear it's great for war reportage." A big smirk. "You going to the Hartleys' thing tonight?"

I nodded. "Catch you later, then," Gary said and walked off.

Fifteen minutes later, I was still fuming.

"Can you believe that asshole?" I said, sipping a beer at the restaurant.

"Language, Ben."

" 'When I was talking to Avedon last week . . .' 'Leibovitz suggested *Vanity Fair* send me to Sarajevo.' *Vanity Fair* wouldn't send that jerkoff to Coney Island."

"Why are you so pissed off?" Beth said.

"Because he's a name-dropping nobody."

"Big deal. He's always been that way. You know that—so why suddenly get bent out of shape about it?"

"I am not getting bent out of shape. I just hate his smugness."

"You hate that he talks a good game."

"Don't you?"

"Yeah, it's bullshit. But I see it for what it is."

"Which is what?"

"I don't know. Defensiveness, probably. Strip away the dumb bravado and he's just a guy still trying to make it as a photographer. Maybe not doing very well . . . but at least he's trying."

Ouch. "Thanks a lot."

"That was not meant to be a comment on you."

"Sure," I said, sounding sullen.

"Why do you keep trying to pick fights—"

"I am not trying to—"

". . . and always personalize everything I say."

"At least I don't keep putting the knife into you—"

"You are so goddamn thin-skinned—"

"The great novelist speaks."

Beth flinched, as if slapped.

"I'm sorry," I said.

Her eyes welled up.

"Beth . . ." I reached for her hand. She pulled it away, staring blankly at the table. I felt like the biggest shit on earth.

"Mommy's crying," Adam said.

"Mommy's fine," Beth said, wiping her eyes.

And I called for the check.

Silence in the car on the way home. Silence when we reached the house. Silence when I tried to apologize again. Silence when I announced that—as Adam was happily watching *The Jungle Book* for the thirty-second time that week—I'd sneak off to my darkroom for an hour or two.

Silence. She really knew how to wield it, turning it into a blunt instrument that inflicted maximum pain, maximum guilt. As soon as the revolving door of my darkroom closed behind me, the silence really hit home as a waterfall of acid drenched the walls of my gut. Maalox time yet again, and, reaching behind my enlarger, I found the bottle of white chalky elixir that I kept on hand for moments like this.

A long slurp. Count to twenty. Presto. You no longer feel like an ulcerated inferno. The Maalox has done its work. You can cope again. For a few hours, anyway.

Three thousands dollars I've spent on my stomach. I've had barium meals. Telescopic inspections of my large intestine. Even the insertion down my esophagus of a little microscopic probe on the lookout for carcinomas, malignant growths, and other things that go bump in the abdominal night. Not even the mildest peptic ulcer was found. A clean bill of health.

"It's certainly not cancer," the specialist at New York Hospital told me. "There are no signs of benign tumors. And your duodenum is still in one piece."

"So what is it then?" I demanded.

"Bile," he said. "You have a surfeit of bile."

Three thousands bucks to discover that?

I powered up the enlarger, loaded a negative into its carrier, snapped on the safelite, and began to finger the electronic auto-focus button. Slowly an image emerged out of the blur: a hefty middle-aged man—trebled-chinned, his suit crumpled—emerging from the doors of the New York Stock Exchange, his eyes as wide and fearful as those of a deer blinking into the headlights of an oncoming truck.

I caught this shot a few weeks ago. Sneaking out of the office early one afternoon with my Nikon in my briefcase, I loitered for an hour or two in a Wall Street doorway, shooting four rolls of Tri-X as I watched the comings and goings of brokers and Exchange personnel. Naturally, I felt like a truant schoolboy, but still delighted in this small act of subversion— especially as the 144 exposures managed to yield three or four interesting pictures (not a bad return for me, as I'm ferociously selective about what I'll even bother to print). And from the moment I hung up the negatives to dry, I knew that this image of bloated midlife anxiety had hit the bull's-eye, that it transcended mere clever composition and had accidentally stumbled into the realm of gravitas, of uncomfortable truth.

That's the thing about photography—if you set out with high-minded notions about using your lens as a naked arbiter of verité, you will inevitably come up with stilted, self-important images that never really touch the heart of the matter. The best shots are always accidents. Think of Weegee's lurid SpeedGraphic take on New York sleaze, or even Capa's famous image of a dying Spanish Republican soldier (his arms outstretched, crucifix style, as a bullet tears into his back). Their finest work was a shotgun marriage between brilliant technique and *being there*. Happenstance is *all* in photography. You can spend hours waiting for *the right moment*. Ultimately, though, you never really get what you're lingering for, and instead discover that a few shots you rattled off while hanging about have a spontaneity that is simply lacking in any of your attempts at consummate composition. Rule number one of art: You can never pick the right moment; you just stumble into it and hope to Christ that your finger is on the shutter release at the time.

Using the motorized auto-focus, I sharpened the framing of the negative, cropping some background in order to tighten up the image of that world-battered broker staggering out of the portals of the Stock Exchange. Then, sliding an 8-by-10 piece of Galleria bromide paper into the frame, I clicked off the enlarger lamp, pressed the auto-print button, and watched as the image beamed on for three seconds. Red light. A sixty-second dunk into developer, followed by stopper, then fixer, then a switch back to normal fluorescent light. But as I pulled the paper out of this final chemical bath and hung it up to dry, I immediately saw a flaw in the print: the broker appeared to be shadowed by a second image. Technically, you could call this "ghosting," a slight double exposure that creates a specter that haunts the portrait, making it appear to have a phantom underside. A man behind the man.

Immediately, I rattled off four more prints, yet all of them displayed that telltale ghost, that hint of another life hidden beyond this one. Perhaps the camera shook ever so slightly when I snapped the shot. Perhaps I made a small chemical error when developing the film. But after I checked the roll of negatives again, I saw that it was only this specific frame that suffered from ghosting. All the other stockbroker shots were free of double exposure. Yet, without question, this spectral image was the best of the bunch. How did I fail to notice it when I initially developed the film? How did it get there in the first place? What exactly was that lurking phantom?

Using a magnifying cube, I studied and restudied the four ghosted prints again, trying to find some sort of answer to those questions. Then a knock came on the darkroom door.

"Baby-sitter's here," Beth said.

"Coming," I said. "Got a sec? I want to show you . . ."

"No," Beth said. By the time I managed to open the revolving door, she had gone up the stairs.

In the car, she continued to freeze me out.

"I said I was sorry."

"I don't care," she said.

"I know it was a dumb thing to—"

"I do not want to talk about it."

"I didn't mean it—"

"Yes you did."

Silence.

"Beth . . ."

Silence.

"Beth, come on . . ."

Silence. Conversation closed.

Bill and Ruth Hartley lived less than a mile away from us. Their house was a red-shingled Cape Codder with white shutters and an array of children's playthings on the front lawn. I always found the sight of those swings and slides a little spooky, because their only son, Theo, had been born with Down's syndrome and spent most of the year boarding at a "special school" near New Haven. They'd wanted more children, but had never conceived again: "God's way of telling us that we should leave well enough alone," Bill once remarked dryly. Bill was a stockbroker, the heir apparent at AJP Hartley & Co., a small Wall Street brokerage firm that had been run by assorted Hartleys for the past four generations, and which dealt with a small but select core group of clients. "A nice, steady business," as Bill described it, though he could also have been talking about his own life because Bill and Ruth were models of nice steadiness. They'd met twenty years ago at U. Penn and had one of those rare marriages that seemed to coast gently along without any seismic disturbances. Ruth was a successful public relations executive in New York; Bill liked the fact that his small-time brand of stockbroking was removed from the usual Social Darwinistic whirl of the big Wall Street firms. They made good money. They had a pleasant house. A pleasant thirty-foot sloop moored nearby (on which Bill frequently took me sailing). A pleasant way of appearing close, yet never cramping each other's style. And the quiet underlying strength of their marriage was accentuated by the fact that, when the tragedy that was Theo happened, they managed to maintain their equilibrium and hang together.

I envied them such equilibrium, such stability. Unlike Beth and myself, they had decided to embrace their limitations. Instead of looking upon their suburban life as a terrible and limiting compromise, they accepted with grace the cards that had been dealt them. In the process, they had discovered something that had always eluded the two of us: a degree of contentment.

I didn't envy Bill his receding hairline, however. Or the inner tube of flab that was forever expanding around his waist. Or his taste in sweaters. As he greeted us at the door, he was wearing a dark green crew neck decorated with small penguins.

"Who gave you *that?*" I asked him. "Nanook of the north?"

Ruth popped her head around the corner of the doorway. "I did."

Beth gave me an exasperated look, muttered "Jerk" under her breath, and headed off into the already crowded sitting room.

"Oh dear," Ruth said, her eyebrows arched mischievously. She wore a sweater embroidered with polar bears.

"Sorry."

"Don't worry about it, Ben," Ruth said, following Beth into the crowd.

"More fun on the home front?" Bill asked. He was the closest thing I had to a good friend.

"Don't ask."

"Double Scotch, then?" Bless Bill. Unlike just about everyone else in New Croydon, he didn't worship at the abstemious altar of designer water. He still believed in the medicinal pleasures of booze.

"Treble," I said.

"Got some twenty-five-year-old Macallan with your name on it," he said, about to lead me toward the kitchen. But the doorbell rang and he turned back to answer it.

"Ah, our emissary from the world of culture," Bill said.

I spun around. Standing in the doorway was Gary, draped in black, his smirk on overdrive.

"Brought you a special little number." He handed Bill a rectangular gift box. Bill opened it, inspected the label, appeared impressed.

"Well, you can stay," he said. "Go find yourself a drink." Gary gave me a smarmy nod, and headed off in search of the bar. As soon as he was out of earshot, Bill whispered, "He may be a pretentious bozo, but he really knows his wine. Ever heard of this stuff?"

He handed me the bottle. Cloudy Bay Sauvignon Blanc, 1993.

"Yes," I said. "I've heard of it."

7

THE REST OF THE PARTY was a bit of a blur. No doubt, Bill's liter of twenty-five-year-old Macallan had something to do with this. It was rarely out of my company for the entire evening. And by the time I ended up calling Wendy Waggoner "Meat Loaf," more than half the bottle was sluicing around my bloodstream.

For some curious reason, Wendy didn't like that nickname. Her "I-am-a-big-swinging-dick" husband, Lewis, also took umbrage—though this wasn't what caused him to take a swing at me. Rather, the punch was thrown after a somewhat discursive moment during which I wondered out loud if (given his penchant for ruthlessness in business) his idea of charity was buying up the life insurance policies of AIDS victims. Fortunately I managed to dodge his left hook. Unfortunately, it landed on the jaw of Peggy Wertheimer—the most seriously neurotic woman in New Croydon (and with good reason, as her husband had just run off with a Mexican tennis pro named Carlos). Thankfully, the blow did not fracture or dislocate anything, but it did break up the party. Peggy began to shriek in shock. Wendy shrieked at Lewis for being such a hotheaded shit. Lewis shrieked at me for allegedly provoking him. Beth stormed off for home without me. And Gary smugly turned to me and said, "Remind me to invite you over the next time a couple of my Serb and Croat friends are in town."

Gary. Impossible. Unbelievable. She abhorred him. Hated his arrogance, his vanity, even his clothes. No way he could be the guy. No fucking way.

Picked up that salmon I ordered, and a bottle of that amazing New Zealand Sauvignon Blanc. Cloudy Bay Sauvignon Blanc, 1993, to be exact. Nothing more than a coincidence, right? Then why did Beth lie about where she obtained the bottle?

Even though I spent most of the party throwing back shot after shot of the Macallan, I still managed to keep Beth under discreet surveillance. For the first two hours, she studiously ignored Gary. Not a passing glance, not a circumspect smile between them. And I began to think: Stop being a jerkoff paranoid. A coincidence is a coincidence (and she probably had her own abstruse reasons for not telling me where she bought the wine). Then I happened to glance in her direction while she was standing on the staircase, chatting with Chuck Bailey (our neighbor, the Porsche-driving ad man). As Gary squeezed by them, on his way up to the first-floor bathroom, he managed to lay his hand atop Beth's fingers and stroke them quickly. Though she didn't look up at him, a blush colored her cheekbones, a dreamy smile flickered across her lips, and I felt as if three Pershing missiles had just landed in my gut. As I didn't have any Maalox on hand, I reached again for the Macallan, and shortly thereafter found myself inspired to call Wendy Waggoner "Meat Loaf."

"Blame it on Madame Beth Bovary and that goddamn creep," I felt like screaming as everyone else screamed at me. But having already committed the uncharacteristic sin of being drunk and disorderly, some modicum of lawyerly restraint finally kicked in, and I avoided the sort of appalling *j'accuse* scene that would've had tongues wagging in New Croydon for months to come. Instead, I retreated to a corner, smiled weakly when Gary made his Serb and Croat comment, shook his hand good-bye after he proffered it, and even nodded politely when he said, "Any time you're in the mood, drop over to the house and we can talk cameras."

Jesus. Talk about chutzpah. Sure, Gary, I'll stop by, sink a few cold ones, and shoot the shit about Leicas—but preferably on a day when you're not screwing my wife. Okay?

My wife. As soon as Gary made his good-byes, I staggered toward the door, having decided that I must get home, must confront Beth, must finally have it out with her, must . . .

"Ben."

It was Ruth, blocking my path, a restraining hand on my shoulder.

"Ruthie, Ruthie." My words were slurred. "I . . . I'm . . ."

". . . drunk," she said gently. "Very, very drunk . . . and in no condition to go home."

"But . . . but . . . I gotta—"

"You've got to sleep it off. I'll call Beth, tell her you're crashing here tonight."

"You don't under—"

"Ben. Don't go home. Not until morning. Not until tempers cool down."

I tried to lean against a wall for support, but began to slide to the floor. Ruth called for Bill. He came rushing over and caught me before I hit the parquet.

"Come on, big guy," he said. "Let's introduce you to our spare bedroom."

"Sorry, Ruthie," I said. "I fucked up your party."

"We'll live."

The next thing I knew, it was morning, and the inside of my head was my own private Nagasaki. Ground-zero devastation, as if every brain cell had been nuked into oblivion. And then the guilt hit. I had behaved like an asshole, and I knew that Beth was going to make me pay, big time, for it. And as the guilt turned into fear, I found myself wondering: might Gary be occupying my side of our bed right now?

A knock on the door and Bill waltzed in, carrying a glass of effervescent orange.

"Room service," he said brightly.

"What's the time?" I muttered.

"Noon."

"Noon! Jesus! I've got to call Beth . . ." I struggled to sit up, but didn't get very far.

"Ruth already has. Everything's fine. Beth's taken the kids, gone off for the day to see her sister Lucy in Darien . . ."

I groaned. "I'm dead. Lucy thinks I'm Mr. Head Up My Ass."

"That's good, coming from someone who lives in Darien."

"Ruthie say how Beth sounded?"

"Cheerful."

"Bullshit."

"Okay, I'm a liar. Drink this."

"What is it?"

"A killer dose of Vitamin C. Should make you feel semi-human again."

I took the glass, downed the fizzy orange liquid, let out a sigh of relief.

"Better?" Bill asked.

"I might just live. Where's Ruthie?"

"Up visiting Theo."

"She ever going to forgive me?"

"She already has."

"And you?"

Bill flashed me one of his sardonic smiles.

"A memorable night. A real doozy. But, hey, I hate the Waggoners, so . . ."

"Thanks."

"Don't mention it. Up for an afternoon on the Sound? Nice northwesterly blowing."

"I've got to call Beth first, at Lucy's."

"Don't bother."

"It's that bad?" The alarm in my voice was tangible.

"It will be if you call."

"I'm in deep shit, that's what you're telling me?"

"You'll sort it out. But not on the phone. And not this afternoon. So hit the shower. I want to be out on the water in an hour."

We made it to the boat in forty-five minutes. It was a peerless autumn day on Long Island Sound: a hard, cobalt-blue sky, a sharp tang to the air, the wind steady and bracing. Bill's boat—christened the *Blue Chip*—was a thing of beauty. A white fiberglass hull, scrubbed wooden decks, a two-bunk cabin with a full galley kitchen and a compact head. And stowed above a small fitted desk was just about every mod-con navigational device imaginable. A global positioning system, an autopilot, a digital anemometer that electronically measured wind speed, and assorted computers that gauged climatic conditions, navigational progression, even your craft's relationship to polar curves.

"Quite a collection of toys," I said.

"You mean, like your cameras?" Bill asked, all smiles.

"Touché, asshole."

"Beer?"

"Definitely."

"Grab two out of the icebox while I get the sails raised."

The little icebox was located next to a small gas stove that was hooked up by heavy rubber tubing to a large natural gas canister, housed in a wooden compartment on deck. The canister had two hose outlets, the second of which led to a small radiator bolted to the starboard wall. While opening the icebox door, I accidentally jostled one of the hoses and checked it carefully to make certain I hadn't dislodged it. Then I grabbed two cans of Kirin from the box, and headed back on deck.

"Banzai." Bill toasted me with a can.

"Great setup," I said, toasting him back. "Bet you could go places in this baby."

"I keep wanting to take her down to the Caribbean for a couple of months . . . but when do I have a couple of months?"

He finished cranking up the jib, then turned his attention to the halyard that hoisted the mainsail. It flapped wildly as it inched its way up the mast.

"I'd guess twenty knots of wind," Bill said.

I popped my head into the cabin and spied the digital readout on the anemometer.

"Nineteen," I reported. "Impressive."

"Yeah, it's tough being so good. Feel like heading east to Sheffield Island? It's an easy two-hour run from here."

"And it's right off the coast from Darien too."

"You want to go pick trouble with your wife, you'll have to swim ashore."

"All right, I'll shut up."

"You're learning."

As soon as the sail was hoisted, Bill cast off the mooring. Then he trimmed the mainsail. With a decisive *whoosh,* it grabbed the wind and sent the boat sharply to port. Immediately, he spun the captain's wheel and the *Blue Chip* steadied at a twenty-five-degree angle of heel. Within minutes, we had cleared the final headland of New Croydon Harbor. Bill shouted "Coming about," I ducked as the boom swung over to starboard, and with the sail trimmed down, another *whoosh* of wind sent us east.

"Take over," Bill yelled over the sudden gust. As soon as I had the wheel in my hands, the wind picked up another five knots and we whipped along, leaving assorted small dinghies in our wake as we sailed due east into open seas.

"The hell you think you're heading?" Bill yelled.

"Europe," I shouted back. Suddenly, we were skimming the surface of the Sound—flying low thanks to a full-throttle northwesterly, the hull slicing through the now choppy waters.

"Twenty-five knots," Bill roared over the wind. "Goddamn speed demon."

I squinted into that burnished autumn sun, the mounting gale at my back. My lungs felt chilled by the salted air. And for a few tantalizing minutes, my head emptied: that much craved, seldom-encountered perception that you are a tabula rasa, wiped clean of all guilt, all fear, all loathing. The sheer velocity of speed held me in its thrall. I was racing, leaving everything behind—and nothing, *no one,* could catch up with me.

For nearly an hour, Bill and I didn't exchange a word, or even a glance. We both stared straight ahead, mesmerized by that tantalizing sensation of limitless forward motion—a life without frontiers or barriers to stop your progress, to keep you within bounds. And I knew he was thinking what I was think-ing: *Why stop?* Why not tack east and make a dash across the Atlantic? Why not make a run for it? We all crave latitude in life, yet simultaneously dig ourselves deeper into domestic entrapment. We may dream of traveling light but accumulate as much as we can to keep us burdened and rooted to one spot. And we have no one to blame but ourselves. Because—though we all muse on the theme of escape—we still find the notion of responsibility irresistible. The career, the house, the dependents, the debt—it grounds us. Provides us with a nec-essary security, a reason to get up in the morning. It narrows choice and, ergo, gives us certainty. And though just about every man I know rails against being so cul-de-saced by domes-tic burden, we all embrace it. Embrace it with a vengeance.

"You wanted to keep going, didn't you?" Bill asked as we dropped anchor off Sheffield Island.

"Wanted to? Sure. Would've?" I paused, then shrugged. "Nah."

"Why not?"

"You can run, but you can't hide."

"But you *do* want to run?"

"All the time. Don't you?"

"No one's ever totally satisfied with their situation, are they? But some of us are a little more accepting of their circum-stances . . ."

"You have a lot going for you."

"And you don't?" he countered.

"At least your marriage seems intact."

"And at least your children are healthy, properly functioning kids . . ."

"Sorry."

"Ease up, Ben. Ease up on yourself."

I cracked open another beer, and turned my gaze toward the wooded Connecticut coast. It seemed so unsullied, so pas-toral from this perspective, with not a swimming pool or sta-tion wagon in sight.

"Ease up? Me? That's a good one."

"All right, so you're not doing exactly what you want to be doing . . ."

"Do you know how mind-numbingly dull T&E can be?"

"Probably about as mind-numbingly dull as stockbroking. Still . . . you chose it. Just like you chose to marry Beth, have kids, live in New Croydon . . ."

"I know, I know . . ."

"But, I mean, those are not *bad* choices. Shit, you want for nothing . . ."

"Except stimulation . . . on all fronts."

"So what are you going to do? Spend the next twenty-five years thinking life is elsewhere?"

"I don't know . . ."

". . . because I'll tell you something, chum—life is *here*. And if you keep hating where you are, you're going to wind up losing it all. And, believe me, once you lose it, you'll desperately want it all back again. It's how it works."

I took another long swig of beer, then asked, "Say Beth has already decided that it's gone beyond the point of no return?"

"With two kids in the picture and no career of her own, she's not going to get cavalier about leveling your marriage. Trust me—she's not that self-destructive."

Then what's she doing fucking Gary? I felt like shouting. Just as I also desperately wanted to ask Bill if he had heard any grapevine gossip about my wife's extramarital dalliance. But I avoided entering this line of inquiry. I didn't want to arouse suspicions or appear paranoid. And I genuinely feared the truth.

Instead I downed the dregs of my beer and simply said, "I'll see if I can talk to her."

"Try talking to yourself while you're at it too."

I threw my eyes heavenward. "Thanks, Dad," I said.

"All right, end of homily," Bill said. "Take us home."

We made New Croydon by nightfall. I navigated us back into the harbor without the use of any of Bill's fancy technology.

"Very impressive," Bill said as we docked. "The old Bowdoin training?" He knew I'd spent three years on my college sailing team.

"Never leaves you."

"You should get yourself a boat. Give you a nice little escape hatch—and the boys will really enjoy it once they're older."

"I've got enough overhead as it is."

"Well, any time you feel like borrowing mine . . ."

"You serious?"

"No, just stupid."

"I might just take you up on that."

"Just don't go running away with it, all right?"

Bill drove me back to my house. It was dark. I checked my watch: seven P.M. No cause for alarm. Yet.

"Hang in there," Bill said, proffering his hand. "And, for Christ's sake, lighten up."

How strange it was to enter a silent, empty house. I would have enjoyed this temporary respite from domestic din had I not noticed the flashing message light on our answer phone. I hit the playback button.

"Ben, it's me. I've decided to stay up here with the kids for the next few days. I think some time apart might do everyone some good—and I would appreciate it if you didn't try to contact me while I'm at Lucy's. I must inform you, however, that I will be consulting a lawyer in the next few days. I think you should do the same."

Click. I sat down slowly on the sofa and shut my eyes. "I must inform you, however." So formal. So detached. So arctic. She really meant business this time. And it scared me shitless.

I picked up the phone and speed-dialed my sister-in-law. She answered.

"Ben, she doesn't want to—"

"I have to speak with her."

"I said, she doesn't—"

"Put her on the goddamn—"

Click. I hit the redial button. Phil—my laconic cost-accountant brother-in-law—now answered.

"Not the right moment, Ben."

"Phil, you don't under—"

"Yeah I do."

"No, you don't fucking understand—"

"Think I could live without the language, Ben."

"I am about to lose my family, Phil."

"Yeah, so Beth said. Real bad, huh?"

"*Real bad! Real bad!* That's all your number-crunching mind can come up with. *Real bad!*"

"No need to yell, Ben."

"I'll yell all I want, you dumb-shit simian."

"Now, that's getting real offensive, Ben. Real negative. So I think we're going to bring this conversation to a conclusion. But when Beth gets back, I'll tell her you—"

"Beth is out?"

"Yeah, left around an hour ago. Said she was going to see Wendy somebody . . ."

In the background, I heard Lucy shouting: "Phil, you retard. I told you . . ."

I shouted into his other ear. "She's driven back here to see Wendy Waggoner?"

"Well, hey, it's only a thirty-minute drive."

The phone was wrestled out of his hand by Lucy.

"Ben, if I were you—"

"You said she was there. You said . . ."

"I said, she doesn't want to speak with you. And she—"

"What the fuck is she doing at Wendy's? Having a cooking lesson?"

"Getting legal advice, so she said."

"Wendy's no goddamn lawyer—"

"She has this divorce-lawyer friend—"

"She couldn't use the phone to call this 'friend'? She had to leave the boys—"

"The boys are just fine."

"What have you done with them?" I shouted.

"*What have I done with them?* I'm their aunt, not David Koresh."

"Tell me . . ."

"I tucked them into bed. I changed Josh's diaper. I read

Adam a story and wished him sweet dreams. Hope that sounds *reasonable* to you."

"I'm coming to get them—"

"Ben, *don't*—"

"They're my kids—"

"If you show up here, I will get the police. You don't want the police."

"You haven't a legal leg to—"

"It would still look bad. Very bad."

"You wouldn't dare—"

"I've never liked you. I *would*."

And she hung up.

I kicked a table. I smashed a Steuben glass ashtray. I stormed out of the house, jumped into my Mazda Miata, and sped down Constitution Crescent, heading toward Interstate 95 and a fast sprint to Darien. Let that Laura Ashley bitch call the cops. Let her fucking try . . .

Suddenly I slammed on the brakes, then reversed back down a road called Hawthorne Drive until I pulled up in front of a mature three-story clapboard house set back from the road amid two manicured acres. The home of Lewis and Wendy Waggoner. Dark. Silent. With no cars in the driveway.

I punched the steering wheel. The bitch. Using Meat Loaf Wendy—and her so-called "divorce-lawyer friend"—as a cover.

I knew what I was going to do: charge up Gary's front lawn at full speed, ram my Miata through his front door, and crash right into his living room. But as I was about to roar onto Constitution Crescent, a little voice in my head whispered: Prudence. Don't do anything irretrievable. Exercise restraint. Size up the situation and then decide on a course of action. And though I wanted to disobey that cautious, judicious voice—so wanted to play reckless for a change—inevitably I heeded its advice. And slowed down. And cruised the backstreets until I found our Volvo parked on the road running parallel to Constitution Crescent. Smart move, Beth. After all, leaving it in Gary's driveway might just raise a suspicion or two.

I steered into Constitution Crescent. Cutting my headlights, I slid the Miata into my driveway, killed the engine, and
closed the door as quietly as possible. Then, cutting around to
the backyard, I unlocked the basement door. Once inside, I
grabbed my new Canon, a roll of Tri-X, a massive telephoto
lens, and a tripod, then headed up to the second floor. Adam's
bedroom faced out on to Constitution Crescent. The curtains
were open, the lights were out. I quickly unfolded the tripod,
attached the Canon at its base, loaded the film, twisted on the
telephoto lens. Pulling over a chair, I sat down, peered
through the viewfinder, aimed it across the road at the front
door of Gary's house, and waited.

An hour went by. Then, just after eight-thirty, the front
door opened. Gary poked his head out, looked up and down
the road, and nodded behind him. Twisting the focus, I sharpened up the image just in time to see Beth step into the door
frame. Gary pulled her toward him and kissed her deeply. She
ran one hand through his stringy hair while her other five fingers gripped his denimed ass. I flinched, jerking my head
back from the viewfinder as my finger depressed the shutter
release. It took less than a minute for the motor drive to whizz
through the thirty-six exposures. When I reluctantly put my
face back to the camera again, the embrace was just ending.
Looking nervous, Beth glanced in the direction of our house.
Seeing nothing but the lights behind the drawn curtains of
our sitting room, she turned back to Gary. A final full, deep
kiss on his lips, a final glance at the empty road. Then, with
her head lowered, she hurried off into the night—praying, no
doubt, that she wouldn't meet a neighbor out for a mid-
evening stroll as she walked briskly away.

I was on my feet, running down the stairs, running toward
the front door, about to make a dash up the road and catch
her before she reached the Volvo. But again I hesitated—and
instead flopped on the sofa.

That kiss. Definitely not a "passing fling" sort of kiss. It was
so unbridled. So ardent. So *serious*. The last time Beth kissed
me that way, George Bush was president. What the fuck did

she see in the bastard? But I knew that if I ran up to her now and staged a big confrontational scene, it would be like shooting myself in the foot with a machine gun. All hopes of any future reconciliation—as dim as they seemed right now—would be flattened. She'd use the fact I'd spied on her as further proof that our marriage was a sham. We would cross the frontier of no return—and never find our way back again.

I began to pace up and down the sitting-room floor. I was a man who was about to lose everything. Images flooded my brain: a divorce judge granting Beth full custody of the two boys, the house, the cars, the stocks and bonds, and three-quarters of my income. My new life in some tiny one-bedroom box in the East Nineties. Yet another trip to the Bronx Zoo with Adam and Josh during the one weekend a month I was granted access to them. Adam developing Gary's world-class smirk. Josh turning to me at the age of four and saying, "You were once my daddy, but Gary's my real daddy now."

Gary. Suddenly I found myself on autopilot, marching purposefully across the road toward his front door. I didn't know what I was going to say to him, didn't know what (if anything) this would accomplish. But there I was on his doorstep, ringing the bell.

Beth couldn't have been gone for more than five minutes, so when Gary swung the door open, the sight of me threw him completely. He blanched in shock, but then did his best to recover his poise. There was a long silence during which language failed me completely, and I found myself wondering, the fuck you doing here? Finally Gary broke the silence.

"Ben . . . ?"

I managed one word. "Cameras."

"What?"

"Cameras. You said I should drop by sometime, talk cameras with you . . ."

He was totally bemused by this line—and I could see him studying me cautiously, trying to gauge whether or not my arrival on his doorstep really was just the stuff of bizarre coincidence.

"Yeah . . . guess I did. But, uh, kinda late on a Sunday, isn't it?"

"Just past eight-forty," I said, glancing at my watch. "Not late at all. Anyway, Beth and the boys are away . . ."

"Yeah, I . . ."

He caught himself.

"What?" I said.

". . . noticed the Volvo wasn't in your driveway."

"You noticed that, did you?" I suddenly felt emboldened.

"Just noticed . . . yeah." Now words were failing him.

"Didn't know you *noticed* my house so much."

"Well, I don't make a habit of . . . Lookit, Ben, I'm kind of tired. How 'bout . . ."

"Just a fast glass of wine," I said.

He hesitated, and I could almost hear him deciding: Can I handle this? The telltale smirk that crossed his face gave me his answer. He gestured grandly with his right hand. "Entrez, dude."

I stepped inside. Though Gary's house was a Cape Codder, crossing its portals took you out of New England and into some ersatz Tribeca "environment." Walls had been broken down and then distressed in a gray-blue tint. Carpets had been pulled up, floorboards painted black. Four pinpoint spotlights dangled from the ceiling. And the only piece of furniture in the entire space was a long black-leather couch.

"Quite a place," I said.

"Yeah, my dad had some weird ideas about interior design," Gary said.

"Who was your decorator? Robert Mapplethorpe?"

"Very witty. Actually, I did all the work myself, back in '91."

"Right after your dad died?"

"Good memory. Almost a year exactly after my mom went. Think her fucking Alzheimer's killed him too. Wore his heart down real good."

"Must've been hard, being the only child . . ."

"'Losing one parent is unfortunate, losing two is careless.'"

"Never knew you read Oscar Wilde."

"Never have. Saw the quote in a magazine somewhere. Drink?"

He motioned for me to follow him into the kitchen. It too had been gutted—old pine cabinets and work tops replaced with a messy assortment of chrome and steel fixtures. Like the living room, it appeared half finished, underdeveloped, absurd. For a moment, I almost felt sorry for Gary and his desperate attempt to replicate Tribeca cool in the suburbs. But my empathy for his lack of New York success was short-lived. It ended as soon as I saw two wineglasses on a countertop, one of which was dappled by the pink lipstick that Beth always wore.

Nodding toward the glasses, I managed to mutter, "Been entertaining?"

He worked hard at suppressing a smile. "Yeah, guess you could say that." He opened the fridge and pulled out a bottle of Cloudy Bay Sauvignon Blanc.

"Ever try this stuff?" he asked.

"Beth brought a bottle home once."

Another little smile as he uncorked the wine. "She's got good taste, your wife. Cloudy Bay's the best Sauvignon Blanc on the planet."

"So she said."

He grabbed the bottle, two clean glasses. "Darkroom's this way," he said, leading me down a narrow flight of stairs to the basement. It was a cramped, dark space, cluttered and reeking of damp. One wall was taken up with domestic appliances—a washer, a dryer, a large freezer. The other wall held his printing equipment: an old Kodak enlarger, battered chemical trays, a guillotine for trimming paper, and crisscrossing clotheslines on which were pinned several dozen recent prints.

"Your basic, utilitarian darkroom," Gary said, flicking on the fluorescent overhead light.

"Does the job, I'm sure."

"Yeah—but compared to your setup, it's kind of Third World."

"Don't remember ever showing you my darkroom, Gary."

He turned away, and busied himself pulling a few prints down from the clothesline.

"Just conjecturing, counselor."

"Conjecturing *what?*"

". . . that you have a spiffy darkroom filled with spiffy equipment."

"But you've never seen it. Have you?"

That smirk again. How I wanted to rip it off his face.

"Nope. Never have."

Liar. Beth must have entertained him there one afternoon when the kids were out, and given him a guided tour of my basement.

"Then why do you automatically presume . . . ?"

"Because a spiffy Wall Street guy like you can afford the best, and therefore probably *has* the best. That's all." He dropped a stack of prints into my hands. "Here—tell me what you think of these."

I shuffled through the half-dozen prints, all of them bleak monochromatic portraits of assorted lowlifes, all posed against the entrance to some sleazy hellhole of a welfare hotel. It was quite a freak show. An overweight biker with three steel teeth and a sprawling birthmark covering half his face. Two black transvestites in vinyl hot pants with discernible track marks on their naked arms. A one-legged amputee sprawled on the pavement, drool cascading off his lips. But while the imagery itself was shocking, there was something about Gary's composition that irked me. It was too self-consciously artful, too postured in the way it called attention to his subject's physical aberrations.

"Impressive," I said, handing him back the prints. "Arbus meets Avedon's drifters."

"You're saying they're derivative?"

"It was meant as a compliment."

"I've never been a big Arbus fan," he said, pouring some wine in a glass, then handing it to me. "Too much verité, not enough compositional clarity."

"Oh, come on. Arbus was a genius at composition. That

classic shot of the Christmas tree in the Levittown living room, the way each object in the room—the couch, the television, the lamp with the plastic cover on the shade—enhances the terrifying sterility of the image . . . that's compositional genius."

"She loved the subject, but she didn't love the picture—that was her philosophy . . ."

"Sounds like a proper photographic philosophy to me . . ."

"Only if you believe in artlessness . . ."

"You're saying Arbus was *artless*?"

"I'm saying that she always tried to play the passive spectator . . ."

"Nothing wrong with that—unless you're the sort of photographer who likes to call attention to his so-called quirky eye."

"So you *do* think they're derivative?" he said, brandishing his prints.

I chose my words carefully. "Not derivative. Studied. Too much you. Not enough of the passive spectator . . ."

"What bullshit. The photographer can *never* be a passive spectator . . ."

"Says who?"

"Says Cartier-Bresson."

"Another friend of yours?"

"I met him once or twice, yeah."

"And I suppose he personally told you, 'Gary, ze photographer, he must never be ze passive spect-a-tor.'"

"He wrote it." Reaching behind him, he grabbed a Cartier-Bresson book off a shelf, rifled through some pages, then read out loud:

"'The photographer cannot be a passive spectator; he can be really lucid only if he is caught up in the event.'"

"Well, how 'bout that," I said. "He personally autograph that book for you?" Gary chose to ignore the sarcasm and continued to read on.

"'We are faced with two moments of selection and thus of possible regret: the first and more serious when actuality is there, staring us in the viewfinder; and the second when all the shots have been developed and printed and we have to reject the less effective one. It is then—too late—that we see exactly where we failed.'"

He looked up at me, his face flushed with acrimony. "That touch a chord with you, counselor?" he asked. "Not that you'd know anything about failure. Especially when it comes to photography. And your wasted year in Paris. And your stint behind the counter at Willoughby's, and . . ."

I heard myself whispering, "How the fuck . . . ?"

The smirk was now epic, triumphant.

"Guess," he said.

Silence. I stared at the linoleum floor. Finally I muttered, "How long?"

"You mean, Beth and me? Couple of weeks, I think. Can't remember exactly."

"And is it . . ."

He cackled. "*Love?* That's what she's calling it."

Another punch to the gut. "And you?"

"Me?" he said brightly. "Well, I'm having fun. A lot of fun. Because, as you probably know, Beth's one hell of a fuck. Then again—from what's she told me—maybe you don't know that."

"Shut up."

"No, no, no—*you* shut up. And listen good. She loves me. And hates you."

"She doesn't—"

"Oh yes she does. Hates you big time . . ."

"Stop it . . ."

"Hates your job. Hates her life up here . . ."

"I said—"

"But really, really hates the fact that you hate yourself. Your self-pity. The way you act so entrapped—while all the time refusing to accept that it was you who couldn't cut it as a photog—"

"And you've cut it, loser?"

"At least I'm out there, man . . ."

"You're a bullshit artist with a trust fund . . ."

"At least I'm still pitching. At least I'm still in with a shot . . ."

"You are *nowhere*—"

"And you've made it?"

"I'm a goddamn partner in one of the biggest—"

"Face it, you're just some corporate stain who can't even get it together to fuck his own—"

And that's when I lashed out. And hit him. With the Cloudy Bay bottle. Swinging it wildly and catching him on the side of the skull. The bottle shattered in two, the broken stem still in my hand. Gary was knocked sideways. As he fell away from me, I lashed out again and suddenly the jagged glass was in the back of his neck. It all couldn't have taken more than five seconds—and I was drenched. Drenched in a geyser of blood.

The blood caught me full frontal in the face, momentarily blinding me. When I managed to wipe it from my eyes, I saw Gary staggering around the darkroom, the bottle protruding from his neck. He turned toward me, his face a chalky mask of shocked bemusement. His lips formed a word. *What?* Then he fell forward, facedown into a tray of developer fluid. The tray upended. His head slammed into the floor.

Silence. My legs gave out. I slumped to the linoleum. A curious echo reverberated between my ears. Time seemed swollen, distended. And for a moment or two I didn't know where I was.

But then my mouth felt dry. So dry that I licked my lips. And tasted that sweet sticky liquid running down my face. A taste that told me:

Life as I knew it would never be the same again.

PART TWO

WHY ARE HIS FINGERS MOVING?

I snapped out of my reverie and watched with horror as one of Gary's fists slowly unclenched. An involuntary spasm, no doubt—but terrifying nonetheless. Especially as fifteen minutes must have passed since . . .

The fingers stopped unlocking. I looked at him carefully. Still lying facedown on the floor, the bottle jutting out of his neck like an abstract sculpture, blood still leaking from the wound, mixing with the developer fluid to form a reservoir beneath his outstretched arms. No signs of life.

Fifteen minutes. Could I have sat here this long?

Fifteen minutes. A quarter of an hour ago, I was a model American: an industrious, economically productive, child-rearing, mortgage-paying, two-car-owning, actively consuming, Gold Card–carrying resident of the top-income echelon. And now . . .

Now . . . total decimation.

And it didn't even take fifteen minutes. A mere five seconds from grabbing the bottle to . . .

Can everything you've built up—all that domestic and professional striving—be demolished in five unhinged seconds? Is everything so tenuous, so finely balanced, so easily obliterated? One moment a perfect citizen, the next . . .

A murderer? *Me?*

There was blood on my lips. My tan Shetland sweater was sodden, crimson. So too my khakis and Docksiders. And though I was in deep netherworldly shock—though I still couldn't exactly fathom what had happened, and stared at Gary's ever stiffening body with disbelief—a curious lucidity began to undercut the free-floating trauma and fear. And in those moments of pure clarity, a scenario of future horrors began to unspool in my head.

They would come for me at the office. There'd be two of them. They'd both wear cheap overcoats and cheap suits. Flashing their shields, they'd identify themselves as homicide detectives with the Stamford, Connecticut, police department.

"Benjamin Thomas Bradford," Cop One would say while Cop Two cuffed my hands behind my back, "you are under arrest for the murder of Gary Summers. You have the right to remain silent; anything you say can and may be used in a court against you . . ."

I'd be led out of the office. Estelle would stare at me with tears running down her cheeks. Jack, looking apoplectic, would still manage to yell, "Ben, don't tell 'em anything until Harris Fisher gets there" (Harris being the Street's leading white-collar criminal lawyer). Then we'd negotiate the central office hallway. Every partner, associate, and low-level employee of Lawrence, Cameron and Thomas would line the corridor, gaping in silent shock. When we reached the elevator, Prescott Lawrence—the firm's most senior partner, the man who hired me because he played baseball with my dad at Yale—would be waiting. He'd speak not a word. He wouldn't need to. His arctic gaze would say it all. You have ruined your life. You have disgraced the name of this firm. Expect no empathy, no legal assistance, no support. We are washing our hands of you. You are dead meat.

Silent stares in the elevator. A curious crowd of onlookers in the downstairs lobby. And outside, a battalion of photographers, television cameramen, radio hacks. We'd push through them, eyes lowered to avoid the flashbulb pyrotechnics, the shouted questions. An unmarked car would be waiting for us. I'd be shoved into the backseat.

"Take a good look, Bradford," Cop One would say, motioning toward the glass. "You won't be seeing the Street again for a very long time."

"If ever," Cop Two would add. "Murder one might just mean life without. Especially if the jury decides to make an example of some white-bread yuppie who thinks he's so above the law he can slash the dude who's boning his wife."

"You're gonna be famous, though. Front page of the *News,* the *Post,* maybe even the *Times.*"

"Fuckin' sure the *Times.* If it was a brother done the cutting, they'd bury the story in Metro news. But a preppy perp from Wall Street? Man, I expect an editorial and two op-ed pieces by Friday."

"Not to mention all that cheap-ass tabloid TV. *Inside Edition, Hard Copy,* crawling all over your house, trying to get an interview with your stricken wife, bribing Gary's housekeeper to let 'em do some close-up shots of the bed where they sinned, the black basement where you took his life . . ."

". . . and I'm sure they're gonna be after little Adam too. Or at least his homeroom teacher. 'Ma'am, how do you tell a little boy that his father's a murderer?' Close-up of the teacher fighting back tears . . ."

After reaching Stamford, I'd be fingerprinted and booked, then cuffed to a desk in a grubby interview room and left waiting for five hours until Harris Fisher arrived. Around fifty—country-club tan, thinning silver hair, double-breasted silver-gray suit, serious French cuffs, an ambulance-chaser smile that he'd flash at the two arresting cops, but not at me.

"A bad business, counselor—a very bad business," he'd say as soon as the two detectives were out of the room.

"How bad?" I'd manage to croak.

"Put it this way—I've just spent the past three hours with Morgan Rogers, district attorney for Fairfield County. And he wants your balls. Especially as it is an election year. Especially as he believes he has enough evidence to win a murder one conviction. Seems your fingerprints are all over Mr. Summers's house, you have no one who can vouch for your whereabouts at the time of his murder, your wife has made a statement that she and Mr. Summers were, uh, *involved,* and, of course, there is the unfortuate matter of those photographs you took of your wife and Mr. Summers in mid-embrace. Pity you forgot about the camera in the window. First thing the police found when they searched your house."

Hanging my head, I'd ask, "Did he offer any sort of plea-bargain possibilities?"

"Man one—eighteen to twenty-five."

"Twenty-five *years?* I can't do twenty-five years."

"Probably just eighteen with good behavior . . . though I can't guarantee that. We could, of course, go to trial. But Rogers informs me that, if we do demand a jury, he will press for life without. Though we could naturally build some sort of case, the evidence is overwhelmingly stacked against you. And when it comes to motive—they've got you by the *shlong,* counselor. Husband murders the guy *schtupping* his wife. Oldest scenario in the book—and without mitigating circumstances, one that carries heavy time in the eyes of the law.

"I have more difficult news. I spoke with your wife this afternoon on the phone. She was in a rather distraught state, but she still made it very clear that she will be willing to testify against you should this go to trial."

Lowering his voice, he'd avoid my gaze.

"She also said that, if you made bail, she would seek a court order barring you from any contact with your boys."

"Can she do that?" I'd gasp.

"You know she can. A man has been murdered. You are the prime suspect. No judge is going to grant someone under indictment for homicide access to his children. I'm sorry.

"The arraignment hearing won't be until tomorrow. I'd think long and hard about the few options that you have. If you really think we can mount a defense, then we'll naturally take on your case—but you must realize that proving your innocence is going to be quite an uphill task. And it will also be a very costly process. But I don't have to tell you about the high cost of legal work."

I'd now want to die, and would ask Cop One for his service revolver, and a bullet, and a shot of whiskey to steady my nerves. Turn your back for a moment, guys, I'd tell them, biting down on the barrel of his .38, and let me save the taxpayer some money . . .

The screen inside my head was suddenly filled with light. I was jolted back to the basement floor. To blood drying on my lips, and the broken bottle in Gary's neck gleaming under the fluorescent lights.

How I wanted to confess. Get up. Call 911. Tell all to the cops. Purge myself of the shame. Embrace the catastrophe.

But. But. But. After the cathartic release of confessing all, where would I be? In the Connecticut state pen, probably dodging the affections of some psychotic behemoth named Moose. Even if I did manage to get off on a lesser charge, I would still be disgraced, defiled, despised (not to mention disbarred). And I would do time. Serious time.

Upon my release—in late middle age—I'd be permanently estranged from my sons (Beth having long since divorced me). I'd end up living in a rented room over some garage in Stamford, seeing out the remainder of my working days stacking books in a public library, Adam and Josh refusing to talk to their ex-con dad . . .

Fuck confession. *Think*. Think of a way out of this. You're a lawyer, after all.

2

FINDING THE BASEMENT BATHROOM was my first bit of luck. It was tucked away next to the washing machine and freezer—a grubby little toilet and shower stall that looked like it was last cleaned in '89 and was stacked with half-filled paint cans, turpentine bottles, dried-out rollers, and other home-decorating detritus. I didn't care about the mess. The fact that there was a working shower in the basement was a huge relief. It meant that I wouldn't have to go upstairs in my bloodied clothes, and leave tiny smudges of DNA-rich evidence around the house. I could contain the gore down here.

I stripped off everything, rolled it into a tight bundle, and dumped it all into a black plastic bag I found among the cleaning supplies. Then I stepped into the shower. The water was hot. I soaped up with a dirty cake of Ivory, and found an old bottle of Prell shampoo to clean the matted blood from my hair. I stayed in the shower for over ten minutes. There was a lot to wash away.

The only towel in the bathroom was communion-wafer thin and had once belonged to a Motel 6. It barely stretched across my midsection. After turning it into a makeshift toga, I walked quickly across the basement floor and up the stairs. When I reached the door, I hesitated for a moment, remembering that Gary had left the lights on in the kitchen. The windows faced a backyard. The backyard faced . . . ? Probably another house. Might a nosy neighbor be able to spot me? *And Mrs. Rifkin, is the man you saw with just a towel around his waist in this courtroom today?* Better not to risk an accidental sighting. So I cracked open the door, and slid my hand along the wall until I found the switch for the kitchen and the hallway. Once all the lights were off, I carefully negotiated my way down the corridor that led to the front door, then turned left up the stairs, trying to touch as little as possible.

Gary's bedroom was at the rear of the second floor. It was dark, and remained so until I closed all the blinds. When I flicked on the main switch, two bedside lamps jumped into life. The room continued the house's crash-pad theme, with half-stripped floorboards, strewn clothes, messy piles of glossy magazines, and an expensive futon on a varnished frame. Its duvet was in a state of postcoital disarray; a large stain adorned its bottom sheet. I shuddered. She did it with him *here?* In this slum? Ultratidy Beth, who was always rearranging her sock drawer, who was obsessive about the way her art books were displayed on our coffee table? She actually put up with such disorder? And maybe even enjoyed it? Getting off not just on the thrill of illicit sex, but also on hanging out with a hip slob?

I found what I was looking for near the bed. A pair of black sweats; top and bottom, both in black. Gary was about my height and had the same lanky frame, which meant that his sweaty clothes fit reasonably well. So too did a pair of his black Nikes. I checked my watch. 9:30. Around fifty minutes since . . .

I sat down slowly on the bed, woozy, disoriented, my adrenaline in overdrive. Did someone see me cross the road, knock on Gary's door, go inside? If they did, I'm toast. If they didn't . . . it'll just be two or three days before questions are asked about his whereabouts. And then . . . it will only be a matter of time. They'll put it all together, figure it out, come for me. And there'll be no escape. No way out.

Easy now. *Easy.* Don't go Dostoyevskian. It's not the moment for guilt, remorse, shame, existential soul-searching —unless you really want to walk the plank. Forget the crime.

Think of it as . . . *a problem.* And problems can be solved. If you work them out. One step at a time.

Alibi? Do you have one? You called Darien twice at around seven. And then? There are two hours to account for. You could always say you were watching television. All right, Mr. Bradford, can you remember what Murphy Brown was up to that night? . . . Oh, you were watching CNN . . . what was the lead story? Forget television. You could always say you were reading and had an early night. But how are you going to prove that you were at home all the time? The phone bill will show those early calls to your appalling in-laws. But after that . . . ?

I had to get on the phone now, call Beth, and have some sort of record on my Southern New England Telephone bill to show that I was in our house around the hour that the murder was committed. It wouldn't totally clear me—far from it—but it might just toss up some "reasonable doubt" questions in the jury room.

But before I made the dash back to my house, I needed to do some basic housekeeping here, to get rid of as much evidence as I could, just on the off chance that Gary was expecting a late-night visitor. Or had given an extra set of keys to a friend who was crashing in the spare bedroom for a few days. Or . . .

A dozen other paranoid scenarios flashed through my head. Don't waste any more time. Clean up the mess.

Motel 6 towel in hand, I crept back into the dark kitchen, pulled down the two venetian blinds, hit the lights. Beneath the sink I found a pair of rubber gloves, a rag, and an aerosol can of Pledge furniture polish. Donning the gloves, I used the spray and the cloth to rub the kitchen cabinet I had just touched, along with the cord for the blinds. In fact, I sprayed and buffed every surface I could find—just in case I'd inadvertently fingered any of them during my conversation with Gary. Then I went back to the basement.

As I descended the stairs, I saw his face. Half his face; the other side rested flat against the linoleum. One eye stared up at me with glassy reproach. I didn't return its gaze, but instead noticed that the flow of blood had ceased. First things first. The bottle. I approached the body, doing my best to steel myself for the task ahead. Crouching down, I grabbed the bottle neck and quickly pulled. But it wouldn't come away, as it appeared to be stuck on some vertebrae, bone, or muscle. Another go. This time Gary's entire head lifted up with the bottle. I instantly dropped it, the head slamming into the floor. I tried twisting the bottle slightly, then pulling. Still no give. Placing my left foot squarely on his head, I yanked hard, and the bottle finally gave way, escaping from his neck with a loud, repulsive slurp.

I had the towel over the neck wound, just in case it started bleeding profusely. But only a light trickle baptized the white terry cloth. Grabbing both his arms, I pulled him out of the small crimson pool surrounding his body. Blood and developer fluid streaked the linoleum as I tugged. Then I turned him over. Reaching into his pockets, I found his house keys, his car keys, his wallet. I pocketed them all. As I stood up, my back bumped against the chest freezer. An old Frigidaire model. I opened it. Bachelor provisions: a couple of pizzas, three lasagnas, four tubs of Ben and Jerry's Cherry Garcia, nothing more. Perfect. Absolutely perfect. My second bit of luck. I dumped all the food in the black plastic bag. Then I sat Gary up and leaned him against the freezer. Crouching down, I took a deep, steadying breath and pulled him toward me, wrapping my arms beneath his arms. As I clutched him in a bear hug, his head fell forward against my shoulder and lay there cozily, like some teenage girl slow-dancing at a high school prom. He must have weighed only 170, but it still took a monumental effort to haul him up.

When he was finally standing, I let go and gently pushed him backward. His skull landed in the middle of the freezer. Using his legs as a rudder, I maneuvered his body, steering his head into one corner and doing my best to squeeze as much of his torso and thighs into this small compartment. But his height was a major problem, because no matter how I positioned him, his knees and legs still dangled over the side. And it was crucial that they fit fully inside that box. After all, I didn't know how long I might have to keep him chilled, and the freezer had to be closed properly, otherwise he might start to decompose in a day or two—a prospect I certainly didn't relish. But how would I get his goddamn legs into the freezer? I tried folding them on top of him. Crossing them at his side. Sitting astride the freezer lid in an effort to jam them in. This was hopeless. He wouldn't fit. I wouldn't be able to store him here, and would be forced to get rid of the body in haste. And if there's one thing the law teaches you, it's this: Haste always leads to a fuckup.

Then I saw a hammer, tossed among the cleaning supplies in the bathroom. Its head was large, formidable. And I realized, swallowing hard, very useful for my purposes.

I opened the freezer. I pulled out Gary's left leg and dangled it over the side. I shut the lid. I grabbed the leg in my left hand, pulled it as tautly as possible, and slammed the hammer down, hitting a spot four inches below the knee. It took five more blows, but eventually the bone cracked in two, and the lower part of his leg suddenly became floppy in my hand. Then I pulled out the other leg and repeated the process. The bone was even tougher this time. Seven blows were needed before it too fractured in half.

Now I was able to take each broken leg and fold it back, so that the foot fit under the knee. It reduced the length just enough to jam him completely into the box. When I closed the freezer lid, it shut perfectly. He could now stay there for weeks—until I decided what to do with him.

I checked my watch. A minute before ten. I needed to get back home and make that phone call soon. I quickly grabbed a mop from the bathroom, dumped the remaining contents of a Mister Clean bottle into a bucket, and got to work on the floor. Within twenty minutes, the blood and developer fluid were gone.

I snapped the mop in two and tossed it into the plastic bag. The bucket followed, along with the developer tray, the smashed Cloudy Bay bottle, any remaining glass fragments, the soap and shampoo. I worked fast, but thoroughly. I was taking no chances.

Two rinses of the basement sink and shower. A comprehensive rubdown of all basement surfaces, all door handles, all banisters, all light switches, and everything I touched in Gary's bedroom. Finally, it was time for the most dangerous stage of this damage-limitation exercise: leaving.

A fast peek out the door. Constitution Crescent was silent. No traffic. No moon. An overcast sky. Though I was certain there were lights on in the homes that adjoined Gary's, I had to gamble that none of the neighbors would happen to be glancing out their front windows as I made my dash across the road.

I pulled my head back in and shut the door. My adrenaline shifted into overdrive. I couldn't move, and found myself rooted to the spot. But I had to make that phone call.

I hoisted the bag and let myself out, shutting the door silently behind me. My first instinct was to run. Make a mad dash for it across the road. But the lawyer in me counseled calm demeanor. Don't run. Walk. But for God's sake, don't look back.

It was like strolling through Sarajevo during the height of the sniper season, dreading the faint gunpowder report in the distance that might be the last thing you ever heard. I walked out onto the little sidewalk that fronted Gary's house, stepped off the curb, and moved briskly across the empty road, fully expecting to hear, at any moment, the "Hey you! Stop!" that would signal the beginning of the end.

But all I heard was the sound of my own footsteps, moving from paved road to the gravel of my driveway to the soft crunch of late autumn leaves as I made my way to my back door. Reaching into the sweats' pocket for my keys, I found both sets of Gary's keys. But mine were missing.

Immediately, I was on my knees, scrambling in the dark through the plastic bag until I found my khakis. I dug straight into the pockets. No keys. All the bloodied clothes now came tumbling out. No keys. Then I saw the hole in the bottom of the bag.

I quickly repacked the bag and left it by the basement door. Then I started retracing my footsteps, my eyes firmly rooted on the ground.

I didn't have to walk far. Just to the edge of the road, where the keys lay a few inches from the curb. Reaching down to grab them, my relief was huge. Until I heard a voice.

"Something wrong with you, guy?"

I looked up anxiously. It was Chuck Bailey, the ad man who lived down the road. Late forties, thick, dyed black hair, dressed now for jogging in a Calvin Klein tracksuit with a battery-operated lamp strapped to each bicep.

"Chuck," I said, trying to sound collected. "Evening. Dropped my keys."

He jogged in place.

"You sure there's nothing wrong with you?" he asked. "A death wish, a need for grievous bodily harm . . ."

I was getting more than a little nervous. "I don't under—"

"The sweats, Ben. The shoes. All black. Makes you kind of invisible on the road. Car comes along, you're toast. Who you trying to be, Zorro?"

I managed a laugh.

"Just like our asshole neighbor, Gary. Always see him out jogging at night, dressed just like you. The invisible fucking man." He glanced down at my feet. "Same Nikes too."

"How's biz?" I asked, trying to change the subject.

"Crap. Just lost the Frosty Whip account. And the multinational assholes who now own us are talking words like 'restructuring,' 'downsizing.' Scaring the shit out of everyone."

"Life in the nineties . . ."

"Yeah—one long panic attack."

He checked his watch.

"Gotta go," he said. "Knicks versus the Clippers tonight from L.A. Best to Beth and the kids. And buy yourself some lights, you gonna jog in the dark. You're a family man."

"Tell me about it."

A male bonding laugh from Chuck Bailey. "I hear ya. Later, guy."

I watched him jog up the road. That went well. More than well. *And, Mr. Bailey, you say that you met Mr. Bradford jogging on the evening of the murder?* What nice, respectable guy goes jogging after committing a murder? *You said that Mr. Bradford was wearing black Nikes—the same sort of Nikes that Mr. Summers usually wore. And—let me get this straight —before that night you'd never seen Mr. Bradford in black Nikes?*

Mental note: Buy a pair of black Nikes tomorrow. And get that camera out of the window, now. You can just about see it from the road.

I walked to the back door, turned the key in the latch, grabbed the plastic bag, and ducked inside. Leaving the bag near my gym equipment, I raced upstairs, snatched the camera and the tripod from the darkened bedroom, and returned to the basement. Flipping open the back of the Canon, I removed the film canister, popped it open, and yanked out the film, exposing all thirty-six frames. That additional evidence destroyed (and laid to rest in the bag), I reached for the phone and dialed Darien. Phil answered.

"Put her on," I ordered.

"Ben, I told you—"

"Put her fucking on."

"You talk to clients this way?"

"No—just to assholes. Now get her—"

He hung up so loudly I had to pull the receiver away from my ear. When I redialed, the answering machine was on. So I left a message.

"Beth, it's me. I am upset. Very upset. And I think, before you go running off to see Wendy's divorce-lawyer friend, we should, at the very least, try to talk it out, see if we can—"

She suddenly came on the line.

"There is nothing to talk about," she said quietly.

"There is everything to talk—"

"No. I have done enough talking. And I have nothing more

to say to you except this: I've decided to remain up here with the boys for the week. I've also called Fiona and informed her that she has the week off. And I'd like you to find somewhere else to stay by the time we're back next Sunday."

"It's not just *your* house—"

"There are two ways we can handle this, Ben. Politely, or with injunctions."

The phone shook in my hand.

"They're my boys too," I finally said.

"And I won't keep them from you. So if you'd like to drop by some evening this week and see them, that would be nice. But don't call back tonight. We won't answer."

And she hung up.

I put the phone back in the cradle and covered the back of my head with my hands. I stayed in that cowed position for what seemed like an hour, replaying over and over that moment when I reached for the bottle.

Go on. Get it over with. Grab the garden hose, some heavy adhesive tape, a bottle of Irish, a vial of tranquilizers. Then drive off to some secluded spot, insert the hose in the exhaust, tape it in place, thread it through the window, tape the rest of the window closed, pop twenty Valium, chase them with a large swig of Black Bush, turn on the ignition, and surrender to the inevitable. You'll pass out, won't feel a thing. Face it, you'd never be able to live with the guilt. Every waking hour would be overshadowed by the fear: Today they'll find out . . . today they'll come for me . . . today is the last time you'll ever see your boys again. And even if you somehow managed to dodge detection for a while, the agony of inevitable arrest would be unbearable. You're going to lose everything anyway. End the agony now. Cleanly. With the minimum of fuss.

I stood up. My legs buckled. I fell back on the couch, weeping uncontrollably. Crying for my sons. And for myself. I was guilty not just of murder, but of self-hatred—a loathing that had made me despise the life I'd built for myself. And now, in the final hour or two of that existence, I would bear witness to the cruelest of ironies—the fact that I so desperately wanted to keep what I once so wanted to flee. Had I believed in some sort of supreme being—some Mr. Fixit in the sky—I would have sunk to my knees and pleaded: Give me back everything that I once found so stifling. Give me back that mind-numbing commute, the dreary hours spent pouring over codicils, the corporate ass-kissing. Give me back the domestic drudgery, the marital squabbles, the sleepless nights. Give me back my kids. No more would I think life was elsewhere. No more would I curse my compromised fate. Just give me one more chance.

I was on my feet, lurching through the house. I grabbed a bottle of whiskey before bolting up the stairs. In the bathroom I found a bottle of Valium. I upended the dozen pills into my mouth and flushed them down with as much Black Bush as I could swig. But the excessive overdose of whiskey set my gut aflame. I was suddenly, convulsively sick. Projectile vomit. Over the bathroom walls, the floor tiles, the sink, the toilet.

I remember little beyond the final monumental retch. When I drifted back into consciousness, the enveloping aroma nearly had me heaving again. Fully clothed, I staggered into the shower stall, turned on the cold water, and shoved my face under the spray, opening my mouth wide, blasting away the noxious tang of a botched suicide.

I stripped off the sweats, leaving them in the shower. Without bothering to towel off, I fell out of the bathroom and into bed.

And then it was Monday morning. And the phone was ringing. I answered it with a grunt.

"Mr. Bradford, is that you?"

Shit. Estelle. My eyes tried to focus on the bedside clock. 10:47. Shit. Shit. Shit.

"Mr. Bradford, you there . . . ?" Her voice was thick with worry.

"Sick. I'm sick."

"You sound it, Mr. Bradford. Your wife with you?"

"Away with the kids at her sister's."

"Then I'll call a doctor right . . ."

I was suddenly awake.

"No doctor, no doctor . . ."

"Mr. Bradford, you sound like death."

"Food poisoning, that's all. Bad can of soup."

"Could be botulism. Or hepatitis. I'm calling the company doctor . . ."

"Estelle, the worst is over. A day in bed is all I need now."

"You can never be too careful with bad soup, Mr. Bradford."

"I'll live. Cancel my appointments. Tell Jack. And I'll call in later when I'm feeling . . ."

"No, I'll call you, Mr. Bradford. And if you want me to phone Mrs. Bradford at her sister's . . ."

Absolutely not. I needed Beth to stay in Darien as long as possible.

"I'll deal with that, Estelle."

"At the very least, let me call your own doctor . . ."

"I'm going back to sleep now. Talk to you later."

I hung up. And spent an hour staring at the ceiling. I didn't want to leave this bed. Ever. I wanted to think of that scene in the basement as nothing more than a psychotic bad dream. And when the lingering perfume of the bathroom hit my nostrils, I cursed my bile-filled gut for failing me again. A nice, calm gut and I would have been happily dead by now.

The stench finally forced me out of bed. I spent an hour cleaning the john. By the time I finished, the washing machine had also rid Gary's sweats of any residual odor. I shoved them into the dryer and returned to bed, hiding my head under the duvet.

I stayed there for hours. Mental paralysis. Physical paralysis. I didn't know what to do next.

The phone rang again at four. Estelle. I assured her I was on the mend. Hanging up, I made my way to the window and peered out of the blinds at Gary's house. He's dead, I'm dead. Tomorrow I'll pay our doctor a visit, tell him my nerves are still shot, walk away with a nice big Valium refill, and do the job properly this time. With water, not whiskey.

I climbed back under the duvet. I started to cry and slammed my fist against the bedside table. It connected with the television remote control, snapping me out of my crying jag. The picture tube blurred into life. On the screen was a deranged televangelist in a polyester suit, holding forth before a spellbound audience of Christian rednecks in some mammoth prefab church.

"And then," thundered the reverend, "Jesus said to Nicodemus, 'You come by night, but I'm gonna turn on the light. Except a man be born again, he cannot see the Kingdom of God.'

"Now why d'you think Jesus said, unless you get born a second time, you sure won't see no Kingdom of God? And what does getting born again mean? Well, it don't mean going back to your zero years. You're not gonna revert to being a baby again.

"No . . . what it means is this: Though your mother brought you first into the world, unless you're born again and accept Jesus as your Lord and Savior, you still have Satan in your heart. Hell without God is where you're heading. But when you're born again, it's like you're being given a second chance. The blood of the lamb washes away all your sins. You walk new, you talk new, you *are* new. It's as if you've killed off your old life and come back with a second chance. Reborn a new man . . ."

I sat bolt upright. My tears subsided. My watery eyes suddenly cleared. For the first time since reaching for that bottle, a wave of calm descended over me. *We are born, but only if we are born again can we start life anew.* What a simple, reassuring precept. That fleshy Bible thumper rumbled on. And I found myself thinking:

Yes, I must die. For there is no other way out. But after I am dead, why can't I begin life anew? Why can't I have that second chance? Why shouldn't I be born again?

The more I considered it, the more clearly I realized: You don't need Jesus to be reborn. You just need a lot of careful planning.

3

THINK OF IT as a moon walk, I kept telling myself. You ponder and reflect upon every move you make, remembering all the time that a false one might just send you winging into deep stratospheric shit from which there is no return. Take one slow, calculated step at a time. And don't chance anything.

So I didn't return to Gary's house until late Monday night. As I didn't want to bring any more of my potentially traceable clothing fibers across his threshold, I dressed in his freshly laundered black sweats and Nikes. Before leaving, I locked the plastic bag of evidence in my darkroom, shoved a penlight in my pocket, and put on a pair of surgical gloves (I buy them in bulk to use while handling photographic chemicals). When I finally crept out my back door after midnight, there were no signs of life on Constitution Crescent. With commuter trains awaiting early morning go-getters at dawn, and kids due at school by eight-thirty, even the most nightowlish of the road's residents were always down for the count by eleven. But not wanting to chance another encounter with Chuck Bailey—or someone returning home late after a weekend away—I still exercised extreme caution, loitering in the shadows of my driveway, making certain the coast was absolutely clear before light-footing it across the road.

Once inside, I used the penlight to guide me to the basement. After negotiating the steps, I turned on the overhead fluorescent tubes and made an inspection of the linoleum floor. No noticeable traces of blood. Then it was time for a very quick glance inside the freezer. Gary's face now had a light-blue tint, and when I tried to close his eyes, the lids were so chilled that it took some effort to force them shut. Not a pleasant experience, but at least I had evidence that the freezer was doing its job properly.

Penlight in hand, I found my way upstairs to a spare bedroom on the second floor that Gary used as an office. The blinds were closed. I turned on a small desk lamp and found myself surrounded by chaos. Stacks of bills, correspondence, unopened junk mail, old newspapers, general detritus. Sweat clothes and dirty socks were thrown everywhere, papers littered the floor, his desk and IBM Thinkpad were covered with dust. I shuffled through his bills and bank statements. His Amex and MasterCard accounts were both long overdue. Southern New England Telephone had sent out a final notice for $484.70, and Barneys wasn't going to honor his charge card until the long outstanding balance of $621.90 was paid off. When I inspected his Chemical Bank statement, there was a credit balance of only $620 in his checking account. But judging from the pattern of previous deposits, he was due a quarterly trust-fund installment of $6,900 tomorrow, on the first of November. Gary was evidently one of those clowns who never paid his bills on time, and probably took great pleasure in annoying the hell out of credit departments. But as I rifled through more creditor demands, I also gathered that he found it difficult to maintain a fast-lane life on $2,300 a month. Nothing I found hinted at any income other than his trust fund.

In a pile of correspondence, there was a recent letter from the photo editor of *Vanity Fair*.

> Dear Mr. Summers:
> Thank you for your recent submission. *Vanity Fair* does not accept unsolicited photographic material for publication, so I am returning your work to you now.
> Sincerely,

A form letter. Not even signed by the editor. Digging around his pile of correspondence, I found other recent brush-offs from *National Geographic, Condé Nast Traveler, GQ,* even *Interview.* I had been right all along—Gary's bravura talk about knowing Avedon and Leibovitz was pure, unadulterated bullshit. Yet reading those cold little rejection notes didn't give me much satisfaction. Instead, I felt a peculiar sadness, and pictured Gary sitting here, trying to come to terms with yet another dismissive letter, yet another professional setback. Suddenly, his public arrogance seemed understandable. It was not just pompous bravura, but a form of self-defense—a way of bolstering himself against rejection and disappointment, of staving off self-doubt.

I opened his IBM Thinkpad, powered it up, and accessed my way into his WordPerfect files. There was a directory named PROFCOR. It contained three dozen or so PROF-essional CORrespondences. Letters offering his services to just about every glossy magazine and ad company in New York. There were also begging letters he wrote to the ten top photographic agencies in the city. One of them, dated the twelfth of September of this year, read:

Mr. Morgan Grey
Grey-Murcham Associates
54 West 44th Street
N.Y., NY 10011

Dear Mr. Grey,
Thank you for your letter of September 5th, and for your enthusiastic words about my work. I was, however, deeply disappointed that you wouldn't take me on as a client—especially as this is the third time in three years that I have approached you about representing me (It's becoming something of an annual event!).

I appreciate the fact that you might have too many clients on your books at the moment. But I also know that, once launched by you, I would prove to be one of your most lucrative photographers. As you saw in my portfolio, I

am versatile, eminently adaptable to the demands of commercial and photojournalistic work, and not rooted in a
specific visual genre. I know I can compete with the big
boys when it comes to major assignments. I know I have
what it takes to break through. And with your agency
behind me—without question, the only photographic
agency in New York I'd want as my representative—I know
I could cut it big time.

Please reconsider. It would be just one more name to
add to your books—and a decision I know you'll never
regret.

Sincerely,

The self-assurance, the chutzpah, was breathtaking. I
quickly opened up the next file, anxious to know if such Dale
Carnegie salesmanship had paid off. The letter was dated
October fourth.

Mr. Morgan Grey
Grey-Murcham Associates
54 West 44th Street
N.Y., NY 10011

Dear Mr. Grey,
Thank you for yours of September 29th, and for
dealing with my letter so soon after your return from Cap
d'Antibes (hope you had a great vacation, by the
way).

Yes, I do understand the problems your agency has with
client overload, and yes, I do realize that, even for your
established clients, the economic downturn has meant
leaner times all around.

But I also know this: you *will* take me on one day. And
when you do, you'll discover that I am one of the best invest-
ments you've ever made.

I'll be back to you in six months. And six months after
that, if need be. All I ask for is a shot.

Sincerely,

There was something truly gruesome about this sort of self-aggrandizement. The man had no shame. Gary pretended to be a winner, always just on the precipice of success. In private, he must have despaired of ever living up to such a confident public image. And quietly wondered: Am I a failure? I'd always mocked his pretensions, his delusions of grandeur. Because, perhaps, I secretly envied his persistence, the fact that, unlike me, he didn't surrender to corporate inevitability. Instead, he kept banging on doors, kept traveling hopefully.

I flipped through the rest of the PROFCOR directory. The last letter, dated just six days ago, was dispatched to a Jules Rossen, the photo editor of a new travel magazine called *Destinations*.

> Dear Jules,
> Great seeing you last week. I'm pleased you like my port-folio and hope that the commission will happen. I really love the idea of a photojournalistic essay covering the California/Baja California border—especially as it would allow me the opportunity to point up the vast contrast between First and Third World realities, not to mention the nuances of frontier town sleaze. The fee you mentioned—$1,000, including expenses—is considerably lower than what I'm usually paid. But I do appreciate that, as a new publica-tion, *Destinations* does not yet have the wherewithal to match the fees paid by other, more established magazines. And—as I was dead impressed by the dummy issue you showed me, and would certainly like to be a member of the *Destinations* photographic team—I'd be willing to accept the terms you offered.
> I have a small gap in my schedule at the moment, and could therefore head west as soon as you give me the green light.
> Once again, I really look forward to developing a rela-tionship with *Destinations* and now await the go-ahead from you to "make a break for the border."
> Best,

A small gap in my schedule . . . The fee you mentioned is considerably lower than what I'm usually paid. By whom? *The New Croydon Shopping Gazette?* I had little doubt that this Jules Rossen guy was probably canny enough to read between the lines and realize that no successful photographer would accept an assignment three thousand miles from home for an all-in fee of a mere thousand bucks. Arrogance often masks desperation.

I searched the desktop pile of correspondence for a reply to this letter. Nothing. So I returned to the Thinkpad, switched out of the PROFCOR directory, and opened one cryptically labeled "B." There were nine files. I read them sequentially.

9-12-94

B:

Ten on Wednesday just fine. Will take pep pills in anticipation.

Later,

G.

○   ○   ○

9-15-94

B:

Back scratches still healing . . . but just about recovered otherwise. You are deranged. Can't do Monday—meeting in the city. Tuesday, lunchtime? Await your call.

G.

○   ○   ○

9-21-94

B:

I leave another of these notes in my letter box, I'm gonna start thinking I'm in a bad Le Carré novel. Tomorrow at two works.

G.

○   ○   ○

9-24-94

B:

Off to Boston on biz. Don't worry—I won't call (though I really think you're being just a little paranoid about me phoning. He's not there during the day, and if the nanny answers, I can always say I'm the plumber).

Be in touch when I'm back. And, yeah, I'll miss you.

G.

○ ○ ○

10-3-94

B:

Back from Beantown. Tomorrow anytime.

G.

○ ○ ○

10-5-94

B:

Thinking long and hard about what you said yesterday. Stop worrying—he's too preoccupied to suspect anything. And when you do finally give him the heave-ho, we can keep playing it low-key for a while. Does that calm your bourgeois conscience? At home Monday morning, if you wanna party.

G.

○ ○ ○

10-10-94

B:

Got your message. You sounded like you were auditioning for *Oprah*. Can't figure why you need to turn our nice little arrangement into bad psychodrama. But it's your call, your guilt trip. So . . . hasta la vista. Might see you and the kids at the Safeway sometime.

G.

P.S. No rush, but do leave the back-door keys under my mat when you have a chance.

○ ○ ○

10-17-94

B:

Well, you do surprise me. Yeah, I'm around later today if you want to drop over. Say 4 p.m.?

G.

○ ○ ○

10-27-94

B:

Great news. Assignment in the offing to Baja California.
Might have to head west in a hurry. But, still around tomorrow a.m.

if you want to play. Yeah, I've been invited to the Hartley thing on
Saturday. If you're uncomfortable with me being there in the presence
of hubby, missing it won't kill me. But we can talk that through on
Friday.

    G.

By the time I read this final file, my gut had turned into a
furnace. Reaching for Gary's Filofax, I rifled through the
pages of his diary, and discovered that, in addition to every liaison mentioned in his letters, there were at least half a dozen
others on different dates, all annotated with the letter "B."
These additional trysts were obviously set up when they saw
each other, while all other rendezvous were arranged through
the "note in the mailbox" method. No doubt, it was ultratidy,
ultracareful Beth who came up with the idea of Gary leaving
her missives in the old-style mailbox at the edge of his front
lawn. I had to admire her ingenuity.

It worried me that she still might be in possession of Gary's
back-door keys—especially as his diary entry for ten A.M. this
coming Wednesday was also marked with a "B." They'd probably arranged this future liaison on Sunday night. And come
Wednesday, Beth would undoubtedly make up some excuse to
leave the kids with Lucy in Darien and pop down here for a
few hours. Unless, of course, Lucy was in cahoots with her, and
knew all about Beth's extramarital dalliance. No—that wasn't
Beth's style. She was, by nature, intensely secretive. And it was
also pretty clear from Gary's notes that, while she was uncer-
tain about whether to bust up our marriage, she found it
equally difficult to give him up.

She loves me. And hates you. I didn't believe it then, but
now, after reading the "B" files, I felt I had proof that Gary was
speaking the truth. If she was that smitten with him, then she'd
be more than a little curious as to why he wasn't here for her
on Wednesday. And if she decided to let herself in the back
door and started snooping around . . .

Gary would have to be called out of town. Check that: Gary
would have to be called out of town . . . and then decide to stay

away permanently. A note must be waiting for her in the mailbox on Wednesday morning. And sometime after Sunday—when she returned home from Darien with the kids—I would have to be dead.

I was beginning the last week of my life.

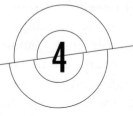

DURING MY FIRST YEAR at Lawrence, Cameron and Thomas, there was a small interoffice scandal when one of the junior associates in the M&A division was nabbed after forging the signature of a vacationing senior partner on an urgent contract.

"Dumb schmuck," Jack Mayle said after the hapless young associate was shown the door. "He should've known that if you want to fake a guy's signature, you always copy it upside down. Oldest trick in the forger's book."

Good advice, Jack. Pulling Gary's Amex card out of his wallet, I turned it over to the signature side, reversed it, reached for a yellow legal pad and a Bic pen, then began to practice copying his upside-down signature.

It was easy to reproduce. A large bold "G," a sweeping "Y," with a swiggly line bridging these two letters. He signed his last name with a big-deal "S," followed by a bumpy mountain range of consonants and vowels before ending with another slalom course of an "S." After ten or so attempts, I had the signature reasonably perfected. Then I turned back to the Thinkpad, opened the directory named MONEYBIZ, and found out everything I needed to know about his banking arrangements and his ongoing relationship with Concord, Freeman, Burke and Bruce—the law firm that administered his trust fund. Thankfully, there was little in the way of correspondence with his attorneys, bar the occasional begging letter, asking if it was possible to dip into the principal (and two follow-up whines after the request was, naturally, denied).

Turning to a battered gray filing cabinet near his desk, I found myself confronted with more paper anarchy. But after some serious digging, I hit gold. I unearthed a fat, dirty manila file that contained his birth certificate, his Social Security card, the title deeds to his house, his parents' last will and testament, and the all-important trust documents. More good news here. The house was fully paid off and Gary was sole owner. He was also the sole beneficiary of the trust, currently yielding an annual income of $27,600, paid quarterly to his Chemical Bank checking account. There were no tricky codicils or conditions attached to the trust (bar the fact that the principal was inviolate). Gary's own will was also reassuringly straightforward. He had never married, never spawned any dependents, and was an only child. In the event of his death, therefore, the entire bulk of his estate was to be left to his old alma mater—Bard College—on the stipulation that . . . I couldn't believe this . . . a chaired professorship in photography was to be created in his name.

I had to laugh. The guy's vanity knew no limits. And it didn't at all surprise me that Gary was an old Bard grad, as it was an institution that catered to well-heeled "artistes" who generally majored in advanced pretension. The Gary Summer Professor of Photography! Bard would have to wait a long time for that chair to be established. A very long time.

For the next few hours, I attempted to sort out Gary's paperwork, bundling back correspondence into two large piles, separating bank statements, excavating car and home insurance documents, gathering up all bills in need of payment. By five in the morning, I had brought some order to his office—but couldn't risk working on, as Constitution Crescent's early risers would soon be out for their predawn jogs. So, grabbing the legal pad on which I practiced his signature, I moved quickly around the house, turning off every light. Then I cracked open the front door, gently closed it behind me, double-locked it, and slipped back across the darkened street.

Once inside my house, the legal pad and the surgical gloves joined the other evidence in a black plastic bag. I stripped out of Gary's sweats and Nikes, hid them away in a cabinet beneath the darkroom sink, then showered and shaved and dressed for work. While knotting my tie, I caught sight of myself in the bedroom mirror and didn't like the picture. My complexion was as chalky as Maalox, and two blackened smudges were inked beneath a pair of deeply spooked eyes. Exhaustion, fear, terror, hit like a domino effect. I shut my eyes because the room was now swimming.

I ran the taps and plunged my head into a sink of cold water. Two voices ricocheted 'round my head. The first howled, I can't do this. I can't . . . The second coolly replied, You have to do this. You have no choice. And I knew I had no option but to heed the counsel of that second voice.

I dried my face, opened the medicine cabinet, and chased three large tabs of Dexedrine with a long slurp of Maalox. Within twenty minutes, the Dexedrine would kick in, giving me the energy to overcome my lack of sleep. I pocketed the pills. I was going to need a lot of chemical assistance to make it through today.

A clean shirt and tie, a trip to the laundry room with some dirty clothes, and once the laundry machine was operating, I tossed the bag of evidence into the Miata's minuscule trunk. Tuesday mornings were always the day when I paid a precommute visit to the local recycling plant, so I also managed to stuff three additional bags of empty bottles, aluminum cans, and newspapers into the passenger seat.

New Croydon was far too high tax bracket and protectionist to ever allow a dump to take up residence within its municipal limits. You moved here to get away from garbage, after all, and you paid big money to insulate yourself from the animate and inanimate trash of modern American life. So there was no way that its good citizens would ever allow a litter mountain to loom over the townscape. Especially as they had that grubby minimetropolis called Stamford just ten miles up the road.

The Stamford dump was situated in a grim corner of the city, a slum dominated by rundown frame houses, graffiti, and car dealerships. The sun was just gaining altitude by the time I reached its main gates. I was relieved to see five other cars lined up in front of me, waiting for the gates to open at six-thirty, as I didn't want to be the first face that the dump employees saw at the start of the business day. I only had to wait five minutes before some guy in overalls lifted the barricades and waved us through. After tossing the recycling bags into their respective bins, I drove over to the area earmarked for household garbage.

"Anything inflammable or possibly explosive in the bag?" asked the yawning guy at the Dumpster.

I shook my head and suffered a nervy moment—because sometimes they actually checked the bags to make certain you hadn't laden them down with eruptible aerosol cans or anything other than kitchen waste.

But it must have been too early in the morning to start inspecting garbage, as he grabbed the bag and tossed it into a Dumpster overflowing with last night's debris. As I drove out, I craned my head and saw a forklift truck hoisting the Dumpster and moving it toward a large truck. Within minutes, all that deeply incriminating evidence would be buried under two tons of other trash, and then dispatched to its final resting place—that fragrant corner of New Jersey where Connecticut now interred all its garbage.

I made it back to New Croydon in fifteen minutes, parked my car at the station, and caught the 7:02 into the city. En route, I hid behind *The New York Times*. From time to time, I peeked out from behind its gray pages to make certain no one was staring at me. Surely it was obvious, written all over me, impossible to hide. Someone was bound to notice, call for the conductor, whisper into his ear. The conductor would then stare at me with alarm and hurry off down the corridor. When we pulled into Grand Central, the cops would be waiting.

But no one paid me the slightest heed. To them, I was just another suit. And for the first time in my adult life, I was grateful for such gray-flannel anonymity.

Estelle was surprised to see me in the office at eight-thirty.

"You had me worried yesterday, Mr. Bradford," she said.

"I'll live."

"You still look a bit peaked," she said, taking in my ashen face. "You shouldn't have come in so early."

"You're early too," I said.

"Mr. Lawrence called a partners' meeting . . ."

Red alert. "For when?" I asked.

"This afternoon. So that's why I'm here now. Thought I'd better get in before nine to deal with all the documentation you'll need—"

"A partners' meeting! Christ almighty, Estelle!"

"It's not until three. And I'll have everything ready for you . . ."

"Why wasn't I informed?"

"You were sick, Mr. Bradford."

"You called me twice yesterday. You could have called me again."

She looked startled by my angry tone.

"Mr. Lawrence's secretary only informed me of the meeting at five-thirty. I didn't want to disturb—"

"Well, you should have disturbed me."

"I just thought—"

"You thought wrong. A partners' meeting! You know I need to prepare for these things, Estelle. You know I'm going to have to stand up and account for my life for the past three months. And you also know it's not the sort of thing I need dropped in my fucking lap first thing on a fucking Tuesday morning. I mean, I'm the one who's going to look like an asshole, walking in there unprepared. What am I going to tell them? 'Sorry, guys. My dumb-shit secretary forgot to . . .'"

I caught myself in mid-rant. Estelle was staring at me in shock. I put my elbows on the desk, lowered my head, and pressed it hard against my open palms.

"I'm sorry," I whispered. "I'm really—"

She slammed the door behind her as she rushed out.

I felt a deep, horrified shiver run through me. The window. It's right behind you. Five small paces, a quick upward shove open with both hands, then a fast nosedive into the void. Fourteen stories. Ten seconds of terror. It's pretty instantaneous, they say. You might even be dead before you hit the ground. A nice, clean, free-fall coronary to black you out before . . .

There was a knock on the door. I lifted my head from my hands, suddenly aware that ten minutes had passed since Estelle had run out. Jack Mayle was standing in front of me, looking deeply worried. He closed the door behind him, approached my desk. I waved him away.

"Please. I know. I didn't mean to . . . Don't know what . . . Really wrong thing to . . . I'll apologize. Promise. Promise . . ."

"Ben," Jack said gently, putting a steadying hand on my shoulder. "What's going on?"

I started to sob. Loudly. Jack let go of my shoulder, sank into an office chair, and waited silently until my crying jag subsided.

"Tell me," he said.

How I wanted to tell him. Everything. To divest myself of the whole appalling business. And beg him for some sort of absolution. Which I knew he couldn't—and wouldn't—supply. Especially now. A day and a half later. With Gary on ice. And all his legal documents neatly stacked on his desk. A crime of passion now looked like a carefully premeditated murder. And there was no way that Jack would keep quiet after I confessed to him. For all his fast-and-loose legal style, he was a by-the-book guy when it came to matters of right and wrong. And no matter what sort of spin you put on it, taking a life was never "right."

So all I said was:

"Beth wants a divorce."

"Shit," he hissed under his breath. He liked Beth, liked the kids. He didn't want to hear this. He had enough grim news to cope with. "When did she drop this?"

"Sunday night."

"After a fight?"

"Sort of."

"Maybe just a flash of anger . . ."

I shook my head.

"Heat of the moment, all kinds of dumb things are said," he reasoned.

"It's been building up for months. Years."

"Someone else involved? A third party?"

I looked at him squarely. "No. Beth's not the type—"

"I was thinking of you."

I managed a grim laugh. "I'm not the type either."

"Then what's the problem?"

"Mutual disaffection. We just don't get along anymore."

"That happens in all marriages. Give it time, equilibrium gets established again."

"She doesn't want it back to the way it was. She didn't *like* the way it was."

"Then why'd she have two kids with you?"

"Because . . ."

"Yeah?"

"Accidents will happen."

"Life is a fucking accident."

"Tell me about it."

"You love your kids, love her?"

I nodded.

"Then sort it out."

"It's not that simple. She won't listen—"

"She has to listen . . ."

"She *won't*. As far as she's concerned, it's over. Finished. Dead."

"No hope at all . . . ?"

"None. And I know how she operates, Jack. It takes her a long time to make a decision. But when she does, it's final. And irreversible."

Jack lapsed into troubled silence. He suddenly looked old, sickly.

"I'm sorry," he finally said.

"Estelle . . ."

"She's pretty upset."

"I didn't mean . . ."

"I know."

"Asshole thing to do."

"It happens."

"I'll go and apologize—"

"Not just yet. Let me smooth things over with her first. And listen, the partners' meeting this afternoon . . . think it would be best if I handled it."

"I'll be fine. Really."

"No, Ben."

"It was just an outburst, Jack."

"I understand. And sympathize. But you're kind of shaky right now."

"Of course, I'm a little shaky. Wouldn't be human if I wasn't . . ."

"*Exactly.* So why give yourself the grief of a partners' meeting on top of everything else? Know what I want you to do—take a week off. Eight days if you like. Come back next Wednesday. Have a little break."

"What are you telling me, Jack?"

"That I think you need some time to—"

"What are you telling me, Jack?"

"You look like shit, Ben. Not just tired. Spooked. You've looked that way for months. And questions have been asked—"

"Asked by whom?"

"Guess. Prescott Lawrence, Scotty Thomas—every senior partner in the firm—"

"My work has been fine."

"Without question. But they're still concerned, Ben. You know these assholes—image is everything. And recently, you've been giving off the image of someone with big troubles. They may tell me how much they empathize with you—'We're family here'—but, believe me, they secretly despise it. Despondency, depression, despair—it's not in their lexicon, pal. Because they don't know how to handle it. Never allowed it across the front door. It's a business. The firm *über alles*. And in a business, the illusion of confidence is as important as your professional competence. You have not appeared confident for a long time, Ben. And it's making them nervous."

I turned away, swiveling my chair toward the window. Five little steps. That's all it would take. One. Two. Three. Four . . .

"Now don't worry about Estelle," Jack continued. "Send her some flowers, a nice, contrite note, and I'll make sure she stays *shtum* about this morning—because the last thing we need is that coffee klatch of hers talking this up on the office internet. And I'll also have a word with Prescott Lawrence—explain about the problems at home, say this has been building up for a while, taking its toll, but how I have every confidence you'll pull through, crap like that. At Yale with your dad and Georgie Bush, wasn't he? I think he'll buy it. He likes you, Ben. We all do."

I said nothing. I just kept staring at the window.

"You'll be all right. You know that. I need you to be all right. Time isn't exactly on my side."

He stood up. It took some effort.

"Now go home," he said.

"No one to go home to. Beth took the kids to her sister's in Darien. She wants me out by the time she's back on Sunday."

Jack regarded the carpet at his feet. "What can I say?"

"Nothing."

"Go hit the city then. Have a five-martini lunch. Sleep it off in a movie. Wander around. Make believe you don't have to work for a living. Clear your head."

He opened the door. "One last thing," he said. "Mel Cooper. The king of hard-ass New York divorce lawyers. Not showy—just a ruthless shit. A friend of mine. I'll make a call."

"Thank you."

"We'll talk," he said and left.

Time isn't exactly on my side. Nor on mine either. I took those five steps to the window. I hoisted it open and was nearly knocked back to my desk by a blast of cold, late-autumn air.

Gripping the sill, I bent forward, staring down into the congested hum of Wall Street. Even from a fourteenth-floor prospect, the noise was still resonant. My hands were drenched. I was losing my grip, about to let go. Into the great wide open. But just as I was on the verge of tottering forward, I pushed myself backward and landed on my office floor.

The wind howled through my open window. The cacophony of traffic blared below. I had peered into the void and flinched. Now I knew that the void would never be an option, that I'd never have the courage or reckless abandon needed to make that long, final plunge. I was stuck with myself, stuck with my crime.

I quickly closed the window and returned to my desk. I removed a sheet of office stationery from a drawer, picked up a pen, and wrote Estelle a note apologizing for my abominable tantrum ("I am not taking Beth's decision to end our marriage very well. This does not excuse my outburst—but, please understand, my anger had nothing to do with you"). I also included a line saying how she was the best secretary imaginable, blah, blah, blah, and informed her that, on Jack's advice, I'd be taking the next few days off, but would check in from time to time just in case any urgent business was pending. Folding the letter into an envelope marked "Estelle," I left it in a prominent position on the front of my desk. Then I called Interflora and ordered a $100 bouquet of roses to be sent to her at the office this afternoon.

Act of contrition completed, I reached into a lower desk drawer and pulled out a file containing my own last will and testament. Naturally, I'd drafted it myself—a stark, airtight document leaving the entire bulk of my estate to Beth and the kids. She would do well out of my death. Mortgage insurance would ensure that she owned the house outright. There was $250,000 in assorted stock options. There was an additional $750,000 in corporate and personal insurance policies. Lawrence, Cameron and Thomas would also pay her in compensation an entire year's salary and my annual bonus. And then there was the $42,000 I received annually from the estate of my father. All told, she could expect around $1.4 million—which, properly managed in the trust I'd established, should yield her an annual income of just under $100,000. Not a vast sum, but with the house paid off, enough to keep her and the boys in relative New Croydon comfort.

I also did a thorough fine-print inspection of all my insurance policies. They covered every potential possibility for my demise (bar death in a war zone), so there was no chance that they'd renege on the payout.

Locking all the documents back in my desk, I chased another Dexedrine with Maalox, grabbed my coat and briefcase, and waited until I heard Estelle leave her desk before beating a fast retreat out of the office.

I hailed a cab on Broadway and told the Lithuanian driver to take me to Columbia University—my old turf during the six-month lost-soul period following Paris. I couldn't remember the last time I'd paid a visit to that distant corner of the Upper West Side. When you live in the 'burbs and work on Wall Street, your social circle generally doesn't extend to that cerebral slum called Morningside Heights. The cabby actually knew his geography (probably one of five New York hack drivers who'd ever bothered to study a map). But he had some sort of advanced death wish, racing up the West Side Highway at toxic speed, barely dodging other vehicles and ominously muttering to himself in some Vilnius dialect. Still, it took only twenty minutes to reach Broadway and 116th Street—though I needed another slug of Maalox to calm my stomach when my feet finally felt the secure pavement beneath them.

I walked south three blocks and entered a sprawling old bookshop I used to frequent years earlier. I was rather conscious of my suit and trench coat, wondering if it would make me stand out (or look like a Fed) amid all the student types. But the shop was so crowded with lunchtime browsers that no one seemed to take any notice of my arrival, and I quickly made my way to the back of the store where there were a couple of shelves marked "Alternative & Anarchist."

I used to peruse these shelves for laughs, as they contained a specialist assortment of obscure books from rather worrying small presses that catered to the more paranoid fringe groups in American society—Aryan militias, subversive Trotskyites, guys who wanted to set up their own republic in the Ozarks. Now, however, I was grateful for their subversive expertise, and after a few minutes' browsing, I found exactly what I was looking for: *The Anarchist's Cookbook*, which contained everything you needed to know for making delicious homemade explosives. Heading straight for a chapter entitled "Explosives and Booby Traps," I rifled through it until I found the recipe I was after and copied it down in a little notebook, occasionally casting a glance around to make certain that no one saw me cribbing from this highly seditious "cookbook." I then returned it to the shelf and went digging around until I encountered a paperback entitled *Directory of Mail Drops in the United States and Canada* ("A listing," according to its back-cover blurb, "of over 700 mail drops and re-mailing services all over the world, descriptions of their services, and tips on using them"). Under "California, Bay Area," I found the phone number of one such service in Berkeley, added it to my notebook, placed the directory back on the shelf, then calmly left the shop.

My next stop was a bank, where I withdrew $500 from a cash machine and handed over a $10 bill to a teller in exchange for a roll of 40 quarters. Walking down to Broadway and 110th Street, I entered a phone booth, dialed the Berkeley number, and deposited $5.25 for three minutes when requested to by the operator (I could have used my AT&T card, but I didn't want any account record of this long-distance call). After three rings, a guy answered. His voice was beyond laconic.

"Berkeley. Alternative. Post. Office. Yeah?"

"Hi," I said. "Are you the people who can provide me with a mailing address?"

"Yeah. We're. Those. People." It was like listening to maple syrup being poured.

"How does it work?"

"Twenty dollars a month. Minimum six months. Payment in advance. You give me your name now. When we've received the money, the service starts. When you have a new address, you call us. And we remail everything. To you."

"You never give out that new address to anyone, do you?"

"Fuck, no. We're the Alternative Post Office. We keep. Cool."

"I want the service to start tomorrow."

"Then you gotta wire us. The money. Via Western Union."

He gave me their Western Union number and the address to which all mail was to be redirected:

10025-48 Telegraph Avenue
Berkeley, California 94704

"Like, you never use our name. You just have everything addressed to you. Here. So, like, this becomes the place. Where you're supposed to be at. You got a name?"

"Gary Summers," I said.

"Okay. Gary. Wire me the money. Then we take care. Of the rest. Later, dude." And he hung up.

I couldn't help but wonder how many brain cells he'd lost during the late sixties. The guy had spoken so slowly I used up most of my remaining quarters, but I did have enough left to call Directory Assistance and discover that there was a Western Union office in a drugstore on Fifty-first and Second. Perfect. I jumped in a cab heading downtown, got to the pharmacy, and wired $240 to the Berkeley Alternative Post Office, enclosing a terse cover note:

12 months' payment. Re: Gary Summers

That business concluded, I walked over to Grand Central and caught the 1:46 back to New Croydon. When I reached the station, I collected my car, drove the ten miles to Stamford, and paid a visit to the large central post office downtown. Approaching the window, I asked the clerk for a "Change of

Address" form. Finding a quiet counter, I filled it in, indicating that, as of tomorrow, Gary Summers of 44 Constitution Crescent, New Croydon, Connecticut 13409 would like his mail rerouted to 10025-48 Telegraph Avenue, Berkeley, California 94704. Quickly slipping Gary's wallet out of my pocket, I turned his Amex card upside down, then inverted the postal form and copied his scrawl onto the line marked "Signature." I admired my handiwork. Not bad—but I'd soon have to master his signature right side up, and without the aid of a credit card.

"You're supposed to hand-deliver this to your post office," the clerk said as she inspected the form.

Yeah, but the two postal clerks in New Croydon know everyone in town.

"I was running some last-minute errands in Stamford," I said, "so I thought I'd take care of it here."

"Well, I can't accept it. Either you take it to New Croydon or you mail it to them."

I returned to a counter and scrawled "New Croydon P.O." on the front of the prepaid change of address card. Before popping it into the mailbox, I noticed some fine print in the top left-hand corner of the card:

NOTE: The person signing the form states that he or she is the person, executor, guardian, authorized officer, or agent of the person for whom mail would be forwarded under this order. Anyone submitting a false or inaccurate statement on this card is subject to punishment by fine or imprisonment or both under Section 2, 1001, 1702 and 1706 of the United States Code.

Another felony to add to my expanding rap sheet.

As I walked back to my car, I wondered: Did the clerk notice my face? Was she at all suspicious? I wasn't acting nervous, was I?

Don't think about it. It was just a routine question. You're just one of several hundred faces she sees every day.

I spent the next fifteen minutes cruising around Stamford

until I found a large multistory parking lot on Broad Street. I circled it twice. According to a sign out front, it was open twenty-four hours. It offered long-term weekly rates. It had one thousand spaces. It was a low-rent operation with no video surveillance—not the sort of place, I figured, where they took much notice of cars left for several days.

I drove on to the Stamford Town Center Mall, parked on the eighth level of their lot, and fed the meter with enough quarters to cover the maximum one-day parking allowed in the mall. Hiking down Atlantic Street to the train station, I waited fifteen minutes, until a southbound local came by. Boarding it, I was back in New Croydon in six minutes. It was now 4:15. If anyone noticed me walking home, they would simply think that I was making an early day of it from work.

No messages on the answering machine. No mail of interest. I changed out of my suit and collapsed on the bed. Drained, depleted, running on one cylinder, I wanted to give in to sleep. But I knew that I couldn't afford a nap yet. Jumping up before I drifted off, I popped another Dexedrine and carefully dressed myself for my next outing.

Gary's standard around-town outfit was a pair of Levi's, a denim shirt, a leather jacket, a black baseball cap. I had reasonable facsimiles of all these clothes in my closet (well, we all shop at the Gap). I put them on, then waited another forty minutes until early-evening darkness had arrived. My anxiety level was now in the deep-red zone because the next maneuver was going to be tricky.

Just after five, I let myself out the back door. I was banking on the fact that most of my commuting neighbors never got home before six, at the earliest, and that this was the hour when children were being bathed and fed and subdued yet again with *Big Bird's Story Time.* In other words, an hour when movement on Constitution Crescent was minimal. I guessed right. The occasional car passing by. But no beleaguered daddies slouching home from the station.

I pulled the cap down until it almost touched my nose. Crossing the road, I approached Gary's car (parked in the driveway), opened it, climbed inside. The interior of the MG was a disaster zone. There was a big gash in the driver's seat. Empty Coke and Budweiser cans littered the floor, along with some McDonald's bags and a few aging editions of *The New York Times*. But I was relieved to discover the all-important car registration in the glove compartment. And though Gary may have been a slob, he still kept his twenty-five-year-old car in perfect under-the-hood condition: the engine fired on the first go and hummed sweetly.

I revved the accelerator, threw the stick into reverse, and backed up fast. A bad mistake. Suddenly, there was a screech of brakes behind me, followed by a blast of a car horn. My heart was now halfway out of my mouth. I stared up into the rearview mirror and saw a UPS van skidded to a halt, inches from my rear bumper. The driver had his head halfway out the window and was roaring, "Way to go, asshole!"

I didn't turn around. Keeping my head lowered, I rolled down my window and acknowledged my stupidity with an apologetic wave.

The next few seconds were dreadful, as I waited to see if he was one of those hotheads who was going to approach my vehicle and threaten to rearrange my face. But he simply put his van in gear and headed off down the road.

I gripped the wheel. I said a silent prayer of thanks. That was bad. That was close. Easy now. *Easy.* Just don't fuck up again.

I checked the rearview mirror three times before finally backing up. Turning away from the direction of the station, I drove at low speed through assorted backstreets, avoiding any of New Croydon's main thoroughfares. Finally reaching I-95, I stayed well within the speed limit all the way to the parking lot I had cased earlier in Stamford.

Entering it, I didn't make eye contact with the attendant as his hand shot out from his booth, giving me a ticket. I slipped it under the sun visor and found a space on the third floor. I took the stairs down and exited through a side door.

It was a fast, nervy walk through some very dark mean

streets to the Town Center Mall. Immediately, I headed to the multiplex cinema, scanned the show times, and bought a ticket for the film that was starting next. I still had fifteen minutes to kill, so I went to a pay phone and called Darien. Beth answered.

"Oh," she said. Her tone was glacial. I tried to sound cheerful. It took work.

"What have you been up to today?" I said.

"This and that. Where're you calling from?"

"Stamford. The mall. Made it an early day, decided to hit a movie. Want to join me?"

"Ben . . ."

"Leave the kids with Lucy and Phil; you could be here in ten minutes . . ."

"*Ben.* I told you—"

"I just thought, maybe—"

"No."

"But—"

"I said *no.* I don't want to see you. I don't want to discuss *anything.* Not now, anyway."

A long silence. "Can I at least speak to Adam?" I said.

"Hang on," she said and put the receiver on a table. I heard her shouting Adam's name in the distance, followed by his excited yell, "Daddy, Daddy, Daddy," as he ran toward the phone. I felt my eyes sting.

"Daddy, why aren't you here?" he asked after picking up the receiver.

"Because I have to go to work while you and Josh and Mommy are having a vacation at Aunt Lucy's and Uncle Phil's. You having fun?"

"Okay. I don't like Eddie." He was referring to his five-year-old cousin—a pudgy little brat whose temper tantrums were the stuff of legend. I couldn't stand the little freak, and admired my son's good judgment.

"You being good for Mommy?"

"I'm good. I want to go home, Daddy. I want to see you."

"I want to see you too. But . . ."

I bit my lip. Hard. And tried to continue.

". . . I'll come up in a couple of days. Okay?"

"And we go to McDonald's?"

"Yeah—we'll go to McDonald's."

I suddenly heard Beth's voice in the background. "Adam, *The Aristocats* is starting."

"I'm going to watch *Aristocats!*" Adam said with delight. "Big hug for Daddy."

"Big hug for Adam," I whispered, hardly getting the words out.

Beth came back on the line. I tried to regain my composure.

"Got to go now," she said. "Josh needs a bath."

"He sleeping okay?"

"Off and on."

"Tell him I love him."

"Of course."

"Beth . . ."

"I'm hanging up now, Ben . . ."

"Hang on. I'm coming up to see the boys on Saturday afternoon. That's the least . . ."

"I know that," she said, cutting me off. "Saturday afternoon will be fine. Let's try to keep this amicable."

"*Amicable?* You call this *amicable!*" I was shouting.

"Good night." And she was gone.

I staggered into the movie. It swam before me, a muddle. Some "cop on the edge protecting some woman on the run" thing. Didn't even notice the lead actor. Stallone? Willis? Van Damme? They all blur together, don't they? A noisy soundtrack. A lot of machine-gun fire, surface-to-air missiles, car bombs. A South American heavy in a white suit, screaming "I want her dead!" And the obligatory fuck between the cop and the blonde babe he's safeguarding. It all rolled over me like tepid surf. I couldn't engage with a single moment of it. Because all I saw in front of me was Adam and Josh. And all I could think was, after Saturday you will never see them again.

Why didn't I have the nerve to make that leap? It would have been easier. Easier than what was to come. I might learn to live with it. But the ache would never go away.

The end credits rolled. The brightening houselights disoriented me. But the fluorescent glare of the mall was even worse, and when I heard my name being called out, it took a moment before Bill and Ruth Hartley came into proper focus.

"Hey, life of the party," Ruth said, kissing my cheek.

"Night off alone?" Bill asked.

"Yeah. Thought I'd kill it in a movie."

"What'd'you see?" Ruth asked.

"Some action junk. You?"

"Ruth's dragging me to some arty English film. A lot of static camera work. A lot of down-and-outs screaming about their miserable lives and getting sick after sex."

"It got terrific reviews," Ruth said.

"Cultural enlightenment," Bill said, flashing Ruth a smile. "How's Beth?"

"Still in Darien with the kids."

"Oh," Bill said. "Everything okay?"

"Uh . . . no."

"Bad?" he asked.

"Very bad," I said. "Kind of irreparable, I think."

"Oh Christ, Ben . . ." Ruth said, taking my arm and gripping it tight.

"Fuck the movie," Bill said. "Let's—"

"No, really—"

"Ben," Ruth added, "you can't be on your—"

"I'm fine. Honestly."

"You don't look fine," Ruth said.

"All I need now is sleep," I insisted. "I haven't—"

"That's pretty obvious," Bill said. "The shape you're in, you're not gonna make it home."

"I'm not that bad."

"You should see yourself," Bill said.

"Not tonight, *please*. I need bed."

"Tomorrow, then," Ruth said.

"All right."

"Right after work, you promise?" she asked.

"I'll be there."

"And later on tonight, if you can't sleep—" Bill said.

"I'm not going to sleep tonight. I'm going to die."

They glanced at each other with disquiet. Bill tried again. "I really wish you'd let us—"

I had to end this conversation now.

"Please," I said, gently shrugging off Ruth's restraining grip. "I'm handling it. And after eight hours' sleep, I'll probably be handling it even better."

I gave Ruth a fast hug, pumped Bill's hand.

"Tomorrow," I said. "And thanks."

Then I walked off, not turning back. I didn't want to see their concerned faces, and hoped to hell they wouldn't call me late tonight at home. Or, god forbid, stop by to check that I wasn't opening my arteries while chain-popping Valium.

Because I wouldn't be there.

I was back in New Croydon by nine. A call on the answering machine from Estelle, thanking me for the flowers and the note of apology.

"Of course, when Mr. Mayle told me what was going on," she said, "I forgave you in a New York second. I'm really sorry for your problems, Mr. Bradford. And having been there myself, I feel for what you're going through. Don't worry about coming in for a few days. We'll hold the fort. And—if you don't mind a small piece of advice from a veteran of all this—the moment you start forgiving yourself, the easier it gets."

If only, Estelle. If only.

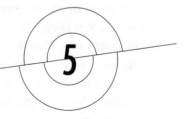

5

I HADN'T EATEN in about a day. Possibly because I had no appetite. But after I finished listening to Estelle's message, I forced myself to ingest a plate of scrambled eggs and toast. And four cups of coffee. There was a long night's work ahead, and I didn't think my body could cope with another jolt of Dexedrine.

I returned to my darkroom, changed into Gary's sweats and Nikes, covered my hands with a fresh pair of surgical gloves, checked my watch.

I had so much to do at Gary's that I decided to take a small risk and venture over just after ten. It was an unseasonably cold night—a distinct hint of impending winter in the air—so I gambled that no one would be out training for the marathon at this hour. I gambled right, and let myself in unseen after first grabbing a pile of mail from the box on his front lawn.

First things first. Using the penlight, I made my way to the basement and opened the freezer. He was still there. Considerably bluer than last night, but showing no signs of decay. My inspection lasted ten seconds. It was more than enough.

I headed upstairs to the office and leafed through the mail. Mainly junk—magazine subscription offers, an "invitation" to join America Online, a "You can own your very own piece of

Florida Paradise" brochure from some suspect property company. And a letter from *Destinations* magazine.

> Dear Gary,
> I hate to be the bearer of bad news, but we've decided to go with a San Diego–based photographer for the Baja California story. This decision was made reluctantly, as we really liked your work. We simply felt that—as the San Diego freelancer could do the job in the next few days (being essentially right on the border)—it would be easier to give him the commission.
> Sorry for the disappointment. Keep in touch. I'm sure there's some story we can do together soon.
> Sincerely,
> Jules Rossen

Talk about asshole behavior. They told Gary he was a virtual cert for the job, then strung the poor schmuck along, raising his hopes when, all the time, they knew that this San Diego hack was their ace in the hole.

Suddenly I was taking Gary's side. Defending his corner. Wanting to fire back a letter to Jules Judas Rossen, informing him that he was a low-level shitbird who didn't deserve a photographer of my talents.

My talents? Fuck me, it was starting.

This rejection letter did fit in very neatly with my plan. No one at *Destinations* would be chasing after Gary, making phone calls, wondering when he'd be delivering the photographs.

No one would be looking for him at all. Except Beth.

I opened up his Thinkpad, switched into the "B" directory, created a new file, and wrote:

> B:
> Big news this morning. Landed the Baja California gig. They want me on the border pronto, so I'm hitting the road tonight. Wanted to tell you, but didn't think it cool to call Darien. Be gone two, three weeks. Don't worry: no post-

cards. You'll know I'm back when you see my car in the driveway.

   Gonna miss you big time.

I reread the letter several times, carefully comparing it to
the other notes in the "B" directory. Stylistically it was fine. But
that line about calling Darien . . . No, she wouldn't have given
him the number. And the business about the car in the driveway—a little too overexplanatory. So I used the Delete key and
tightened it up.

   B:
   Big news this morning. Landed the Baja California gig.
   They want me on the border pronto, so I'm hitting the road
   tonight. Wanted to tell you, but . . . Back in two, three
   weeks.
   Gonna miss you big time.

Much better. Terse. A little distant. Vague. I hit the Print
key. Using Gary's upside-down Amex card, I signed it with his
characteristic big, self-important "G," and popped it in an
envelope.

   I now turned to the pile of debt demands on his desk.
Altogether, he owed $2,485.73. Switching into his MONEYBIZ
directory, I discovered that he paid all his bills via his bank.
Whenever his creditors started threatening legal action, he'd
simply fax a letter to Chemical Bank, authorizing a list of transfer payments from his checking account. This was a relief. I
didn't want to use his checkbook—for the simple reason that,
other than his signature, I didn't have an extended example of
his penmanship. And I feared that some sharp-eyed bank official might get a little curious if he noticed that, though the signature was roughly the same, there was a vast difference
between the way Gary printed "one hundred dollars" a month
ago and how he scribbled it now.

   Opening up a new file in MONEYBIZ, I wrote a terse, busi-
nesslike communiqué to the bank, informing them that—as

soon as the quarterly trust-fund payment hit the account later this week—they should pay the designated amounts listed below to Amex, Visa, MasterCard, Barneys, Bloomingdale's, Southern New England Telephone, and Yankee Power and Electric. I retrieved the bank's fax number from a previous letter. I hit the Print button. I did another ever improving rendition of Gary's signature. I fed the letter into the machine and pressed Send.

Gary Summers was now out of debt.

There were more letters to write. Every credit card and utility company received faxed instructions, asking them to set up a direct billing arrangement with Gary's bank. In turn, Chemical Bank was dispatched copies of these letters. Any debts he ran up in the future—and any nominal utility charges accrued on his house in his absence—would be cleared automatically. When it came to paying his bills, he would now be a model citizen.

Correspondence completed, my eye fell on a file marked NUMB. Hitting the Enter button, I couldn't believe my dumb luck. NUMB was shorthand for "NUMBERS"—and here was a list of PIN numbers for all his cards, most important, his ATM bank card. I had really struck pay dirt. It would now be possible to call on Gary's trust-fund money at any cash machine in the country without ever having to write a check or deal with the bank.

MONEYBIZ completed, I turned my attention to the anarchic state of his office and bedroom. If he was leaving town for a while, surely he would have made some nominal effort to tidy up (especially if there was a chance that he might not be coming back and would possibly be renting out the house at a future date). So, finding a couple of empty cardboard boxes in a closet and some black plastic bags, I spent several hours sorting through his papers. Anything of reasonable importance went into the boxes. Everything else was bagged. Moving on to his bedroom, I folded and stored clothes, cleaned the floor of scattered periodicals, stripped the bed. Then I did a basic cleanup of the living room. By the time some domestic order had been restored, it was almost four-thirty. Time to finish business for the night. Slipping quickly out the back door, I deposited two bags of trash in the bins at the side of his house, then popped the note to Beth inside the mailbox. But as I was about to cross the road, I remembered that I would need Gary's birth certificate today, so I quietly retraced my steps and let myself back inside.

I'd left the file containing his certificate (and all his other vital documents) on his desk. Picking it up, my legs abruptly turned to rubber as the effects of a sleepless night (and an excess of Dexedrine) finally hit me. I sat down on the office daybed, leaned back against the wall, and shut my eyes, waiting for this moment of exhausted delirium to pass.

Out of nowhere, I heard Beth's voice.

"Gary," she said in a loud whisper. "Where you hiding, babe?"

I jolted awake. Sunlight was streaming through the office blinds. I glanced at my watch. 10:08 a.m. Wednesday morning. Shit. Shit. Shit. I'd passed out. For over five hours.

"Gary!" The voice was foxy, playful. A voice I hadn't heard in years. "Come out, come out, wherever you are."

Beth had let herself in through the back door and was now downstairs.

I sat up and frantically looked for a place to hide. The closet? Dangerous—she might just open it. The bathroom across the hall? Forget it. Underneath the bed? Bingo.

As silently as possible, I lowered myself to the floor. Clutching the file close to me, I managed to squeeze myself into the tiny foot-high gap between the carpet and the bed. The box spring sagged in the middle, so I couldn't get in very far, with the result that my head was just a few inches from the edge of the bed.

"Gary, for God's sake . . ."

I heard Beth open the basement door and trot down the stairs. If—for some bizarre reason—she opened the chest freezer, I was a dead man. A few dreadful minutes passed.

"Gary, is this hiding game some kind of joke?"

She was back on the first floor, wandering from room to room. Then I heard her footsteps on the stairs. Sucking in my breath, I lay motionless as she entered the office.

"What the hell . . ." she said, stunned by its sudden tidiness. I could see her shoes less than a foot from me. Suddenly, her entire weight dropped down on the bed and I had to fight the urge to scream as the box spring dug into my back. Sweat was cascading down my face. She sat there for what felt like hours, evidently confused. Finally, she jumped up, left the room, opened a few more doors, then headed down the stairs and let herself out the back.

As soon as I heard that rear door close, I struggled out from under the bed, my back aching, my nervous system in extreme overdrive. But I still made it to the window. Without opening the blinds, I managed to peer out as Beth executed a fast, furtive search of Gary's mailbox, grabbed the note, hurried across the road and into our front door.

For the next half hour, I paced the floor of Gary's office (staying well away from the blinds), willing myself to calm down. Dumb. Dumb. Dumb. And near fatal. Had she not yelled out Gary's name, she would have found me asleep on the daybed. And that would have been that. Checkmate. Endgame.

At least I had gotten some semblance of rest. But what a fucking wake-up call.

Footsteps on the front path, followed by the front door letter slot clanging open, and a loud metallic rattle as something landed on the hallway floor. I froze, waiting until I heard the footsteps retreat. Another quick squint between the blinds. Beth was crossing the road, her head lowered. She got into our Volvo station wagon, slammed the door angrily, gunned the motor, backed out, and shot off down the road.

A good ten minutes passed before I dared to go downstairs. When I figured she wouldn't be coming back, I raced to the door and saw a bulging envelope. As I picked it up, its rear flap fell open and a set of keys landed at my feet. I grabbed them and returned to the office. A letter accompanied the keys. Not a letter, really—more of a hastily scrawled fuck you.

Given what's going on right now, your timing is impeccable. So much for your bullshit about sticking around while I told him it was over. You're just like him—totally self-absorbed, always putting yourself first. I need the two of you like cancer. Here are your keys. I have no use for them anymore.

It was unsigned.

Totally self-absorbed? Always putting myself first? That's a little harsh, Beth. And why give Gary a hard time about taking his first job in years? All right, he might have promised that he would be here for you during this trying time. But, hey, work is work. And the road is the road.

I didn't believe for a moment that she was really ending it. It was Beth's way of upping the emotional ante, using guilt as a strategic weapon. But I was pleased that she decided to get melodramatic and return his keys. It meant that she wouldn't be able to make a surprise visit to his house again.

I placed the note and the keys back inside the envelope, and pressed down firmly on the flap until it was resealed. Then, picking up the file containing Gary's birth certificate, I shoved it under my sweatshirt, turned off all the lights, moved quickly downstairs, and redeposited the envelope by the door (just in case Beth came by late one evening and peered through the mail slot to see if it was still lying there).

Leaving Gary's house was a worrying experience, as I'd yet to emerge from it in full daylight. I decided on a diversionary tactic (just in case anyone might be glancing out a neighboring window). Swinging left, I headed for a little jog up the road, my hands buried deep within my sweatpant pockets, hiding the surgical gloves. A quarter mile down Constitution Crescent, I looked up and saw Chuck Bailey jogging right toward me.

"Hey, Zorro, how you . . ." He didn't get to finish that sentence as he ground to a winded halt. His face was tinted scarlet, his breathing bronchial, his eyes heavy with debility. He looked like a candidate for a coronary, and leaned against my shoulder for support. I was about to grab him by the arm, but then remembered the surgical gloves and decided to scrap the Good Samaritan gesture.

"You okay, Chuck?"

"Fuck, no."

"Want me to call a—"

"No doctor necessary. Just gimme a sec."

His fingers dug into my shoulder. As he struggled to regain his breath, I kept rubbing my right hand against my inside pocket in an effort to pull off one of the gloves. It wouldn't budge.

"Okay now," he eventually said.

"You sure?"

"Think so. Christ . . ."

"You should get yourself checked out, Chuck . . ."

"Just did. Ticker's fine. It's just—"

He turned away for a moment, gritted his teeth.

"Assholes. Fucking assholes."

"What gives?"

"The bullet, that's what."

"You?"

"Yep."

"No way."

"Caught it yesterday. Right before I was about to leave. Called to the chairman's office. The fucking Frosty Whip account, and another client who went AWOL three months ago. 'We don't like doing this,' he said . . . and in a minute it was all over. Twenty-three years at the same shop. Always profitable, except for this year. And then they end it all in sixty seconds. Not only that, when I staggered back to my office after getting the news, some security goon was there with my coat and briefcase. 'Sorry, sir. The office is sealed.' Nearly took his fucking head off."

"Jesus," I said. "They give you a parachute at least?"

"Six months' full pay."

"Guess it's something."

"Not with Emily at Smith and Jeff at Choate, it isn't. With what I've got stashed away, I might be able to stagger on for two years. Then—"

"You'll find something."

"I'm fifty-three years old. I won't."

"Consultancy?"

A bronchial laugh. "That's just another way of saying you're corporate dead meat. Tell anyone you're now a consultant, and they file you away under loser."

"Shit, Chuck. I'm really—"

"Save it. Sympathy gives me the shits. You out of a job too?"

"Me? Just a day off. Woke up this morning, thought: Fuck it."

"That's the luxury of being a partner. Me, I never got beyond the executive-vice-prez grade. Up for a drink? Decided to spend the day making the acquaintance of Mr. Johnnie Walker."

"Got plans. But maybe later in the—"

"What's wrong with your hand?" Chuck interrupted, staring at the up-down motion taking place within my sweatpants pocket. I halted it immediately.

"An itch."

"Interesting itch?"

"Crabs."

"I should be so lucky. You change your mind about that drink, I'm going nowhere."

"Be careful, eh?"

"Why? A coronary would solve all my problems."

And before I could offer him another dreaded word of solace, he jogged off home.

When he was out of sight, I quickly withdrew my hands, stripped off the gloves, shoved them back into my pockets. Walking back toward my house, I thought: It's all so fragile, isn't it? It can all be taken away in a moment. And we spend most of our working lives fearing that that moment is near.

I was relieved to get into my house. Relieved to see that I hadn't sweated up the documents hidden beneath my shirt. Relieved that there were no messages on the answering machine. After a shower, I dressed again in Gary-style clothes, pocketed his birth certificate, and headed for the highway.

It was just after twelve. Five hours of available light. Just about enough time to run a few crucial errands before dinner at the Hartleys'.

The first errand involved a trip to the motor vehicles bureau in Norwalk, a midsized commuter-belt town around twenty miles north of New Croydon. Before reaching it, I stopped in a gas station, tanked up, and asked to use their phone. I dialed Information and obtained the number for the Connecticut Department of Motor Vehicles. I punched it in and chose General Information from the list of Touch-Tone phone options provided by the computer-generated voice. After being told I would be waiting five minutes before my call could be connected, I finally found myself speaking with a civil servant named Judy. I explained that I had lost my license and wondered if I needed a new photograph for the replacement document.

"Of course you'll need a new photograph," Judy said. "It's state law."

"Now I know this sounds kind of silly," I said, "but, well, it's just that I really liked my old photograph and was wondering if you might have it on file."

I heard her suppress a laugh. "Can't help you out there, sir. The state of Connecticut doesn't keep computerized photo records of drivers' licenses."

It was the news I was hoping to hear. I retreated to the station toilet. Once inside a cubicle, I pulled out Gary's driver's license, noted the number in my notebook, then extracted the scissors on my Swiss Army knife and turned the license into confetti. Three flushes and it had vanished from view.

I'd chosen the motor vehicles bureau in Norwalk because it was never particularly crowded (Norwalk being one of those nowhere suburban townships that everyone aspired to leave), and because I'd already renewed my own license in Stamford six weeks earlier and didn't want to risk bumping into the same clerk again.

There were only five people in line ahead of me. While

waiting, I filled in a Lost License form, noting the number of Gary's "misplaced" driver's permit.

"How'd you lose it?" asked the buck-toothed nerd behind the desk.

"At home."

"Got your birth certificate and Social Security card?"

I handed them over. He inspected the document and my application.

"You forgot to sign the form," he said, pushing it back to me.

Brilliant. I couldn't exactly pull out Gary's Amex card and do my upside-down forgery trick. So, trying to steady my hand, I quickly inked a replica of his signature at the bottom. A passable job. The clerk glanced at it quickly.

"Over there for the eye test," he said, pointing to another line.

It took two minutes to call out the letters on the eye chart and be certified as a sighted driver. Then I was shunted along to a photo machine, had my mug shot taken, and did another decent imitation of Gary's signature on the card that, when processed, would become the new laminated license.

There was a ten-minute wait while the processing took place. And when someone called out "Gary Summers," it took me a moment or two to realize: That's me.

I approached the counter with trepidation, expecting a policeman to emerge from a back office and arrest me for impersonation.

"Here you go, Mr. Summers," said the clerk, handing over the new license and counting the cash I pushed toward him. "Try not to lose it again in the future."

As I rolled north up I-95, I gave thanks to the overbureaucratized state of Connecticut for not having the software necessary for keeping a record of license photos. And I also congratulated myself on obtaining the key piece of identification needed within the United States.

The rest of the afternoon was spent shopping. Heading first to a big mall in that industrial slum called Bridgeport, I used my own ATM card to withdraw another $500 from a cash machine. Then I entered an auto-supply place and bought two plastic gas cans. Now north to New Haven, where I found a large sporting-goods store in some suburban shopping center and dropped $195 on a small inflatable rubber dinghy, a foot pump, and a pair of oars. A forty-minute drive onward to Hartford. I used the Yellow Pages to find the address of a chemical supply company. $27.50 bought me a four-ounce bottle of acid. Moving south to the city of Waterbury—a fast half-hour on the interstate—I hit a gardening outlet that sold assorted weed-killing chemicals. Then I shot farther south on I-84 and tracked down a hardware outlet in Danbury, where I bought some large black plastic sheeting, a jeweler's hammer, a long rubber hose, a lunch box, and a large bottle of Drano. Back now to Stamford on Route 7 (passing Darien along the way) and a mall on the western outskirts of town. Here I stopped at three different shops to pick up a pair of black sweats and sneakers, a large green car tarpaulin, two large duffel bags, a roll of industrial-strength tape, a foot-long cardboard tube, and two glass vials with cork stoppers.

I paid cash for every item I purchased. I never asked a shop assistant for help. I never made idle chat with a checkout girl. And though I'd clocked nearly 200 miles in an afternoon, I still considered this extended tour of Connecticut a necessary safety precaution. One-stop shopping—especially for a mass purchase that included inflammatory chemicals and a rubber boat—might have raised a few eyebrows and made someone remember my face.

I was back in New Croydon by seven. I stored all my purchases in assorted locked corners of my darkroom. Then I drove over to the Hartleys'.

They plied me with good Scotch and good Chablis. They fed me Dover sole. They listened with attentive sympathy as I gave them the large-print edition of the disintegration of my marriage. They made all the usual kind/practical noises about counseling, mediation, the potential for reconciliation. They looked at each other when I mentioned that Beth wanted me out of the house by Sunday.

"Take our spare room for a while," Ruth said.

"I couldn't," I said.

"You must," Bill said.

"You don't need the grief," I said.

"What grief?" Ruth said. "Anyway, why go through all the hassle of finding a place—"

"I'm sure the firm would let me have the company apartment for a few weeks . . ."

"Yeah, but at least if you're staying with us," Ruth said, "you'll be near the boys. And Beth. A couple of weeks apart, who knows? Maybe everything will cool down."

"It's hopeless."

"Never believe that," Ruth said.

"I don't believe it. I know it."

"Anyway," Bill said, "the spare room is yours for as long as you need it."

"Really, I'd rather—"

"It's settled," Ruth said.

"I don't know what to say."

"Say nothing," Bill said. "Just keep drinking."

He refilled my glass. I sipped the wine and then dropped a question I'd been waiting to drop all evening:

"I'm thinking of staying out of the office until the middle of next week. Don't suppose you're up for a day or two on the Sound?"

"Love to," Bill said, "but we're visiting Theo in New Haven on Sunday. How about Saturday?"

"Up seeing Adam and Josh in Darien."

"Well, if you want to go by yourself on Sunday, you're welcome to the boat. Head off for a night or so if you like."

"No way I'd take that baby out on my own."

"Why not? From what I saw last week, you certainly seemed to know what you were doing. A few days out alone might just do you some good. Give you a little perspective."

"Wouldn't want to risk anything happening to the *Blue Chip*."

"Fuck it, it's insured."

"Heavily," Ruth added. And we all laughed.

"You're both too kind," I said.

"Hey," Bill said, "what are friends for?"

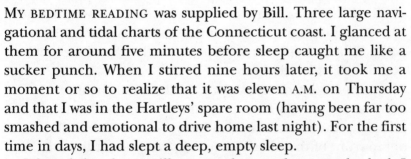

6

MY BEDTIME READING was supplied by Bill. Three large navigational and tidal charts of the Connecticut coast. I glanced at them for around five minutes before sleep caught me like a sucker punch. When I stirred nine hours later, it took me a moment or so to realize that it was eleven A.M. on Thursday and that I was in the Hartleys' spare room (having been far too smashed and emotional to drive home last night). For the first time in days, I had slept a deep, empty sleep.

I found the charts still scattered around me on the bed. I also found a note and a batch of keys on the bedside table.

> We've gone to work. Didn't want to wake you. Make yourself at home. Hang on to these keys, and move stuff in whenever. The little key unlocks the *Blue Chip*'s cabin, in case you want to have a look around.
>
> Hang in there.
> Love,
> R & B

I didn't deserve friends like Ruth and Bill. They were too decent, too trusting. And I was going to take advantage of their hospitality in a very big way.

Still, I was exceedingly grateful for the keys to the *Blue*

Chip. After a fast shower in their guest bathroom, I took a run down to the New Croydon docks and climbed aboard. Letting myself into the little cabin, I did a quick inspection. There was a reasonable amount of storage space beneath one of the two bunks. There was an engine if you wanted to go off sail and power-drive the sloop for a while. The engine was strong enough to battle modestly tricky currents—especially if you put it on autopilot while sleeping and let Bill's global positioning system keep you moving in the right direction. According to one of the operational manuals I found on a cabin bookshelf, you could travel up to 200 miles on a full tank of diesel. There were three jerry cans full of motor diesel stored in a little utility closet near the head (Bill was taking no chances when it came to the possibility of running out of gas in a becalmed sea). And in the galley, I noted that the hose connecting the stove to the outside gas canister was a bit worn and had been haphazardly repaired with a Band-Aid application of black electrical tape.

I stepped out on deck, locking the cabin behind me. An overcast day, the sky bone gray, an encroaching Nordic chill. I pulled up the collar of my leather jacket and laid Bill's charts out in front of the wheel. I carefully read up on the tidal conditions for this Sunday and Monday, then turned to navigational information about Long Island Sound. Running my finger along the jagged teeth of the Connecticut coastline—a craggy sequence of little harbors and inlets—I didn't find what I was looking for until my finger came to rest on a tiny spit of land east of New London called Harkness Memorial State Park.

Two hours later, I was there. It was a hundred miles northeast of New Croydon. I drove up I-95 to the maritime city of New London—home of that center of academic excellence, the Coast Guard Academy—and then slinked a few miles down Route 213 until I hit the entrance to the park. Rolling acres of green lawn, picnic tables, wooden boardwalks leading down to the beach, and the imposing old Harkness mansion, now a museum and looking like a haunted house from a Vincent

Price movie. There were low wooden gates at the park entrance—and a sign saying that they closed at sundown. Beyond them was a sentry box. As it was the third day of November, the park police weren't manning it in the off-season. In fact, I had the place to myself on this bleak Thursday. Strolling down to the beach, I liked what I saw. A few pleasure boats out on the water, the occasional coast guard speedboat, and a clear, unimpeded stretch of sea that—fifteen miles due east of here—would become the Atlantic Ocean. I also noticed that this was the only stretch of nearby shoreline that didn't have a house fronting the water—which meant I could land here without being observed. I worried a bit about the coast guard presence. Might all those cadets-in-training swoop down on every boat that strayed across their path? Then again, their job was to defend the coast, so why would they hassle a pleasure craft heading straight out to sea? Yes, this was the spot. And as long as the currents were on my side, it would be a smooth passage out into the Atlantic.

I lingered for a while on the beach, breathing in the salt spray, staring out at that void of water, momentarily incapacitated by a guilt that I knew would never go away. Fear defines every waking moment of life, doesn't it? You stagger on, always plagued by the thought: Today, everything will be revealed. Your petty crimes and misdemeanors—the little lies you make to get through the day—are nothing compared to that dread of having your worthlessness, your fraudulence, laid bare for all to see. And this dread stays with you. Until, perhaps, you cross that shaky frontier between civilized and primitive behavior. A frontier we all fear—for we all secretly know it is so easily broached. In a nanosecond. All we have to do is reach for that bottle.

And then? Then you wonder why you so squandered so much of your life awaiting the moment of dreaded revelation. Suddenly, you *are* guilty. You have done the unspeakable. You need not fear the dark anymore. You are there. It is a moment of terrible liberation. Because, as you scramble for a way out of the dark, you also know that you will now suf-

fer the most unbearable of bereavements: the loss of your children.

I sat on the beach for around an hour, until the sun began
its gradual decline. Making my way back to the Miata, I left the
park and turned left. Around a half mile down the road, I
braked suddenly in front of a dilapidated farmyard gate.
Behind it was a field—around two acres in size—with a large
clump of trees. The trees were tightly clustered together, but
there was room enough to drive a small car between them. I
looked around. The land appeared unused, overgrown. The
nearest dwelling—a large red clapboard house—was around a
quarter of a mile away. The field was perfect for my needs.

Returning to New London, I clocked the mileage to the
local train station, then followed the signs to I-95 and pointed
the car in the direction of New Croydon.

Back home, I called Beth. I was quietly hoping that Gary's
sudden departure might just thaw her out. I thought wrong.

"It's late," she said after hearing my voice.

"It's seven-thirty," I said. "Not exactly the middle of the
night."

"You know Lucy and Phil don't like calls after seven."

"Disturbs their karma, does it?"

"Is there a point to this call?" she said.

"I just wanted . . ."

"Yes?"

". . . to see how the boys were."

"They're well."

"Great."

"Anything else?"

"I'll be up Saturday."

"We know that."

"Around two."

"Fine," she said. And the line went dead.

A thaw? More like the fucking Ice Age. Hopeless. Finished.
Kaput.

I swallowed hard and called Jack Mayle at home in
Scarsdale. He sounded depleted.

"Little fuzzy tonight," he said. "Must be the pills Dr. God has got me popping. You hanging in there?"

"Finally got some sleep last night," I said. "Guess that's something."

"Beth see reason yet?"

"Not a chance."

"Gevalt."

"Says it all."

"Seen the boys?"

"I'm being granted a visit Saturday afternoon. You need me back at the store before then?"

"Think we'll manage. Just. The Dexter case is turning nasty. That Santiago ambulance chaser has dug his heels in at one-nine a kid, and the fifth Mrs. D. is having conniptions. And I had a very distressed Deborah Butt Bowles on the phone, saying that the board of her co-op was about to serve her papers for six months' back maintenance."

"Good."

"She is a client, Ben."

"She's a flake. And a nasty one, to boot."

"Can't argue with that. But we'll still have to find her some bridge finance."

"Estelle okay?"

"Estelle is Estelle."

"I was such a schmuck."

"Ancient history. Put it behind you."

"You bearing up?"

"Well . . . I'm still here. Which is something, I guess. But lookit: I gotta have you back here on Wednesday. You're needed."

"I'll be there," I lied.

"Try to get some rest, eh? Best thing for you."

"Thanks for everything, Jack. You've been the best."

He detected the note of finality in my voice.

"You sure you're okay, Ben?"

"Just tired. Beyond tired."

"Courage, kid."

I hung up. And realized that we would never speak again. The first good-bye. With harder ones to come.

A covert dash over to Gary's house. A quick examination of the chest freezer. I prodded his gray-blue lips and heard a slight crackle. Three cheers for Frigidaire—when it comes to keeping a body on ice, their freezer is a world-beater. I closed the lid and turned my attention to his darkroom area. Unlike me, he had only three cameras: a battered Rolleiflex, a relatively new Nikkormat, a pocket-sized Leica. I packed them all into his camera bag, along with an auto-flash, two extra lenses, and a small tripod.

Carrying the bag upstairs to his bedroom, I found a black duffel in his closet and filled it with assorted jeans and shirts and sweaters and underwear. I also grabbed his brown Avirex flight jacket, his Filofax, his toilet kit, and a pair of RayBan Wayfarers that he always wore in public. I tried on his brown Tony Lama cowboy boots. Snug, but they would eventually loosen up with constant wear. They joined his other clothes in the duffel. One last item: his IBM Thinkpad. The carrying case was stored under the desk and also contained a portable Canon printer. How convenient. I slotted the Thinkpad into the case and hoisted the bags.

A fast, nervous hobble across the road. Once I was in my driveway, the bags were stored in the trunk of the Miata. After a quick trip to my darkroom, they were joined by the green car tarpaulin and the file of Gary's documents.

Then it was off on a late evening drive to Stamford. Another half-awake attendant in the booth of the parking lot. He didn't look up from his *Sports Illustrated* as I collected my ticket and drove in. I found a space three cars away from Gary's MG. The lot was empty of drivers, so no one saw me as I quickly transferred everything from the trunk of the Miata to that of the MG. Needing to kill some time (I didn't want to prod the attendant's attention by driving out again five minutes after arriving), I walked down the stairs and over to an Indian restaurant on a nearby backstreet. I killed an hour over tandoori chicken and a few beers, keeping my head buried in that day's edition of the *Stamford Courier.*

No notice was taken of me when, at eleven-fifteen, I drove out of the lot in the Miata. And there was a new attendant on duty when I arrived back on foot early the next morning (having caught the 6:08 local from New Croydon). It was Friday and I looked like I was starting the weekend early, dressed for a country walk: hiking boots, a thick sweater, a day pack on my back. Gary's MG fired on the first turn of the ignition key. I forked over $24 for two days' parking and yawned my way up I-95, my brain fogged in after a restive night.

I kept well within the speed limits and reached the entrance to Harkness State Park. I bypassed it, traveling on down the empty road until I reached the ramshackle farmyard gates. I jumped out, threw open the gate, drove in, closed the gate behind me, then headed straight for the trees. Creeping along at five miles per hour, I tried to steer the MG as far as possible into this dense cluster of elms and oaks. After fifty feet, I could travel no farther. I turned off the motor, unwrapped the tarpaulin, and covered the car. Then, using my hands, I piled the tarpaulin high with loose leaves. Not exactly a Green Beret camouflage job, but when I hiked back to the main road I could just about make out a humpy mound of leaves deep within this forest.

Pulling a baseball cap and a pair of shades out of my day pack, I began the five-mile trek back to New London. I stuck to the grassy path by the side of the road. Only a few cars passed me. No one stopped and offered me a lift. No one paid me the slightest attention. I was just a fresh-air freak out for a long hike.

At the New London train station, I cooled my heels for a half hour in the waiting room, trying to concentrate on some paperback Tom Clancy junk that I'd brought with me. Jack Ryan was saving the United States from crazed Islamic fundamentalists who were threatening to nuke Cleveland. There was a scene in the Oval Office in which the president told Ryan,

"The nation is counting on you, Jack." There was a scene where Ryan told his wife, "The nation is counting on me, dear." There was a scene where Ryan told one of his subordinates, "The nation is counting on us, Bob." Clancy wasn't a writer; he was a committee in the CIA. But I owed him a debt of thanks. One purple patriotic passage appalled me so deeply that I lifted my eyes up from the page in embarrassment and, through the waiting-room window, suddenly saw my brother-in-law, Phil, standing right in front of me on the station platform.

Not that Phil saw me. Because he was currently staring into the eyes of a woman around forty. She was tall, with heavily permed hair, and dressed in an ordinary business suit. I couldn't tell much else about her, as they were suddenly locked in a very deep, tongue-down-the-throat embrace. Instantly I was on my feet, heading for the rear exit. And I kept on walking until I was out of the station and en route to the nearest bar.

A steadying boilermaker, followed by another glass of Bud. That was close. Thank Christ I was still in the waiting room and not on the platform. Of course I was now stuck here for two more hours until the next southbound train pulled in. But it was almost worth it to discover that my emaciated geek of a brother-in-law—a man who physically and spiritually resembled a sharpened pencil—was two-timing the godawful Lucy. Who, I wondered, was the femme fatale? Some fellow cost accountant he fell for while verifying the books of Johnson Depilatories Inc. (auditing cosmetic companies was a Phil area of specialization). Or maybe just someone, like him, seeking refuge from a dead-end marriage. Wanting a little reminder that they might still be desirable. Way to go, Phil. You've got a secret life too.

When I finally got on the next southbound train, I took a seat near the bathroom, just in case I needed to hide from some other familiar face.

A hazardous job awaited me upon my return to New Croydon. Opening a locked cabinet in my darkroom, I extracted the assorted chemicals I had purchased. Then I dug out my little notebook containing the recipe I'd copied down from *The Anarchist's Cookbook* and went to work. Using a mixing bowl, I played mad scientist, measuring out assorted doses of each chemical before blending them together. Retrieving the foot-long cardboard tube I'd bought, I secured the plastic cover on the bottom end with heavy electrical tape. After filling the tube with the chemical compound, I taped shut the top end and employed a scissors to bore a half-inch-diameter hole in the plastic cover. Two pieces of Scotch tape were then placed over this little aperture. Picking up the second tube, I repeated the process. When I was finished, I packed them away in a small carry-on bag, tore up the recipe, and gave it a burial at sea via the toilet.

Using a tiny funnel, I now filled two vials with acid, sealed them both with blu tack (a substance chosen because of its noninflammable properties), then taped a cork stopper to the side of each bottle. Bringing out the lunch box, I employed several lengths of electrical tape to secure the bottles to opposite ends of the box. Once fastened in place, I shut the box and gave it a vigorous, nerve-racking shake. The two vials didn't move; the acid didn't leak. And I didn't suddenly go up in flames—though when I cracked open the first of six beers I downed that evening (while sprawled mindlessly in front of the television), a geyser of foam drenched my face.

These precautions with the acid were necessary ones as, the next morning, I stored the vials aboard the *Blue Chip*. I'd rung Bill the previous night, telling him that I'd like to get my supplies on the boat before sailing off on Sunday. "No problem," Bill said and promised to give the harbormaster a call, just in case he wondered what a stranger was doing snooping around the sloop.

"How do," the harbormaster said as he walked down the dock toward me. He was around sixty—stringbean thin, with a face as craggy as granite.

"Morning," I said.

"You're Hartley's friend, right?"

"Ben Bradford," I said, proffering my hand. He gave it a quick, stern shake.

"Saw you here yesterday," he said.

This stopped me short. I didn't know I was being observed.

"You should've said hello," I bantered.

"Was about to, but then saw you had the key for the cabin—so I figured you were legit. Going to Europe or somethin'?"

"Just up the coast for two days."

He stared at the bag of groceries and the duffel I had already loaded on deck.

"Amount you're stowing aboard, looks like you're planning to do the Atlantic."

"You never know."

He noticed another giant duffel still on the dock.

"The hell you got in that?" he asked.

My palms began to sweat. I shoved them into my pockets.

"Scuba gear."

"Ain't nothing to look at in these waters, 'cept sewage," he said. "Need a hand with it?"

Before I could decline the favor, he was grabbing one end of the duffel. I jumped down onto the dock and grabbed the opposite side.

"Sonfabitch weighs a ton," he said, helping me hoist it. "Feels cold as hell too."

"Keep the tanks in my garage. It's like an icebox in there."

We managed to lift the duffel onto the boat, then lowered it gently.

"Thanks," I said, hoping he would now get out of my life.

"You setting sail today?"

"Tomorrow at dawn."

"Harbor gates open at six-thirty."

"I know."

He kept staring at the duffel. I tried to remain calm.

"Scuba diving in November?" he said, shaking his head. "Better you than me."

He kicked the bag with his left shoe. Thankfully, it connected with the steel tank, making a muffled *bong*.

"Sounds like a pretty big tank," he said. "How long can you stay under with it?"

"'Bout an hour."

"Guess that's long enough in these waters. Well . . . happy sailing."

"Appreciate the hand," I said.

He gave me a curt nod, climbed down onto the dock, and strolled off.

I went down below, into the cabin, flopped on a bunk, and tried to stop hyperventilating.

Harbor gates don't open until six-thirty. That's why I brought this duffel here now. Because I knew I couldn't sneak it aboard in the middle of the night and didn't want to raise Bill's suspicions by showing up with it tomorrow morning. Thank God I tossed the scuba tank into the same bag.

Why the hell was he being so nosy? Did he suspect something? Was I acting noticeably shifty? Or was he just a prying old man with nothing better to do than make my business his business?

I decided to go with the "nosy old bastard" scenario. He had no reason to distrust me, after all. And he certainly didn't realize that he had just helped bring aboard the frozen body of Gary Summers.

Getting Gary into the bag had been quite a job. Around one this morning—after I'd completed the *Anarchist's Cookbook* recipe—I'd backed my Miata into Gary's garage, closing the door behind me. The garage was empty, except for a collection of home-improvement tools adorning one wall. I carried with me the largest of the duffels I'd bought the previous day. The garage's interconnecting door led right down into the basement. I went straight to work, unzipping the duffel and laying out black plastic sheeting on the basement floor. Opening the chest freezer, I managed to get Gary sitting upright, but nearly slipped a disk trying to hoist him out. He was rock solid with rigor mortis and impossibly cold. So cold that, when I wrapped my arms around his midsection, I could barely hold him for more than a few seconds. After several attempts, I finally had his torso dangling over the side of the freezer. Then I reached down, grabbed his legs, and heaved-ho. He landed headfirst on the floor, his skull hitting the linoleum with an awful thud. It looked badly contused, but thankfully it was so well chilled that there was no blood. I rolled him over onto the plastic sheeting and immediately realized that, even though his broken legs could be folded back to reduce his length, the duffel still wasn't long enough to contain him. Radical surgery would be required. Returning to the garage, I found a soldering iron and a power saw: a Black & Decker model with a very sharp rotary blade.

Back in the basement, I hit the Black & Decker's power button. The blade made a maniacal hum as it whizzed into action. I turned it off. *No way, no way.* So, for the next half hour I tried fitting Gary into that duffel. But every time I thought I'd solved the problem, the bag wouldn't close properly. There was no choice but to proceed. Taking out a spare plastic sheet, I ripped open a hole in the middle and stuck my head through it. This makeshift poncho would hopefully protect me from any splattering. I took a very deep breath. Can I do this? You have no choice. Go to work.

The job took twenty minutes. Gary's half-dismembered body was then wrapped in black plastic sheeting and securely taped shut. It fit comfortably into the duffel bag. In fact, there was now an extra two feet of spare room at one end—so I decided to load it up with scuba gear as soon as I got back to my house, in an attempt to mask its actual contents. Getting it up the stairs was a chore. I had to drag the bag step-by-step into the garage before hoisting it into the trunk of the Miata.

The basement cleanup job was immense. Before beginning, though, I spent several minutes getting sick in the basement toilet—my stomach heaving with guilt at the task I had just completed. Then I used three bottles of disinfectant to scour the Black & Decker power saw and every basement surface. I poured Drano down all drains, washing them free of any blood, hair, or anything else that might be traced through DNA tests. I bagged all other potential evidence and tossed it into my car. A final inspection tour. The aroma of singed flesh was almost masked by all the Mr. Clean I had used. The freezer was now unplugged, along with every other major appliance in the house. Curtains and blinds were drawn, doors double-locked. The house was now closed. And would remain that way until, some months from now, Gary would decide to put it on the market. Rid himself of it completely.

I eased the Miata out into the driveway, locked the garage behind me, and drove without lights across the road. I didn't look back. I didn't want to lay eyes on that house ever again.

A few hours later, I was at the New Croydon docks, unloading my gear. Once I bade the harbormaster farewell and retreated to the cabin, I waited a good fifteen minutes before going back on deck. He was now harassing the crew of some pleasure boat that had just docked. It was flying Canadian colors. No doubt, he was currently searching it for illegal Nova Scotia stowaways. Hauling the duffel down below, I unpacked the scuba equipment, then stored Gary in the cabinet beneath the portside bunk; the second duffel (containing the inflatable dinghy) went into the fuel stores. Locking the cabin, I walked back to my car and headed off, hoping that the carcass wouldn't thaw overnight.

It was now time to head to Darien. I didn't take a direct route, however. Instead, I did a fast tour of Fairfield County. Needing to part company with those final bags of evidence, I made quick stops at Dumpsters I spotted in outlying corners of New Canaan, Wilton, and Westport, divesting myself of a bag at each locale.

Phil and Lucy lived in a dead-end enclave called Franklin Avenue. Their house was a throwback to the Eisenhower era—natural wood shingles, with a redbrick porch adorned with thin white columns. Two big flowerpots were suspended over the porch. A large American flag drooped from a pole above the front door. I steered my car into the driveway and spent a moment or two trying to control my dread. Then I got out and rang the front doorbell: a loud ding-dong chime. Lucy answered. She was wearing a cream Shetland sweater, a white turtleneck, white jeans, black Gucci loafers. A black silk head-band held her blonde hair in place. She did not smile when she saw me.

"Ben," she said tonelessly.

"Hi, Lucy." The anxiety in my voice was palpable.

"He's here," she yelled over her shoulder. Then, turning back to me, she said, "You might as well come in." As soon as I was in the door, she headed off to the kitchen, leaving me alone.

Chintzy fabrics. Heavy floral wallpaper. Victorian bric-a-brac. The Laura Ashley school of interior design.

"Daddy! Daddy!"

Adam came charging up from the basement playroom and threw himself at me. I grabbed him and held on tight.

"Daddy's here, Mommy," he announced loudly.

"So he is."

Beth was standing on the opposite side of the room, with Josh asleep against her shoulder. She gave me a fast nod. She was dreading this meeting too.

"You well?" I asked.

"Okay," she said quietly.

"We're going to McDonald's," Adam said. "We're going to get toys."

"Whatever you want," I said.

"No chocolate milkshakes," Beth said. "It makes him hyper."

"I want chocolate milkshake!" Adam said.

"Strawberry is just as nice," I said.

"Chocolate!"

"No, Adam," Beth said.

Adam began to cry. "I want—"

"We'll see," I whispered into his ear.

"Ben, I told you—"

I held up my hand. She gave me a tired nod.

"Go get your coat, big guy," I said. Adam went hurrying off downstairs. An awkward silence. Beth broke it.

"The house okay?" she asked.

You should know. You were there three days ago.

"Fine," I said. "Josh keeping you awake much?"

"He went down for five hours last night."

"Something of a record. Can I . . . ?"

"Of course," she said and gently handed him over to me. His head nuzzled against my neck. I kissed his warm cheek. He still smelled newly minted. I rocked him back and forth. I didn't want to let him go.

Adam came running back into the room, dragging his brown duffel coat behind him. He didn't like seeing the baby in my arms.

"No Josh! No Josh!" he said, brimming with first-child jealousy. "Just Daddy and Adam."

"That's not very nice, Adam," Beth said.

"I want Daddy!"

"You've got him," I said. I handed Josh back to Beth with reluctance, a chill running through me. Adam took my hand.

"Can you have him back by five?" Beth asked. "He's been invited to a friend of Eddie's for dinner."

"Don't like Eddie," Adam said. "He hit me."

"Hit him back," I said.

"Ben, Eddie's in the kitchen with Lucy . . ."

"You shouldn't let him bully Adam."

"Of course I don't let him—"

"Fine," I said, cutting her off before she shifted into angry high gear. "Can I take the Volvo? I won't have to transfer the booster seat then."

"Here," she said, handing me the keys. "Five, please. No later."

"I heard you the first time."

We left. As I strapped Adam into the baby seat, he said, "Daddy doesn't like Mommy anymore."

"I do like Mommy. We just—"

I broke off, lost for words. How do you explain disaffection to a four-year-old? You don't. You simply lie.

"There'll be no more fights, Adam."

He smiled. "We all go home soon?"

I lied again. "Yeah. Real soon."

At McDonald's Adam had his usual Chicken McNuggets and French fries. He slurped his strawberry milkshake, never once complaining that it wasn't chocolate. He played with the little Disney toy that accompanied his meal.

"When are we going to Disney World?" he asked. He'd been begging for a trip to Orlando for months, having endlessly rewatched the propaganda for Mickey's Kingdom that preceded some Disney video.

"We'll get there sometime," I said, reaching into my pocket for a bottle of pills.

"Christmas? Can we go at Christmas?"

I swallowed hard.

"Sometime, Adam. Sometime."

I opened the vial and popped two pills, washing them down with Diet Coke.

"Daddy takes medicine," Adam observed.

Daddy's taking Dexedrine. Daddy needs Dexedrine. He hasn't slept. He's been doing unspeakable things in a neighbor's basement. Daddy also wishes he had some Valium on him. Because all this talk of Disney World and Christmas is about to make Daddy fall apart.

"Just Daddy and Adam go to Disney World. No Josh."

"You should be nice to Josh," I reasoned. "You're his big brother. He's going to need you . . ."

"Daddy's *my* daddy."

Please, kid. Stop it. Or I'll go under right in front of you.

"Where to next?" I asked, trying to change the subject.

"Toys! You buy me a present?"

"A big present."

We drove into Stamford and parked in front of the Baby and Toy Superstore on Forest Street. Adam tore into the shop, with me in hot pursuit. Within moments, he had found the bicycle section and mounted a pint-sized red Schwinn with training wheels. He'd obviously had his eye on this model for a while.

"Mommy bring you here this week?" I asked.

"Aunt Lucy bring me when Mommy was away."

You mean, while Mommy was off discovering that her lover had left town.

"Did Mommy say where she was going when she left you with Aunt Lucy?"

"Away." He pressed down on the pedals and started riding in circles.

"Please, Daddy. Buy me this one."

"Only if you wear a helmet."

A saleswoman standing nearby chimed in: "We have them in six different colors."

"Red, I think," I said. "It'll match the bike."

She returned a few moments later with a box.

"I wear it!" Adam said, halting momentarily while the saleswoman covered his blonde locks with the helmet and strapped it under his chin. Then he was off again, wheeling around the bike department.

"A lovely boy," the saleswoman said.

"He is that," I said. Adam looked up for a moment and gave me a grin of utter delight. My son. My beautiful son.

"You know the bike is self-assembly," the saleswoman said. "But it shouldn't take you more than an hour and all the tools are provided."

My heart sank. A scene danced across my brain: Adam watching sadly as Phil—his new surrogate Dad—struggles to put the chain on. "Where's my daddy?" Adam cries. "Daddy makes my bike for me."

"Don't you have one already assembled?" I asked the saleswoman.

"Just the one he's riding," she said. "But we're not supposed to sell display items."

"Could you make an exception, please?"

"It's really a simple job."

"I'm sure it is, but I don't have much time with him today . . ."

The penny dropped. She nodded understandingly as she categorized me as yet another divorced dad, trying to assuage his guilt with yet another expensive gift for his little boy. If only you knew, lady. If only you knew.

"I'm sure the manager will let you take that Schwinn," she said.

Before we left the Baby and Toy Superstore, Adam also scored a Solar System floor puzzle, a remote control Cookie Monster car, a Lego fire station, and three more Thomas the Tank Engine trains. At the checkout counter, I nearly reached for Gary's wallet, but caught myself in time and paid for it all on my own Amex card. There was so much booty that a shop assistant helped me carry it out to the Volvo. It was now three-thirty. Just ninety minutes left. And a cold drizzle was leaking down from a dingy sky.

"Can we go to the park?" Adam asked as I strapped him into his seat.

"It's raining, big guy. Parks aren't fun when it's wet."

"I want to ride my bicycle!"

"Not in the park. You'll catch a cold—"

"Please, Daddy. I ride my bicycle!"

And that's how we ended up inaugurating Adam's bicycle up on the top floor of the Stamford Town Center Mall. On Saturday afternoon, it was the quietest corner of the complex—there were only a couple of fast-food joints up here—so Adam was able to bike up and down an entire side of the mall without too many disapproving looks from the security guard on duty. I followed him at first. But after twenty minutes of chasing his bicycle, fatigue hit, so I parked myself at a snack-bar counter and watched as he wheeled his bike endlessly up and down this pedestrian corridor. Twice I tried to convince him to give it a rest, enticing him away with the offer of an ice cream. Twice he said:

"I ride my bike, Daddy."

Eventually, he did tire of this cycling marathon and accepted a vanilla cone. 4:20. Down to just forty minutes. We moved to a table. His free hand was proprietorially gripped around the handlebars of the Schwinn.

"You're really good on the bike, Adam."

"I want to ride without the little wheels."

"Maybe in a year or so you can take them off."

"You teach me, Daddy?"

I bit hard on my lip.

"I'll teach you, big guy."

"And we take the bike to Disney World. And we take the bike to school. And Daddy and Adam take the bike on the train to the city. And go to the big park. And go to the zoo . . ."

As he sang this sweet litany of future times together, I lost a battle I had been fighting for hours.

"Why are you crying, Daddy?"

His eyes were wide with fear. They grew wider as my sobbing became uncontrollable. I clutched him against me. And held on tight, as if he could somehow protect me from harm, make everything right again, lead me back to the life I was about to lose.

"Stop it, Daddy. *Stop.*"

He stiffened in my arms, terrified. But I couldn't stop, couldn't apply the emotional brakes. I had lost everything. I was now in free fall.

"Hey, hey? *Hey?*"

I felt a strong hand clutch my shoulder, shaking me hard. I relaxed my grip for a moment and Adam sprang out of my arms, running down the corridor. I looked up. The manager of the snack bar was standing over me, his face aghast.

"You okay?" he asked.

I shook with disorientation, my vision blurred by the cascade of tears.

"Hang on, I'm gonna call for a doc—"

"No need, no need," I managed to say. "Upset, that's all."

"So's your little boy."

"Adam . . ."

I stood up in panic, unable to see where he was.

"Adam!"

Then I heard him, crying. He was cowering against a nearby wall, regarding me with dread. I tried to move toward him, but the snack-bar manager—a beefy man in his forties—held me back.

"Is that really your kid?" he asked.

I tried to shrug him off, but his hand grabbed my collar and yanked hard.

"I'm asking you again, pal. Is that your kid?"

"Of course it's my—" I struggled against him, but he now had me in a menacing grip. I was marched over to Adam. He was white with fear, a large wet stain now visible across the crotch of his jeans.

"Is this your daddy?" the manager asked him.

Adam managed a terrified nod.

"You absolutely sure it's your daddy? You don't have to be afraid, son."

Adam stood, paralyzed for a moment, then threw himself against my legs, weeping loudly. The manager finally let go of my collar. I knelt down and gathered Adam in my arms, whispering, "I'm sorry, I'm sorry, I'm sorry." I rocked him gently until his tears subsided, and until I felt my own fragile equilibrium return.

"Daddy don't cry anymore," Adam finally said.

"Everything's okay now," I lied. I picked him up, holding him against my chest with one arm. As I rose to my feet, I saw that a small crowd had gathered and was gawking silently at us. As soon as they met my gaze, they turned away in voyeuristic embarrassment. The manager was still standing beside me, blocking my path.

"You want me to call someone?" he asked.

"We're fine now," I said.

"No, you're not."

"Lookit, my wife and I are—"

"I don't want to know your problems, pal. I just don't want to see you here again. Understand?"

"You won't. Believe me."

"You sure you want to go home with Daddy?" the manager asked Adam. "You don't have to if you don't want to."

"I go home with Daddy," Adam said and buried his face against my neck.

The manager was still looking hesitant about letting us leave. I tried to mumble an apology. But he cut me off.

"Get some help," he snapped and walked back into his snack bar.

Still holding Adam, I managed to pick up the bicycle in my free hand and get us to a bathroom. Adam said nothing as I used a stack of paper towels to dry his urine-soaked jeans. He said nothing as we rode the elevator down to the parking lot. As soon as he was strapped into his seat, the shock of the last fifteen minutes knocked him out cold. He slept all the way back to Phil and Lucy's house. Post-shopping traffic was heavy. Every time I was forced to halt, I glanced into the rearview and saw him blissfully asleep. The tears started again. Because I knew that he wouldn't wake now until morning. And I would be gone.

We didn't reach the house until 5:40. The moment I pulled into the driveway, Beth was storming out the door into the rain. She did not look welcoming.

"Congratulations. Well done."

"The traffic was terrible," I said, getting out of the car.

"I told you, five o'clock, no later. He's missed the dinner now . . ."

"I'm sorry . . ."

"Christ, he's all wet," she said, lifting him out of his seat.

"He had an accident."

"Didn't you take him to the toilet?"

"Of course I took him to the—"

"Don't lie. He's soaked. And—"

She finally caught sight of all the booty in the back of the car.

"Are you crazy?"

"He wanted a bike, so—"

"No way, no way—"

"I wanted him to—"

"We're not accepting it. I don't want your guilt. I don't want anything from—"

"Please, Beth. Let him keep—"

She snatched the car keys from my hand.

"Just go, will you? *Go.*"

She turned and ran with Adam through the driving rain into the house. I gave chase, but she slammed the door just as I reached the step. The rain was now frenzied. But I didn't care. I kept pounding on the door, screaming, begging to be let in. Minutes passed, but I kept up my tirade, certain that she would relent, see reason, at least offer me temporary shelter from the storm. But there was only silence from within.

My fists were raw from pounding, my body drenched. I backed away from the door, defeated. And then I saw her. Staring out at me through a window, looking cheerless, forlorn. For one brief moment our eyes locked. A moment of terrible indecision. A moment when the veil of enmity lifted, and all we could behold was sadness. A moment when we realized we were both alone now.

But then the moment ended. She mouthed two words: "I'm sorry." Not an apology. Just a statement of finality.

The light in the window went out. It was over. All over. It was time to end it all.

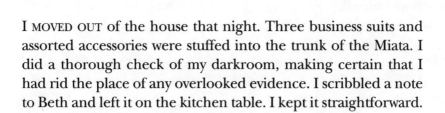

7

I MOVED OUT of the house that night. Three business suits and assorted accessories were stuffed into the trunk of the Miata. I did a thorough check of my darkroom, making certain that I had rid the place of any overlooked evidence. I scribbled a note to Beth and left it on the kitchen table. I kept it straightforward.

> Borrowed Bill's boat for the weekend. Back late Tuesday night. I'll be staying at Bill and Ruth's for the next few weeks, while I look around for a new place. Will drop over to see the boys on Wednesday evening after work.
> I love you all.

I signed the note. I left $50 on the table for our maid Perdita, having pushed back her cleaning day from this past Thursday to Monday. I took a shower and changed into the clothes I'd be wearing tomorrow: khakis, a button-down shirt, a heavy sweater, deck shoes, a Nautica windbreaker. I re-checked my pockets, just to be sure that Gary's wallet, car keys, and house keys were stowed separately from my own items.

It was now time to leave. To slam the door behind me. To make that final move. I sat, frozen, at the table, staring aimlessly at all the domestic minutiae of the kitchen. The white-washed walls. The handcrafted pine cabinets and countertops.

The array of kitchen appliances. The white Wedgwood plates stacked neatly in a plain Shaker rack. The family photos pinned to a bulletin board. The school notices and Adam's drawings adorning the fridge. So much stuff. So many acquisitions. I marveled at it all. Marveled at the way your life is a series of accumulations—an ongoing search for things to fill up the space, fill up the time. All done in the name of material comfort, yet always masking the terrible realization that you are just passing through; that, one day, you will be dispatched into the unknown with just the clothes on your back. You accumulate in an effort to cheat your inevitable extinction—to fool yourself into believing there is a permanence, a solidity to what you have built. But the door slams anyway. And you leave it all behind.

I walked over to the bulletin board and took down a photo of Josh sitting on Adam's lap. I remembered taking that shot— and just how hard it was to convince Adam to hold the baby. When I finally had them posed, Adam managed a big, toothy smile, while Josh gazed up at his big brother with charmed bemusement.

I'd always loved that picture—and, for one brief moment, decided that I had to have it. But as it shook in my hand, I knew that no evidence of the past was allowed where I was going.

I stood by the bulletin board for several terrible minutes. The phone rang. I jumped—and quickly pinned the photo back to the board before grabbing the receiver. It was Bill.

"We're about to turn in," he said, "so I was just wondering if you were getting over here tonight."

"Just leaving."

"No rush. You have the key, right?"

"I've got it."

"Let yourself in, make yourself at home. I'll give you a wake-up call around six-thirty, if that's not too brutally early."

"Fine. I want to make an early start."

"How was Darien?"

"Uh . . ."

"That bad?"

I stared at the photo of my sons for one last time.

"Yeah, that bad."

Bill and Ruth were asleep when I arrived at their place thirty minutes later. I unloaded my clothes and hung them up in the guest-room closet. A bottle of Laphroaig and a glass had been left on the bedside table, along with a note: "Guaranteed Cure for Insomnia." I climbed between the sheets, downed a glass, poured another. Surely Beth would let Adam have the bicycle, wouldn't she? Especially when he started crying for it this morning. But if she was stubborn about it, she'd definitely change her mind by Tuesday. When the phone rang at home and she heard the news.

Another large belt of Laphroaig finally delivered the knockout punch. The next thing I knew, Bill was shaking me. Thin light was streaming through the bedroom blinds. My mouth tasted like Highland turf.

"Rise and shine, sailor," he said.

"I'll rise, but I won't shine," I muttered.

"Half a bottle of malt does have that effect."

Ruth was still asleep as Bill and I drove over to the harbor in his Cherokee Jeep.

"I wanted to say good-bye to her," I said, yawning. "Thank her for everything."

Bill looked at me curiously. "Well, you are going to see her Tuesday night, right?"

I'd made a half-awake gaffe, and did my best to cover it.

"Of course, of course. I just appreciate everything you guys have done."

"Our pleasure. But listen . . . are you sure you're up to being by yourself at sea for two nights? I mean . . ."

"Yeah?"

"How can I put this?"

"Try being blunt."

"You have us both worried."

"I'm not going to jump overboard in a moment of despair, if that's what you mean."

"That's what I mean."

"Not my style."

"Good."

"You don't sound convinced."

"Benson the harbormaster called me yesterday."

"Jesus."

"Yeah, he's a prying old pain in the ass. But he also mentioned to me that, when he came aboard the boat yesterday, you seemed kind of nervous, jumpy."

"I am nervous. I am jumpy. My wife is leaving me."

"I explained that to him. Know what he said? 'Hope you know what you're doing, lending him your boat.'"

I took a big gamble and said, "Well, if you're in any way worried about me . . ."

"No, no, no."

"You sure about that?"

"I'm sure, now that we've talked. Just don't go scuttling it, okay?"

"How about disappearing to the Windward Isles?"

"Is that why you packed the scuba stuff?"

"Benson really is a pain in the ass."

"Hey, you want to play frogman in offshore slime, that's fine by me. But if you do run away to Barbuda, call me and tell me where to meet you."

We both laughed. The moment of danger had passed.

At the harbor, Bill gave me a crash course in the *Blue Chip*'s glittering array of hi-tech equipment. He showed me how to work the autopilot, how to make contact with the coast guard on the radio, and how to plot a course using the complex components of his global positioning system. Then he sat on the bunk containing Gary.

"You know what's beneath here?" he asked.

I shook my head.

"The food stores. You need any additional supplies, you take off the mattress and you'll find a couple of hatches. Lift them up and there they are."

"Right," I said.

"Want me to show you?" he asked, pointing to the mattress.

"I'm sure I can work it out."

Instead, he showed me the drill for hoisting and handling the sails. He showed me how to hoist a spitfire (a small storm headsail) in case a nasty blow or squall threatened. He gave me the rundown on the diesel engine and assured me that, as long as I was less than 200 miles from shore, there'd be enough diesel aboard to get me to land.

"But you're not going to be venturing that far from the coast, are you?" he asked.

"Might aim for Block Island."

"If you do, make sure you stay well within its waters. You stray too far, you're in the Atlantic. And that might get a little tricky—even for someone with coast of Maine experience like you."

"Don't worry. The Atlantic isn't my idea of a good time."

We pored over charts. Bill mapped out an easy route east to Block Island, pointing out a harbor on the eastern tip of the island where I could duck in for the night. By now it was eight o'clock. The sun was up. The sky was a deep, azure blue. There was a nippy northwesterly blowing. A perfect sailing day for reaching east on Long Island Sound in a twenty-knot wind.

"Well," Bill said. "Better shove off now. Theo is expecting us at the school by ten."

"He doing all right?"

"He's the best," Bill said.

"Send him my love."

"When you dock on Tuesday night, give me a call, I'll come pick you up. And, of course, if there are any problems, use ship to shore to reach my mobile."

"There won't be any problems."

I tossed him my car keys, in case he needed to move the Miata out of his driveway. We shook hands. Bill seemed reluctant to go ashore. I could tell that he now regretted offering me the boat.

"Go easy," he said, finally stepping down onto the dock.

"Thanks again, friend."

I moved to the wheel, turned the ignition key, and listened as the motor hummed to life. Bill untied the *Blue Chip* from the dock and tossed the docking line back aboard. I pulled down on the gearshift, raised the throttle, turned the wheel, and slowly began to power out of New Croydon harbor. I gave Bill a final nod. He raised a hand slowly, a somber, apprehensive gesture of farewell.

I motored for around half a mile until I reached the outer edge of the harbor. Then I cranked up the mainsail and the jib, and set an easterly course down a soft, swelling Long Island Sound.

Trimming the sails carefully to make the most of the northwesterly, I was soon sailing at hull speed, the sails well filled as a freshening breeze now had the *Blue Chip* speeding along. I glanced at the anemometer. A twenty-two-knot wind was blowing—hardly dangerous, but I still kept my eyes fixed on the Sound, making certain that this seascape of moderate waves and whitecaps remained manageable. The sun was now at full wattage, and spray was flying out from the lee bow as she plunged down the Sound.

Maintaining an even keel, I raced east up along the Connecticut coast, passing Long Neck Point near Stamford and the archipelago of islands off Norwalk. It was a clean, steady reach.

Still, I had a good working breeze and, around one, was bypassing New Haven. Lunch was a Diet Coke and a hunk of cheese that I forced myself to eat, though I had little appetite. As I was making excellent time, I could have pulled in toward shore and docked near Vineyard Point to give myself a short mental break from the exactitudes of sailing. But I feared stopping, feared that if I halted my inevitable progress toward New London, I would abandon control. So I kept going. Never looking back.

A coast guard cutter passed me somewhere near Hammonasset Point, its officers on duty saluting me as they sped by. I was pleased to see their receding wake. Near Old Lyme Shores, light began to dim. By the time I dropped anchor a mile off Harkness State Park, day had become night.

I was the only craft in the immediate vicinity. There were no other boats or launches on the horizon. Scanning the shore with my binoculars, I saw no hints of campfires in the state park. Thank Christ it wasn't summer, when this area would have been filled with vacationers who considered it romantic to grill hot dogs on a moonlit beach. Thank Christ there was no moon tonight. I needed the dark.

After carefully stowing the sails, I went below deck. It was time to begin. I could feel my stomach caving in, but I steadied myself, thinking: Just take it step by step.

One. I pulled on surgical gloves, then dug out the duffel containing the dinghy. After inflating it on deck with the foot pump, I attached a length of line to the hook on its bow, stowed its oars aboard, and carted it out on deck.

Two. I undressed completely, changing into a new pair of black sweats and black sneakers. Then I shoved Gary's wallet and keys into a back pocket and zipped it closed.

Three. I unwrapped Gary. Using heavy-duty scissors, I cut off his clothes and dumped them into a black plastic bag. He was still cold to the touch, his skin the color of cigarette ash. Balancing the top half of his body up on the edge of the port bunk, I dressed his torso in the shirt and sweater I'd just taken off and slipped his legs into my khakis. Stripping off the blankets, I laid his torso out flat on the bunk. I shoved my wallet and housekeys into his pocket and tucked the blankets back in, leaving his hands outside. He looked like he was enjoying a sweet sleep.

Four. I withdrew the little jeweler's hammer from the duffel. Opening his lips wide, I set about destroying his teeth, chipping away until identifying Gary through dental records would be almost impossible. It was a long, tedious job, chewing up nearly forty-five minutes.

Five. I excavated the two jerry cans of diesel. Attaching a hose to one can, I threaded the other end straight down Gary's esophagus until it bumped into his stomach (or, at least, what

I presumed to be his stomach). Inverting the can, I heard the liquid slurp through the tube. I held the can upside down for around three minutes—until, suddenly, diesel started to leak out of Gary's mouth. He was now primed for cremation.

Six. Using the second can of diesel, I drenched his head, his legs, and his hands. I gave his fingers a particularly good soaking, just to be sure that all fingerprints would be quickly charred away. Then I doused the cabin walls and floors with all the remaining diesel before tossing the two cans into the plastic garbage bag.

Seven. I taped the two prefilled cardboard tubes to the port and starboard walls. Trying to keep my hands as steady as possible, I inverted both vials of acid and inserted them, cork-first, into the top of each tube. I had now primed an incendiary devise known as a nipple bomb. In around seven hours—according to those Betty Crocker folk at *The Anarchist's Cookbook*—the acid would eat its way through the cork and flow right into that most inflammable compound of chemicals. The result would be two huge fireballs on both sides of the diesel-soaked cabin, quickly engulfing diesel-fed Gary. He would be burnt beyond recognition.

Eight. Using the *Blue Chip*'s global positioning system, I charted a southwesterly course at a maximum motorized speed of seven nautical miles per hour. The boat would travel by autopilot straight across the Sound, then ride the ebb tide through the Race—a narrow passage of water with strong tidal currents south of Fishers Island. Having studied Bill's tidal charts, I knew that the tide was in my favor for the next six hours—and would add as much as four knots of speed to the boat, thereby carrying it through the Race. After clearing this passage, it would leave Montauk Point to starboard and Block Island to port, eventually entering the Atlantic. By the time the nipple bombs kicked in, the craft would be thirty miles from the nearest landfall. It would be three in the morning. The fire would rage. Gary would erupt. The gas-stove canister would finally detonate. And—given that it was the middle of the night—it would be at least five hours before any forensic experts were on the scene to inspect whatever wreckage of the *Blue Chip* still remained. Five hours in seawater was enough time to mask the excessive amounts of diesel used to destroy the boat and scatter evidence. In short, it would all look like an accident. A very bad accident.

Nine. I stuffed the plastic bag into one of the duffels and went on deck. Placing the duffel in the dinghy, I lowered the inflatable boat into the water, tying it to the stern. I returned to deck and pulled up the anchor, stowing it on board. Then I powered up the engine, pulled the gearshift into forward, and raced to the stern as the boat began to move.

But as I tried to board the dinghy, I slipped on its wet rubber stern and plunged into the arctic waters of the Sound. I hung on to the side of the dinghy, gasping for air. The *Blue Chip* was now moving quickly. I swam madly toward its stern. A fast unscrambling of the knot and I fell back into the Sound as the *Blue Chip* left me behind. I gripped the rope as if it were a life raft, yanking the dinghy toward me. When I had finally reeled it in, I hoisted myself onboard. It nearly capsized under my angled weight. Using my hands, I bailed out as much water as possible, but there was still a good foot sloshing around. Grabbing the oars, I rowed for shore, shivering with cold. In front of me, the *Blue Chip* was sedately chugging out to sea.

It took a half hour to reach the beach. Along with everything else in the duffel, my flashlight was waterlogged, dead. A wind was blowing, my sweats were sodden, and I had no light to guide my way through the park to the road. I deflated the dinghy, folded it up, and added it to the duffel. Then I started to walk, the heavy duffel hoisted atop my right shoulder. I found the boardwalk and crept up it until I reached a paved path. I followed it through the pitch-black park, the duffel's weight becoming heavier with every step. There were no lights on in the Harkness mansion, but a wind was blowing, chilling me further. And I was numb with worry. What if I couldn't find the car until first light? What if there was a nighttime patrol of the park by the local cops? What if I tripped and broke my leg?

It took me twenty minutes to reach the park gates. They were only four feet high. Tossing the duffel before me, I climbed over. Half a mile to go. I kept off the road, staying near the trees. A car passed. I flattened out on the ground to avoid being spotted by its headlights. Picking myself up, I continued my slow hike. When I reached the red clapboard house I froze for a moment, as lights were ablaze in every window. Crouching down commando-style, I made a quick, stealthy dash by its front door and didn't stop running until I had disappeared into the dark again.

The final quarter mile was agony, the duffel now a torturous deadweight. It landed at my feet when I reached the farmyard gate. I tossed it over, followed it, and headed for the trees. When I reached them, I kept colliding with branches. My free hand was extended in front of me, guiding me through this black wood. My pace accelerated and suddenly my outstretched hands connected with something hard and metallic. I dug through the leaves and found the car tarpaulin. Pulling it off, I reached into my sweats for the keys. Springing open the trunk, I grabbed a clean set of clothes and a towel from Gary's travel bag, then flung the duffel inside. I unlocked the passenger door, hit the ignition, set the heater on maximum and climbed out again. As the car interior heated up, I stripped out of my wet clothes and toweled myself down. After changing into Gary's clothes— jeans, a denim shirt, his leather jacket—I jumped into the now warm MG.

Camouflaged by the trees, I sat there for ten minutes, the car's heater helping stave off hypothermia. I still stank of the sea. I tried to comb my hair with my fingers, but ended up looking like a haunted, waterlogged refugee. If a cop were to stop me now on the road, I wouldn't exactly inspire confidence. Nervously, I put the car in reverse. But as soon as I had backed up a few feet, I screeched to a halt and jumped out. I had forgotten my sodden clothes and the tarpaulin. Brilliant—nothing like leaving some interesting evidence in your wake. Wrapping them up in a big ball, I tossed them next to the duffel in the trunk. Driving without lights, I slowly inched my way through the trees until I reached the open field. A fast U-turn, a quick opening and closing of the gate, and I was on the road, headlights now aglow.

I wanted to bolt now, to hit the interstate and put a thousand miles between myself and Connecticut. A series of terrible scenarios flooded my head. The nipple bombs failing to detonate. The *Blue Chip* veering off course and running aground. The coast guard boarding the boat. My appearance on the FBI's Ten Most Wanted list.

But around 500 yards down the road, I passed a clearing that fronted an inlet of the Sound. Pulling onto the shoulder, I killed the engine, killed the lights, and stared out at the inky water, relieved to see no sign of the *Blue Chip* on the horizon. It had vanished from view.

An eerie hush. A black sky, devoid of stars. A void to match my own. I wondered how my death at sea would be interpreted. A tragic mishap? A spectacular suicide? No doubt, the police and coast guard would question Beth and Bill and Ruth and Jack and Estelle. No doubt, they would all say the same thing: He was not a happy man. Their guilt would be huge. So too their anger. And Adam? I hoped they would mask the truth. Tell him I had gone to a place from which it was impossible to return. His four-year-old mind wouldn't grasp the finality of this news. He'd mourn my absence for a while. In time, however, I'd be nothing more than a blurred memory from his early childhood. A photo on the mantelpiece that he would stare at quizzically from time to time, any recall of me ebbing with the years.

Forget me quickly, Adam. And with little pain. Because I chose this way out. In my panic, I saw no other option. In my panic, I also spied an opportunity. A chance few of us ever have. Or take.

I turned the ignition key. I hit the headlights. I drove away. Thinking:

My name is Gary Summers. I am a photographer.

PART THREE

I DROVE ALL NIGHT. I drove all day. I kept myself awake by popping Dexedrine and mainlining gas-station coffee. I stopped only to fill the car, empty my bladder, grab fast food, and dispose of stuff from the boat. I scattered evidence in municipal dumps across three states. When I was running low on gas I avoided small service stations, sticking to the big, crowded truckstop plazas that lined the highway. I paid cash for everything. I was on the road for nineteen hours. I blared heavy metal on the car radio to stay awake, paying scant attention to the passing landscape. I concentrated on numbers. Interstate numbers: 95 to 78 to 76 to 70. I bypassed New York and Newark and Harrisburg and Pittsburgh and Columbus and Indiana-polis and St Louis. I never exceeded the speed limit. I never switched lanes suddenly. I never tailgated. I did nothing that might draw attention to myself. I just kept moving west.

On the outskirts of Kansas City, my brain went haywire. Triple vision, an icy sweat, a surge of nausea, Dexedrine over-load, impending delirium. I needed a bed fast. I sidestepped two small mom-and-pop motels and checked into a large, anonymous Day's Inn. $49.95 a night. I handed over five $10 notes, registered under G. Summers, and gave New Croydon as my home address (it was still too early to use the Berkeley mail-drop address). The room was a little tatty. There were cigarette burns on the carpet and a large stain on the bed-spread. I didn't care. I drew the blinds. I hung out the "Do Not Disturb" sign. I climbed in between the stiff, frosty sheets. I turned out the lights and died.

I didn't stir for twelve hours. The digital bedside clock said 6:07 A.M. For a few befuddled minutes, I believed I was at home in my own bed and suffered momentary panic as I wondered: Why isn't Josh crying? But then reality hit. Good morning, you're dead.

I fumbled for the remote control and stared, half awake, at CNN's *Headline News.* A White House cabinet resignation. Another budgetary battle on Capitol Hill. More fun in Bosnia. An Algerian bomb made safe in Paris. Nothing about an explosion aboard a small pleasure boat early Monday morning off Montauk Point.

I channel-surfed, eventually finding a financial news station. Surely they would cover the death at sea of a Wall Street lawyer. But the hourly news bulletin on CNBC didn't mention Ben Bradford.

I showered, but didn't shave; I was trying to camouflage my features under some stubble. I put on dark glasses and a base-ball hat. I checked out. On my way to the parking lot, I fed quarters into two vending machines and bought copies of *The Kansas City Star* and the national edition of *The New York Times.* I scrutinized both papers, page by page. Not even a three-line item on the "accident." I went through them again, thinking I must have missed the story the first time around.

I hit the road. I stayed on Interstate 70, crossing the state line into Kansas. I kept the radio tuned to an all-news station. The terrain grew flat. Fields of grain stretching into infinity. The sky was cloudless, empty. The hours clicked by. The radio kept spewing news, but failed to report the one story I needed to hear. Kansas was endless, the road sucking me deeper into visual nullity. Counties vanished behind me—Ellsworth, Russell, Ellis, Trego, Gove. There was no respite from this horizontal void. The world was flat and I felt like driving off its edge. Because I was now a wanted man.

Night. The Colorado state line. And, coming up fast on my rear, the blue lights of a highway patrolman. My pulse went berserk. I kept my foot on the accelerator. They found the boat. Intact. With Gary's severed body. And two dud nipple bombs. They'd searched Gary's house, realized his car was missing, issued an all-points bulletin for an MG with Connecticut plates. And now the Colorado cops were going to make the collar.

The sirens began to shriek. I didn't slow down. The lights of the patrol car filled my rearview. I was blinded by the glare. I knew what I was going to do. As soon as they were right on my bumper, I'd veer left, cross the divider, and go right into the path of an oncoming truck. But just as the cop car closed in on my tail, it swerved left and sped off in pursuit of a pickup doing ninety in front of me. I didn't wait around to see if an arrest was made. I took the next exit and checked into the first motel I could find.

I spent the night flipping among television news channels, willing my death to be broadcast. In an attempt to stay calm, I kept telling myself: Had they found the *Blue Chip* adrift with a dead body on board, the story would be everywhere by now. But still I couldn't sleep, convinced that it was just a matter of time before the knock came on the door.

I was back on the interstate just after sunrise. I reached the outskirts of Denver by ten. I stopped at a McDonald's. I bought a *Rocky Mountain News* and a *New York Times*. Nothing in the local Denver paper. Nothing in the first section of the *Times*. Then I turned to the second section. On the bottom corner of page four, I saw the headline:

LAWYER MISSING,
FEARED DEAD AFTER BOAT EXPLOSION

Benjamin Bradford, a junior partner at the Wall Street law firm of Lawrence, Cameron and Thomas, was feared dead after the sailboat he was piloting went ablaze seventeen miles east of Montauk Point, L.I.

The blaze was spotted by the Montauk lighthouse shortly

after 2:30 A.M. Monday. According to the lighthouse keeper, James Ervin, the fire was followed by a massive explosion. A coast guard launch was immediately dispatched to the scene, but bad weather conditions and lack of light hampered rescue efforts.

"From what we can ascertain so far, a fire engulfed the cabin of the craft and quickly combusted," said coast guard spokesman L. Jeffrey Hart. "Though we can't rule anything out at this point, we are currently treating this as an accident."

The boat—a 30-foot sloop christened *Blue Chip*—was registered in the name of Wall Street stockbroker William T. Hartley, a friend of Mr. Bradford.

"I'd loaned Ben the boat for a few days," Mr. Hartley said yesterday. "He was an experienced sailor, the craft was fitted with every safety device imaginable, and he wasn't a smoker. Maybe the fire started when he was cooking something on the gas stove and, instead of abandoning ship, he tried to put out the flames."

Mr. Bradford, a resident of New Croydon, Connecticut, is married, with two children. The coast guard will continue their search for more wreckage this morning.

I reread the story several times. It took a while to sink in. "We are currently treating this as an accident." My mind shifted into overdrive. After the cops ascertained that I didn't have any homicidal enemies, hadn't borrowed money from the Mob, and would have jumped overboard if I'd been a suicide, they would file my death away under misadventure. Unless, of course, some suspicious insurance investigator decided to run extended tests on all that waterlogged wreckage. But what would they find? Maybe the occasional fragment of Gary's body, but forty-eight hours in saltwater would hamper any detailed forensic examination. A surfeit of diesel, perhaps? Under questioning, Bill would acknowledge that he kept four full cans of the fuel aboard. And the investigators would surmise that, if the fire did start at the stove and spread across the cabin, I was probably trying to fight it off when it finally reached the diesel stores. But I didn't succeed in quelling it. Instead, as the diesel ignited, I was baptized in a ball of flame. It charred me beyond recognition. The fueled fire then triggered off the gas-canister explosion. I was shredded like confetti. End of story.

I was going to pull it off. I was going to get away with it. And yet I didn't feel triumphant. Just numb.

My past had been eradicated, snuffed out. No responsibilities, no demands, no ties, no former life. It was like being in a vacuum. Question: When you wipe a slate clean, what do you end up with? Answer: a blank slate. Alternative answer: freedom. The burdenless life you've always craved. But when you're finally confronted with that freedom—that blank slate—you feel nothing but fear. Because freedom—of the absolute, no-strings variety—is like staring into an unchartered void, a realm without structure.

I left my Big Mac and fries untouched. I went back to the car. I drove. Direction: nowhere.

For the next few weeks, I just drifted. I wandered the interstate system like some motorized Flying Dutchman. Leaving Denver, I took 25 South and traversed New Mexico. At the town of Las Cruces, I joined 10 West, then spliced onto the 8 for the run to San Diego. Up 15 through Vegas into Salt Lake City. Across the empty quarters of Nevada on 80.

Numbers, numbers. You connect with the 5 at Sacramento. Grab 84 East at Portland. Take a spur road at Ogden in Utah to connect to 80 East. Run across Nebraska, then hop the 29 to Fargo. The 94 gets you out of North Dakota and into Minneapolis. The 35 sends you running south to Des Moines before you reconnect with the 80 to Iowa City. And then . . .

A pattern developed. A day on the road, a night in a motel. Cash only. And no conversations. Just a few phrases, spoken over and over again: *Fill 'er up . . . Can I have a shake with the cheeseburger . . . Need a room for a night.* I never stayed more than one night anywhere. I never ventured into bars, clubs, cocktail lounges, or any other place where I might stray into idle chat. I never crossed into a city. I never left the interstate system—

because I feared small towns where people might just be interested in a stranger passing through.

The 80 connects with the 55 near Joliet, Illinois. At Jackson, in Mississippi, you can grab the 20 to Dallas. Then it's the 35 North up to Salina in Kansas. And then you're back on the 70 again . . .

Every day, I obsessively checked the car's internal mechanics, as I had a deep fear of breaking down on some nowhere highway and being forced to seek help from a state trooper. Every day, I scoured *The New York Times*.

LAWYER STILL MISSING AFTER BOAT FIRE

The body of Benjamin Bradford, a Wall Street lawyer, presumed dead after a fire on Monday, November 7th, aboard a boat he was piloting off Long Island, has yet to be recovered.

Coast guard spokesman L. Jeffrey Hart did confirm that fragments of clothing were found among the wreckage, and were later identified as possibly belonging to Mr. Bradford by his wife, the former Elizabeth Schnitzler of New Croydon, Connecticut.

"Like the wreckage of the boat, early forensic tests have shown that the clothing was heavily permeated with diesel," Mr. Hart said. "According to Mr. Hartley, the boat's owner, significant amounts of diesel fuel were stowed aboard the craft. At this stage, we are still calling this incident an accident."

Two days later, my obituary appeared.

BENJAMIN BRADFORD, LAWYER, 38, IS DEAD

The headline startled me. So stark, so final. The obit was a straightforward *New York Times* job. Dead at sea. Born Ossining, New York. Educated at Andover. *Cum laude* graduate of Bowdoin College. J.D. from NYU Law. Joined Lawrence, Cameron and Thomas in 1983. The names of my kids. A keen amateur photographer . . .

An entire life in ninety-four words. No picture, thankfully.

That laurel was given to some former General Foods CEO who had expired on the same day as me. His was a less dramatic leave-taking. Heart failure.

Below the obituary, I also found myself listed in the death notices column.

> Bradford, Benjamin
> Suddenly, after a boating accident on
> November 7th. Much loved husband of
> Elizabeth. Adored father of Adam and
> Joshua. Sadly missed by friends and
> colleagues. Funeral details to be
> announced later. No flowers, please.

Much loved husband. Yes. Once upon a time.

There was another notice taken out by Lawrence, Cameron and Thomas. Respected junior partner. Tragic loss. Devastated colleagues. Photographic scholarship fund to be set up in his name.

Because, after all, he was such a keen amateur photographer.

A week or so later, when I was somewhere outside Provo, Utah, the *Times* ran another Ben Bradford story.

FORENSIC EXPERTS RULE OUT FOUL PLAY
IN BRADFORD DEATH

Twelve days after the boat he was piloting caught fire and exploded in the Atlantic, New York State Police investigators have ruled out foul play in the death of Wall Street lawyer Ben Bradford.

State Police spokesperson Janet J. Cutcliffe issued a press statement today stating that, "After a thorough forensic examination of the wreckage of the sailing boat *Blue Chip*, it has been decided that no further investigation of this case will be undertaken . . ."

It was the news I had been waiting to read. The all clear had sounded. But I still roamed the interstates for another week. Adrift. Rootless. Coasting.

On the last Tuesday in November, I reached Rock Springs, Wyoming. It was a nowhere town on I-80—a collection of fast-food joints and jerry-built houses plonked down amid crimson-colored mesa. I checked into the Holiday Inn. When the receptionist asked, "How long will you be staying, Mr. Summers?" I did a double take. After three weeks on the road, I still wasn't used to being called that name.

"Just a night," I said.

My room overlooked the highway. I had a shower. I flopped on the bed, trying to unwind after thirteen hours on the road. I opened *The New York Times* I had bought earlier that day. A short item in section two caught my eye.

WALL STREET MOURNS LAWYER LOST AT SEA

Several hundred friends and colleagues of the late Wall Street lawyer Benjamin Bradford packed Trinity Church in lower Manhattan yesterday afternoon for a memorial service. The body of Mr. Bradford, who died in a fire aboard a sailing boat on November 7th, has never been recovered.

Several hundred friends? I never had several hundred friends, did I? No doubt, Prescott Lawrence read some psalm. Jack gave the eulogy. Beth looked brave. Estelle cried loudly. And Adam? I hope to Christ he was kept at home with Josh and the nanny, and wasn't subjected to two hundred pitying glances, to tearful strangers hugging him and saying godawful things like, "Your daddy would want you to be a brave little boy."

Several hundred friends. I read those words over and over again. And felt shame.

There was a brief flash when I wanted to pick up the phone, call Beth, tell her everything, beg her forgiveness, and somehow convince her to . . .

What? Close down her life in New Croydon, grab the boys, and join me on the run? She'd be on to the Feds in a New York minute. Especially when she learned of the fate Gary had suffered.

The delusional flash ended. Don't go seeking absolution—because it will never be forthcoming. You've made your choice. You're condemned to live with it.

I left the room. I sidestepped the motel lounge where a group called Four Jacks and a Jill were currently performing. I got into my car, zipping up my leather jacket against the December cold. I cruised down the gasoline alley that bisected Rock Springs. Two-for-one taco joints. A Dairy Queen. A couple of redneck bars. And a large barnlike prefab diner called the Village Inn.

It was the best option in town: a generic dump with bright lights, laminated menus (with color photos of blueberry waffles), and a collection of waitresses who all needed to make the acquaintance of a depilatory. The manager of the diner wore a polyester short-sleeved shirt and a clip-on tie.

"Ready to order?" he asked after approaching my table.

"Grilled cheese sandwich, regular coffee," I said.

"You got it. Staying long in Rock Springs?"

"Just passing through."

"Hope you're not trying to hitch somewhere on a night like this."

"No, I've got wheels."

"Only way to travel," he said and wandered off to deal with my order.

Me, a hitchhiker? I was mildly offended by the inference. But when I paid a visit to the bathroom, the mirror over the sink explained everything. With my thickening beard, highway-jaded eyes, and pasty, bloated face (thanks to weeks of junk food and no fresh air), I really did resemble a road rat. Someone who aimlessly dwelled in the Great American Nowhere. An eternal loser, hoping to thumb a ride out of town.

All journeys have a logical structure—you depart, you return. But mine had become an endless ride down a concrete corridor. And there was no terminus in sight.

The food arrived. I ate the sandwich. I drank the coffee. I settled the check.

"Everything okay for you?" the manager asked as he handed me change.

"Fine," I said.

"Where you bound for next?" he asked.

I muttered, "Heading east," but that was a lie. Because I had no place to go.

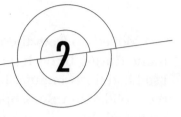

December 2, 1994
Berkeley, CA

B:

Greetings from the People's Republic of Berkeley. I pulled in here last week after finally hauling my ass out of Baja. The assignment didn't go as well as expected. The photo editor at the mag thought my work far too hard-edged and graphic for his purposes. Everyone wants gloss these days. Fuck him.

I know I shouldn't be writing you at home, and I hate to be landing you with some shitty news. But I thought I'd better come clean with you straight away. While hanging out in San Felipe, I hooked up with a photographer from the Bay area named Laura. She was on vacation down there and what we both thought was just a weekend thing turned into something more. So much so that I followed her back to Berkeley, where she lives, and where she's been helping me get work on a couple of magazines.

Though it's too soon to tell, I believe we're really going to make a go of it together. Even if it doesn't work out, the scene here is great. I've already landed a couple of commissions—which makes a nice change after the bullshit treatment I was getting in New York. I think I might just click here.

222 o Douglas Kennedy

Sorry to end it this way—but, let's face it, it was always just a fling and never a long-term prospect. But it will always be a nice memory—and they're few and far between.

Take care.

G.

I looked up from the IBM Thinkpad and stared out at the traffic tearing by on Interstate 80. I checked my watch. 11:30. I still had thirty minutes left before I had to vacate my room at the Holiday Inn Rock Springs. So I reread the letter again. I preferred this draft to an earlier one, in which Gary said that he had read about Ben's death in *The New York Times* and made a lot of appropriate sympathetic noises. Had Beth received that version of the letter she would rightfully have asked: Then why didn't the bastard pick up the phone and call me? Anyway, the whole point of this note was to so enrage Beth that she would never want anything to do with Gary again. Which is why I invented the business about his new squeeze, Laura. Coming fast on the heels of my death, Gary's romantic defection would make Beth write him off as a shit—and ensure that she wouldn't try to make contact with him in Berkeley. Or, at least, that's what I was hoping. I had deliberately omitted a return address on the letter, just in case.

Satisfied with my handiwork, I fed a sheet of paper into the Canon Bubblejet and hit the Print button. Then I typed Beth's name and address on the computer screen and printed out an envelope. I signed the letter, folded it into the envelope, and shoved it in a larger manila envelope already addressed to the Alternative Post Office in Berkeley. I also enclosed a $10 bill paper-clipped to a note that read:

Please mail this for me.
Gary Summers

I sealed the manila envelope, affixing two 29-cent stamps to its upper right-hand corner. I packed my bags. After checking out, I tossed the envelope into the motel mailbox. It would take at least forty-eight hours to reach California (which is why I dated Gary's letter two days ahead). Once received, the Alternative Post Office folk would dispatch Gary's letter to Beth, thus ensuring that it had the necessary Berkeley postmark.

In the motel parking lot, I opened my Rand McNally road atlas. Driving west on I-80 would bring me back into Salt Lake City. East would eventually edge me into Nebraska. Terrific options. The only other route out of town was 191: a two-lane blacktop heading north into mountain country. I had been dodging back roads for weeks, sticking to the anonymity of the highway. But with Ben Bradford's death now officially ruled "accidental," I no longer had to live as a fly-by-night. And the thought of another day on the interstate made me shudder. I opted for the back road.

Badlands. Flat, scrubby prairie. Bloodred rock. And silence. A hushed, solitary muteness—enormous in its expanse, its magnitude. For over an hour, the road was mine. Not another car in sight. I pushed deeper into this domain, gradually gaining altitude, a tentative winter sun casting thin shafts of light across the stark tundra.

The road turned vertiginous—a slow, uphill climb. I downshifted into third, but the MG still struggled against the steep gradient. A light snow began to fall. Traction was bad. I downshifted into second. The engine groaned with disapproval. The snow was thickening, a westerly breeze swirling it across the blacktop. My foot was to the floor. The speedometer was stuck at 25 miles per hour. I was never going to make it up this hill and feared breaking down in this no-man's-land.

But just as I was about to retreat back to Rock Springs, I reached the crest of the hill. And all I could behold in the distance was epic grandeur. Rugged peaks, a vast plateau of lofty pines, glassy lakes. The sheer scale of this domain held me mesmerized. It seemed limitless, all encompassing. I discarded any ideas about withdrawing to the monotonous lowlands of the interstate. Instead, I eased the MG over this hilly apogee and rolled down into the snow-dusted valley below.

The road became a slalom course, snaking its way across this glen before steeply ascending again. For the next hundred miles, I felt as if I were participating in some sort of Alpine Grand Prix—negotiating spindly bends, navigating perpendicular descents, traversing the base of jagged ridges. Visibility was minimal—but I wasn't complaining. Because—for the first time since hitting the road nearly a month ago—I felt a curious sense of liberation. Gone were the paranoid delusions of a posse on my tail. Gone was the flow of nightmare images that dominated every hour of my waking day. All I could think about was the next hairpin turn, the next dangerous plunge down a frosty stretch of blacktop, the way in which every new mile I clocked brought me deeper into a hidden mountain kingdom; a place of formidable natural battlements to keep the outside world at bay. And where you could easily seek refuge from life beyond its frontiers.

This illusion of insularity ended late that afternoon when I rolled into the town of Jackson. It is a big ski resort, brimming with designer clothes outlets, designer delicatessens, and well-heeled corporate types from San Francisco and Seattle and Chicago, parading past the faux Wild West architecture in designer parkas and furs. Within ten minutes of arriving in Jackson, I wanted to hit the road out of town—because I was certain that, were I to loiter here for a while, I'd run into some vacationing West Coast lawyer with whom I'd done business over the years. And transcontinental phone lines would start humming the moment he spotted me.

There was, however, a problem about extricating myself from Jackson. The snow was now reaching blizzard conditions, night was fast approaching, and when I stopped at a local gas station to fill the car, the pump jockey told me that all roads out of Jackson were now impassable.

"No way you're getting outta town tonight," he said. "I was you, I'd find me a room fast, 'fore they all get took."

"Will they have the roads cleared by morning?" I asked.

"Plows usually start right before dawn—but, hate to tell ya this, weatherman's predicting two more feet of snow overnight."

I grabbed a couple of sandwiches and a six-pack of beer at a small package store, then managed to snag the last vacancy at a small motel on the outskirts of town. I remained shuttered in my room for the night, mindlessly soaking up the hours with small-screen junk, not daring to show my face around town.

I was up at six the next morning. I peered out the window. A virtual whiteout. I called reception and inquired about road conditions.

"Blizzard's supposed to keep on hitting us till at least three this afternoon," said the woman at the front desk. "You gonna want the room for 'nother night?"

"Guess I've no choice," I said.

A quick dash to a neighboring convenience store for supplies, then it was back for another extended stint of incarceration in front of the television. I worked my way through a box of jelly doughnuts and a quart of take-out coffee. I watched Geraldo and Sally Jessy: "Senior Citizens Who Marry Drum Majorettes" . . . "Crack Addicts Reunited with Their Policemen Fathers" . . . "Fat Women Who Can't Wipe." Everyone was confessing something, crying big tears, hugging estranged parents, parading their newfound emotional growth. I ate an oily salami hero, drank a sixteen-ounce bottle of Dr Pepper, and spent the afternoon watching reruns of *The Honeymooners* and *I Love Lucy* and other sitcom remnants from my childhood. I tried to read a bad paperback novel about a serial murderer who preys on certified public accountants. I stared at five minutes of *Sesame Street,* but thoughts of Adam and Josh overwhelmed me and I had to switch channels. I sat through *ABC World News* and the MacNeil/Lehrer *NewsHour.* I wolfed down a ham-and-swiss on rye and began drinking the first of six Michelobs. I watched the entire NBC prime-time schedule. I finished the last Michelob. I pulled back the curtains. The blizzard had stopped. I fell into bed—bloated, overfed, junked-out—vowing never to subject myself to such confinement again.

At first light, I was heading west on Route 22. The road was freshly plowed, but still a little tricky. Twice the MG went into a skid. Twice I just managed to gain control of the car before it swan-songed into a ravine. I crept along at 20 miles per hour, my teeth chattering. The car heater tried hard, but wasn't really effective against an outside temperature of 8 degrees Fahrenheit. Gary's leather jacket and cowboy boots also didn't provide the necessary insulation against the Wyoming winter. I'd wanted to buy myself a proper down parka and a pair of insulated boots while in Jackson, but feared that as soon as I walked into the Ralph Lauren factory outlet, I'd hear some deep white-bread voice saying, "Laurie, isn't that the late Ben Bradford over there?" Better to freeze for another day than risk being spotted.

Cold within, cold without. And on the horizon, the most glacial vista imaginable—the menacing, forbidding silhouettes of the Grand Tetons. Craggy summits scraping the sky at 13,000 feet, arrogant in their austerity. There was nothing inviting or user-friendly about these peaks. They had an Old Testament demeanor, solemn, fateful, unforgiving. They dwarfed you. They mocked your temporal preoccupations. They let it be known: You are a negligible transient, destined for obliteration.

I couldn't take my eyes off the Tetons. They chilled me, made me feel as if they were gazing down in judgment. Yet their verdict was one of aloof disinterest. To them, I was the stuff of inconsequence.

The snow started again as I approached the Idaho border. I was now on Route 33—two lanes, hemmed in by freshly plowed snowbanks that limited the horizon. It was like passing through an arctic tunnel. Occasionally, I could glimpse beyond these banked walls. Iced lakes, frosted firs, the all-pervading stillness of an Edenic wilderness. I pushed farther north, the snow now heavy, vision limited to four feet. I didn't care. I pushed on, tempting fate, refusing to turn back and seek shelter. Can I get through this? Perhaps. And if not? Let the elements swallow me whole. Let them smother me. White me out. Render me invisible. And if I do make it out of here? Then, maybe— just *maybe*—there is such a thing as a cosmic joke.

My progress was reduced to a crawl. I slithered along, expecting at any moment to encounter the snowbank that would dead-end me forever. But nothing impeded my path. The hours crept by. My worldview remained limited to a few feet of vanishing road. Yet I continued my steady progress north.

Around one that afternoon, I crossed the Targhee Pass. Then I saw a road sign. It welcomed me to "Big Sky Country." The state of Montana.

There was no sky. There was just that ashen dome of snow. I was on Route 287. In front of me I could see the flashing lights of a plow-cum-sander. I trailed behind it as it opened the road for me. For three slow hours I followed in its wake. Until it led me, safe and secure, onto Interstate 90.

It was now around four. I had been driving since dawn, but the snow was starting to ease and I couldn't face an early retreat to another motel room. So I turned west. Fifty miles down I-90, the snow turned to freezing rain and my radio antenna sprang an icicle. Seventy-five miles down I-90, and I was in a near collision with a pickup when it swerved to avoid a moose. One hundred miles down I-90, the snow started again. One hundred and fifty miles down I-90, the blizzard was so encompassing that I could just about see the exit sign for the town of Mountain Falls.

There were only two motels with vacancies in the town. I opted for the Holiday Inn because it was the first place I could find. A wild wind was blowing. Snow was drifting with such velocity that, when I opened the car door, half an inch of the stuff blew across the front seat. I experienced near weightlessness in the motel parking lot, the gale hoisting me toward the front entrance.

"Is early December always like this?" I asked the receptionist at the front desk.

"Yep," she said. "Winter in Montana."

By morning, the snow clouds had headed south. Light streamed through the plastic curtains of my motel room. I stumbled out of bed, and blinked with disbelief at the marvel of a blue sky.

228 ○ Douglas Kennedy

I left the Holiday Inn in search of breakfast. It was nine in the morning. The roads and pavements were already cleared, and the glare was so strong that I slipped on my RayBans against its reflective sheen. Maybe it was the sight of all that pristine snow. Maybe it was just the rare appearance of a winter sun. Or maybe I was simply ready to get off the road. Whatever the reason, after a five-minute walk through Mountain Falls, I knew I was going to stay there for a while.

The main street was called Main Street. It was a wide thoroughfare. At the northern end of the street, the mountains began. Due south there was a river called the Copperhead. In between there was a half-mile stretch of old redbrick buildings, nicely renovated. There were two or three honky-tonk saloons, a pair of elderly Deco apartment houses, an old general store now reconverted into a collection of cafes and restaurants. And a bar and grill called the Mountain Pass.

When I ambled in for breakfast, there were five hard men drinking beer at the bar of the Mountain Pass. They were all wearing grubby overalls and baseball caps. Their fingers were nicotine stained. Ditto their teeth. They looked up as I entered and did not favor me with a smile. Nor did the eight large women in polyester pants who were playing the slot and poker machines that lined the walls of the cafe. But the waitress—a plump woman with heavily permed hair and a serious mustache—did offer me a welcoming half grin as I slid into a booth near the kitchen.

"Y'hungry?" she asked. I nodded. "Then our 'Mountain Man' $4.95 breakfast special's just for you."

"Sounds good."

"It is."

It arrived a few minutes later on a platter. A steak, two eggs, three pancakes, a huge lump of home fries, four pieces of toast dripping in butter. I could finish only half of it.

"Thought you was hungry," the waitress said when she came by with a coffeepot.

"Not that hungry."

"Y'want a doggy bag t'take with you?"

"No thanks."

Suddenly the door flew open and a thickset man in a battered duffel coat staggered in. He was around forty, with a drinker's face: red and blue veins crisscrossing his cheeks, a bulbous nose, mad, darting eyes.

"Rudy," the waitress shouted, "you git right now."

"Ah c'mon, Joan," Rudy said in a voice with a decided nicotine rasp. "You can't bar me forever."

"Wanna bet?"

"Just a cup of coffee . . ."

"Charlie!" the waitress shouted. A hulk appeared from the kitchen. Around six five, with tree trunks for arms and the head of a pitbull. He had a baseball bat in one hand. Rudy immediately backed off toward the door.

"Got the message, got the message," he said.

"Then don't be showing your face here again," the waitress said. "You barred. And you staying barred."

"Joan, haven't you ever heard of the Christian concept of forgiveness?"

"Yeah. Now fuck off."

"Your wish is my command." And he was gone out the door.

"Thanks, Charlie," the waitress said. Charlie grunted and returned to the kitchen.

"Who's your friend?" I asked the waitress.

"Rudy Warren."

"Oh."

"You mean you don't know him?"

"I'm new in town."

"Must be—'cause if you live in Mountain Falls, you know Rudy Warren. Especially if you read the local paper."

"He's a journalist?"

"He's a drunk. A dumb-shit drunk. But yeah, he writes for *The Montanan*."

"Is he any good?"

"So they say. But get ten beers into him and he turns asshole. Used to drink here all the time. Six weeks ago, he comes in, sits down, throws back a dozen drafts in a half hour, stands up, grabs a stool, tosses it right into the bar, walks out. Musta broke around ten bottles of good liquor and a mirror. Four hundred bucks' worth of damage."

"He pay?"

"Shit, yeah. Cops arrested his ass too. Man was lucky to get off with a warning. But he ain't drinking here again, no way. More coffee?"

I accepted a refill and also bought a copy of *The Montanan* from the vending machine by the rear door. It was quite a respectable paper. Decent national and foreign coverage. Intelligent editorials. Even two pages given over to local arts news—recent gallery openings, reviews of a jazz concert, details of a Wim Wenders retrospective at the town's art-house cinema. And court reports with cases like:

> Billy James Mulgrew, 24, of 238 Snakecharm Drive, was fined $250 and given three months' probation for discharging a shotgun inside the offices of the Mountain Falls Marriage Counseling Service.

Or:

> Willard Mount, 56, of Bellevue Apartments, was fined $75 for wearing a sidearm in public.

There was also a column by Rudolph Warren, accompanied by a photograph that must have been ten years old, as it bore little resemblance to the haunted wreck who'd just fallen through the door of the Mountain Pass.

> At first sight, it still looks like your archetypal cowboy town—the kind of burg where gunslingers once loitered with intent on street corners, where there was a spittoon every ten feet, and where the only cultural divertissement on offer was the local cathouse.
> With its wide dusty main drag and honky-tonk architec-

ture, Bozeman, Montana, used to score a ten on the *High Noon* meter—as you could easily imagine a bunch of heavies in black Stetsons shooting it out on its main street.

But now, Bozeman—where I've just spent a weekend—has joined Kalispell, Bigfork, and our own Mountain Falls as yet another Montana town that has fallen victim to that viral affliction called "Californication."

How can you tell when this disease has invaded your community? Take a look at your local shops. If they're now flogging Ralph Lauren denims and $300 designer cowboy boots, you know they've been infected with the Californication bug. Go into your favorite hash house. Are all their dishes now garnished with arugula? Are the waiters now spouting on about the "blackcurrenty subtext" of a Napa Valley Pinot Noir? And has your local diner been refashioned recently into the sort of upscale coffeehouse that serves seventeen different variations on a latte theme?

If so, then you know that the Californication virus has struck at the very heart of your very own town. And unless the good citizens of this state start sheathing every Montana main street in a giant condom, the virus is going to spread, unchecked . . .

I had to smile. Rudy Warren may have been a drunk, but, as columnists go, he was also a first-rate stylist.

I left the Mountain Pass and took a wander up Main Street. I passed three espresso joints with distressed walls. And two decent bookshops. I cut down a side street. There was a contemporary art gallery. There was a New Age emporium called the Herbalist Apothecary. And there was Fred's Hole—a suspect-looking bar that was advertising an "Amateur Striptease Night" that evening.

I wound my way down to the banks of the Copperhead. It was already a solid chunk of ice. I crossed a bridge, passing the large modern building that housed the offices of *The Montanan.* Beyond this the college began—a large, sprawling, state university campus. On the nearby streets were more bookshops, more cafes, and a place that sold customized gun racks for recreational vehicles.

Rudy Warren was right. Mountain Falls had been gently gentrified, but it still hadn't lost sight of its redneck roots. I took to its mixture of western sleaze and bookish cosmopolitanism. I liked the fact that it was a large town of around 30,000 (according to the "Entering Mountain Falls" signs at the interstate exit)—cozy, yet still big enough to get lost in. A newcomer wouldn't be the subject of intense local interest. The university ensured that there was a high turnover of recent arrivals every year, and I was pretty certain that all those galleries and cafes were catering to a clientele of urban refugees—burnt-out careerists who'd fled to Mountain Falls in search of that most nineties of pipedreams: "lifestyle." My presence here would go unnoticed. I'd be just another city slicker trying to make a new life for himself under that big Montana sky.

The cold was beginning to penetrate my bones. I moved on to a cash machine and withdrew $250 from Gary's account. Then I headed to a sporting-goods store and bought a thick down parka and a pair of insulated Timberland boots. Next door to the shop was a real-estate agency, open all day Saturday according to the hours posted on the front door. I walked in. A woman in her late forties—blonde, dressed in a blazer and a tweed skirt—was seated behind a desk.

"Hi there," she said. "And how are you today?"

"I'm fine, thanks," I said, taken aback by her overfriendly tone. "Do you rent apartments?"

"We sure do, Mr. . . ."

"Summers. Gary Summers."

She proffered her hand.

"Meg Greenwood. What sort of place were you looking for, Gary?"

"One bedroom. Something central."

"For you and your wife?"

"I'm single."

A little smile crossed her lips. "Children? Pets?"

"No."

"How did you slip through the net?"

"Sorry?"

"Just a joke."

"Right."

"Price range?"

"I'm sort of new in town, so I don't exactly know . . ."

"One beds go from around $450 to $700 a month. Wouldn't recommend what we've got at the lower end of the scale. Strictly student. But I've got this nice one-and-a-half for $600 in Frontier Apartments. You know the building?"

"Like I said, I'm new in Mountain Falls . . ."

"From back east, are you?"

"Uh, yeah. How'd you . . ."

"Takes one to know one. Connecticut girl myself. And you?"

"Connecticut."

"No kidding! Whereabouts?"

"New Croydon."

"I don't believe it. I'm Darien, born and bred."

I wanted to run out the door.

"You know it?" she asked.

"I know it."

"Well, this is just great. A New Croydon guy. What brings you to Montana?"

"A photographic assignment . . ."

"You're a photographer?"

I really needed to kill this conversation quickly.

"Yeah . . . and what I'd like to find is a place where I could also set up a small darkroom."

"Do I know your work at all? Seen it in magazines?"

"I doubt it. Now about this place at the Frontier Apartments . . ."

"Well, it's just two blocks from here. You've got ten minutes?"

"Sure."

She stood up, grabbed her coat and a set of keys. On our way out, she flipped a sign hanging in the door, saying "Back in 30 minutes."

Walking over to the apartment house, she bombarded me with questions.

"So what magazines you work for?"

"A couple of travel things you probably . . ."

"*Condé Nast Traveler? National Geographic?*"

"Not exactly . . ."

"And you just decided to stay in Mountain Falls—"

"I'm working on a book about Montana," I lied.

"Who's the publisher?"

"That's to be determined."

"So you're looking for a base for a few months?"

"Exactly."

"Well, you've come to the right town. Real friendly. Lots of interesting people. And for a single guy in his thirties . . . well, you'll have fun."

We reached the Frontier Apartments. A 1920s building, with a dark foyer in need of a paint job. We rode the tiny elevator up to the third floor.

"Lived here myself for a month after my divorce," she said. "'Course, once the money came through from the sale of our house, I was able to buy a nice two-bedroom A-frame in Shawmut Valley. You know the Valley? Real, real pretty. Just ten minutes from town, but feels like you're right in the middle of the woods. Have to get you out there sometime."

Another of her little smiles. The elevator stopped with a jolt.

"'Course my husband was the reason we moved to Montana in the first place. Got a job teaching at the university. Used to be on the faculty at Williams—I loved western Massachusetts— but he didn't get tenure, so we ended up at Mountain Falls State. A year after we get here, he runs off with another teacher. A child psychologist, can you believe it?"

I said nothing.

"Well, here we are," she said, stopping in front of a battered wood door with the number 34.

"Now before we go inside, I have to tell you that the decor is a bit tired. But the space is great."

Tired was the operative word. Elderly floral wallpaper, a rust-colored carpet bordering on the threadbare, two battered armchairs, a gray leatherette couch, a sagging double bed with a crushed velvet headboard, aging appliances in the kitchen.

"This is what $600 a month buys you in Mountain Falls?" I asked.

"The location is fantastic. River view, terrific southerly light, and look at all the space you'll be getting."

She did have a point, as the living room was twenty by twenty feet, the master bedroom was equally spacious, and there was a second narrow study area that would make a nice little darkroom. But the grim boardinghouse decor would have to go.

"You'd have no objections to me fixing it up, would you?" I asked.

"We just manage the property. But the owners live in Seattle, and they just use it as an investment . . . so, yeah, I think I could talk them into it. As long as you're not planning to do anything radical."

"I'm from Connecticut. Radical isn't part of my vocabulary."

She laughed, then added, "The minimum lease would be six months."

Half a year in Mountain Falls? It was worth the gamble.

"That shouldn't be a problem . . . at $550 a month."

"You *are* from Connecticut."

We returned to her office. She made the phone call to Seattle and blathered on to the owner about this wonderful new tenant she found, and how he was willing to renovate the apartment in exchange for a rental reduction of $50 a month. He seemed to take a lot of convincing, but Meg Greenwood was from the school of hard sell and eventually won him over.

"It's yours," she said to me after hanging up.

"At $550?"

"Took some talking, but yeah, that's the price. A month's security deposit and a month's rent in advance, of course. Plus our finder's fee of $275."

I did some fast math. After the withdrawal I made today, Gary's checking account had a balance of $3,165. Moving into the apartment was going to cost me $1,375. There would be another $550 due a month from now—leaving me with a grand total of $1,240 to cover the six weeks until the next trust fund payment hit the account. I would have to live cheap.

"When can I move in?" I asked.

"Monday morning, I guess, if that's good by you."

"Fine. I'll be here to sign the lease at ten, if that suits."

"Sounds good to me. Uh, you wouldn't be able to supply us with some references, would you?"

That stopped me short.

"Might take a couple of days," I said. "My bank's back east and . . ."

"No one here can give you a character reference?"

I gave her a big, flirty smile. And said: "Only you."

She upped the coquettish ante. "Guess I'll just have to accept your New Croydon word of honor that you're good for the rent."

I fretted the rest of the weekend about Meg Greenwood. I envisaged her making calls to Darien. I wondered if she had friends in New Croydon. I feared that she might begin telephoning her divorced pals in Mountain Falls, telling them how she had managed to stumble upon that rarest of species: an unattached man. I needed to throw a barricade around myself fast.

"Hey, there, New Croydon guy," Meg said as I entered her office on Monday morning.

"Morning," I said. I took a seat, reached into the inside pocket of my parka, and brought out a stack of notes, freshly retrieved from a nearby ATM machine. I counted out thirteen $100 bills, seven tens, and one five, and placed them in a neat stack on her desk.

"A check would have been fine," she said, eyeing the cash.

"Yeah, but it would've taken a couple of days to clear my New York bank, so I thought this would be easier. You have the lease?"

She nodded and handed me a three-page document. As I perused it, she tried to make small talk.

"Get up to anything interesting the last couple of nights?" she asked.

"Stayed in my room at the Holiday Inn."

"Gonna have to get you out on the town, show you around."

I ignored this comment, and instead called her attention to a sentence in the rental agreement.

"Uh, clause 4, paragraph 2, kind of worries me," I said. "It's the phrase 'residual ownership rights.' Does this imply that the lessee can have his tenancy terminated if the landlord decides to assert his absolute privileges of householdship as guaranteed by the freehold title deeds?"

She gave me a bemused look. "I thought you were a photographer."

You fucking idiot. Damage limitation bells went off in my head.

"My dad was in the real estate business," I said, trying to smile. "Spent four long summers during college working in his office. So leases are a useless specialty of mine."

"He obviously taught you well. But we don't have tenant-right guarantees out here, so all leasing agreements come with a 'residual ownership' clause."

"Fine," I said, not wanting to pursue this issue further. I picked up a pen and signed both copies of the lease.

"In six months' time," Meg said, "we can negotiate a second lease, though I can't guarantee that the rent will remain at its current discounted level."

"Understood," I said, thinking: In six months time, I might just be a thousand miles from here.

"You'll have to contact the telephone and power companies to get the accounts put in your name."

"No problem," I said.

She handed me the keys. "And if you have any questions, you know where I am."

I shook her hand. "You've been great, Meg."

I stood up.

"One last thing," she said. "You free for dinner some night?"

"Love to," I said, moving toward the door. "But how about in a couple weeks' time, when I've settled in and Rachel's in town?"

"Rachel. Who's Rachel?"

"My girlfriend."

"You said you were single."

"I am. But I do have a girlfriend in New York. Coming out to visit me over Christmas, so if you're around, we'd love to . . ."

She looked at me as if I had just duped her. Which, of course, I had.

"I'm away over Christmas," she said.

"That's a shame. Maybe when she's back in late January we'll all get together. Thanks again."

I was out the door before she could give me another recriminating glance.

I moved into 34 Frontier Apartments a few hours later. That afternoon, I went out in search of a paint store. There was one right near Greenwood Realtors, but I decided to stay away from that corner of Main Street for the time being.

Just two days in Mountain Falls and I was already having to lie low.

3

ON MY FIRST NIGHT in the apartment, it started to snow again. It didn't stop for ten days. This suited me fine. It kept me indoors. Kept me working. Distanced me from the preparations for Christmas that were everywhere to be seen on the streets of Mountain Falls. Christmas was a holiday I was dreading.

I slept badly that first night. The bed sagged in four different places, the sheets were mildewy, the apartment stank of despair. The next morning, I threw out the bed and spent $150 on a futon in a shop near the university. I assembled the base myself and coated it with a light varnish. I dropped an additional $200 on a duvet, a fitted sheet, pillows.

The carpets went next. It took an entire day to remove them all and haul them to a Dumpster two blocks away. I also pulled up the linoleum in the bathroom and kitchen. I rented a sander for $75 and spent a week eradicating the three layers of paint that covered the pine floors. By December fourteenth, all the boards were stripped. Then I turned my attention to the walls. Removing the wallpaper turned out to be a mistake. I uncovered a multitude of plastering sins. So, on the morning of the sixteenth, I drove to a big hardware store on the edge of town and paid over $100 for a dozen rolls of lining paper, glue, and brushes. I also bought a book on do-it-yourself wallpapering. My initial attempts at repapering were moronic. After a roll buckled, one living-room wall looked like a textured collage. Another wall seemed fine until the glue dried and a network of bubbles appeared on the surface of the paper. I had to strip it all off and start again. I finally decided to work on a small area and, by the nineteenth, had relined the walls of my bedroom. By the twenty-fourth, the entire papering business was done. Not the most professional of jobs, but at least the apartment had been freed from its previous dark gloom.

I woke up Christmas morning haunted by images of Adam and Josh. I saw Adam charging down the stairs at home in New Croydon, diving into a pile of presents under the tree. "Where my present from Daddy?" he'd ask Beth. She would point to a gift she bought herself and say it was from me. "Why can't Daddy give it to me?" And Beth would then try to explain yet again that Daddy was . . .

I felt myself getting shaky, so I went to work, spending eighteen hours in the company of a brush and several large cans of white paint I had bought the previous day. Christmas dinner was a cheese omelette and three bottles of beer. My holiday gift to myself was a $30 transistor radio. I blared National Public Radio throughout the day, trying to drown the silence. I opened a package of mail that had arrived the previous day from the Alternative Post Office. Some credit-card statements. A letter from the bank confirming the direct debit arrangement I'd set up before leaving. A handful of Christmas cards— but none, thankfully, from Beth.

By New Year's Day, the apartment was repainted, the floors freshly varnished and sealed, and I was almost broke. After I paid the next month's rent (slipping it under the door of Greenwood Realtors late one night to avoid meeting Meg), I discovered that I had exactly $250 left in my account. There was still a month to go before the next trust-fund payment arrived. I toyed with the idea of getting cash advances on Gary's Visa or MasterCard, but still felt wary about running up any debts. I would have to live on $9 a day.

It didn't prove difficult. I shopped carefully at the local

supermarket, I bought dollar paperbacks at the university book exchange, I laid low. The snow kept falling, I rarely left the apartment, I passed the time with books and National Public Radio and inexpensive domestic chores. I sandpapered all kitchen cabinets and work surfaces by hand, then used the remaining floor varnish to stain them. I killed two days removing all rust from the bathtub and kitchen sinks. I polished taps, stripped the stove of baked-in grease, lined kitchen cabinets with paper, and tried to keep my mind preoccupied with these household tasks.

Nine dollars a day. I used to drop that sort of money on a cab ride in New York. But I liked the ascetic discipline of living frugally. Just as I also took pleasure in the minutiae of redecorating. There was something gratifying about glossing a door frame, sealing floorboards, freeing a cornice of embedded paint, transforming a dingy space into something light, airy, immaculate. It focused the mind, pushed the nagging demons to one side. Though I occasionally tinkered with Gary's cameras—and was itching to peer through a viewfinder again—I held off on anything to do with photography. Just as I also used the nonstop snow—and my lack of cash—as an excuse to avoid exploring the terrain beyond Mountain Falls. Or even venturing back to the Mountain Pass for one of their mammoth breakfasts. I was still in hiding. I would go out for a daily walk at dusk. I would vary my shopping routine, never buying groceries at the same supermarket twice in the same week, hitting the used-book exchange at differing hours to make certain that there was always someone new behind the cash register. I feared friendly smiles, innocent questions, easy acquaintanceship.

On the second of February—when my total net worth was $7.75—I plugged Gary's card into a cash machine on Main Street and hit the button for balance information. After a long minute, the figure $6,900.00 popped up on the screen. My relief was huge. The quarterly trust payment had hit the account. I was flush again. I withdrew $750 and went shopping.

Petrie's Cameras was located opposite the Holiday Inn. I'd passed it many times since coming to Mountain Falls, but had kept myself away from its temptations. Until now.

"How do," said the guy behind the counter. He was in his late thirties—tall, shaggy-haired, with granny glasses and a plaid lumberjack shirt.

"I'm in the market for an enlarger," I said. "Probably something used, if you do secondhand equipment."

"We most certainly do," he said. "What's your price range?"

"Five hundred, tops."

"Got a great buy in the back—a Durst AC707 autocolor. Swiss made, in perfect shape, one owner, a bargain at $475."

"What millimeter lens?"

"It comes with two lenses—a 50 and an 80 millimeter. Want to see it?"

I nodded and he disappeared into the storeroom. $475 for an enlarger—it had to be a piece of junk. After all, my old Beseler 45mx back in New Croydon had cost me $3,750 two years ago. Still, I was not in a position to be cavalier with money. That $6,900 trust-fund payment would have to last me until May first, with three months' rent automatically deducted from its total. $750 was the maximum I could spend on darkroom equipment, especially as the apartment still needed a few basic odds and ends. Like a table and chairs.

The salesman returned with the enlarger. A basic no-frills model. He plugged it in and demonstrated the electric auto-focus. It worked smoothly. I studied the lenses. No noticeable scratches or evident optical distortion.

"It's certainly not top of the line," he said, "but as standard enlargers go, it does the job nicely. Comes with a six-month guarantee too."

"Sold," I said. "I'm going to need some chemicals. You stock Ilford?"

"Of course."

"Galleria bromide paper?"

"Naturally."

"And I'll also need an easel, three trays, a safety light, a neg focuser, a developing canister, a changing bag, and a timer."

"You got it. The name's Dave Petrie, by the way."

I shook his hand and introduced myself.

"New in town, Gary?"

"Yeah."

"This a hobby of yours?"

"No. I get paid for it."

"Thought as much. Well, you'll be pleased to know we offer a 15 percent professional discount to all regular customers."

"Then I'll also take a dozen rolls of Tri-X and a dozen of Ilford HP4."

After he returned with all the goods, he spent several minutes writing up an invoice.

"With tax, that's going to be $742.50."

I withdrew my wad of notes.

"We do take credit cards, if you prefer," he said.

"I always pay in cash."

"Fine by me. You shoot color too?"

"Sometimes."

"Let me throw in a half-dozen FujiPro, on the house."

"No need."

"Hey, it's not every Monday morning I have a pro walk into my shop. Who d'you work for?"

"Bunch of magazines back east."

"No kidding? You know, we've got an amateur photographic society in Mountain Falls. Meets twice a month. I'm sure they'd love to hear about your work . . ."

"Kind of busy right now," I lied, "but maybe in a couple of months, when things ease up . . ."

"What sort of equipment you use?"

"Rolleiflex, Nikkormat, standard stuff."

"Ever own a SpeedGraphic?"

I was about to say yes, but then remembered: Ben Bradford owned one, not you.

"Nah."

"Ever use one?"

"Couple of times."

"Just got a model in the other day. Vintage 1940, perfect condition. Could easily sell it for a grand, but I've decided to hold on to it myself. If you had an hour to spare, I'd really appreciate a couple of pointers . . ."

"Like I said, I'm a bit under the gun with an assignment right now, but . . ."

"I understand. Tell you what. Give me your home number; in a week or so I'll give you a call."

Reluctantly I scribbled down my number.

"Want me to deliver this stuff for you?" Dave asked.

"No need. I'll drop by later in my car."

I walked across Main Street, thinking that Mountain Falls was just a little too friendly for my liking. As soon as I was back in my apartment, I had the strong urge to flee, to pack my bags and light out of town. But where would I run to? A city like Seattle or Portland, where I'd have a better than even chance of bumping into someone I knew? Another midsized place like this one? I'd find myself facing more friendly questions about who I was, where I was coming from. And if I did run out on the lease, Meg Greenwood would be on the phone to Connecticut. I had no option but to stay in Mountain Falls and try to adjust to the inquisitive cordiality of small-town life. Because if I didn't start relaxing here, if I kept regarding every question as a potential threat, I would end up calling attention to myself as a cryptic crank with something to hide.

So, when I returned to Petrie's Cameras later that morning to collect my purchases, I spent half an hour giving Dave a fast lesson on the finer points of SpeedGraphic photography. I even accepted his offer of a cup of coffee, over which we talked tech talk—the high-priced pleasures of working with a Leica, the grainy gradations of Tri-X film, why a Nikon never lets you down. Dave also told me a bit about himself— a refugee from Phoenix who drifted up here after college, and was now married with two kids.

"Running a shop really wasn't what I had in mind when I came to Montana," he said. "But the big problem with

Mountain Falls is that, though the lifestyle is great, you can't support a family as a jobbing photographer. Just not enough work to go around. Still, Beth and I . . ."

"You wife's named Beth?" I said.

"Yeah. Anyway, the way Beth and I see it, you want to live in a place like Montana, you've got to make some trade-offs. Guess everything in life is a trade-off, isn't it?"

I left Petrie's Cameras on "good guy" terms with Dave, promising to stop by for a beer once my work pressures eased. As I drove away, I regretted the fact that his was the only photographic outlet in town. He wanted to be my friend, and I couldn't afford friends.

I spent the next few days assembling my darkroom. I gave the window in the small bedroom three coats of black paint. I bought two narrow trestle tables. One became my dry bench, housing the enlarger, the easel, and the timer. The other was my wet bench, containing all chemical trays. I rigged up a clothesline for drying prints. I stapled a thick black curtain over the door to trap light. I installed a small extractor fan in the window to make certain that the chemicals didn't destroy an exorbitant number of brain cells. I replaced the existing naked lightbulb with a two-way safety light. I used the Nikkormat to expose a roll of film around the house and test the enlarger. It worked perfectly. Not the absolute, consummate detail that my old Beseler used to provide, but more than adequate when it came to delivering a crisp image.

I hung up the first print to dry. It showed the two windows of the sitting room, whited out after a fresh snowfall. It looked as if the glass had been whitewashed to keep the world at bay.

The snow eased a few days later. I grabbed my camera case and a half-dozen rolls of Tri-X, then headed east on a tiny backroad marked RTE. 200. It was cold. Ten below, according to the local forecast on NPR, and the MG's heater still wasn't delivering the goods when it came to preventing frostbite. But the sky was cloudless, the sun at full wattage, the banked snow incandescent as I twisted my way toward the Continental Divide.

The road bisected the Garnet Range—somber, austere mountains that defined the horizon. Unlike the august imperial Tetons, this corner of the Rockies gave off an aura of melancholia, of being dwarfed by the immensity of the land, the sky. What lonely terrain. It accentuated the feeling that you had entered a realm where geography was immeasurable, where there was no such thing as spatial limits or borders.

Outside the town of Lincoln, I stopped at a roadhouse—a general store and saloon. I grabbed the Nikkormat and sauntered inside. It was like entering a forgotten era. Sawdust floors, old wooden shelves stacked with canned goods, a soda fountain with hand-action syrup pumps, a long zinc bar where a couple of sullen men with lined faces sat drinking neat whiskey. Behind the bar was a gnarled woman in a floral-print smock. She noticed the camera slung over my shoulder.

"Photographer?" she asked as I took a seat at the bar.

I nodded. "Mind if I take a few shots here?"

She glanced at her customers. "Buy 'em a round, there should be no problem."

I tossed ten dollars on the bar and went to work. The light was terrific—slanting shafts of winter sun beaming through the grimy windows, heightening the low cloud of cigarette smoke that hung above the bar. I worked quickly, concentrating on the faces of the drinkers. I also shot a dead-on portrait of the manageress framed between the soda pumps and a large yellowing photograph of Jim Reeves.

"You git what you want?" she asked after I finished shooting her.

"Yes, ma'am. Much obliged."

"What you drinkin'?"

"A little early for me," I said.

"What you drinkin'?" It wasn't a question.

"Bourbon, I guess."

She reached behind the bar for a bottle of Hiram Walker, poured me a shot glass. I downed it in one go. It had a cheap burn. She took out a pencil stub, licked it, and scribbled something on a slip of paper.

"Gonna expect a copy of my picture," she said, handing me the paper. "A deal?"

"A deal," I said.

I drove farther east, negotiating a spectacular high-wire act of a mountain pass that crossed the Continental Divide. I entered Lewis and Clark County. The road was devoid of houses, billboards, truck stops, or any other hints of late-twentieth-century life. Just a long strip of blacktop, snaking its way through high country. Eventually I did come across a gas station. Two ancient pumps, a battered garage. A kid around seventeen came out to fill my car. He had a frizzy beard, bad acne, a baseball cap, and a battered parka worn over oil-splattered overalls. I convinced him to pose in front of the pumps. He obliged, then asked if his wife and baby son could be part of a picture.

"Great idea," I said.

He disappeared into the garage. A moment later, this wisp of an adolescent—she couldn't have been more than sixteen—came out cradling a tiny infant, bundled up heavily against the cold.

"My wife, Delores," the pump jockey said.

Delores chewed gum. She wore a faded Michael Jackson sweatshirt, dabbled with baby-food stains. I found it hard to look at the little boy, so I quickly posed the family between the two pumps, the background framed by that decrepit garage and the empty snowbound terrain beyond. I shot a dozen exposures, paid for my gas, wrote down their address, and promised to send them a print in the mail.

I returned to Mountain Falls just before sundown and went straight to my darkroom. By late evening, I was poring over the developed negatives and circled nine frames with a red china marker. I printed them. I hung them up to dry. I ate a midnight meal of scrambled eggs and two glasses of low-grade California wine. I returned to the darkroom and scrutinized my handiwork, rejecting four of the prints outright. But the five that remained pleased me. The barroom faces were strongly delineated. You saw hard, creased features tempered by an all-purpose weariness. The smoky atmosphere of the general store was understated. It augmented the image, but didn't swamp it. You could tell immediately that this was a mountain dive deep in the American West, but your attention fixed upon the subdued faces of these early-morning drinkers.

The portrait of the manageress was a little arch—she really did look like the original wizened, tough broad—but the surrounding detail made the picture. Her gnarled hand pulling down an old soda spray. The bottle of Hiram Walker at her elbow. Jim Reeves smiling beatifically behind her.

One of the gas station shots also made the cut. It showed the pump jockey and his adolescent wife standing side by side. The baby was cradled low in his arms. They were trying to smile, but the rusty pumps, the tumbledown garage, the forsaken terrain all emphasized the bleakness of their prospects. They looked like kids shellshocked into adult responsibility and now residing in the ultimate dead end.

I drank another glass of wine and continued studying the prints. The ones I rejected showed all my old tendencies toward self-consciousness; the five that worked did so because they didn't impose an artful eye on the subject matter. When I concentrated on faces—and let them define the composition—everything else fell into place. So why not keep concentrating on faces?

The next morning I mailed the promised prints to the general store manageress and the gas station couple. I did not enclose a return address. Leaving the post office, I was on the road again. Heading north past the iced expanses of Flathead Lake to the town of Bigfork. It was gentrified Montana in extremis. New bleached wood houses. Big flashy four-wheel-drive vehicles. Designer denim outlets. Three boutiques specializing in New West artifacts. I persuaded the very blonde, very svelte owner of one such establishment to pose in front of a cigar-store Indian. The price of this artifact—$1,750—was prominently displayed. I shot two young ski dudes—both in Stetsons and RayBans—standing in front of a frozen yogurt emporium. The local bookshop owner—flowery skirt, embroidered vest, waist-length gray hair—was photographed in front of a shelf with a sign: NEW WEST.

I shot four rolls of Tri-X in Bigfork, and managed to cull just three prints that satisfied me: pictures where the faces dominated, where they told you everything you needed to know about the individual and his milieu.

For the next three weeks, I took constant day trips out of Mountain Falls. I went to Whitefish and shot gamblers working the slots at a local casino. I went to Kalispell and photographed the owner of an auto wrecker's. In the town of Essex, the manager of an isolated railway lodge posed for me on the empty station platform. In Butte, two miners stood gazing at sunset over the town slag heap. I roamed everywhere west of the Continental Divide. I ignored landscapes. I kept concentrating on faces.

By the beginning of March, I had sixty prints I could live with. I also had a cash-flow problem, as I had shot over 150 rolls of film, and had bought myself a few photographic essentials (like a decent tripod and light meter). I was down to $1,900. April's rent would still have to be deducted from that figure, leaving me just $1,350 to cover the nine weeks until the next trust-fund payment rendered me solvent again.

"Sure you don't feel like opening an account with us?" Dave Petrie asked me one morning.

"Thanks for the offer, but I'm a cash guy."

"You're also my best customer. And I'd like you to have the ability to stop by, grab some film, and not worry about having to hit a cash machine beforehand."

"Much appreciated, but I hate credit."

"When are we gonna have that beer?" Dave asked. "And when are you gonna have a night free to come over, meet Beth and the kids?"

"When this project is wrapped."

"Must be a biggie, considering the amount of film you're buying. Gonna make you some big money?"

"I doubt it."

I did frequently wonder where I might be able to hawk my burgeoning collection of Montana portraits. For a while, I tinkered with the idea of dispatching a portfolio to that editor at *Destinations* who was on the verge of commissioning Gary. Or maybe reapproaching one of the New York photographic agencies that came so close to representing him. But I was still wary about making contact with anyone who knew Gary. Just as I was also apprehensive about the idea of having anything to do with life back east. Though a university bookshop near me stocked *The New York Times, The New Yorker, Harper's,* and a slew of other Manhattan-based journals, I resisted buying them. I didn't want to know about Gotham life, didn't want to catch up on tristate news, feared maintaining an ongoing interest in Wall Street. I looked upon the Continental Divide as a sort of defensive frontier, not to be breached. So I stopped crossing it, developing a superstitious belief that, as long as I stayed due west of this watershed, I would be safe. And I wasn't going to tempt fate by trying to do business with New York. Nor did I feel secure enough as yet to start making contact with magazines in Los Angeles, San Francisco, Seattle. Best to maintain a low profile and live cheaply off the trust fund.

There was one snow-free week in the middle of March. Then the blizzards started again. Ten straight days of whiteout. It kept me off the road, kept me confined to barracks at the Frontier Apartments, gave me cabin fever. So, one night, I braved the snow and walked up Main Street in search of liquid entertainment. I decided to bypass the Mountain Pass (it was packed with poker-machine junkies). I didn't really want to venture into Fred's Hole. So I figured it was time to give Eddie's Place a try.

It was a loud joint: a huge horseshoe bar three deep with drinkers, a half-dozen pool tables in the back, Bob Seger blaring on the loudspeakers, *Monday Night Football* on the thirty-two-inch television, a mixed crowd of university types and a higher class of redneck.

I managed to secure a stool at the bar. I ordered a Bud Light.

"You always drink low-octane shit?" asked the guy seated next to me. Middle-aged, hangdog eyes, a face I'd seen somewhere before.

"It's not low octane," I said. "You guzzle enough, you get a buzz."

"Maybe . . . but it's still shit," he said. He shouted to the woman working the bar. "Linda, honey—another J&B on the rocks. And pour my friend here a shot of something while you're at it."

"What's it going to be?" she asked me.

"You have Black Bush?" I asked.

"We got it," she said, filling a glass.

"Man's got expensive taste in whiskey," the guy said as Linda lifted a $10 note from the pile of cash in front of him.

"Next round's mine," I said.

"Fine by me," he said. "Rudy Warren."

Yes, I had seen his face before. When he was being thrown out of the Mountain Pass.

"The columnist?" I asked.

"I am flattered."

"Read you all the time. Like your stuff."

"Should have bought you a double. You got a name?"

"Gary," I said.

"Pleased to meet a fan. You're not from California, Gary?"

"No way."

"Good," he said, lighting a cigarette. "Then I'll keep drinking with you. Passing through Mountain Falls?"

"Living here."

"You a masochist? Or are eight-month winters your idea of a good time?"

I gave him my spiel about being on a photographic assignment.

"Oh, you're one of those," he said.

"One of what?"

"An *artiste*. We seem to attract 'em in Mountain Falls. You ask around this bar, you'll find at least a dozen guys writing the great Rocky Mountain novel, painting bullshit New West landscapes, pretending they're Ansel Adams . . ."

"Thank you for turning me into a cultural cliché."

"You offended?"

"Not really."

"I'm disappointed. I usually manage to offend everyone I meet. Just ask my ex-wives."

"How many ex-wives?"

"Three."

"Not bad going."

"And how many times have you been dragged to the alimony cleaners?"

"Zip," I said. "Never married."

"Then you're definitely not from 'round here. Know how you find out if someone's originally from Montana?"

I shook my head.

"You ask him how many car crashes and bad marriages he's managed to survive. If it's over two, you know he's a native."

Rudy said that he was a Mountain Falls lifer. Born and bred here. Educated at the university. Landed a job on the paper in 1976. Never worked or lived anywhere else.

"'Bout five years ago, right around the time I was unloading wife number two, I got approached by the *Seattle Times*. Editor there had read my column, said he liked my style, paid for me to be flown over to meet him. Dumb bastard even offered me a job."

"You didn't take it?"

"The fuck I'd do with myself in Seattle? That town's Yuppie Central. Eighty-two kinds of coffee, aerobics, and they force-feed you sun-dried tomatoes. I was on the next plane back to Mountain Falls."

"There's a cafe near my apartment here that serves twelve different kinds of coffee."

"Tell me about it. Up until 1990, coffee in this state went by the name of Joe. Now you gotta talk Dago to get a cup. And it's all due to guys like you moving here."

I said nothing. He gave me a sardonic smile.

"Still haven't offended you yet, Gary?"

"Nope."

"Shit. I must be off form tonight. Guess I better keep drinking. Linda, two more here."

"It's my round," I said.

"I won't argue with that."

We drank four more rounds, during which Rudy talked nonstop about Mountain Falls.

"Back in the early seventies, you could still buy a house in this town for twenty thousand bucks. Now you're lucky to find a shack for two hundred grand. Fuckin' Californicators. They're killing this state. Y'hear me? Killing Montana acre by acre. Ten more years, we're gonna be a suburb of L.A. *Have a nice day, pardner . . .*"

He was shouting.

"Rudy," Linda the barkeep said, "shut the fuck up."

"Truth hurts, babe."

"Save it for your column, Rudy."

He pointed a finger at Linda. "Know why Miss Gorgeous Ass here hates what I'm saying? 'Cause she's a bitch from Pasadena, that's why."

Linda grabbed Rudy's finger and bent it backward.

"I ain't no bitch, Rudy," she said.

She yanked the finger farther toward the knuckle. Rudy turned white with shock.

"You gonna apologize or am I gonna have to snap your finger in two?"

"I apologize," Rudy said, just on the verge of howling.

She let go of the finger.

"I love a gentleman," Linda said. Then she poured us two more shots.

Rudy fell silent for several minutes. When the pain finally subsided, he downed his whiskey and shuddered.

"You really have a hell of a way with women," I said.

He managed a smile. "Ain't that the truth."

Linda kicked us out at two. We were the last customers in the bar. As we staggered toward the door, she shouted after me:

"Don't let the sonofabitch drive."

"O ye of little faith," Rudy said.

We fell into the street. It was still snowing.

"How're you going to get home?" I asked.

He reached into his pocket, pulled out a bundle of keys. "In my car."

"No way."

"The streets are empty, I am a danger to nobody."

"Except yourself. Give me the keys, Rudy."

"The fuck are you? My nanny, Mary Poppins?"

I snatched the keys out of his hand.

"Shithead," he said, throwing a punch that I easily dodged. He tottered over.

"I'm going home now," I said. "You want your car keys, you follow me."

I turned and started heading up Main Street. After I'd walked a hundred yards, I spun around and was relieved to see Rudy back on his feet, staggering my way. I didn't wait for him to catch up, as the cold was brutal. But it did keep us both moving, and it also served as an antidote to all the booze we'd imbibed. By the time I reached the Frontier Apartments, I felt almost sober again. I waited inside the lobby for a minute or two before Rudy showed up, his shabby black duffel coat dandruffed with snow. The walk had revived him.

"You live here?" he asked as he entered the foyer.

I nodded.

"Think I got up to no good here once with a real-estate broker. Real pain in the ass named Meg Greenwood. Decided a one-night poke was *lurve*. Kept calling me at home, at the paper, finally had to change numbers. Twice. Don't care if your balls feel like concrete—you ever meet that crazy in a bar, at a party, you take a walk. Like, fast."

I laughed. "Come on up, I'll call you a cab."

In the elevator, Rudy asked, "Did I take a swing at you outside Eddie's?"

"You did."

"I connect?"

"No."

"Good."

When we walked into my living room, Rudy emitted a low whistle.

"Will you look at this," he said. "SoHo, Montana."

"Glad you approve," I said. "You know the number of the local cab company?"

"You're one hell of a host. Buy me a beer; then you can kick my ass out."

"I'm tired," I said.

"One lousy beer and I'm outta your life."

I staggered into the kitchen. Rudy followed.

"Man, I ain't seen so much white paint in all my life," he said, eyeing the empty walls. "What you call this school of interior decor? Rocky Mountain Minimalism?"

"Hah," I said.

"Two of those and you'd be laughing."

I extracted two bottles of Rolling Rock from the fridge. I handed him one.

"Much obliged," he said. After taking a long swig, he stared at me long and hard.

"You know, I sure as shit wouldn't want to play poker with you."

"Why's that?" I asked.

"'Cause I bet you're one hell of a bluffer."

I suddenly felt the onset of unease.

"I always lose at poker," I said.

"Don't believe it," he said.

"Try me—you'll make some money."

"No thanks. Poker and me's like the divorce courts—a no-win situation. But I bet you know all the tricks: how to keep your counsel, give away as little information as possible . . ."

"What are you saying here?"

"Just that I've spent the last five hours drinking with you and you've told me shit about yourself. And being the nosy journo that I am, I guess it makes me wonder: *'Why?'*"

"Maybe because, unlike you, I don't need to give everyone the story of my life after the second drink."

"Maybe so," he said, smiling. He had made me uncomfortable—and he was enjoying that knowledge.

"Let's see about that cab," I said.

I walked back into the living room and picked up the phone. I dialed Information. It took twenty rings before the operator answered. She gave me the number of a local taxi company. I called them. After forty rings, I put down the phone.

"They don't answer," I said, heading toward the kitchen.

"Kinda figure they wouldn't. After twelve on a snowy night they always call it quits."

He was no longer in my kitchen. He was in my darkroom, leafing through a stack of Montana portraits I'd left on my dry table. He looked up as I entered.

"All your own stuff?" he asked.

I nodded. He said nothing; he just kept flipping through the pile of fifty prints, a small smile occasionally crossing his lips.

"I've been in that fucking gas station," he said, holding up a shot of the pump jockey and his family. He moved on to the next print.

"Sonofabitch," he said, grinning at the portrait of the road-house manageress. "It's Madge the Menace."

"You know her?"

"Hell, yes. She's barred me from her place at least twice." He held up his now empty bottle of Rolling Rock. "Could you score me another beer, pardner?"

"Getting kind of late," I said. "How are you gonna get home?"

"You got a couch?"

"I guess . . ."

"Then you've got a guest."

I didn't want a guest—especially one who intimated that I had something to hide.

"Listen," I said, "I've got an early start in the morning—"

"You want me outta here, gimme my keys. And if the cops stop me on the way back, I'll just blame you for letting me loose . . ."

"I'll get you the beer," I said.

Still holding the stack of pictures, he reeled into the living room and flopped on the couch. I extracted the last two Rolling Rocks from the icebox in the kitchen. Then I handed him a bottle and collapsed in an armchair opposite him. He drank the beer while working his way back through the pile of photographs.

"Well . . . ?" I finally said.

He looked up. "You're asking for an opinion?"

"I guess I am."

A long pause.

"They're fucking terrific."

"Really?"

"Best gallery of Montana faces I've ever seen."

"You serious?"

"They were bogus horseshit I'd be the first to tell you. But you've got something here, I look at these faces and I think: *my* people, my fucking Montana. And y'know why these pictures are so good? Because you aren't trying to be *authentic.* Aren't trying to make everyone look like some quaint fucking Western character. You've just shot 'em as is. And you've gotten 'em bull's-eye."

He flashed a skeptical smile. "So you really are a photographer."

I didn't know what to say. "I suppose so."

"You don't sound convinced yourself," he said.

"I'm just . . . flattered, that's all."

"What are you gonna do with 'em?"

"A book, I suppose."

"Hell, it's gotta be a book. And I'll even give you a title: *Faces from the No-Bullshit State.*"

He kicked off his shoes, stretched out on the couch, handed me back the photos.

"Now get me a blanket," he said. "Preferably one without fleas."

I dropped the prints back in the darkroom, then dug out the old bedspread that came with the ancient bed I threw out. It still stank of mildew.

"Gracious living," Rudy said as I threw it over him.

I tossed his car keys on a table. "Sorry," I said. "I'm not really equipped for guests."

"Or for drunks. Two bottles of beer is piss-poor hospitality. But, seeing that you're up, how 'bout a glass of water. Just half full."

"Okay, Your Highness."

When I came back from the kitchen, Rudy reached into his mouth and extracted two full sets of upper and lower dentures. Then he dropped them in the glass and set it down by the couch. I flinched. He noticed.

"You sure I still haven't offended you yet?" he said, his toothless mouth making him sound like a rubber-voiced children's comedian.

"Night," I said. "And thanks for the kind words about the photos."

"I'm never fucking kind," Rudy Warren said. "Just accurate."

I flicked off the room light and pitched into bed.

I woke at eleven, vowing to convert to Mormonism, Islam, the Moonies or any other faith that proscribed the use of alcohol. It took about five minutes to empty my bladder. It took an additional ten minutes to clean up the urine-sprayed bathroom floor. A shower helped restore a degree of equilibrium. But I was still feeling shaky when I lurched into the living room, fully expecting to find Rudy Warren comatose on the couch.

But the couch was empty. So too was the glass that contained his teeth. The car keys were no longer on the table, their place taken by a near empty beer bottle with a cigarette floating in its base.

"Rudy?" I said, thinking he might be in the kitchen.

No response was forthcoming. He was gone. And the gracious sonofabitch hadn't even left a note.

I made myself a mug of weak instant coffee. I gagged on the first gulp. The second gulp went down a little easier, so I carried it with me into the darkroom, flipping on a light switch as I entered.

The red whorehouse glow of the safety lamp suited my toxic condition. But as soon as I glanced over at the dry bench, I was fumbling for the other switch that turned on the overhead fluorescent tubes.

As the room convulsed with white light, I blinked with shock. My stack of Montana prints was gone.

4

I PANICKED. I paced the floor of my living room, not really knowing what to do next. I cursed myself for going to Eddie's, for allowing myself to get sucked into conversation with a lush, and—worst of all—for playing the Good Samaritan and inviting Rudy back here. Why didn't I do the right thing and let the bastard crash his car? Or freeze to death on the street?

And why the fuck did he take the prints? A dozen story lines raced around my skull, all of them paranoid. Sensing that I was "A Man with a Past," he'd absconded with the photos and would demand a ransom for their return (Dumb scenario: if he really wanted to screw me, he'd have taken the negatives—which, thankfully, I found untouched in the darkroom). Maybe he was going to hawk the prints as his own. Or organize an exhibition—"Rudy Warren: A Montana Eye." Or perhaps—and this crazed scenario alarmed me the most—he had a friend who was a cop. Some drinking buddy named Cliff or Wilbur on the verge of being drummed out of the local force and therefore in need of a big, redemptive arrest. "Check this new guy out," Rudy would say, spreading my prints out on the bar. "Dude says he's a photographer from back east, but the minute you give him the third degree he breaks out in a sweat . . ."

I picked up the phone. I dialed *The Montanan* and asked to be put through to Rudolph Warren. I got an answering machine.

"Hi, Rudy Warren here. If you're calling to complain about something I've written, here are a few ground rules. I don't answer letters and I certainly don't answer crank calls. If, however, you're just calling to leave a message, you know what to do: name and number after the beep."

I forced myself to sound very calm, very friendly.

"Rudy, Gary Summers calling. Hope you got over your hangover. Could you give me a ring at 555-8809 when you have a chance? Thanks."

I hung up and immediately dialed Information, in search of his home number. It was unlisted. Shit, shit, shit.

Over the next two hours, I called *The Montanan* three more times. I kept getting connected to his answering machine. I left no further messages.

To try to stay occupied, I went to my darkroom and began the slow, laborious process of reprinting the fifty shots that he had stolen. Eventually, around four, the phone rang. I dove for it.

"Gary Summers?" It was a woman's voice, a voice I'd never heard before.

"Yes."

"Hi. You don't know me, but Rudy Warren told me all about you . . ."

"Really?" I said, bracing myself for what might come next.

"Sorry, I should introduce myself. I'm Anne Ames—the photo editor at *The Montanan*. Anyway, Rudy walked into my office this morning with a bundle of your prints. Tossed them on my desk and said that I should hire you on the spot."

I let out a little laugh. A laugh of immense, overwrought relief.

"So that's what he wanted with the prints," I said.

"You mean, he didn't tell you he was going to show them to me?"

"Uh, no. But, from what I can gather so far, Rudy is a man of ongoing surprises."

Now it was her turn to laugh. "That is the understatement of the year," she said. "Anyway, I think they're great. As you can imagine, I see a lot of 'Real Montana' stuff, but you've really done something fresh here. And I was just wondering if they were already promised to another paper or periodical?"

"Not yet."

"Great—then maybe we can do some business. You free tomorrow around noon?"

As soon as I agreed to the appointment, I wanted to cancel it, to call back this Anne Ames and feed her some lie about a New York magazine just calling me to buy all the photographs. But my free-floating fears were tempered by vanity. Someone in the professional photographic game had seen my work, liked it, and now sounded as if she wanted to buy it. All right, it was just the picture editor of Montana's biggest newspaper— but still, a door had opened. It was an opportunity, a shot. I had to take it.

So I showed up at the offices of *The Montanan* at noon the next day. The reception area overlooked an open-plan news-room—a tidy, functional sprawl of desks and computer termi-nals and neatly dressed reporters going about their business with technocratic calm. Even in Montana, journalism had been corporatized—and it struck me that, within this sterile, sedate environment, Rudy Warren must have seemed like the Wild Man of Borneo, a role, no doubt, he worked hard at per-fecting.

"Well, hi there."

Anne Ames was in her mid-thirties. Tall, willowy, stylishly cut strawberry-blonde hair, clear skin free of makeup. She wore well-pressed denim jeans and a denim shirt open to the sternum. I glanced at her hands. No wedding ring.

Her handshake was firm. I could see her taking me in, siz-ing me up. I'd lost all the weight I'd put on during my initial Flying Dutchman month on the interstates. My face had become as gaunt as Gary's, I'd gotten used to tying my now shoulder-length hair into a ponytail, and had even learned to live with permanent designer stubble. When I stared at myself in the bathroom mirror, I no longer saw Ben Bradford; rather, an emergency edition of Gary Summers. I still hadn't perfected the smirk, however—so I returned Anne's greeting with a nervous smile.

"First time at our offices?" she asked, leading me through the newsroom.

"That's right."

"We only moved into this building a year ago. Before that, we were in a big old warehouse right on the river. It was a dump, but at least we all knew we were working on a newspaper. Now, every time I come through the door, I have to remind myself that I'm not working for IBM."

She arched her eyebrows mischievously.

"You can now see why Rudy does most of his writing up at Eddie's Place. Know what he did the first day we moved in here? Installed a spittoon next to his computer terminal. Stu Simmons—that's the editor—got the point. Told Rudy he could work from home—which, for him, means Eddie's. That's where you met him?"

"I'm afraid so."

"Not exactly the most salubrious spot in town, but compared to the Mountain Pass, it's like the Oak Room at the Plaza."

"You're from New York?" I said, suddenly uneasy.

"The 'burbs. Armonk."

"Home of IBM," I said.

"I know," she said with another touch of amusement. "My dad ran their public-affairs department for thirty-four years."

Her office was a chaotic tag sale of prints and negatives and marked-up page proofs. There was something reassuring about its untidiness—a hint of a rebellious streak lurking behind her well-scrubbed appearance.

"Welcome to the photo junkyard," she said, motioning me

toward a chair on which lay a half-eaten sandwich. I didn't sit down.

"Jane, honey," she said, "what's your lunch doing there?"

Jane—a chubby-faced kid around twenty-two—turned away from a filing cabinet and immediately scooped the sandwich off the chair.

"Thanks for not squishing it," she said to me.

"That's the mark of a real gentleman in Jane's book," Anne said. "Jane—this is the famous Gary Summers."

"Oh yeah, the faces guy," she said. "Love the pics."

"Thanks," I said.

"Jane's my assistant. How 'bout making us two cups of coffee, honey? And this time, try to boil the water first."

"Milk and five sugars as usual?" Jane said sweetly, then left the room.

"Great kid, Jane," she said, digging through a pile of papers on her desk. "And almost as disorganized as me."

She found my photos under a pile of requisition forms.

"So, Mr. Gary Summers," she said, flipping through the prints, "on the basis of what I've seen so far, you are one hot-shit photographer. Which leads me to ask: What the hell are you doing in Mountain Falls, Montana?"

I was about to give her my usual spiel about the book I was allegedly working on, but sensed that she might see through this ruse. Just as I also sensed that, were I to bullshit her about being on assignment for assorted New York magazines, she'd spend an hour or two on the phone, checking out my credentials. So I decided to play it straight. Well, sort of straight.

"I was freelancing in New York. I wasn't really scoring much in the way of work. I was getting sick of just missing out on commissions. I decided to head west, maybe try my luck in Seattle. I pulled in here for a night, liked what I saw, thought: Why not stay a while? End of story."

I could tell she liked my directness, the fact that I didn't try to gloss over my failure to cut it in Manhattan.

"And what made you decide to start shooting faces?"

"A total accident," I said and told her about stopping at the roadhouse near the Continental Divide.

"Best ideas always start as accidents," she said. "And we'd like to benefit from this one. Now that I've shown your pictures to the editor, he's as keen on them as I am, and what he suggests is running a photographic feature every Saturday inside our weekend section. We'll call it 'Montana Faces,' and use one of your prints each week. Initially we're going to try it for six weeks, and we're willing to pay a hundred and twenty-five dollars a picture."

"That's kind of low, isn't it?" I said.

"Welcome to Montana," she said. "We're not exactly *Vanity Fair* here, we already have four photographers on staff, and what I'm offering is well above our normal rates."

"It's still below what I'd be prepared to accept," I said, deciding to hold my ground.

"Which is what?"

I plucked a figure out of the air. "Two-fifty a print."

"In your dreams," she said. "One-seventy. Final offer."

"One seventy-*five*."

"What are you, a lawyer?" she said.

I managed a laugh. It took work.

"Absolutely," I said. "Can't you tell? One seventy-five, then?"

"You push a hard bargain, mister."

"You're still getting me cheap."

"They'll kick my ass at the next budget meeting."

I found myself giving her a flirtatious smile.

"I'm sure you're able to kick ass back."

She returned the smile. "Charm will get you nowhere. But I'm not going to argue over five bucks. One seventy-five. Done deal."

We shook hands. She said that she'd like to hold on to the stack of photos for a few more days to decide on the final six prints that would eventually run in the paper. The phone rang on her desk. She answered it, then put the call on hold.

"Got to take that—it's the editor," she said. "Nice doing

business with you. I'll be in touch in a day or two."

I stood up.

"One last thing," she said. "Are you really from New Croydon, Connecticut?"

I suddenly wanted to evaporate.

"How did you know that?" I said.

"Meg Greenwood."

"Friend of yours?"

"Everyone knows each other in Mountain Falls," she said, giving me a final flirty grin. "I'd better not keep the boss waiting. See you around."

On my way back to the apartment, I found myself in the pincer grip of major anxiety. Questions, questions. How much had Meg Greenwood told her? Did she call me a sleaze? Inform Anne how I'd managed to wangle the apartment from her at a cut-rate price and without a reference? Said how I charmed her until the lease was signed, then fed her some garbage about a phantom girlfriend back in New York? (What name did I give her again?) And why—Jesus, *why*—did I flirt with Anne Ames? Because I'm a dimwit, that's why. No doubt, she's on the phone to Meg right now. "Yeah, I met him," she's saying. "And he really does act as if he's got something to hide . . ."

I spent the next two days locked in my apartment. I finished reprinting my collection of Montana faces. I fought the urge to leave town. Late one afternoon, I found myself staring out the window and watched as a guy my age walked down the street, holding the hand of his four-year-old son. I turned away, drew the blinds, retreated back to my darkroom. The darkroom was the only place I felt secure anymore.

Around six that evening the phone rang.

"Gary Summers?" Another woman's voice I hadn't heard before.

"That's right."

"This is Judy Wilmers. I run the New West Gallery on Cromford Street. I'm also a friend of Anne Ames and she dropped over this afternoon with your photographs. Very impressive work."

"Uh, thanks."

"Listen, if you're not too busy tomorrow, might we be able to meet for coffee?"

Why, oh why did I land myself in a small town?

5

THE NEW WEST GALLERY was located on a narrow side street off Main. It was an old showroom redecorated to look like the sort of generic art emporium you now found on every street corner in Soho or Tribeca. A concrete floor painted black. Stark white walls, spot lighting, a cafe with chrome tables and chairs. There was a collection of abstract canvases—under the collective title "Prairie Earth Dreams"—currently on view.

Judy Wilmers wore a long denim skirt and a lot of Native American bangles. Her gray hair cascaded down to her waist. She smelled of sandalwood soap and seaweed shampoo. We sat in the cafe. She drank rosehip tea; I slurped down a double espresso. She gave me the *Reader's Digest* version of her life. She was from the Bay Area and used to run a small gallery in Pacific Heights, but moved here in '86 when her first marriage broke up and she needed to "re-alter the parameters" of her middle age.

"Like, here I was with a thousand square feet of prime Pacific Heights shop frontage. Bought in '79 for $22,000, mortgage cleared, now valued at $415,000 in February of '86, thanks to Ronnie Reagan and his voodoo economics. I mean, there's positive equity and then there's *karmic* positive equity, know what I mean?

"Now around this time, my husband, Gus, is deep into this midlife thing involving an acupuncturist from Sausalito. I'm distressed, I'm conflicted. But eventually I decide—if he wants closure, I'll give him closure. So I sell the gallery, book myself in for a retreat at this great holistic five-star resort in Idaho. Anyway, one day when I've had enough of the ginseng diet they've got me on, I rent a car, drive east two hours into Montana. Mountain Falls is the first town I pull into. I look around. I see the university. Note the burgeoning arts scene. Like the regenerative vibe. Within half an hour, I pass by this place. A Goodyear showroom up for sale. I call the realtor, make inquiries. The boom hasn't hit Montana. He's asking $29,000. We settled on $26,500. Another $18,000 for the renovation and Mountain Falls has its first major gallery of contemporary Western art."

"It must be worth a little more than 47k today," I said.

Without batting an eye, she said: "If market trends continue to hold, $319,000. Of course, my accountant now wants me to diversify—to open branches of New West in Bozeman and Whitefish, maybe even consider a gallery in Seattle. But you know that diversification has an inherent risk structure that needs to be backed up by considerable liquidity. And why, I asked myself, should I gamble with equity?"

I nodded, wondering if she too had once gone to law school.

"I mean, this is the nineties. Small is beautiful. You have a vision, you expand that vision within manageable synergistic boundaries, otherwise you endanger the purity of that vision through overextension. But that doesn't mean that you don't look at the potential for market growth. And when Anne showed me your photos, I knew I wasn't just looking at a potential exhibition, but also a remarkable overview of the New West weltanschauung. And one with far-reaching potential."

I decided to cut to the chase. "You mean, you think they'll sell?"

"Like hotcakes. What you've done—magnificently, in my opinion—is capture the true conflicted spirit of this state today. You look at those faces, you think: Here is the grit, the pained *texture* that is contemporary Montana. And even real Montanans have responded well to them—and, believe me, a native here *never* has a good thing to say about an outsider. Especially if the outsider has had the chutzpah to photograph or paint their sacrosanct state. So to get someone like Rudy Warren telling me that you are going to be the Walker Evans of Montana—"

"You know Rudy Warren?" I asked.

She looked at me strangely. "Of course I know Rudy. He was my second husband."

"*You* were married to *the* Rudolph Warren?"

"Don't look so shocked," she said. "Everyone's entitled to a mistake or two. Anyway, it only lasted six months."

I finally understood why Rudy had such a thing about Californication.

Judy got down to business—a negotiating game she played with karmic ruthlessness. A show had just fallen through; she had a slot in just six weeks' time, but she needed a wider range of prints from which to "compose" the exhibition. She was pleased to hear that I had around thirty other recent photographs that I might consider putting forward for inclusion. The gallery would pay for framing, naturally. She was gauging a price of around $150 per print and wanted a 50/50 split on all sales. She also wanted a 35 percent taste of all subsidiary rights (books, print journalism, postcards, calendars, even reproduction on the Internet), not to mention a 15 percent kickback on all future gallery sales, both within the contiguous forty-eight states and abroad.

I told her to get a life. But this was standard gallery practice, she countered. Then I didn't want a show here. But it would be more than just a show, it would *metamorphose* into an entire national marketing campaign that would make my name. You want the show, I said, you agree to a sixty-forty split, with no future hold over any subsidiary rights. She wouldn't budge from her position. Fine then. I stood up, picking up my prints.

"Thanks for the coffee," I said.

"Don't you think you're being a little vain for someone who has never exhibited before? I mean, who are *you*, Gary? From what Anne told me, you even admitted that you came to Mountain Falls because things weren't working out workwise back in New York. And now, when the best gallery in Montana offers you your first major exhibition—and on the basis of unsolicited work—you get difficult about contractual matters. Don't you want this show?"

"Not if I'm going to be manipulated out of a significant share of future terrestrial copyright . . ."

I caught myself before I descended into further legal jargon.

"If you want to renegotiate terms," I said, "you have my home number."

With that, I left.

I was, at first, relieved to have blown off Judy Wilmers. It would have been far too much exposure, I kept telling myself. Best to let the six pictures run in the newspaper, then withdraw quietly from view. But though I continued to reassure myself that I had done the right thing, a vainglorious voice inside my skull kept niggling me with comments like: She loved the work, she offered you a show, for Jesus' sake . . . and what do you do? Throw it all away by getting all anal and legalistic.

Still, at least I would never have to hear her use the word "conflicted" again. Even though I myself was deeply conflicted right now.

On my way back to the apartment, I stopped at Benson's— the department store on Main Street—and shelled out $70 for a cheap answering machine. I rigged it up as soon as I was home. I didn't change the robotic recorded message on the tape. Instead, I picked up a camera and hit the road, driving down through the Leantree Forest due south of town—mile after mile of slender firs, fronting the rushing waters of the Copperhead. It was a fine day, snow quilted the landscape, the mercury was considering the warm high twenties, and the sun was radiating a nice hangover haze. Around twenty miles out of town, I pulled off the road, hiked down to the river, and happened upon two banker types engaged in a spot of ice fishing. They were both in their fifties, well padded, bespectacled—small-town Babbitts, wearing expensive hip boots and Gore-Tex parkas. They'd found a small corner of the river that wasn't frozen and were seated on little canvas fold-out stools, passing a flask of whiskey, shooting the shit about some new bond issue and other outdoorsy matters. I broke a rule of mine and decided not to ask permission to photograph them. Instead I stood, sniper style, behind a tree, the telephoto lens focused on their jowls, clicking away, the rapid flow of the water masking the sound of the camera motor. I felt like a spy and relished the role of hidden observer. They couldn't pose because they couldn't see me. I was the invisible eye. It was the part I was happiest playing. You drifted through life unnoticed. I wanted to stay the invisible eye. Permanently. But Mountain Falls was gradually forcing me out of this role, because, as I was discovering, you can never remain invisible forever in a small town. It was simply not allowed.

When I reached the apartment just before sunset, there were four messages on my new answering machine. The first and the third were from the karmically challenged Judy Wilmers, asking me to reconsider the show.

"I am sure we can reach creative and commercial détente, Gary," she said in message number one. "Not just détente, a true rapproachment. Muse on the nature of potential . . . and call me back."

In her second message, she excised the meditative bullshit and got down to proverbial brass tacks.

"Okay, here's how the deal's going to work. I agree to a 60/40 split in your favor; you give me a twelve-month option to act as your international agent and handle subsidiary rights for 35 percent of all sales, and 10 percent of your commission on all gallery shows I set up. At the end of the year, all rights revert to you. Believe me, as a friend, you'd never land such an advan-tageous deal in New York or San Francisco . . ."

"As a friend." Did this woman have any sense of irony?

In between the two sales shticks from Judy there was a monologue from Rudy Warren. Judging from the blaring background din of bad music and bad behavior, he was calling from Eddie's Place.

"Hey, photographer. Gather you hit it off with Ms. Ames and you're about to become a regular at *The Montanan*. I also gather that you refused to be cowed into submission by that larcenist known as ex-wife number two. I like you more and more. But do understand: Having set you on the path to suc-cess, I will now expect undying fealty. You will also be required to pick up all future bar bills. Which brings me to the point of this message: I'm at 'my office' all evening if you want some low-rent company."

The final message was from Anne, asking me to call her mobile phone. She was in her car when she answered.

"Don't the natives here take a dim view of cellular phones?" I asked.

"Yeah—but they all have them. Listen, I've chosen the six prints we're going to use. Want to see what I've picked . . . and scam dinner off *The Montanan* at the same time?"

"Didn't know the photo editor had an expense account."

"It's a real generous two hundred bucks a year—which means I'm going to blow half of it tonight. Be outside your door in five minutes."

And then she hung up before I could try to wangle out of the evening.

She took me to Le Petit Place. It was the best restaurant in Mountain Falls. Located in a disused railway station at the end of town, it was all redbrick walls and angular black post-modernist tables, and George Winston on the stereo system and a menu that described itself as New Pacific . . . even though we were around 500 miles from that body of water. Our "waitperson" was called Calvin. He recommended the sea bass with shiitake mushrooms, garnished with vegetable tempura. The special salad this evening was hydroponic lettuce with crème fraîche and dill. The wine of the week was a "beauty from Oregon"—a Rex Hill chardonnay—"with just the right oaky atmospherics."

"You know how to make a martini?" I asked.

"Of course," he said, sounding slightly offended by my patronizing tone.

"A Bombay Gin martini then, straight up, very dry, with four olives."

"And madame?" Calvin asked.

"Madame would like the same," she said.

"*Madame,*" I said with a laugh. "The guy's probably never been east of Bozeman."

"No need to give him a hard time," she said.

"I wasn't giving him a hard time. I was simply inquiring as to whether he had a degree in martini science. It is a science, you know."

"You were playing the SEA."

"What's that?"

"Superior Eastern Asshole," she said, smiling sweetly.

The drinks arrived; we ordered our food. She lifted her glass.

"To our collaboration," she said.

We clinked glasses. I sipped my martini and felt its liquid novocaine numb the back of my throat.

"A decent martini," I said.

"Don't sound so damn surprised."

"I just never expected martinis or hydroponic lettuce in Montana."

"Oh, I get it. You're one of these blow-ins who hate the idea that interesting food, foreign films, and decent bookshops might just have a place in Mountain Falls. You want 'the Real West'—greasy steerburgers, *Debbie Does Dallas* at the local fleapit, and a cigar store where you can buy *Hustler* and other stroke books. No wonder you hit it off with Rudy Warren."

I laughed. "Was he really married to that Bay Area flake?"

"Life can be stranger than fiction. I think Judy saw him as the ultimate Montana character and kind of fell for his rough-and-tumble charms."

"It only lasted like six months, right?" I asked.

"More like two hours. Judy was new here at the time . . . and not exactly tuned to the right frequency."

"You think she is now?"

"Don't let the Grace Slick appearance fool you. She really knows how to sell her artists."

"Knows how to screw them too, from what I can gather."

"Yeah, I heard that you two ran into a little contractual conflict . . ."

"News travels fast."

"It's Mountain Falls, what d'you expect? Anyway, I believe she's made you a new offer. You going to accept it?"

"I haven't decided yet. Her Marin County bullshit gets on my nerves."

"Tell me about it. We're sort of friends, but after an evening with Judy, I want to go out and shoot a Sufi mystic. Still, she runs a great gallery, and she does have connections on the Coast. I would try to reach some kind of accommodation with her."

"Well, the terms are still outrageous."

"You are one tough-assed negotiator, Mr. Summers. Makes me wonder if you were something on Wall Street in a previous life."

"Didn't know you believed in reincarnation," I said, dodging the question.

"Everyone who comes to Montana believes in reincarnation. That's why they ended up here. Forget that 'Big Sky Country' bullshit. This is the personal reinvention state."

"Did you reinvent yourself?" I asked.

"You could say that—considering that Mountain Falls is a long way from Armonk, New York. But it wasn't a straightforward transition from Westchester County to Montana."

"Bet you went to one of those progressive colleges back east. Sarah Lawrence. Bennington. Hampshire."

"Wrong. Skidmore."

"No shit. Why aren't you wearing a plaid skirt and married to some orthodontist in Mount Kisco?"

"Because I've never conformed to type. Whereas you . . . let me guess. Antioch? Oberlin?"

I was about to say Bowdoin, but then remembered that Gary went to . . .

"Bard."

"Ha! I was on the right arty track. *Bard.* What a joke. What'd you major in? Advanced macramé? Nicaraguan resistance literature? Living off Daddy's trust fund?"

I was anxious again.

"How did you know I had . . . "

"I didn't. I just guessed. Thirtysomething guy like yourself, no visible means of income, decides to move to Montana on a whim, sets himself up in an apartment, isn't exactly banging down doors when it comes to work . . . the way I figure it, you're either a retired drug dealer or you're one of those lucky bastards who was left just enough money to avoid worrying about little things like earning a living."

"It's not that big a trust fund," I said, sounding defensive. "Just enough to cover basic bills."

Anne gave me an amused smile. "Hey, the fact that you might have an annual family income doesn't matter a shit to me. Especially since you actually have talent." She covered my hand with hers. "Serious talent."

"You really think so?"

"I'm certain of it," she said, withdrawing her hand nervously, like someone worried that they may have played a card too early. "Which is why you have to let this exhibition happen."

"We'll see," I said.

"Why this reluctance to grab an opportunity?"

"I'm not reluctant—"

"You most certainly are. I mean, when I met you at the paper, you gave off this air of diffidence. As if you didn't care if I bought your pictures, and would've almost preferred if I turned them down."

"I was just being cautious, that's all."

"I know. And I rather liked it. Even found it attractive—especially compared to the jerks I get hustling me for jobs, coming on like they're the next Robert Doisneau. But it still made me wonder: Why?"

"Why what?"

"Why are you so hesitant about selling your work?"

Calvin saved me from answering that question by showing up with the food. The wine did have a noticeable oaky nose; the hydroponic lettuce tasted like lettuce. And the interruption afforded me the opportunity to steer the conversation away from "My Reticent Career" and back to Anne's life after Skidmore.

"Ended up in Boston after college," she said. "Finally landed a job on a glossy lifestyle magazine with the highly original name of *Boston*. Worked as a photo researcher—which, at *Boston* in the early eighties, meant scrambling around for interesting portraits of sushi. Anyway, I was living across the river in Cambridge, and the guy in the little apartment next to mine was named Gregg. Finishing a doctorate in English. Within a year, we were sharing an apartment. Within two, we were married. Within three, we were yanked out of Boston and plopped down in Bozeman, when Gregg got a job at Montana State."

"How long did the marriage last?" I asked.

"Five years."

"Why'd it end?"

"Something happened."

"What?"

"*Something.*" Her tone hinted that it would not be wise to further pursue this line of questioning.

"Anyway, after we split, I certainly didn't want to stay in Bozeman, but I also didn't want to leave Montana, which I'd fallen for in a big way. So I paid a little visit to Mountain Falls, and got a friend of a friend to set me up an interview with Stu Simmons, the editor of *The Montanan*. Timing was on my side—a week earlier, his photo editor had quit. I got the job. I moved here."

"Sounds like the perfect Mountain Falls story," I said.

"Yeah—everybody ends up here because things went wrong elsewhere."

"Everybody has troubles in Casablanca."

"Or in New York. What kind of troubles did you have, Gary?"

I could see that she now expected me to fess up and give her the rundown on my failure to cut it in Manhattan. So I essentially took some of the basic details of Gary's life and embellished them. I was surprised at just how fluid I was when it came to the business of elaboration. I told her how I hit the city after college, thinking that I'd be shooting covers for *Vogue* in a matter of months. Instead, I lived in crappy Lower East Side apartments, doing menial jobs, getting nowhere. Then my parents died and, as I was the only child, the house was left to me. It was incredibly hard to move back to the 'burbs after all those years in Manhattan, but, financially speaking, I had no choice. Especially as I was still being strung along by assorted photo agencies and magazines like *Destinations*.

Then I mentioned the affair with Beth.

"Was it serious?" Anne asked.

"Nah. Just self-destructive. You only get involved with a married woman if you really want to do yourself some damage."

"Did her husband ever find out?"

I shook my head. "He was a Wall Street lawyer. Totally preoccupied by the fact that what he really wanted to be was a photographer."

"Oh Jesus," Anne said with a laugh.

"You should have seen this guy's darkroom. State of the art. And his camera collection . . . it must have been worth forty thousand easily."

"But still, she ended up falling for you. The real photographer."

I stared down at my plate.

"Yeah," I finally said. "You seeing anyone right now?"

"There was a guy—a journalist on the paper, but he left town around three years ago. Got a job in Denver. Wasn't really that serious anyway. Since then, just a couple of dumb mistakes."

"I'm surprised," I said.

"Don't be. Mountain Falls may be a great place, but for a single woman the pickings are slim."

"There's always Rudy Warren."

"Yeah, right," she said. "Mind you, he did try it on once . . ."

"And?"

"Give me a break. Sleeping with Rudy would've been a serious taste crime."

We drank the wine, ate the sea bass, ordered another bottle of wine, and began to laugh a little too loudly.

"Want to hear the best Rudy Warren story of all time?" Anne said. "One night he talks Meg Greenwood into bed with him . . ."

"Yeah, I heard," I said.

"Anyway, after they've finished, Meg snuggles up against him and whispers, 'That was really nice, Rudy.' Know what he says? 'Don't tell me. Tell your friends.'"

We lurched out of Le Petit Place around midnight.

"I hope to hell you're not planning to drive home," I said.

"No way," Anne said. "Because you're going to walk me back."

She linked her arm with mine. We said nothing as we strolled the three blocks back to her house. She lived on a quiet tree-lined cul-de-sac of 1920s shingle homes. The streetlamp cast the street in a warm sepia tint. As we approached her front door, I kept telling myself: You're loaded. Just give her a quick peck on the cheek and walk away. Don't complicate things . . . When we reached the front steps, Anne turned and gave me a hundred-watt drunken smile. The glow of lamplight fell across her face. I thought: She is beautiful.

"Well . . ." I said.

"Well . . ." she said.

"That was fun."

"A lot of fun."

"Well . . ." I said.

"Well . . ." she said.

I leaned forward to peck her cheek, but suddenly kissed her fully on the lips. Her mouth opened, she threw her arms around me, and we started lurching backward. We fell into the house. We landed on the hallway floor. We began to tear off each other's clothes.

Later, in bed, she said, "I could get used to that."

"Don't tell me, tell your—"

"Shaddup," she said, kissing me deeply.

"I could get used to that too," I said.

"Could you really?"

"Sure."

"Wish I could believe that."

"Why can't you?"

"Because I wonder . . ."

"Yeah?"

". . . if you're just another of those fly-by-night heartbreakers who blow into a place, hang around until they start getting bored with the scenery, then slink off down the road one night when nobody's looking."

"Do I strike you as the type . . . ?"

"You're in your late thirties, you've never been married, things didn't work out in New York, so you drifted out here. In a couple of months, you'll probably start thinking Mountain Falls is small potatoes, so you'll—"

"Aren't we getting a little ahead of ourselves here?" I asked.

"Yeah, we are."

"We?"

"Okay, *I* am. But I've been burned about three times too many and I'm not going to let it happen again. I'm too old . . ."

"You're not old."

"I'm thirty-five."

"Sorry. I was wrong. You're really old."

"Bastard," she said and kissed me again.

When I woke in the morning, she was gone. A note had been left on the pillow.

Gary:

Some of us have to work.

Call me later. I could be persuaded to cook
you dinner tonight.

Coffee, tea, gin in the kitchen.

Love,

A.

I wandered through her house. It was far less cluttered
than her office. Simply decorated, with whitewashed stone
walls, bleached floorboards, New Mexican throw rugs, piles
of books and compact discs, and a small darkroom in what
was once a second bathroom. An elderly Kodak enlarger,
strips of newly developed negatives, and two recent prints
clipped to the drying clothesline. The first showed a billboard—BUTTE ELEGANT MOTEL . . . HONEYMOON SUITES . . . HEIR
CONDITIONED—riddled with bullet holes. The second was of a
small backwoods church, totally buried in snow, its makeshift
steeple adorned with the slogan "Jesus Is Coming." I smiled.
Anne Ames had a splendidly sardonic eye and—judging from
the expert composition—she also knew what she was doing
with a camera.

There was a phone in the darkroom. I picked it up and
rang her at the paper.

"You never got around to showing me the six prints of mine
you'd chosen," I said.

"That was just a ruse to get you into my bed," she said.

"I really like the shot of the Butte billboard. And the buried
church."

"You've been snooping."

"You leave me alone in your house, of course I'll snoop
around. The photos are great. You going to show me more?"

"If you like."

"I like."

"Dinner invitation accepted, then?"

"Absolutely."

"See you around seven," she said. "Bring plenty of wine."

You shouldn't be doing this, I told myself. I know, I know, another voice said. But, do me a favor. Stop talking.

I made myself a cup of coffee and wandered into the living room. There were three family photos on the mantelpiece—Anne with an elderly couple (her parents, I presumed), a teenage portrait of two acned guys in school blazers (no doubt, her brothers), and a picture showing her in her late twenties, cradling a tiny infant in her lap. Must be a niece or a nephew, I thought to myself, as she'd mentioned nothing about children. I checked out the magazines and newspapers on the coffee table. *The New Yorker, The New York Review of Books, The Atlantic Monthly, The New York Times,* and—buried at the bottom of the pile—a copy of *People.* Well, we all have a secret weakness for junk. I broke my rule about reading anything from back east and leafed through the previous day's edition of the *Times.* When I reached the obituary page, my eye immediately fell upon a headline:

JACK MAYLE, LAWYER, DEAD AT 63

Jack Mayle, a senior partner at the Wall Street firm of Lawrence, Cameron and Thomas, died on Saturday at Mount Sinai Hospital after a long illness. He was 63.

Mr. Mayle, the head of his firm's trusts and estates division, joined Lawrence, Cameron and Thomas in 1960. He was made a partner in 1964 and was widely regarded as one of New York's foremost experts on estate law.

He is survived by his wife, Rose, and two children.

I put my head in my hands. Jack. After my dad died, he really became my surrogate father. Someone who silently *understood.* Because, like him, I was an outsider. We recognized that in each other the first day we met—two corporate types who played the Wall Street game, yet secretly abhorred everything to do with it. The best time of his life, no doubt, was that year in the mid-fifties when he lived in some atelier off MacDougal Street and painted his crazed Kandinsky-influenced canvases. But as soon as he buckled under to parental pressure and entered law school, he threw the canvases away. And he never picked up a paintbrush again. Poor Jack. I probably hastened his death with my own. Another of my victims.

I closed up Anne's house and walked back to the Frontier Apartments, the harsh morning sun reminding me of just how much I had drunk last night. When I opened my front door, I knew immediately that something was wrong. A stale aroma of cigarette smoke hung in the air and I could hear protracted wheezing coming from the living room. Someone was there—and I was suddenly very scared. Until I heard a half-awake voice.

"That you, photographer?"

I poked my head into the living room and there, sprawled on my sofa, was Rudy Warren. Three dead bottles of beer were lined up by his mud-caked shoes, along with a saucer full of dead butts. His teeth were sunk in a glass of water.

"For fuck's sake, Rudy."

"Morning," he said. Then, hoisting the glass, he downed the water before shoving his teeth back in his mouth.

"That's better," he said.

"Charming," I said. "How the hell did you get in here?"

"Keys," he said.

"What keys?"

"The keys I stole the other night. You know, the spare set you keep in the kitchen . . . "

"I know them," I said. I also hadn't checked to see if they had been missing since Rudy's last visit.

"Meant to tell you I borrowed them," he said, sitting up.

"Just like you meant to tell me about the prints you also stole?"

"So this is the thanks I get for jump-starting your career? Not to mention setting you up with the delicious Ms. Ames? Had a good night, had we?"

"The keys, Rudy. The keys."

He shrugged, reached into his pocket, and tossed them to me.

"You make copies of these?" I asked.

"Don't be a jerkoff. Just took 'em in case I needed an emergency bed sometime."

"Which you did last night?"

"Yep. Couldn't drive a tricycle, let alone my car."

"You could've called me first."

"But you were out, romancing Ms. Ames. Anyway, if you check your answering machine you'll see there's at least three messages from me, begging you for a place to crash."

"You have no other friends in town?"

"None that'll talk to me anymore."

"You didn't consider a hotel? Or even a cab?"

"Hell, they cost money. Pardner, you wouldn't put a pot of coffee on the stove, would you? I need an intravenous of caffeine pronto."

"I am not your fucking manservant, Rudy. And I want you out of here now."

"You're kind of pissed off at me, aren't you?"

"Very perceptive."

"Can't figure why. I mean, it's not like I slept in *your* bed, shat in the sheets . . ."

"Rudy, good-bye."

"Not until I've had that fast cup of coffee."

"I don't want to make you coffee—"

"Once I get my Joe, I go. You want me out, put on the pot."

He lit up a cigarette and immediately had a coughing fit. He sounded like he was chasing a gold medal in the phlegm Olympics.

"Okay," I said, "I'll get you the coffee."

When I returned a few minutes later, his coughing had just about subsided.

"Don't you think you owe your lungs a little vacation from the smokes?" I said.

"Nah," he said.

He accepted a mug of coffee and tasted it.

"Instant?" he said with disdain. "Thanks a lot."

"Only the best for you, Rudy."

"What's the time now?"

I checked my watch. "Ten thirty-five," I said.

"Shit," Rudy said. "Got a deadline at two."

"Will you make it?"

Rudy gave me a withering look. "I always make it. I'm a pro."

"No offense," I said.

"You should learn a thing or two about friendship, photographer. And about small towns. You want to play Mr. Aloof, buy yourself a ticket back to New York. Out here, we kind of like living in each other's pocket. And we also like having a sense of who—and *what*—we're dealing with. I mean, Dave at the camera shop tells me you're a great customer, always pleasant, always polite, even gave him a pointer or two about some old camera he bought, if I'm not mistaken. But he must have asked you to dinner about half a dozen times. And every time you've dodged it. Now, why's that?"

Because he has a wife named Beth, that's why. And two sons.

"I don't like mixing business with pleasure."

"What a bunch of horseshit. You just want to stay nice and removed from people. Last week, I could instantly tell just how much you regretted inviting me back here, and how you wished you could've hustled my ass back out into the snow. Don't mean to pry—"

"Yes you do."

". . . but did something happen back east that you're trying to duck? You running out on alimony? A paternity case? A very precocious twelve-year-old who assured you she was eighteen . . . ?"

I attempted a laugh. As soon as I emitted it, I realized just how tense it sounded.

"Nothing that picaresque. I was just a guy who couldn't get arrested, let alone hired, in New York. Professionally speaking, I was a fuckup."

"We've all got a past, pardner. Just some of us are a little more comfortable talking about it than you. Like when you walked in here today, I could tell immediately that you'd gotten some sort of bad news. Anything happen? Someone die?"

Was I that transparent? I shook my head.

"Okay," he said. "Remain a closed fucking book." He finished the dregs of his coffee. "Better get my ass in gear, find myself a typewriter."

"What are you going to be sounding off about this week?" I asked.

"The ingratitude of Easterners."

"Better than Californication. How the hell did you ever envisage a life with Judy Wilmers?"

"Ain't she a piece of work? Hell, you know how these things are? Winters are kind of long up here, you're in the mood for company, next thing you know you're hitched to some crazy bitch who's convinced she's channeled into the soul of some Cherokee war goddess. Well, you know what the guy said: 'Experience is the name men give to their mistakes.'"

"Oscar Wilde?"

"Sonny Liston."

He stood up, grabbing his duffel coat off the floor.

"One last thing," he said. "I've got a real soft spot for Anne Ames. In fact, we all do at the paper. So don't mess her around. She's a great kid and she's been through enough in the past."

"What, exactly?"

"I'm sure she'll get around to telling you about it. In time. But I warn you—you break her heart, I kick your ass."

He opened the door. And said: "See you at Eddie's sometime. If you ever fucking deign to grace it again with your presence."

He left. I threw open all the living-room windows in an effort to clear the room of Rudy's stale smoke. I washed the dishes he'd used. I went to my darkroom and started developing the film I'd shot the day before on the banks of the Copperhead. I tried not to think about what people might be saying about me in town.

After lunch, the phone rang.

"Finally, the great man answers."

It was Judy Wilmers.

"Besides your talents as a photographer, you're also very good at playing hard to get."

"I've just been busy, Judy."

"Yeah, I know. She's a class act, Anne. So, don't blow it, y'hear me?"

I wanted to scream. Instead I said, "I hear you, Judy. Loud and clear."

6

LATER THAT AFTERNOON, Judy Wilmers and I achieved *closure*. Sitting in her gallery cafe, chain-drinking cups of rosehip tea, she complained loudly every time I raised an objection to her contractual terms. At first, I struck a Mr. Nice Guy pose and told her that the 60/40 split for this exhibition was acceptable to me. But then I became the shit. I would only allow her a six-month period in which to market my work, and wanted to give her only 25 percent of all subsidiary sales (though I did agree to her 10 percent take on any exhibitions she set up during this time). She dug her heels in, saying that if she could only have six-month control on the rights she would insist on a 30 percent cut. I was willing to concede her the additional 5 percent, but on the condition that she agree to the insertion of a contractual clause. It imposed a thirty-six-month ceiling on all royalties payable to her from the sales achieved in the time she controlled subsidiary rights. She was not amused.

"This is, like, totally outrageous."

"I'm just covering my back," I said. "Anyway, a clause stipulating length of royalty is commonplace in most contracts."

"You're not a photographer," she said. "You're an ambulance chaser. I want a sixty-month ceiling."

"Forty-eight," I countered.

288

"Done," she said.

She would have contracts ready for my signature by tomorrow. The exhibition would open on May eighteenth and run until July first. She was going to call it "Montana Faces: Photographs by Gary Summers." There would be a poster, using the picture of Madge the Menace, which would be distributed statewide. There would be an opening launch party. It would be attended by "important dealers" from San Francisco and Portland and Seattle and Denver. She wanted at least another thirty new portraits in her hot little hands within two weeks.

"That'll make eighty prints all together. I'll choose forty for the show. Naturally, you'll have a say about what makes the cut. But—as the owner of the gallery—I retain final veto. No doubt, you've got a problem with that too."

"I wouldn't give you anything I didn't want exhibited, so . . . yeah, I'll give you final veto."

"You sure you're feeling well?" she said.

"Very funny."

"But lookit, I'd rather you didn't let *The Montanan* have any more pictures after the six they're running. Of course, their spreads will have a big local impact—which will be great pre-publicity for us. But after the show, I'm gonna want to start selling the pictures to big-time places, so I'm afraid *The Montanan* is going to be out of the frame."

"Anne's going to love this bit of news."

"Hey, it's business."

I didn't initially say anything about Judy's contractual terms when I saw Anne that evening. Because as soon as she opened her front door we were all over each other. A word wasn't uttered between us for at least a half hour. Until, snuggling up against me in bed, she put her chin against my shoulder and said, "Well, hello there."

I had come armed with two bottles of Washington State Shiraz, and after dinner, I mentioned that our previous night together seemed to be the stuff of public knowledge around Mountain Falls.

"Don't look at me," Anne said. "Advertising my private life isn't exactly my idea of a good time."

"Well, how is it that the walls have ears and eyes here?"

"Not a lot else to do," Anne said. "But, hey, are you worried that people know you spent a night here? I mean, it was just a night. Tonight's just another night . . ."

I returned her smile.

"And tomorrow," I said, "is also just another night."

She leaned over and kissed me deeply.

"That is exactly what I wanted to hear."

The next morning, as we finished breakfast in her kitchen, she finally brought out the six prints she had chosen for the paper. Madge the Menace, the gas station couple, the boutique owner in Bigfork, a fundamentalist preacher outside his trailer chapel in Kalispell, a real estate agent in Whitefish wearing a blue blazer and a Stetson, a tattooed biker playing a poker machine inside the Mountain View.

"You approve of my choices?" she asked.

"I approve."

"Now, I was thinking about the next half dozen we might run . . ."

"I'm afraid that there's a little contractual problem," I said and informed her of Judy's insistence that I sell *The Montanan* no further pictures from this series.

"That devious bitch," she said. "Did you agree to this?"

"I don't have much choice in the matter."

"Gary . . ."

"But once I deliver the last of the portraits," I said, "there's no legal reason why I can't start shooting other pictures for you."

She gave me a conspiratorial smile.

"Sounds good to me."

The next two weeks were frantic ones, as I rushed to shoot forty more portraits for the exhibition. Every morning I was up at first light and on the road. Every afternoon I would return and spend a few hours developing the day's film in my darkroom before heading over to Anne's for a late dinner. I would always show up with wine and just-dried contact sheets. Inevitably, we would fall into bed as soon as I arrived. After the paucity of passion that characterized my last year or so with Beth, there was something deliriously adolescent about such unbridled ardor. We couldn't keep our hands off each other—and I spent each of my long photographic day trips out of Mountain Falls ticking off the hours before I would land back on her doorstep.

"Oh, it's you again," she would say with studied detachment before reaching across the threshold and pulling me into her arms.

The wine would be cast aside, the contact sheets scattered across the floor, we'd have each other half undressed before we even made it to her bedroom.

Afterward, one of us would eventually stagger down to the kitchen to throw together a fast dinner. We got into the indolent habit of eating in bed—and whenever it was my turn to cook, Anne would spend the half hour or so I was absent going through my contact sheets with a magnifier and a china marker, choosing the best shots of the day.

"What sort of flash did you use for the picture of the gun salesman?" she asked one evening after studying my recent portrait: the proud proprietor of Ferdie's Firearms in Butte.

"None," I said. "Just available light."

"No kidding. How'd you get that spectral glow on his face?"

"Got lucky with the late afternoon sun. Streamed right through the front windows just as I was shooting."

"Lucky, my ass," she said. "You posed him right in it."

"Well . . ."

"When it comes to your pictures, luck has nothing to do with them. They're calculating as hell—but what saves them is your lack of pretense. Bet you started off shooting really affected stuff."

"Maybe."

"Bet you saw yourself as a real artiste, as befits a boy from Bard."

"Got me in one."

"I'm not surprised. It takes a long time as a photographer to trust your eye, to resist the temptation to overeditorialize. I've still not gotten there myself."

"Those shots I saw in your darkroom were terrific."

"Witty—yes. Terrific—nah. They're too clever by half. Too attention-getting. Whereas your portraits . . . you manage to make them look happenstantial, even though it's clear that each shot is carefully thought out. That's a neat trick."

"I only learned it recently."

"I kind of figured as much. So when you get big and the magazines eventually start writing profiles of you . . ."

"That'll never happen . . ."

"Don't be so sure. But if and when they do, you'll be able to tell them that coming to Montana was the moment you 'found your eye.' "

"Yeah. Montana was my liberation."

"From what?"

"Professional failure. Self-doubt."

"Anything else?"

I chose my words carefully.

"Everyone has a history, Anne."

"I know. It's just you're still a little selective about telling me yours."

"It's only been ten days . . ."

"True."

". . . and you've also been a bit selective about your own past."

She looked at me squarely.

"You want to know why my marriage ended?"

"Yes. I do."

She fell quiet for a few moments. "You know the photograph on the mantelpiece downstairs with me and the baby?"

I nodded.

"My son," she said. "Charlie."

She paused. "He died."

I shut my eyes. Her voice remained very calm, very controlled.

"It happened around a month after that photo was taken," she said. "He was just four and a half months old at the time. Still sleeping in the same room as us. Still waking up two, three times a night. Only on that night, he didn't stir once. Gregg and I were so damn tired from weeks of broken sleep we crashed right out, didn't move until seven the next morning. I was up first. And when I didn't hear a sound from his crib, I knew immediately that something—"

She broke off, avoided my gaze.

"Sudden Infant Death Syndrome. That's what they call it. The doctors at the emergency room, the pathologist who performed the . . . they all kept telling us that there was no rhyme or reason to this . . . *syndrome.* It simply 'happened.' It was 'just one of those things.' We 'mustn't blame ourselves.' But, of course, we did. If only we'd checked on him in the middle of the night. If only we hadn't been so tired, so greedy about getting a solid night's sleep. If only . . ."

I closed my eyes again, unable to look at her. In that darkroom of my brain, Adam and Josh came into sharp focus.

"A marriage has to be pretty rock solid to survive a child dying," she said. "Ours wasn't. Within eight months, I'd moved to Mountain Falls. And, y'know—seven years later, I've never been back to Bozeman. Never made contact with Gregg again. I can't. You don't get over it. You just learn to *deal* with it. To keep it hidden from view. Tucked away in a room of your own—a place only you know exists and which you visit, every waking hour of every day. And no matter how hard you try, you know that you'll never rid yourself of that room. It's with you now forever."

She looked back up at me.

"You're crying," she said.

I said nothing, rubbing my eyes with my shirtsleeve.

"I'd like a whiskey," she said. "Large. I think you could use one too."

I went down to the kitchen, retrieved a bottle of J&B and two glasses, then returned to the bedroom. As I sat down on the bed, Anne put her head on my shoulder and began to sob. I held her until she stopped.

"Never ask me about that again," she finally said.

Later that night, I woke suddenly. The digital clock by the bed said 3:07. The room was black. Anne was curled up, dead to the world. I stared at the ceiling. Adam and Josh appeared before me again. My lost sons. Anne was right: Grief is a dark room all your own. Only unlike hers, my loss was self-inflicted. When I killed Gary, I killed my life, a life I didn't want. Until it was dead.

Now everything was a falsehood, a fabrication. My name. My credentials. My so-called history. If there was to be a future with Anne, it would be one constructed on that grand fabrication—because it was all I had to play with. I should have obeyed my first instinct and sidestepped involvement. But now—even after just ten days—I didn't want to let her go.

The next morning—a Saturday—Anne roused me out of bed by dangling a copy of *The Montanan* in front of my face.

"Rise and shine," she said. "You're in print."

I was awake within seconds. And there, on the second page of the "Weekend" section, was my picture of the gas station couple and their little baby. It covered around a quarter of the page. There was no editorial comment attached to it, no caption beneath the photo explaining who the individuals were. Anne had kept it starkly simple. There was just a tidy headline—FACES OF MONTANA BY GARY SUMMERS—and nothing more.

"Pleased?" she asked.

"Amazed."

"Why?" she said, suddenly concerned.

"Because it's the first picture of mine ever to make it into print."

"I still don't believe that."

"You did a great job with the layout and the reproduction. The clarity's first-rate. Thanks."

She kissed me.

"Anytime, toots," she said. "I'm sorry about last night."

"Never be sorry about that," I said. *"Never."*

"Got any plans today?"

"I'm yours."

"I like the sound of that. Feel like an overnight jaunt out of town?"

"You're on."

We took my car and first stopped at my apartment, so I could pick up a change of clothes and a camera.

"Quite a place," Anne said, sizing up the stark decor. "We could start using it as our this-side-of-Mountain-Falls pied-à-terre. You ever bump into Meg Greenwood?"

"Not since she showed me around here," I said, deciding not to mention the fact that, every month, I still shoved the rent under her office door late at night to avoid her company.

"I have to ask you something," Anne said, "and you must be straight with me."

"Yes?" I said hesitantly.

"When I first mentioned to Meg that I'd met you, she said, 'Oh, he's spoken for. He told me there's a girlfriend back in New York.' Is there?"

"No way," I said.

"Then why did you tell her . . . ?"

"Because it was the only way I could convince Meg that signing a lease didn't mean I wanted her to be the mother of my children."

"Bastard," she said, trying to stifle a laugh. "But, yeah, she does tend to overplay her hand a bit whenever there's an available man in the room. So . . . there really is no one else?"

"Trust me," I said.

"I do," she said, taking my hand. "I do."

Back in the car, Anne told me to take Route 200, heading east. There had been an unusual dry spell for the past two weeks. With the temperatures steadily above freezing for the first time since December, the ever present snow had vanished at ground level. And today the landscape looked thawed out— the terrain brown, the trees still barren of leaves.

"So winter really ends around here," I said.

"Don't kiss it good-bye yet," Anne said. "This dry spell's a total fluke. And I've seen six inches of snow in May. So anything's still possible in mid-April. Blizzards, ice storms, famine, pestilence, plagues of locusts . . ."

"Why the hell did I ever move to Montana?"

"To find your muse," she said archly.

"Oh please . . ."

"And to meet me."

"I suppose you're worth eight months of sub-zero temperatures."

"I'll take that as a compliment."

"Why did you wait so long to ask me about the phantom girlfriend in New York?"

"I decided to remain in denial about it. Until . . ."

"Yeah?"

"I started thinking you might be nice as part of the furniture."

"What kind of furniture might I be?"

"A BarcaLounger," she said.

"Thanks a lot."

"Anytime."

"Where are we going, by the way?"

"You'll see."

Around thirty miles down Route 200, Anne directed me onto a tertiary road—a narrow, winding strip of blacktop that snaked its way through a forest of towering pines. They were so densely packed together, so vertiginous, that the sky seemed to disappear. It was like being in a vast, lofty cathedral. Ten minutes into this timberland, Anne directed me to make a left-hand turn onto a tiny paved track. The two-seater MG was almost too large for this nonentity of a road, the surface of which was so jagged that I had to slow down to 15 miles per hour.

"If we blow out a tire here, I'm going to expect some help," I said.

"I might just have to assist you."

The car began to vibrate as we hit a stony stretch.

"Hope this is worth it."

"Believe me, it is."

Around five minutes later, the blue began. Not blue, exactly, more of an aquamarine. In front of us was a boundless lake. At first sight, it seemed like a sea. You could barely discern its opposite bank. Two tiny islands floated in the middle of its expanse, both empty of habitation. We parked the car near the water's edge and got out. I looked north, south, east, west. Occasionally, you spied a house tucked away within the trees—but you really had to look hard to find it. For this was an Eden—freshly minted, unsullied, enveloped within a giant primeval forest.

"Good God," I finally said.

"It is pretty impressive," Anne said. "Moose Lake. Second biggest in the state. Here to the western shore must be twenty-five miles. You go out in a boat, you can sometimes lose direction, forget which way you're heading, it's so damn big."

I asked her how long she had been coming here.

"Ever since I bought that."

She pointed toward a tiny cabin around 200 yards from us, tucked away within the pines. It was something of a shack. Rough-hewn, weatherbeaten wood, small aerielike windows, a crude stone chimney spouting from its roof. The inside consisted of one large room. Bare floorboards, a wood-burning stove, an old tin sink, a pair of beat-up armchairs, an old iron double bed, a large wicker basket overflowing with chopped wood, shelves piled high with paperback novels and tins of food, a wine rack with a dozen dusty bottles. A transistor radio provided the only link with the outside world.

"There's no electricity," Anne said. "Just kerosene lamps. It does have a toilet, however, and a bathtub—but the only way you get hot water around this place is by boiling it on the stove. Still, it's my very own escape hatch, where I can slam the door on everything. My summer vacation last year was two weeks here on my own. Didn't see another soul the entire time."

"You do amaze me, Ms. Ames."

"It's not exactly an amazing place," she said, reaching for a box of Domino matches in the kitchen area. "Kind of a dump, actually."

"Yes, but there's no way you'd ever get me up here alone for long stretches of time."

"You really do get to like the isolation after a while. Even an urban rat like you could develop a taste for it."

"How long have you had it?"

"Four, five years. Paid next to nothing for it—and it shows." She opened the door of the stove and lit it.

"I always clean the stove and lay a new fire before leaving. It means that I don't have to spend an hour chopping wood and gathering up kindling when I return. Especially as, winter or summer, it is always fucking freezing in here when I arrive."

I didn't disagree.

"Two hours from now, once the stove is warmed up, this place should be tolerable. C'mon, let's take a hike."

We set off down a narrow path that fronted the water's edge. The sun was now at full strength. It made the still lake appear as glossy as a freshly waxed floor. The air was champagne crisp and a light wind swayed the pines. The calm was enveloping. We said nothing as we walked. As we trekked farther along the shore, it struck me that what I loved most about this state wasn't only its lonely roads and grand skies, but also its respect for stillness. What was that old line of Pascal's about all of man's troubles deriving from his inability to sit alone quietly in a room? Montana instinctively understood this conundrum, and had done its best to block out the white noise that so dominated life elsewhere. Here quiet was considered a virtue, a necessity.

Close to an hour into our hike, Anne suddenly reached out and gripped my shoulder. When I turned around, she had her finger to her lips, then silently pointed into the woods. There—around thirty feet from us—was a large grizzly bear and her two cubs. She was giving them a bath—licking them all over with her huge, outstretched tongue. Anne and I stood motionless, knowing full well that any sudden movement might startle the mother—who, in turn, might think that her cubs were under threat. As any dedicated reader of *National Geographic* remembers, the fastest way to get yourself mauled by a grizzly is by triggering her protective maternal instincts. So we remained very still, secret onlookers to this sweet domestic scene. At first, I resisted the temptation to reach for the little Leica in the pocket of my parka. But when it became clear that the mother still wasn't aware of our presence, I quietly withdrew the camera and slipped off the lens cap. Anne's eyes grew wide with disbelief. She tapped me on the shoulder and vehemently shook her head no. I gesticulated back, my hands telling her not to worry. Then I peered through the viewfinder and squeezed off eight shots of the grizzly and her cubs. I regretted the lack of a telephoto lens—and, in an effort to get closer to my subject matter, I took two stealthy steps forward. A huge mistake. As soon as my boots crunched on the ground, the mother bear froze. She clutched her cubs to her. Scanning the horizon, she saw the two of us and, stepping in front of her cubs, she gathered herself up to her full, ferocious height. Over the sound of my heart in metabolic free fall, I heard Anne's sharp intake of breath. The mother bear was as motionless as we were. A Mexican standoff ensued—it lasted no more than thirty seconds, but it seemed like an hour. Finally, she backed down off her haunches, nudged her cubs with one of her large, outstretched paws, and herded them with her deeper into the woods.

We waited several minutes before moving again. Once the bears had vanished from view, Anne exhaled. I knew what was coming next.

"You are a total jerk," she said in an angry whisper.

"It was an accident—"

"Accident my ass. I told you not to move—"

"I really didn't think—"

"That's right—you *didn't* think. And you nearly got us killed. Next time—"

". . . I'll have much better bear sense," I said, trying to defuse her anger. A bad tactic.

"Don't try to fucking humor me, Gary." With that, she stormed off back toward the cabin. I didn't give chase, I just brought up the rear. During the hour we retraced our steps, she didn't look back once. She was nearly five minutes ahead of me. I heard the cabin door slam in the distance. When I entered, Anne was standing near the kitchen, uncorking a bottle of wine. The stove had done its work—the cabin had lost its meat-locker chill. Anne splashed a little Shiraz into a glass, took a hefty sip, and shrugged me off when I tried to put my arm around her.

"I'm sorry," I said.

"You should be," she said.

"I wasn't thinking . . ."

"You *were* thinking . . . as a photographer."

I smiled. "They're going to be great shots."

"I know," she said. "And if you want to make amends, you'll give them to me for the paper."

"Done," I said and reached over to stroke her cheek. She took my hand and held it tightly.

"She would have mauled you with two swipes of her paw. Because I was behind you, I might have been able to dodge her . . . but you wouldn't have stood a chance. Don't you ever go putting yourself at risk like that again—"

"Come here," I said, pulling her toward me.

The bed creaked, the sheets were a little clammy, and though there were two thick blankets covering us, we still clung to each other for warmth.

"Let's not go back tomorrow," I said, leaning down to retrieve the bottle of Shiraz and two glasses from the floor. "We'll hole up here and let everyone believe we've vanished without a trace."

"This cabin ain't big enough for the two of us, pardner."

"What sort of romantic are you?"

"I'm a practical romantic . . ." she said.

"Isn't than an oxymoron?"

". . . who would very much like to hold on to you. Which is why I would never, *never* agree to two weeks alone with you here."

"Why not?" I said, sounding offended.

"Ever heard of cabin fever? Guaranteed to kill a romance stone dead. Two weeks alone in such a small, isolated place, and we'd either be screaming to get out of each other's company . . . or we'd decide to form our own militia."

"Great Montana pastime," I said.

"Know why this state leads the country in gun-obsessed, government-hating, separatist lunatics? Because so many people here live in small cabins."

She climbed out of bed and quickly began to pull on her clothes.

"Now you're about to discover the wonders of my backwoods pasta sauce," she said.

Four kitchen shelves were stacked high with cans of soup, vegetables, baked beans, chili, tuna fish, clams, sardines, condensed milk. There were assorted packets of pasta and rice, bags of wholemeal bread mix, jars of coffee, tea, and Ovaltine, and small vials of dried spices. Anne poured some olive oil into a hefty frying pan and placed it on top of the stove. Within a few minutes, the oil began to bubble.

"So it really does work," I said.

"You are such a city boy," she said, tossing some dried garlic and rosemary into the pan.

"How do you adjust the heat?"

"Simple," she said, opening the stove and throwing in three more chunks of wood. "That's it."

"You are such a frontier girl."

"You going to lounge in bed all evening while I cook?"

"It had crossed my mind."

"How about opening some more wine?"

I forced myself out of bed and dressed. Anne added two tins of tomatoes and a splash of the remaining Shiraz to the saucepan. She filled a pot with water and placed it at the rear of the stove.

"When you go shopping for this place," I said, eyeing the vast array of tinned goods, "do you always worry about being unprepared for Armageddon?"

"Nah . . . but there is a fallout shelter in the basement."

"Really?"

"Pu-leeze."

"You've got yourself a pretty impressive larder."

"I do two big shops for the cabin each year, and then I don't have to think about it again."

"So you really could disappear without a trace if you wanted?"

"Not anymore," she said.

"Why's that?"

A hint of a grin. "You'd know where to find me now."

She added a tin of clams to the tomatoes and tossed a handful of pasta into the pot of boiling water. I uncorked more wine, lit candles, set the table.

"Linguini alla vongole," she said, placing a steaming bowl of pasta on the table. "An old Montana favorite."

We ate. We drained the second bottle of Shiraz. I found a bottle of port in the wine rack and began to pour us two glasses. She insisted on just a small measure.

"I'm going to have an appalling headache tomorrow morning," she said.

"Misery loves company," I said, handing her a glass.

"You're really trying to get me drunk, aren't you?"

"Absolutely—then I can take total advantage of your body."

The candlelight flickered. She leaned over to cover my hand with hers. The glow of the flame radiated across her face.

"Happy?" she asked.

"Very happy."

"Me too."

We fell silent. Then she asked:

"Do you have a kid somewhere?"

Without thinking, my free hand clenched. Thankfully, it was under the table.

"No."

"I'm surprised."

"Why?"

"Because when I told you about Charlie, you got very upset."

"It's a very upsetting story," I said.

"Yeah—but of the few people I've told, the ones who don't have kids usually don't react so emotionally. Naturally, they say 'how terrible' and stuff like that . . . whereas anyone who is a parent finds the story unbearable. Like you did."

I shrugged. I figured it was the safest response.

"Don't get me wrong," she said. "I was very touched by your reaction. It just . . . surprised me, that's all. A single man with no kids . . . you don't expect him to understand the depth of feeling that a parent has toward a child." She paused, stared me straight in the eye. "You want kids?"

I returned her gaze. "I might. And you?"

"I might too."

She took a nervous sip of her port. I drained my glass. We quickly dropped the subject.

I slept fitfully, and jumped upright in the middle of the night after hearing the maniacal buzz of a Black & Decker power saw deep within my comatose brain.

"You all right?" Anne asked, half awake.

"Just a bad dream."

"Go back to sleep," she said, wrapping her arms around me. "You'll have forgotten it all by morning."

If only that were true.

I finally did pass out again and fell into an empty black void. The true sleep of the dead.

7

SUDDENLY, I FELT A HAND clasping my shoulder and shaking me hard.

"Gary, Gary . . ."

I snapped into consciousness. Anne was standing over me. She was dressed and looking anxious. Very anxious.

"We've got to go," she said.

"What . . . ?" My brain was still blurry. I glanced at my watch. Nearly noon. No wonder I was fogged in.

"We've got to leave right now," Anne said.

"Jesus, why?"

"I'll show you when you get up. But you've got to get up *now*."

"I don't get this—"

"Gary . . ." She all but pulled me out of bed. "Move!"

I did as instructed, throwing on my clothes, tossing some dirty laundry into my overnight bag. Anne, meanwhile, raced around the house, closing it up. She worked fast.

"Ready?" she said as I pulled on my hiking boots.

"Yeah. Why all this drama?"

"Step outside," she said.

I hoisted my bag and opened the door.

"Jesus Christ," I said. "Jesus fucking Christ."

A fire was raging. It had engulfed part of the forest. It was less than a mile from us, and flames were licking the tops of pines. A dense cloud of acrid smoke colored the sky, eclipsing the sun. A strong wind was blowing, fanning the blaze. I now knew why Anne was so eager to get me out of bed. The fire was heading this way.

I raced to the car, popped open the trunk, grabbed my camera bag.

"Are you crazy?" Anne said.

"Just a couple of shots," I said, flipping open the back of the Rolleiflex.

"Use Ilford HP-4," she said, watching me scramble through the camera bag for film. "It has sharper definition."

I grinned at her. "Yes, boss."

"And be fast about it. We've only got a few minutes."

I twisted on a telephoto lens and squeezed off a dozen shots of the pines in full blaze. Seen through the sniper sight of the telephoto lens, they looked like oversized birthday candles, burning brightly. But then a sudden downdraft turned the fire into a conflagration. There was a discernible, ominous *whoosh*, and the flames seemed to erupt, spreading closer toward us.

"Right, we're out of here," Anne said. "I'll drive."

I tossed her the keys and we jumped into the MG. She turned on the ignition.

Nothing happened.

She turned the key again. Still no sound.

"Pump the accelerator," I said.

She hit the pedal several times, then tried the ignition again. Silence.

The wind was gaining velocity. We could now clearly smell the burning pines, as wafts of smoke drifted toward us.

"What the fuck is going on?" Anne said, desperately pumping the pedal again.

"Stop, stop, stop," I said, "you'll flood it."

"If it doesn't start, we die."

"Throw it into second," I said. "Now turn the key and put the clutch straight to the floor."

She did as ordered. I jumped out of the car, ran to the back and began to push. At first, it wouldn't budge, but once I managed to shove it over a small bump, it began to gently roll downhill.

"Let out the clutch," I yelled as the car slipped away from me. Suddenly, there was a combustible belch as the engine turned over.

"Pump it, pump it," I shouted as Anne tried to sustain the engine blast. But, within seconds, it was silent again.

"Shit, shit, shit." Anne turned the ignition again in frustration. It made a grim, grinding noise. The smoke from the fire was now thickening.

"Get back into second," I yelled, running up to the rear of the car. "Clutch down?"

"Yeah," she shouted back. "Go."

Using all the weight I could muster, I shoved the car again and ran behind it until it developed its own momentum and slid away from me.

"Clutch!"

Anne let it out. There was another convulsive mechanical burp, followed by the reassuring roar of an engine in full throttle. I raced to the car and jumped in. Anne gunned the accelerator, shifted into first, and we took off down the dirt road. Anne pushed the car up to thirty miles per hour, but the uneven surface meant that the MG vibrated like a dentist's drill. It forced her to slow down to twenty.

"Fucking British cars," she said. "All style, no substance."

"They're not exactly designed for forests," I said.

"How about fog?" she asked as the wind whipped up yet again and a thick, toxic cloud of smoke descended on the road. It blew in through the window, making us gag, covering us both in soot. We struggled to roll up the windows, coughing violently. Visibility was now minimal—maybe ten feet, at most. Anne was leaning halfway over the wheel, trying to keep her vision fixed on whatever she could still see of the road. For a quarter of an hour, we didn't exchange a word. We both knew the fire was only minutes from us. And if we didn't clear this part of the woods soon, it would swallow us whole.

The smoke was terrifying. Its noxious odor scalded the air, making breathing treacherous. The soft-top roof of the MG leaked in several places, letting in a trickle of these fumes. Anne looked white-faced. She was grinding her teeth, doing her best to stay calm. The dirt track was now even more pot-holed, more treacherous, but she kept the car moving as fast as possible. Just as the fog momentarily parted to reveal the main road, there was an eruptive bang as the fire closed in behind us. I turned around and saw the track we had just traveled transformed into an inferno. The flames were racing alongside us, tearing through the forest as fast as the MG.

"Oh Jesus," Anne screamed as the top of a large pine cracked in half and dangled over the road, its branches still ablaze. But just when it looked as if it was about to collapse across our path, there was an abrupt, high-velocity blast of water. It flooded the windshield, momentarily blinding us. But when the water cleared away, we discovered that we had reached the main road, and had been saved from immolation by the local fire brigade.

Two uniformed officers ran to the car and pulled us both out.

"You guys all right?"

My lungs felt a little scorched, but Anne had evidently inhaled more smoke, as she was now gagging loudly. One of the firemen immediately shoved an oxygen mask across her face. I grabbed my camera and went running to her side.

"You okay?" I asked.

She nodded, then pulled the mask off and said, "Go to work."

"Gotcha."

"And I want color as well as black-and-white."

I leaned over and kissed her.

"We'll get you to a hospital as soon as—"

She interrupted me. "I'm not going to a hospital. I'm going straight to the paper as soon as you've got the pictures—"

"Miss," one of the firemen said, "put the mask back on."

But she was digging in the pocket of her jacket for her mobile phone.

"Miss, you need oxygen. The mask. *Now.*"

"Not until I call my paper. Gary, get on with it."

I began to shoot two firefighters losing control of a spurting hose.

"Who the hell is the guy with the camera?" I heard a senior officer shout.

"He's a photographer with *The Montanan,*" Anne shouted back. "Let him do his job."

"The mask, lady. The mask."

I began to run up the road. One young firefighter, his face blackened by soot, leaned against a vehicle, looking shell-shocked. I managed to get five shots of him before turning my attention to four officers silhouetted against two blackened trees. Overhead, light seaplanes had arrived, bombarding the fire with water, then returning to the lake to restock their pontoons with more water. Using a telephoto lens, I got a terrific shot of one pilot casually glancing out of his cockpit as the sheet of water showered down from his pontoons—a nonchalant "right stuff" expression on his face, as if a major forest fire were nothing more than another's day's work.

I switched over to Fujicolor just as a wall of flame was being doused. I nabbed a fantastic close-up of an older officer—his skin as cracked as petrified cement—wide-eyed with disbelief as the red glow of the flames bathed his face. I ran through nine rolls of film in less than thirty minutes. Three seaplanes were now working overhead, while four engines madly pumped water. The heat around me was so acute that I was drenched in sweat. But I kept working, my brain running on high octane. The extremity of the situation—the fact that Anne and I had escaped immolation by seconds—was overridden by the kick of danger, of finally being in the picture. I now understood why combat photographers always ran toward gunfire. There was something irresistible about edging so close to death. Yet you actually believed that, because you were looking at everything through a viewfinder, you were immune to danger. The camera became something of a shield. Standing behind it, no harm would come to you. It granted you absolution from jeopardy.

Or, at least that's what I thought as I raced up and down the forest road, reeling off shots, oblivious to the flames that encircled this backcountry thoroughfare like a fiery circus hoop.

"You, photographer!"

I spun around and saw the officer in charge pointing directly at me.

"You're finished here."

"Ten more minutes and I'll be gone."

"I want you out—"

He didn't get to complete his sentence, as a sheet of flame suddenly leaped out from the trees, enveloping a firefighter standing ten feet in front of him. Immediately, three of his colleagues were charging toward him. I trained my camera on his torched body. My finger kept squeezing the shutter release as he spun around in agony—his clothes and hair aglow—while his fellow firefighters desperately attempted to put out the flames. But once the fire had been doused, the poor bastard pitched forward and lay very still on the ground. I nabbed four exposures as he fell. I clicked away as the senior officer frantically attempted cardiac massage, then finally felt for a pulse. My final shot was of the officer kneeling by the body, his face in his hands.

"Oh God . . ."

It was Anne. She was standing behind me, looking on in shock.

She asked, "Is he . . . ?"

I nodded.

Moving her lips toward my right ear, she whispered, "Did you get it all?"

"Yeah. How are your lungs?"

"Still operable."

An officer approached us.

"Time for you to go," he said. *"Now."*

We drove like bandits. Within ten minutes, we were back on Route 200. As we turned toward Mountain Falls, I stopped the car and jumped out, using up another roll of film as I got a terrific high-altitude view of the conflagration in the valley below. The flames were still so ferocious they seemed to be licking the hovering seaplanes, and a huge, menacing cloud of smoke was suspended above the once verdant canyon.

Anne was standing by me as I finished shooting.

"Guess that's the end of my cabin," she said.

"You might be lucky," I said. "The fire wasn't burning close to the lake."

"Even if the cabin survives, who's going to want to spend time in a barbecued forest?"

Her mobile phone rang. She answered it and was engaged in a rapid-fire conversation.

"Yeah . . . yeah . . . color and black-and-white . . . one dead so far . . . yeah, he got that . . . right, we'll be there in an hour. No later."

She turned to me. "That was the editor. He is thrilled we were almost charred alive . . . and that you happened to be packing a camera at the time. He is also holding the front page, so we have to hurry."

Barreling down Route 200, Anne cranked the MG up to ninety.

"How many rolls you shoot altogether?"

"Seven black-and-white, four color."

"Great. We'll probably go black-and-white on the front page and do a color spread inside. And the color shots are going to be exceedingly marketable."

"To whom?"

"*Time, Newsweek, USA Today,* maybe even *National Geographic.* Whoever pays the highest price."

"And who's going to sell them?"

"I am—in my capacity as photo editor of the paper."

"I didn't know I had agreed to *The Montanan* owning subsidiary rights."

She threw her eyes heavenward. "You really are a romantic."

"So are you, Ms. Marketing."

"All right, let's get this over with," she said. "How much for the first run of the pics in our paper?"

"Two grand."

"Go to hell."

"I nearly got cremated giving you the photographic scoop of the year. You can afford to be generous."

"And you have to be realistic. We're still a smalltown paper. Even a thousand dollars would be an excessive amount for us."

"Then I'll have to sell them elsewhere."

"Fifteen hundred. And a fifty-fifty split on everything we sell on."

"Fifty-five–forty-five."

"I hate you," she said.

I leaned over and kissed her hair.

"Well, I love you," I said.

She turned suddenly and stared at me in shock.

"Keep your eyes on the road," I said.

She returned her gaze to the windshield.

"What you just said wasn't a negotiating tactic, was it?"

"Oh, you are a piece of work, Ms. Ames."

"Well . . ." she finally said, "I guess I'll have to agree to your terms."

We made the paper in forty minutes. Jane was pacing the front lobby, waiting for us. She was very taken aback by the grubby state of our clothes and faces.

"Fuck me, look at you guys," she said. "It really was a fire, wasn't it?"

"An A plus for deduction, honey," Anne said. "Now rush Gary's film to the lab. I want contact sheets in an hour, no later."

A middle-aged man in a tweed jacket, blue button-down shirt, and knit tie came striding purposefully toward us.

"Good God, Anne . . . why aren't you at the hospital?"

"It's just a little pine ash, Stu."

"You must be Gary Summers," he said and proffered his hand. "Stuart Simmons."

"Our boss," Anne added.

"You two made it out of there okay?" he asked.

"She should be checked out by a doctor right away," I said.

"I'm fine," she said.

"Smoke inhalation is never 'fine.'"

"I'm going nowhere until those pictures are printed," Anne said.

The editor turned to the receptionist. "Ellie, call Dr. Braun at home, ask him to make a house call to the paper immediately."

Anne groaned.

"Don't complain, Anne," Stu said. "Anyway, I want you here until the pages are laid out. And Merrill and Atkinson on the city desk want to talk with you. They're doing the words to accompany the pictures."

"You have a reporter out at the scene now?" Anne asked.

"Yeah, Gene Platt."

"Not that old hack?"

"Anne . . . that's not your call. Anyway, he's just doing color. The city desk boys will write the thing."

"How about follow-up pictures for tomorrow?" Anne asked. "Especially as there's no way they are going to have that fire under control by the time we go to press tonight."

"Gary, you feel like going back there?" Stu asked. "Maybe do some night shots?"

"I was hoping to hang here until the current batch of pics is developed."

"Leave it to Anne's judgment," Stu said. "She's the best."

"Damn right I am," she said, arching her eyebrows at me. The editor noticed the seductive glance, yet tried to act as if he hadn't noticed it—though, undoubtedly, he knew all about Anne and me, Mountain Falls being Mountain Falls.

"So, you up for another stint at the front?" he asked.

It was hard to resist the battlefield analogy. I said yes.

"Great," Stu said. Ellie the receptionist interrupted him.

"Mr. Simmons," she said, "I've got Gene Platt on the line. Seems another firefighter died."

He shook his head and said, "This is turning into a real biggie." Then turning to me, he added, "You be very careful. And give me a call sometime tomorrow. I'd like to talk to you about something permanent around here. Really like the 'Montana Faces,' by the way."

Before I could say anything, he turned and headed back into the newsroom.

"Well, well, a job offer," Anne said.

"If it means working under you, forget it."

"You are a charmer."

"Please see the doctor."

"Please watch your ass out there."

She was about to reach out for me, but then hesitated, remembering the all-observant receptionist behind us.

"You still want a color and black-and-white mix?" I asked.

"Absolutely. And keep in mind that, though stark news stuff may work for us, glossy will really sell elsewhere."

She handed me her mobile phone, in case either of us needed to make contact. She touched my arm.

"Don't get hurt," she said.

I was back at the fire within an hour. I returned to the ridge where I had done the valley shots and got very lucky, as the declining sun bathed the smoke-filled canyon in a perfect whiskey glow. I kept shooting for over a half hour, then drove down into the main action. The fire was still untamed, and the scene on the main forest road had now turned into quite a little media circus. Four television crews. Two or three radio types. A handful of hacks from the other in-state papers. And Rudy Warren.

"What the fuck are you doing here?" I asked.

"You think I'd miss this show? Biggest thing to happen west of the Divide in years. Anyway, Simmons called me just after he sent you back here, telling me he wanted a thousand-word commentary by eight tonight."

"I thought this guy Gene Platt and the city desk boys were doing the coverage . . ."

"Yeah, they're covering *the facts.* But Simmons also wants a proper writer on the scene . . ."

"That wouldn't be you, by any chance?"

"You're very perceptive . . . for a photographer."

He disappeared into the fray of hacks and firemen. I didn't talk to him for over an hour, but did occasionally grab sight of him carefully sizing up the order of command among the fire-fighters, scrutinizing the actions of the men as they handled unwieldy water hoses and guarded each other's backs. Occasionally, Rudy would pull out a notebook and jot some-thing down. But basically, he just observed. Seeing him at work, I was reminded of the fact that writers were like scav-engers—they foraged a scene for details that, when joined together, would beget the Big Picture. Photographers were always on the lookout for that one bold image that would define a story. But a writer—if he was any good—knew that his craft was, in part, all about transfiguring small incidents into a compelling narrative. And it was a balancing act—a story with-out potent detail inevitably seemed bland, prosaic. Yet one without a critical overview left you with the uneasy feeling that the writer hadn't grasped the larger implications of the events he'd observed.

Rudy Warren may have been one of Montana's major drunks, but, when it came to the writing game, he still under-stood this need to balance detail with an underlying theme. An hour after he arrived at the fire, he found me shooting a team of medics treating a firefighter for smoke inhalation.

"Lemme borrow your mobile phone," he said.

I turned it over to him. Then, standing next to me, he called the paper, asked for a copy-taker, and began to. dictate his essay straight down the line. He had nothing written. Once or twice, he paused to refer to his notebook. But essentially it was a masterful, off-the-cuff performance. I listened attentively, amazed by his ability to spontaneously compose his copy, and by his shrewd use of revealing images:

> After battling in this acrid, pine-scented hell for over three hours, firefighter Chuck Manning sat slumped by Engine Number Two, wanting nothing more than a cold beer and a comforting cigarette. The beer wasn't forthcoming, but he did have a pack of Marlboros in his uniform. He fished one out, shoved it between his blackened teeth. Slapping his pockets, however, he realized he didn't have a light. Ten feet away from him, a gush of flame suddenly incinerated another corner of Montana's biggest forest preserve. He blinked with shock in the face of this inferno. His cigarette remained unlit.

When he finished filing, he handed me back the phone.

"Now I need a drink," he said.

"That was impressive, Rudy," I said.

He grinned, revealing his decayed dentures. "Yeah, it was."

He managed to collar an officer passing by us.

"Sarge," Rudy asked, "you got things under control here yet?"

"Just about," he said. "And the good news is that the damage has been contained to around a ten-square-mile section of the forest. Could've been a whole lot worse."

"You figure out what caused it yet?" Rudy asked.

"Probably some dumb-ass tourist tossing a cigarette out of a car window."

"Betcha he was Californian," Rudy said under his breath.

I had a question for the sergeant—did any of the lakefront cabins survive the blaze?

"Believe it or not, the fire managed to skirt the entire shoreline. No loss of property whatsoever."

"Anne'll be pleased to hear her cabin made it," Rudy said.

"How'd you know about her place up here?" I asked.

Rudy rolled his eyes. "You still haven't figured out this town yet, have you?"

The mobile phone rang. It was Anne.

"How are your lungs?" I asked.

"All clear, according to the quack. You still in one piece?"

"Yeah. And so's your cabin."

"No way."

"Someone up there likes you."

"Someone down here likes you too. Your pics are fantastic. And ever since we put them out on the AP photo service—"

"You did *what?*"

"AP was on to us as soon as news of the fire reached them, wondering if we had any visuals. I said 'Damn right we do,' and got ten of your best shots on the wire immediately. They've been picked up everywhere."

I was flabbergasted. And more than a little nervous.

"Oh," I said.

"Don't sound so happy," Anne said.

"I'm just a little amazed, that's all."

"You shouldn't be. They are phenomenal pics. You got more film for me?"

"I do."

"Well, get it back here pronto . . . and I may just buy you a beer."

She hung up. Rudy—the all-knowing schmuck—immediately sniffed my unease. And said, "You look like a man who's not exactly coming to terms with success."

I followed his beat-up Bronco back to Mountain Falls. He parked in front of Eddie's and staggered in for a drink. I continued on to *The Montanan.* As I walked in, the first edition was just rolling off the presses. Anne came running toward me, holding a freshly inked copy. The front-page headline read:

TWO KILLED AS FIRE RAVAGES STATE FOREST

Beneath this, covering five of the page's eight columns, was my black-and-white photograph of the senior fire officer kneeling by the body of one of his fallen colleagues, his face hidden in his hands. Five more of my pictures adorned the local news inside pages, and there was also a "special" two-page, full-color spread of ten pictures, most of which concentrated on the heroics of the firefighters.

Stu Simmons strolled over and joined us.

"Amazing work, Gary."

"Told you he was a find," Anne said, then nudged me with her elbow. "Let's get your new film into the lab. Jane!"

Jane was seated at a nearby computer terminal, her eyes fixed on the screen, oblivious to Anne's voice.

"Jane!" Anne said, "Stop playing Nintendo. We've got work to do here."

Jane finally looked up. "Gary, you've to see this. It's *awesome*."

We all joined her at the terminal. She was scanning the Internet, calling up the front pages of several major newspapers around the country. One by one, the first-edition front pages of *The New York Times, The Washington Post,* the *Los Angeles Times,* the *Chicago Tribune, The Miami Herald,* and *USA Today* flashed in front of us. All of them carried my photograph of the dead firefighter and his grieving boss. All of them also carried the credit: Photo by Gary Summers/ *The Montanan.*

"Looks like you're famous," Jane said.

8

THAT FUCKING PHOTO. Everyone ran it. It was picked up by forty papers across the United States (according to Jane, who was assigned to track its placement). Overseas, it made *The Guardian, The Daily Telegraph, The Scotsman, Liberation, Corriere della Serra, Die Frankfurter Allgemeine, El Mundo, Al Ahram, The Times of India, The South China Morning Post, The Australian, The Sydney Morning Herald,* and about a dozen other journals in the Philippines, Malaysia, assorted parts of Scandinavia, Mexico, Brazil, Argentina, Paraguay, Chile, Japan, and Papua New Guinea.

Yes, Papua New Guinea.

"You're even famous in Port Moresby," Jane said when she called me to read out this ever growing list of foreign sales.

Then there was the television coverage. On the morning after the fire, Anne roused me out of bed to catch Bryant Gumbel and Katie Couric discussing my photo on NBC's *Today.*

"They say a picture's worth a thousand words," noted Katie solemnly as the photo flashed up on a screen behind her. "Well, this one's worth a million."

Bryant came in here. "Taken by Montana photographer Gary Summers during the fire that threatened to destroy a state forest yesterday, it is a moving reminder of the human cost of environmental disaster. Two firefighters lost their lives saving the forest. This was one of them—Mike McAllister of Lincoln, Montana, who had just joined the force three months ago. That's his captain, Don Pullman, kneeling by his side. His private grief is now our public grief, as we salute the heroism of Mike McAllister and all our nation's firefighters this morning."

Bryant and Katie looked at each other, and sighed deeply (that "we're near to tears" sigh), then brightened up to deal with an item about Claudia Schiffer's new catwalk colleague: a chimp named Buttons.

"Sanctimonious bullshit," I yelled at the screen as Anne channel-surfed in search of further coverage.

"Hey, don't complain—it's priceless publicity. Your name is going to be everywhere."

That's what terrified me, remembering that Beth watched *Today* most mornings.

"It's just a photo," I said. "It's no big deal."

"Remember that photo of the bombing victim at the World Trade Center—all covered in soot, eyes wild with disbelief? That was also 'just a photo,' but it grabbed everyone's attention. Want to know why? It encapsulated an entire godawful, senseless tragedy in one single image—an image that everyone could relate to. That's photojournalism at its best—when you can find the human dimension in something terrible. It's exactly what you've done in that picture. And that's why everyone wants it."

She was right. Too right. By Monday evening, the photo had also been the source of commentary by Peter Jennings on ABC *World News Tonight* and by Tom Brokaw on NBC *Nightly News*. Brokaw really made a big deal about it—well, he does own a large ranch out here—going on about how "At a time when we tend to disdain the whole concept of public service, Gary Summers's moving picture is a tribute to those who serve us by safeguarding our natural habitat."

Beth watched Tom Brokaw most nights too.

I lay low at Anne's place for the day, sidestepping her offer to come in to the paper and help oversee a big follow-up spread they were running in Tuesday's edition, a spread that would incorporate my night shots.

"I'll leave it to your judgment," I said.

"Fine by me," she said. "You're slightly underwhelmed by all this, aren't you?"

"Just whacked, that's all. It was a hard day yesterday."

"Know what you need?" she said. "Copious amounts of wine, pasta, and deranged sex."

"In that order?"

"We'll see."

When she arrived home at nine, she brought with her a first edition of the next day's paper and two bottles of champagne.

I scanned the center pages. They used six of my night shots, alongside another Rudy Warren column about the aftermath of the fire. It was called "Landscape After Battle" and it read beautifully.

"It all looks great," I said. "What's with the French fizz?"

"Big news," she said, yanking the cork out of a bottle of Mumm and pouring two glasses. "I was going to mention this earlier—but I was still in negotiation with New York until two hours ago."

"New York?" I said. "Who in New York?"

"*Time* magazine."

I gulped.

"They saw your photos on the AP wire, called us, discovered that we still hadn't sold fifty of your color transparencies, and asked us to get them down the Net right away."

She paused for dramatic effect.

"Around seven tonight, their photo editor rang back. They loved the work. 'Who is this guy . . . and why have you been keeping him to yourself?' His exact words. And then he said they'd decided to go with a two-page color spread, accompanied by a Lance Morrow essay. You know Morrow's stuff, don't you? One of their resident prose stylists. *Très* highbrow. I'm sure he'll find something profound to say about the primeval nature of fire and the despoliation of the Old West . . .

"Anyway, the fact that they're attaching a Morrow essay to the spread means that they consider it a biggie. And they're paying big too. It took some negotiation, but I got them to agree to thirty grand."

I felt as if I were in free-fall.

"Thirty *thousand* dollars?" I asked.

"Yep. That's sixteen-five to you. Throw in all the other sales, and I figure you're going to see nearly twenty-seven grand. Not bad for a night's work."

"Indeed," I said, not really knowing what to say.

"And then there's going to be all the spin-off offers of work. I mean, a photo spread in *Time* is a huge thing."

She raised her glass, clinked it against mine.

"Jane's right. You are going to be famous."

I sipped my fizz. I said nothing. She covered my hand with hers.

"Tell me," she said.

"There's nothing to tell," I said.

"Then explain to me why you aren't enjoying all this."

"All what?"

"Success. In the last twenty-four hours you have done something that, for years, you thought would never happen. You have broken through. You've finally *arrived.* You're not going to need Stu Simmons's job offer on the paper, because just about every big-time magazine in the country will start vying for you. And if you play your cards right, you'll be quickly graduating from Judy Wilmers's gallery to some heavyweight dealer in New York. But only if *you* want it. And what's baffling the hell out of me right now is that you definitely *don't* seem to want it. That—for some reason—the idea of success is scaring the shit out of you."

"I'm just . . . adjusting to the idea, that's all."

"Well, adjust fast. Otherwise this is going to be nothing more than your fifteen minutes of fame."

By the end of the week, I had come to understand one of the great underlying truisms of American life—once you are perceived to be hot, everyone wants you. The guy who's struggling is always a despised figure in our culture. Because he's viewed as a nobody, a loser who's desperately trying to convince a publisher, a magazine editor, a producer, a gallery owner, an agent, that he could be a player, if only the right break came his way. But, of course, no one wants to give him that break—because why should they help a schmuck out of nowhere? And even if they think that he might have some talent, they're usually terrified of trusting their own judgment and backing an unknown quantity.

So the nobody remains a nobody. Unless dumb luck intervenes. And the door opens. And the light streams in. And the incandescent glow of professional good fortune envelops him. And suddenly he's the golden boy, *a major talent,* the dude du jour. Everybody returns his phone calls now; everybody phones him. Because he's been anointed with the halo of success.

Later that week, Gary Summers became one of the anointed ones. It happened on the day *Time* hit the streets. Anne was FedExed an advance copy the night before, and I was reluctantly dragged into *The Montanan* for celebratory drinks in the editor's office. I tried to looked pleased. I accepted all the congratulatory backslapping with a fixed smile. I stared at the two magazine pages of pictures—my byline prominently displayed below the headline IN NATURE'S INFERNO—and willed myself to be gratified, delighted by this massive professional coup. But all I could think was: Everyone will see the pictures, everyone will see the name, and it will all start unraveling.

Anne and I both drank too much, so we ended up staggering across the bridge to my apartment. We slept until ten—when the phone began to ring. Constantly. I let the answering machine deal with the calls.

The first was from Judy Wilmers. She was in a state of frantic mercantile fever:

"What can I say? What *can* I say? I saw it, I love it, you're a genius. And what this is going to do for 'Montana Faces' I can't begin to tell you . . . I'm getting on to New York pronto. I promise you a book contract within ten days. And that's just the start. Call me, genius. Call me."

I pulled the duvet over my head. Anne began to tickle my chest, repeating in a shrill Judylike voice, "You're a genius, you're a genius, you're a genius, you're a genius . . ."

"When you're from Marin County," I said, "everyone's a fucking genius."

The next call was from Morgan Grey of Grey-Murcham Associates. The name didn't register at first. Then I remembered that he was that photo agent in New York to whom Gary had written several letters, begging to be taken on as a client.

"Gary, Morgan Grey here. It's been quite a job tracking you down. *Time* told me to call *The Montanan*, a woman named Jane on the photo desk gave me your number . . ."

"Goddamn Jane," I said out loud.

"Chill," Anne said.

Morgan Grey continued with his message

". . . anyway, long time no speak—and I just want to congratulate you on that brilliant spread in *Time*. I always knew you had it in you, and I'm just sorry that we couldn't have worked out some sort of representation deal earlier. But if you still are in the market for representation, we are most certainly keen to have you on our books. Could you call me at . . ."

"Asshole," I said after he hung up. "*I always knew you had it in you.* That clown wouldn't have broken wind for me a year ago."

"It's how it works, Gary."

Ten minutes later, the phone rang again. Jules Rossen, photo editor at *Destinations*.

"Hey, Gary! Just got your phone number from Jane at *The Montanan* . . ."

"I'm going to kill her slowly," I said.

"No," Anne said, "that's my job."

". . . loved the pics in *Time*. Great vérité, great drama, and fantastic composition, given the stress you were undoubtedly under. We need to do some business, hombre. We want you on the *Destinations* team. And, as you know, that screwup on the Baja story wasn't down to me. But, hey—that's past tense. It's the present now—and we should talk. So ring me at . . ."

"Another asshole who played me along," I said.

"They're all going to come out of the woodwork now," she said.

Anne left for work. She called ten minutes later to reassure me that Jane and the switchboard had been instructed not to divulge my phone number. I retreated to my darkroom and tried to get on with some printing. But the phone just kept ringing. Art Pepys, the photo editor of *Time.* Three other photo agents from New York with whom Gary had once been in touch. The photo editors of *National Geographic, GQ, Los Angeles, Vanity Fair,* and *Condé Nast Traveler.* I phoned the telephone company and arranged to have my number unlisted as of tomorrow.

I certainly wasn't going to reply to Jules Rossen or Morgan Grey—because they'd both had face-to-face meetings with Gary, and might wonder why his voice had altered so dramatically since moving west. Getting in direct contact with the magazine editors who phoned also wasn't the best of ideas—one of them might just have stumbled on Gary when he was trawling for work. I needed a go-between, a buffer zone that would allow me to maintain a low profile. I picked up the phone.

"Judy?"

"Gary, *bello,* I was just on the verge of calling. How are you enjoying stardom?"

"It has its moments."

"Listen, you ever hear of Cloris Feldman? New York literary agent extraordinaire? You're her new client. For the book only, of course. And her commission comes out of my fee, you'll be pleased to know."

"You'd've been in breach of contract otherwise," I said.

"Yeah, yeah, yeah. Anyway, I'm DHLing her the transparencies of the 'Montana Faces' exhibition. She can think of at least five publishers who would vie for it as a big coffee-table book."

"You are an operator, Judy," I said. "You wouldn't want to represent me for magazine work, would you?"

It took her a nanosecond to say yes. It took her two nanoseconds to assent to a commission of 15 percent. And she also agreed to make a tape for my answering machine, informing anyone who called me that all professional inquiries were being handled by Mr. Summers's agent and giving her phone number. She could be my switchboard from now on.

I supplied her with a list of the agents and editors who had phoned.

"Right," she said, "I'll politely tell the agents to go fuck their mothers and see what kind of assignments and money the editors are offering. And I'll make sure they know you don't come cheap. 'Bye, genius."

Within five days, Judy had four assignment offers on the table. Two of them tempted me—a *National Geographic* proposal to contribute to a future issue devoted entirely to Montana and a glossy *Vanity Fair* gig that would involve shooting portraits of a dozen or so of the big actor honchos who had bought ranches in the state.

"They're calling the story 'Hollywood, Montana,'" Judy said, "and you basically know what they want: Jane and Ted in denims and boots, looking home on the range under some big, fucking sky. It's glossy bullshit—but you've gotta grab this one. Because celebrity is what sells these days. You get established as a guy who can handle famous faces as well as gritty lowlifes, you can write your own ticket for the rest of your career."

I still made reluctant noises about rubbing shoulders with the rich and fabulous. Until Judy mentioned the fee involved: twenty-five hundred a day for twelve days' work. And I could wait to start work on the assignment until after my exhibition opened in two weeks. This would give me enough time to knock off the *National Geographic* commission—a small portfolio on the subject of Montana roads.

"They've asked six photographers to concentrate on a specific aspect of the state's landscape," Judy explained, "and they thought you might like to be the highways guy. It's a terrific chance to strut your stuff as a 'Big Picture' photographer. Do the 'Lonesome Road' routine. Capture that two-lane blacktop disappearing into the sunset, blah, blah, blah."

"How much are they offering?"

"Four grand, plus expenses. Not bad, considering it's a shared assignment. And it'll get you out of town in the weeks running up to the exhibition. Which, selfishly speaking, would suit me fine. I don't care how cool a customer you might be, a week before the opening you're going to get hit with PET."

"What's that?"

"Pre-Exhibition Tension."

I laughed. "And what are its manifestations?"

"The artist turns into a complete pain in the ass."

Thirty-four thousand for two assignments. It didn't make sense. The absurdity of success terrified and mesmerized me. I accepted both commissions.

On the afternoon before I headed off in search of the perfect Montana road, a packet of mail arrived from the Alternative Post Office in Berkeley. In the midst of all the bills and catalog junk was a handwritten envelope. I recognized the graceful, poised penmanship immediately. The letter I had been dreading since heading west had finally arrived.

Gary:

After I received your kiss-off letter in December, I wrote you off as a complete son of a bitch and vowed never to contact you again. Please don't think that your spread in *Time* and Bryant Gumbel's genuflection in front of your photo on the *Today* show has suddenly made you a nice guy in my eyes. You behaved like a shit. And your letter arrived just after the most appalling few weeks of my life.

Ben was killed in a boating accident on November 7th. He'd borrowed Bill Hartley's boat for the weekend, there was a terrible fire in the cabin—a faulty gas stove, everyone thinks—and the conflagration was so massive that his remains were never found.

It was a desperate shock—and what made the entire horrible business even more unbearable was the fact that (as you well know) I had asked him for a divorce earlier that week. Though the official coroner's report was "death by misadventure," I can't help but wonder if he flipped while out there on the water and did something irrevocably self-destructive. Everyone I spoke with right after his death—Bill and Ruth, Ben's boss Jack Mayle (who died himself a few weeks back)—did confirm that he was not handling the breakup well. And the last time I saw him—when I was staying at Lucy and Phil's in Darien—there was an awful scene over a bicycle he bought Adam. I was so stressed that I wouldn't let him into the house. Two days later, he was dead. The guilt I now feel is huge. I often fear that it will never go away.

Josh, of course, is too young to realize what's going on, but Adam has been taking it very hard. For weeks after Ben's death, he kept asking when Daddy would be coming home; kept waiting by the door every evening around six, anxiously awaiting his arrival. When I finally screwed up the courage and told him that his Daddy had had an accident and would never be coming back, he ran to his room and cried for what seemed like hours. I tried to comfort him, but he was inconsolable. Four months later, he still is. Just yesterday, he said: "Daddy must be home soon." He just can't accept it. And it's breaking my heart.

I stopped reading. I took a deep breath. I tried to steady myself. I didn't succeed. I went to the bathroom, plunged my face into a sink of cold water. Then I moved on to the kitchen, found a bottle of Black Bush in a cupboard, poured myself three fingers, slugged it back, and picked up the letter again.

Your "Dear John" missive landed on my mat two weeks into this nightmare. Your timing was impeccable. I am going to give you the benefit of the doubt and believe that, because you were down in Baja, romancing your Berkeley squeeze, you didn't see *The New York Times*, which had extensive coverage of Ben's accident. If, however, you did know about his death and still wrote me that letter, then you are a shit beyond redemption.

Up until recently, I really considered myself a candidate for an impending nervous breakdown. Then I met Elliot Burden. You may have heard of him during your trawl of the New York arts scene. Ex–big noise at Goldman Sachs who left Wall Street about seven years ago to open a gallery down on Wooster Street. He's in his late fifties, divorced, with two grown-up kids. We met at a dinner given by a mutual friend. Everyone was a bit shocked when we became an item so quickly. But I don't give two shits what anyone thinks. Elliot may not be the love of my life, but he's affectionate and solid and solvent. And he's already begun to establish a rapport with Adam . . .

I took another belt of whiskey. Elliot Burden. I conjured him up immediately. Andover '55. Yale '59. His first wife was undoubtedly named Babs. Still plays competitive singles twice a week at the New York Racquet Club. Probably looks like George Plimpton. A gentleman bohemian. Ralph Lauren blazers and pressed Armani jeans. And now the surrogate father for my two sons. The man Adam will start calling Daddy before the year is out . . .

I helped myself to a third belt of whiskey.

It was Elliot who convinced me to write this letter. He felt that, until I informed you about Ben, I wouldn't be able to achieve some sort of closure with you. I managed to get your new address from the New Croydon post office, but judging from what I read in *Time,* you're now based in Montana. Does this mean you also broke the heart of your Berkeley squeeze, or did she just get smart one morning and throw you out? Anyway, Elliot also happens to be a friend of Cloris

Feldman. Over dinner the other night, she showed us the transparencies of your forthcoming "Montana Faces" exhibition. Elliot loved the pictures. And though I'd rather not admit it, I was deeply impressed too. You've got it now. You're in the zone. But you're still an asshole.

    Beth

Closure. That inane nineties word. Life can never have any messy loose ends anymore. It must be tidied up; all stories ended cleanly. But, for me, there would never be a tidy finale to this story. When you've killed someone—and lost two sons—closure is impossible. Still, if Beth wanted a neat ending, I'd try to accommodate her. Especially if it meant that she would never write to me again.

I opened up the Thinkpad and began to type.

> B:
> Your letter was waiting for me upon my return from Montana. I'm still maintaining a place in the Bay Area, though I seem to be spending a considerable amount of time in the redneck north these days. No, I hadn't read about Ben before I wrote you last time. Heavy stuff—and it sounds like you've been through the wringer. A sailing accident—what a Wall Street death. Still, this Elliot guy seems like good news—and also someone who will keep you in the style to which you are accustomed. Thanks for the thumbs-up about the pictures. It really does mean a lot to me. Finally, if writing me off as an asshole helps the grieving process, then by all means call me an asshole.
> Take care.
> G.

I reread the letter and winced. It really was the work of a major shitbird—and would hopefully reinforce her belief that Gary was a self-absorbed jerk with whom she should not attempt to conduct an ongoing episolatory relationship. There was only one reply she could make to his letter, and that was to call him a heartless scumbag and wish him an agonizing death from testicular cancer. And once she wished him ill, she might just achieve the closure she was seeking.

I printed the letter and an envelope, and dispatched the lot to the Alternative Post Office, enclosing the usual $10 remailing fee. Then I drove over to *The Montanan*. As I was departing for the eastern extremities of the state the next morning, I'd promised to take Anne out for dinner that night at Le Petit Place, and had arranged to pick her up at the office. But as soon as I walked into the newsroom, I found myself dodging an airborne desk chair. It crashed to the left of my shoulder, but I still ducked right to avoid its trajectory. When I picked myself up off the floor, a computer keyboard came thundering down near my feet.

". . . and that's a little gift for the *Time* man of the year."

I gazed up just as Rudy Warren swung his fist wildly and smashed it straight through the screen of his desktop Mac. Everyone in the newsroom looked on in horror—those, that is, who hadn't scattered, as he'd already overturned two nearby desks and dismembered a couple of phones. Rudy slumped down in his chair, his fist still embedded inside the terminal. Blood began to dribble down the side of his desk. He stared at this circulatory leak with bemusement, as if he were some sort of onlooker to an accident in which he was not involved. That's when I knew he was drunk.

Anne came rushing out of her office, a small first-aid kit in one hand. She surveyed the general office damage, her eyes growing wide as she saw the stream of blood now cascading down onto the floor. She looked up at her colleagues.

"Well, don't just stand there gawking," she said. "Somebody call an ambulance."

"Hey, sweetheart," Rudy said, flashing her a dipsomaniacal grin.

"Forget the sweetheart crap, Rudy. What the hell was that all about?"

"Did I do something wrong?" he said, all innocence itself.

"No," she said. "You just attacked several inanimate objects."

"Well, shit, that's not exactly a crime against humanity, now is it?"

"Of course not," she said, sounding as if she were trying to calm a recalcitrant child. "Shall we try to remove your hand from the computer, Rudy?"

"Might be a good idea," he said.

Before undertaking this delicate proceedure, she glanced up and saw me.

"Meet you in the restaurant," Anne mouthed, then returned to the gory task at hand.

I was working on my second martini when she finally walked into Le Petit Place.

"The suspense is killing me," I said after ordering her a drink. "Is his fist still in the Mac?"

"No, the removal operation was a complete success, and he's currently being stitched up at Mountain Falls General. Hopefully, they'll chain him to a bed for the night. The guy had about a gallon of J&B sluicing around in his veins."

"I don't suppose we're going to be reading any more Rudolph Warren columns in *The Montanan*," I said.

"Stu's going to see him at the hospital tomorrow morning."

"Stu is far too sober and button-down to grant absolution to a lush."

"Don't be too sure of that. Rudy's column is popular. And though they might not like him personally, the boys in the marketing department know that he helps sell the newspaper. These days, a midsized paper like ours needs every sales attraction it can get."

"Why do the marketing boys hate Rudy?"

"At last year's Christmas party, he really got stinko and started calling the head of marketing, Ned Allen, 'a Willy Loman cunt.' That's a direct quote, by the way."

"I'm sure."

"Of course, he apologized afterward. Just as he also apologized to Joan after trashing the Mountain Pass. And just as he'll also say several acts of contrition in front of Stu when he's sober again tomorrow. Around twice a year, Rudy always seems to go ballistic. Probably has something to do with the position of the moon."

"Nah—that's far too Californian an explanation for Rudy. He's just a mean drunk."

"He has his virtues."

"Such as?"

"He is an ace writer."

"This is true."

"And"—she laced her fingers through mine—"if he hadn't stolen your prints, I wouldn't be drinking martinis with you now."

"Yeah," I said. "He does have his virtues."

Around three that morning, I stirred when Anne wrapped her arms around me and held on tight.

"You awake?" she whispered.

"I am now."

"Sorry."

"That's okay. Why can't you sleep?"

"Thinking," she said.

"About?"

"You. Us. I'm going to miss you. A lot."

"It's only for ten days. Then I'm back."

"You sure you'll be coming back?"

"I'm sure."

"I wonder . . ."

"Don't."

"It's just . . . now that you suddenly have *Vanity Fair* and a bunch of other magazines chasing you, why should you stay in a pissant Montana town?"

"Because I want to."

"But why?"

"You."

"No other reason?"

"None."

"Success is a dangerous drug."

"But, according to you, I fear success."

"You'll grow to like it. People will soon tell you how important you are—and you'll start to think they're right. Just as you'll also start to think that your past can be discarded. It's how success works."

"Not in this case."

"I want to believe that."

"Believe it."

A few hours later, an awkward silence dominated breakfast. Anne kept staring into her cup of tea, looking distracted.

I finally said, "It's only a week and a half, Anne."

"I know."

"And I'm only going to eastern Montana, not Iraq."

"I know."

"And I will call you every day."

"I know."

"So don't worry."

"I will worry."

"You shouldn't."

"You really know nothing about loss, do you?"

I was on the verge of saying "That's not true," but I managed to stop myself.

"Loss makes you regard everything as tenuous, fragile," she said. "And you begin to distrust the notion of happiness. If a good thing comes into your life, you know it's only a matter of time before it will be taken away from you."

"I won't be disappearing, Anne."

She took my hand, shunned my gaze. "We'll see."

9

As I CROSSED THE Continental Divide that morning, I found myself thinking: *Anne knows*. She may not have figured it all out yet—maybe hasn't even admitted it to herself—but instinctively she suspects I am on the run from something. And she now fears what I fear—that success will inevitably lead to disclosure, forcing me to vanish from view.

But when I finally spoke to Anne late that evening—after checking into a motel on the outskirts of a place called Lewistown—she was decidedly upbeat again.

"Is the motel romantic?" she teased.

"Only if you're an Anthony Perkins fan."

"Speaking of psychotics, Rudy Warren has disappeared."

"No way."

"Checked himself out of the hospital last night, hasn't been seen or heard from since. Stu had one of his minions scour the town for him. They even got the cops to break into his house. Found nothing."

"Not a clue where he's gone?"

"His car is still parked outside the paper. No one saw him at the airport. My guess is that he's hopped a bus bound for somewhere."

"Or nowhere."

"What's Lewistown like?"

"Total nowhere."

"I hate eastern Montana. Too flat. Too empty. I always think it's going to gobble me up. Don't let it gobble you."

"I won't."

Anne was right—traveling in this quarter of Montana really led you to believe that the world was flat and you were fast approaching its edge. And though it was 280 miles from Mountain Falls, the town of Lewistown wasn't even in the eastern extremities of the state. There was almost three hundred miles of horizontal prairie to traverse before you hit the North Dakota border. Three hundred miles in a visual vacuum. Forlorn country. A bleak, desolate terrain of scrubby vegetation and the occasional truck stop. Mile after mile of unbroken monotony, a howling wind providing the constant soundtrack. It was a world that almost appeared fossilized, extinct.

I wandered its byways for over a week. Passing through towns like Lustre and Antelope and Plentywood. Meandering up unsealed roads that passed through vast swathes of uninhabited land. Daring myself to negotiate its labyrinthine system of dirt tracks, narrow arteries that plunged me into the most isolated corners of these badlands. One day I got so lost in the nether reaches of Prairie and McCone counties it took four hours to find my way back to Route 200 and a speck of a hamlet called Circle. I happened upon lonely road after lonely road. I shot roll after roll of film. I pulled into a motel every evening after sundown and then made two calls to Mountain Falls. The first was the daily business update with Judy.

"So here's how we stand today," she would begin, giving me the rundown on recent developments. "Spoke to Cloris in New York. She's got some guy at Random House on to her twice a day. Seems he loves the photos, sees their potential as a coffee-table book, but—according to Cloris—he's just a junior editor and doesn't have the power to buy without authorization. So he's going to have to plead your case in front of the marketing department next week. Meanwhile, at least five gallery owners called—"

"From where?"

"Manhattan, Seattle, Portland. All really interested in the exhibition for their spaces. One or two said they'll even try to show up for your opening. So it looks like some hotshot art folk might be making pilgrimages to see you in Mountain Falls."

"Uh-huh."

"Your enthusiasm is overwhelming, Gary. When are you gonna be back here?"

"The day before the opening."

"Say these people want meetings with you?"

"They can see me the day after the opening. In the afternoon only."

"Greta fucking Garbo. Still, as your agent, I advise you to maintain this air of sullen indifference to things commercial. It's good for your image as someone who takes himself far too seriously. A little aloof self-importance goes a long way in the art game, believe me. By the way, *National Geographic* rang, asking for a mug shot of you for their contributor's page."

"Inform them that I don't like being photographed."

"Very funny."

"I'm serious. I don't want any pictures of myself appearing in print."

"Tell me you're joking."

"I am not joking."

"An explanation, please."

"I've decided that the world doesn't need to see my face."

"Who the hell are you? Thomas Pynchon?"

"Just someone who doesn't want to play the self-promotion game. That's your job. You can sell my ass anywhere you like— just keep me out of it as much as possible. And no pictures of me in print. Okay, agent?"

"You're the boss. Unfortunately."

I think Judy bought my remote artist routine. Or, at least, I don't think she sensed that I had other motives for keeping my face from public view. Anne, on the other hand, wanted me arraigned for haughtiness in the first degree. A few days later, our nightly phone call began with her question:

"Did you really tell Judy that you wouldn't let your mug appear anywhere?"

"I see the village drums have been beating again."

"You're dodging the question."

"Yeah, those were my instructions."

"That's hilarious."

"I just don't want the attention."

"Or maybe you're gunning for a Pulitzer in Affectation?"

"Well, it will fuel the mystique."

"I did hear an underlay of irony in that last statement, didn't I?"

"You did."

"That's a relief. Where are you tonight?"

"Mildred, Montana."

"Never heard of it," she said.

"Surprise, surprise. It's about six hundred miles from you. Halfway between Ismay and Fallon on Route 335."

"I suppose the locals lined the streets when you pulled into town, wanting a glimpse of the famous photographer who refuses to have his picture taken?"

"They even made me mayor. You know who's living here now? Rudy Warren."

"Ha. Actually, he did finally phone Stu the other day from an undisclosed location. Told him he was heading down to Mexico and wanted six months' paid leave."

"Got to hand it to Rudy—he really understands the concept of chutzpah."

"Stu agreed to the leave. Unpaid, of course. And he also informed Rudy that he could forget his salary this month, as it would be used to pay off the damage he caused to the newsroom. But he didn't fire him."

"I guess old Rudy does sell papers. What's he going to do in Mexico?"

"Kill his liver with cheap tequila, sleep with underage whores—enlightened male stuff like that."

"That's one of the big disadvantages of eastern Montana. No teenage prostitutes. Don't suppose you'd want to join me out here?"

"In Mildred? Not a chance. But if you could wrap things up earlier, it would be nice to have you back in my bed."

"I still need a few days in the high north to shoot some mountain roads. How about meeting me halfway in somewhere like Bozeman?"

"Not this weekend. Jane and I have to deal with the annual overhaul of our photo inventory. You're still Stu's golden boy, by the way. He's gotten great mail on the 'Montana Faces' series—which means that you've made him look good. And the poster for the exhibition is now everywhere in town. It's going to be quite a party, your opening. Le tout Mountain Falls will be there."

"I can't wait."

"Mr. Enthusiasm. You'll enjoy the celebrity, Gary. And, meantime, keep missing me."

"I will."

And indeed I did. But as I started wending my way back west, I couldn't help but feel the onset of dread. Out here, in the great disconnected wilds, I felt safe. No one knew me; I could vanish on cue. But back in Mountain Falls I was a face. And—if Judy was doing her job properly— I might start being *a name.* Once I craved such consequence. Now I wanted to run away from it. Because, inevitably, it would lead to exposure.

And yet, another voice within my head kept whispering: If you're careful, you can get away with it. You can achieve prominence as a photographer. You can have a life with Anne. You'll just have to withdraw from view.

On the evening before I was due to return to Mountain Falls, I pulled into Bozeman and checked into the Holiday Inn. Late that night, I had a complete panic attack and was on the verge of phoning Judy and telling her that I wouldn't be attending the exhibition opening. But, after calming myself down (courtesy of a six-pack of Michelob), I eventually decided that my absence might be interpreted as suspicious. Better to show up at the party for a few hours, then later inform Judy that I found the entire experience of pressing the flesh distasteful—and would therefore never make a personal appearance again. She'd scream and moan—but she'd be shrewd enough to realize that she could turn my reclusive status into a lucrative marketing tool. If it worked for J. D. Salinger, why not me?

I climbed into the MG early the next morning, steeling myself for the final two-hundred-mile run back to Mountain Falls. But as soon as I turned the key in the ignition, the engine sounded as if it had just been diagnosed with tuberculosis. An hour later, a local mechanic arrived with his pickup truck, popped open the hood, and diagnosed severe internal combustion problems.

"We're talking a two-valve job here," he said. "And you ain't gonna see much change from a thousand bucks."

"No way I could limp in it back to Mountain Falls?" I asked.

"No way you could limp out of this parking lot. The sucker's out of commission until them valves is overhauled. But the good news is: I've got a free day. You give me the go-ahead, I can have it back to you by noon tomorrow, good as new."

"You accept credit cards?"

"You bet."

I tossed him the keys and checked back into the Holiday Inn. I called Anne.

"To hell with the car," she said. "I'll come and collect you."

"A four-hundred-mile round trip in a day? Wouldn't make you do it."

"I could sleep over," she said.

"Fine by me."

"Book a table somewhere nice for seven," she said.

An hour later, Anne rang back.

"Chaos here," she said, sounding a little frantic. "Lambert, the chief sub, collapsed in the newsroom thirty minutes ago and was rushed to the hospital. A mild coronary, but at least he's going to pull through. Anyway, it's all hands on deck and I've been pulled in to help with layout for the evening . . ."

"Looks like I'll be eating alone, then."

"I called Judy. She's willing to send someone to collect you."

"Tell her not to bother. The car will be ready by noon tomorrow. I'll be back in Mountain Falls no later than three. That'll give me a good three hours before the opening."

"Come straight to my place when you arrive," Anne said. "I want to ravage your body."

Downtown Bozeman was brimming with bars, restaurants, coffeehouses. But I felt like hiding, so I killed the evening in my room, with a pizza from Domino's and another six-pack of Michelob from the hotel concierge. I slept late. At eleven-thirty the next morning the phone rang. It was the mechanic, saying that the car would be delivered to me by one. At twelve-thirty the phone rang again. It was the mechanic, saying that there was a slight delay, but the car would be, without question, at the hotel by two. I checked out. I ate lunch in the Holiday Inn coffee shop. I called the garage at two-fifteen and demanded to know the whereabouts of my vehicle.

"He's just on his way," said the woman who answered the phone.

The mechanic didn't show up until three, towing my car behind him. He had a little boy seated in the cab of his pickup.

"Sorry for the delay, man," he said. "Bit of a scene with my old lady. Had to pick the kid up from school. You're not, like, in a hurry, are you?"

His son gave me a shy smile. I said nothing. The mechanic lowered the hook that held the MG. He opened the hood. The new valves gleamed and the engine block had been steamed free of grease. When he turned the ignition key, everything hummed sweetly.

"Sounds good," I said.

"You've just bought yourself another hundred thousand miles of MG life," he said. "And all for the bargain price of"— he reached into his pocket, pulled out an invoice—"nine hundred and eighty-four dollars and seventy-two cents."

I winced. I handed over Gary's Visa card. He returned to his pickup and pulled out a credit card machine. He made an imprint of my card and had me sign on the dotted line. He checked my signature and decided it was legitimate.

"Going far?" he asked.

"Mountain Falls. And I have to be there by six."

"Two hundred miles on the Montana-bahn? You'll do that in two hours, no sweat. Happy trails."

The mechanic was right. On the no-speed-limit Montana highway, it was possible to break the 100-miles-per-hour mark and not fear an encounter with a state trooper. I put the pedal to the metal and flew low down I-90. The MG purred. My mind emptied. Speed is the most intoxicating of drugs—and as I approached Mountain Falls, I was half tempted to bypass it all together and roar on.

Anne was pacing outside the New West Gallery as I drove up. Behind her, on the door of the gallery, was the exhibition poster: my portrait of Madge the Barkeep, beneath which was the title:

MONTANA FACES
PHOTOGRAPHS BY GARY SUMMERS

I had to force my eyes away from the poster and direct them at Anne. She was dressed for the opening, looking most fetching in an Annie Hall-ish man's suit with a tight vest.

"Where the hell have you been?" she asked.

I explained the problems with the mechanic.

"There's no such thing as a phone in Bozeman?" she asked.

"I'm here now," I said, putting my arm around her.

"I was certain you'd bought it on the highway."

"Wouldn't that be a nice, glossy magazine piece. 'Racing home for the triumphant opening of his first major exhibition, photographer Gary Summers splattered himself across—'"

"Shut up and kiss me," she said.

I complied. Judy came charging out of the gallery.

"You really know how to give a woman an ulcer," she said.

Still in mid-embrace, I raised a hand in greeting.

"Get your tongue out of that woman's throat and get in here."

I parked the car in an alley two blocks away, then retraced my steps. As soon as I entered the gallery, I took a sharp intake of breath. There—on freshly whitewashed walls—were my forty portraits. They were beautifully framed, perfectly displayed, well lit. Judy and Anne looked on silently as I walked from photograph to photograph, trying to take it all in. I felt a curious detachment as I scrutinized my work—the same sense of disconnection a writer must feel when he's first handed a finished copy of his new book. Did I really do all this? Could this actually be my handiwork? And surely it wasn't worth such attention. But I also felt that peculiar buzz of pleasure and terror that comes from knowing that, at long last, you have inched your way into the arena; that finally, you could be taken seriously as a practitioner of your craft. For years I had fantasized about this moment. Now that it was here, all I could think was: It's too bad Ben Bradford isn't around to enjoy it.

"Well . . . ?" Judy finally said.

"He might just have something as a photographer," I said.

"Yeah," Anne said, handing me a glass of wine, "he just might."

It was now five-thirty. There was no time to go home and change before the opening. So I sat at a cafe table with Anne, nervously guzzling glass after glass of cheap plonk. By six, I was working on my fifth tumbler of California Chablis.

"Go easy on that stuff," Anne said. "You'll fall on your face before seven."

"That's the idea," I said.

Stu Simmons and a gang from the newspaper were among the first guests to arrive. I staggered up from the table and joined them.

"Hope you're not going to abandon *The Montanan* now that you're famous," Stu said.

"I'm not famous," I said.

Dave from Petrie Cameras showed up, along with his wife, Beth, a petite woman in her thirties, wearing granny glasses and denim overalls.

"This is the elusive Gary Summers," Dave said, introducing us.

"Are we ever going to get you over for dinner?" Beth asked.

I never got to answer that question, as Judy pulled me away to meet Robin Nickell, the owner of a big gallery in Seattle.

"Love the work," Robin said. "And I know we'll be able to get you fantastic publicity when we open the show in September."

"You've taken the exhibition?" I said, thrown by this news.

Judy chimed in. "We just did the deal last night."

"The launch will be the first Monday after Labor Day," Robin said. "So keep that week free in your schedule to come to Seattle. We'll fly you over, put you up somewhere nice like the Four Seasons, and set up a bunch of interviews . . ."

"I'll have to check my diary," I said, accepting another glass of wine from one of the gallery assistants circulating with a tray.

"Gary Summers?"

I spun around and found myself facing a hefty, bearded man in a tweed jacket.

"I'm Gordon Craig, head of the fine-arts division over at the university. Wonderful show. Have you ever thought of doing some part-time lecturing?"

Anne saved me from answering that question, as she tapped my shoulder to make another introduction.

"Nick Hawthorne. *Time*'s man in San Francisco."

"Was out here doing a story in Kalispell, and thought I'd drive down for the opening," he said. "Your pictures made quite a splash back in New York. I'm sure the powers that be at the magazine are going to want more from you."

"That's nice to know," I said, gulping down my glass of wine. Anne gave me a stern look.

"If you've got some time tomorrow," Nick said, "I'd like to meet and put a proposition to you. I'm working on a travel book about the New American West and am looking for a photographer to collaborate with . . ."

Judy dragged me off to make small talk with some art dealer from Portland. I didn't catch her name, as the bad wine was finally deadening all cognitive faculties. There must have been over a hundred people now in the gallery. Their collective body heat and babble made me desperate for fresh air. But I kept being passed around from guest to guest, nodding moronically as another person pumped my hand and tried to engage me in small talk.

Anne eventually caught up with me again.

"You're drunk," she said.

"Just numb."

"Please switch to water now. There's still an hour to go; then Judy's taking us out to Le Petit Place. It would be nice if you could still string a sentence or two together at dinner."

"Let's get out of here," I said.

"Gary . . ."

"I've pressed enough flesh," I said, "now I want to press yours . . ."

"How romantic," she said dryly.

"C'mon, Anne . . ."

"It's your party, you've got to stay. Anyway, I know Judy wants to introduce you to Elliot Burden."

I was suddenly sober again. "Who?"

"Elliot Burden. You know, the big Wall Street guy who gave it all up to run a gallery in Soho?"

"He's here?"

"Just arrived a few minutes ago. Really nice guy. So nice he came all the way out to Mountain Falls to make a pitch for your exhibition. And he's here with his squeeze. Says she's a former neighbor of yours in Connecticut. Beth something . . ."

"Beth Bradford," I said, my voice barely a whisper.

"That's it," Anne said.

My eyes scanned the room. It took a second to spot them.

They were by the door, deep in conversation with Judy. Elliot Burden—tanned, lean, patrician in a blue blazer and flannels—was standing right next to Beth, her hand casually resting on his shoulder. She looked wonderful—stylishly dressed in a short black dress, her face no longer a mask of gaunt fatigue. She laughed at something Elliot said, then gave him that easy smile I remembered so well from our first years together. For a moment I couldn't move. But then Judy caught me staring their way and I executed an immediate about-face.

"What's wrong?" Anne said. "You've gone white."

"Just need some air . . ." I said and started moving toward the rear of the gallery.

"Hang on, I'll come—"

But I shrugged Anne off and began pushing my way through the crowd, my vision fixed on a back door.

"Gary!" Anne shouted.

Suddenly I heard the voice of my wife.

"Gary!" Beth said.

I froze for a moment, my back to her. Then I bolted for the door.

The door let into an office, now crowded with the staff who were catering the party. They seemed a little bemused as I scrambled past them, flung open the rear entrance to the gallery, and dashed out. Behind me I could still hear Anne calling out my name. So I sprinted up an alleyway, cut down a side street, and ran like hell for my apartment.

When I reached it, I tore up the stairs two at a time, then burst through my door.

I hadn't been home for ten days, and immediately knew something was wrong. A stench of cigarette smoke and flatulence defined the air. There were empty beer bottles and brimming ashtrays and half-eaten tins of baked beans strewn across the living-room floor. And there was the sound of running water from the bathroom. I kicked the door open and found myself staring at the very fleshy, very naked body of Rudolph Warren, standing under the shower.

"What the fuck are you doing here?" I shouted.

"Hi, Gary," he said, turning off the taps. "Have a good trip?"

"How'd you get in?"

"Had a key," he said, starting to towel himself off.

"You gave me back my key."

"Yeah, but I made a copy before—"

"You said you didn't make a copy . . ."

"I lied."

"Asshole. Aren't you supposed to be in Mexico?"

"Lied about that too. Needed some place to hole up, gather my thoughts. And since I knew you were going out of town—"

"Get the fuck out," I said, grabbing him by the arm. "And I mean now."

He yanked himself out of my grip.

"No need to play the heavy—"

I lost it, screaming, "I'll get as heavy as I fucking well—"

But my rant was interrupted by the repeated ringing of the intercom. I froze. It had to be Anne. Rudy moved toward the buzzer that opened the downstairs door.

"Don't answer that," I said.

"What's going on?"

"Just don't touch it."

We both stood still while the intercom buzzed continuously. After two minutes, it stopped. The blinds in the living room were drawn. I stood to one side of the window and peered out as Anne walked away from the apartment building, looked up and down Main Street in despair, then crossed over to a public telephone.

A few seconds later, my phone began to ring.

"Just leave it," I told Rudy. After five rings, the answering machine clicked into action. I turned the volume down to avoid hearing Anne's voice.

"You gonna tell me what's happening here?" Rudy asked.

"Eventually. Right now, I need you to get dressed."

"You've landed yourself in some shit, haven't you?"

"Maybe."

"Tell Uncle Rudy."

"Later."

"Babe trouble?" he said, grinning broadly to reveal blackened gums devoid of dentures.

"Where are your teeth?" I asked.

"They took 'em off me when I was checked into the hospital. And since I checked out without the doc's permission, the teeth didn't come with me."

"You've survived ten days without teeth?"

"Don't need chompers to eat cold baked beans. Glad you had a full larder, by the way, as I haven't exactly been out showing my face around town."

"I need a favor."

"Depends," he said, pulling on the last of his clothes.

"On what?"

"How much you tell me."

"It's babe trouble, okay?"

"That's kind of vague, Gary."

"I can't say more."

"Then I don't think I can help you—"

"Where are you going to sleep tonight?" I said angrily.

"Good question."

"You want this place for another week or so?"

"It would be helpful."

"Then take a fast walk over to MacDougal Alley and bring my car back here."

"That's kind of dangerous for me. I mean, I'm supposed to be south of the border."

"It's nearly dark—and if you take a couple of side streets and keep your head down, no one will see you. Anyway, everyone is still at my opening . . ."

"Ah," said Rudy, "some shit went down at the gallery."

I held up the car keys. "Either get the car or get out."

He grabbed the keys, then opened the cabinet where I kept my booze and removed a pint bottle of J&B.

"You don't need whiskey," I said.

"Oh yes I do," Rudy said, taking a long swig from the bottle. He flashed me a smile. "That's better. Ready for action. See you 'round the back in five."

Slipping the pint of J&B into his jacket pocket, he headed out the door.

As I hurriedly packed a small bag, a plan fell into my head. I'd drive east and hole up in some motel for a few days. To avoid Anne reporting me as a missing person, I'd call her tomorrow morning and explain that Beth had been the married woman with whom I'd been entangled—and the sight of her, coupled with the anxiety of the opening (and the two bottles of wine I'd consumed), had sent me into gagaland. I'd also beg forgiveness—and tell her that I'd be returning to Mountain Falls within a few days (when Beth and Elliot were safely back east). No doubt, she'd be furious—and might not even speak to me for a while—but dealing with her anger was a more palatable alternative to extradition to Connecticut, a very public trial, and an extended stint in a penitentiary. Thank Christ the gallery was so packed that Beth didn't catch sight of me until my back was turned. Now I just needed to get out of town. Immediately.

I glanced out the kitchen window and saw the MG drive up into the alleyway behind Frontier Apartments. I left the apartment and took the fire stairs down to the rear door. But when I reached the car, Rudy wouldn't move from the driver's seat, saying:

"I think I'll come along for the ride."

"No way," I said.

"You're a bit under the influence," he said.

"You've been drinking too."

"Not half as much as you. So you definitely need a driver."

I grabbed the door handle and tried to yank it open, yelling: "Get out of the car now, Rudy."

"Yell a little louder," Rudy said, "and you'll alert the entire town to your departure."

I ran around to the passenger door, climbed in. But as I attempted to reach over and pull the keys out of the ignition, Rudy gunned the engine and sped off down the alley, throwing me back in the seat.

"So where are we headed?" he asked.

"I should fucking kill you," I said.

"You mean, like you killed Gary Summers?"

I went rigid. For a moment or two I stopped breathing.

Rudy flashed me a dark smile.

"Thought that would shut you up. Now where are we going?"

I couldn't speak.

"Cat got your tongue? How 'bout I take Route 200 east?"

I managed a nod.

"East it is then," he said.

He used assorted back roads to get us out of Mountain Falls. By the time we reached Route 200, light had receded, and the high beams of the car illuminated the narrow, twisting road. He reached into his jacket pocket for the J&B, took a swig, then held the open bottle against the steering wheel. Half an hour went by before either of us spoke.

"How did you find out?" I finally said.

A low chuckle from Rudy Warren.

"If only you had a television in your apartment, I'd never have known. Gimme a boob tube, I can happily veg in front of it all day, never get bored. But as I was kind of confined to quarters, and got fed up with all your books and that highbrow shit on National Public Radio, I started to snoop. Go through your papers and stuff. I mean, how else was I gonna kill the hours? Anyway, one afternoon when I had nothing to do, I opened up your computer and started browsing through all the files. Found all those little love notes you wrote to that woman called B. Very touching, really. Then I stumbled upon that kiss-off letter you wrote her in December, telling her that you'd set up house with some babe in Berkeley. Only then I remembered that, around ten days before Christmas, I ran into that harpy Meg Greenwood on Main Street. She started giving me this big number about how I was a shit for fucking and shucking her, and then broadened her tirade into an 'all men are bastards' speech, telling me how she'd just let an apartment to a photographer guy from Connecticut, a real smoothie who talked her into a rent reduction by coming on as if he wanted to date her, but later fed her some jive about a girlfriend back east.

"Now when I recalled this little pre-Christmas encounter I kind of got to wondering: If Meg rented you the apartment in the middle of December, there's no way you could have been shacked up with some babe in Berkeley around the same time. So I figured there was probably some very good reason why you didn't want this B. woman back in Connecticut to know your new whereabouts.

"But later on, while going through a pile of stuff in your darkroom, I found the letter B. wrote you just a few weeks ago, saying how her husband died in November, how the body wasn't found, and how you were a major asshole for not sending her a condolence note. And when I saw your reply to her letter, I really had to agree with this B. babe. I mean, she pours her heart out to you, and what do you say? 'Heavy stuff.' I love a supportive guy.

"Anyway, when I started snooping around your other files, I noticed that, in the first part of November, you were kind of busy on the correspondence front, writing your bank and everyone, giving them this new address of yours in Berkeley. But, according to your letter to B. in December, you only decided to move to the Bay Area after you'd met some chick a few weeks earlier in Baja. And then I checked back on the last note you sent B. *before* heading west—where you told her you would just be gone for two weeks.

"Now this got me speculating about why you were so eager to shut down your life back east, even though you were only heading off on a two-week assignment. And I also couldn't help but note that your departure dovetailed rather neatly with the death of this Ben Bradford guy—whose wife you just happened to be screwing . . ."

He paused, took a long guzzle of J&B, and gave me another sardonic smile.

"Like the story so far?" he asked.

I stared ahead at the black road and said nothing.

"I'll take your silence as a yes. Anyway . . . I thought it might be interesting to learn a little more about the late Ben Bradford. But as I wasn't supposed to be in Mountain Falls, I couldn't exactly hit the local library and start searching through back copies of *The New York Times*. But I got lucky. Your IBM Thinkpad has a built-in modem and also comes pre-loaded with America Online software. And the little cord that goes from the computer into the telephone jack was still in its carrying case. So I plugged it in, found your Visa number and the card expiration date in your MONEYBIZ files—you really are very organized, aren't you?—and signed you up for the Internet.

"Then the fun really started. I surfed my way over to *The New York Times* and asked them to download everything they had on Ben Bradford. He was quite a little news story for around a week, wasn't he? Sadly, there was no picture of the guy with his obit, so I surfed my way to a bunch of eastern newspapers—*The Boston Globe, The Hartford Courant, The Wall Street Journal.* They all covered the story, but again, no pic. Finally I struck paydirt. The *Stamford Advocate*—his local news-paper. A huge page-three story about his death at sea. With a nice big photo of the late Mr. Bradford . . . who—despite your current scuzzy beard and ponytail—was still a dead ringer for you."

A final triumphant toothless grin. He raised the J&B bottle in mock salute, then gulped down another long shot. His words began to slur slightly.

"Game, set, and match, Ben. I can call you Ben now, I sup-pose."

My mind was racing. I gripped the door handle tightly.

"Pretty impressive detective work, don't you think?" Rudy said. "I mean, *I'm* impressed. Just as I'm also impressed with the way you set up your death and resurrection—though you are lucky the *Stamford Advocate* doesn't exactly have a nation-wide readership. And I presume Gary's was the body on the boat, right?"

"Why didn't you go to the police?" I asked.

"And spoil a secret? The *bond* we now have between us?

No way I'd be a stoolie. A Montana boy is always an anti-authoritarian redneck. Anyway, the guy was boning your missus . . ."

"So you've told no one?"

"I'm supposed to be in Tijuana, remember?"

"What do you want, then?"

He upended the whiskey bottle again. "Spoken like a true lawyer. Well . . . as a member of the New York bar, I'm sure you are familiar with the concept of quid pro quo?"

"Better known as blackmail."

"Or, in this case, the price of silence."

"So you want money?"

"You *are* fast on your feet."

"How much?"

"Terms and conditions to be worked out at a future date. Don't sweat it, pardner—I'm not going to be greedy. But, as you are about to come into some serious dough from your photos—and as I am in some serious debt—a significant sum will have to change hands. But, like I said, that's all in the near future. Meantime, you and I are gonna be hanging ten together, as I don't want you to be doing another vanishing act before this little matter between us is settled. Think we'll hole up for a couple of days at Ms. Ames's cabin."

"Then let me drive us there. You're getting dangerous with that whiskey."

"You ain't taking us nowhere. Anyway, I'm a pro when it comes to drunken driving."

A final long swig of J&B.

"Should be nice and quiet by the lake. No one around. Perfect place to, uh, hammer out a settlement."

"And after I've paid you off, then what?"

"We part friends."

"Until the next time you're up to your ass in debt and decide to hit me for another payment."

"You really think I'd do something as low as that?"

"Yes."

For a moment, he took his eyes off the road to glower at me.

"Put it this way. I ain't gonna be some nasty ole loan shark, knocking on your door in the middle of the night. But, yeah, part of the bond that now exists between us means that, in the event I am flat broke, I will expect you to play Benefactor, Good Samaritan, Sugar Daddy . . ."

My heart was thumping wildly.

"For how long?"

He turned to me again.

"Well . . . forever, I guess. Our bond, Ben—it's kind of a lifetime thing—"

He never got to finish that sentence, as we were suddenly blinded by the overpowering glare of headlights. I yelled "Rudy!" as I realized that an oncoming truck was headed directly for us. Rudy spun the wheel wildly, we dodged the truck, the MG veered sharply right and left the road, shooting down a steep embankment. I yanked open the passenger door and fell out just as the vehicle went airborne. My head slammed into the ground; a seismic jolt went running through my right knee and elbow as I rolled down the hill. A large rock ended my slide. As I slammed against it with my shoulder, there was the sound of a crash, followed by an explosive *whoosh*. I managed to peer over the rock and found myself staring into a deep valley, where the MG had landed and was now on fire. Within seconds, the gas tank ignited with a roar. Flames engulfed the vehicle, burning wildly—the heat so extreme that, even from where I lay, its intensity stung my face.

I tried to get up. It took some effort, but I finally made it to my feet. My vision was fogged. I started to stagger, thinking I must get help. Every step was agony. I forced myself to keep moving for around a hundred yards, finding myself in a dense grove of trees. Then, as if someone pulled a plug, the world went black and I pitched forward on my face.

Birdsong. Tentative shafts of light. A whiff of morning dew. And, in the near distance, the mechanized sound of a large vehicle.

I opened an eye. The world swam. After a moment, optical clarity was restored. Then the pain hit. My skull pulsated like an out-of-kilter metronome. My right arm appeared to be numb. There was a large, deep gash on my right knee. When I touched my face, my fingers turned crimson, smeared with blood.

I groaned. I rolled over on my back. I blinked with grogginess as the morning sun cleaved the night sky. The sound of clanging gears was more distinct now. I managed to ease myself over onto my left side and watched as the MG was winched up from the valley. A group of cops and road workers watched, emitting low whistles and shaking their heads as the remains of the vehicle reached the road. Whatever remained of Rudy must have already been removed from its interior. But judging by its skeletal, charred shell, little probably did. The MG had been incinerated beyond recognition.

I wanted to call out, attract someone's attention. But the world went dark again. And when I finally stirred, there was silence.

I glanced at my watch. Eight forty-five in the morning. Every muscle and joint in my body felt contused. Using a tree as support, I managed to stand upright. The cops and the road workers had gone. It took a moment to get my bearings. I was in a burnt-out wood, the remaining trees blackened and charred. I squinted into the valley where I'd almost met my death, and then remembered standing here several weeks earlier, snapping away as the fire raged below. I was back at the scene of my great professional triumph. Even in my concussed, battered state, the irony of it all hit home. And though I was on the verge of struggling up to the main road and flagging down the first car I could find, I hesitated. Beth might still be in Mountain Falls. There would be a predictable wave of local publicity about Rudy's death. The cops would question me endlessly about the accident. No—it was best to retreat somewhere for a while and consider my next move.

But where?

That's when I remembered that Rudy and I had been en route to Anne's cabin, and it was now only a mile down the road from here. It had survived the fire. It was stocked with food. It was the perfect hideout in which to recover and work out how I was going to explain away what happened.

Though my right knee was badly gashed, I was still able to hobble. I found a thick stick on the ground and, using it as a makeshift cane, I began the slow, aching hike to Anne's place. It took over two hours. I wobbled my way through the woods, frequently halting when the pain threatened to black me out again. But around five hundred yards before I reached the cabin, I was back under a green canopy of spring foliage—the line of demarcation, beyond which the fire hadn't crossed.

When I reached the cabin's front door, I fell inside and collapsed on the bed. I didn't move for around an hour. Eventually, I forced myself up, staggered over to the basket of wood, stoked up the stove, and set it alight. Rooting around the kitchen area, I found a first-aid kit and tended to my wounds, screaming loudly as I painted my knee and face and elbow with mercurochrome. When the stove was hot, I boiled four large pots of water, then dumped them all into the bath. I repeated the process twice over and ended up with a half-filled tub of hot water. Stripping off my tattered clothes, I lowered myself into the bath, wincing. I sat in the tub until the water went cold, shock undulating through me.

In a chest of drawers by the bed, I found a baggy pair of Anne's sweatpants and a large sweater that just about fit me. I had no appetite—except for alcohol—so I uncorked a bottle of red wine and drained four glasses before finally turning on the radio.

I managed to get the three o'clock news on some local rock station. Around five items in, the announcer said, "Police investigating the road death of Mountain Falls photographer Gary Summers . . ."

I choked on the wine and was so stunned that I didn't catch the rest of the item. Frantically I scanned the airways for another news broadcast—but, in the end, I had to wait until four o'clock to hear the item repeated . . . by which time I had finished one bottle of wine and was starting to drain another.

> Police investigating the road death of Mountain Falls photographer Gary Summers say he died last night on Route 200 after swerving to avoid an oncoming truck. According to Montana Highway Patrol spokesperson, Caleb Crew . . .

They jump-cut to a static-laden sound bite with Spokesperson Crew.

> . . . Mr. Summers's vehicle left the road just near the intersection with Route 83. The driver of the truck said that Mr. Summers was traveling at considerable speed, and ran off the road into Moose Lake Valley. That's a three-hundred-foot fall, and no one's going to walk away from a crash like that. The county medical examiner is now performing an autopsy, but I'm afraid the body was so badly burned in the fire that even dental records won't help with the identification.

It took a moment or two to sink in. Thanks to Rudy's lack of teeth, the badly charred body of a lush journalist had been mistaken for me. Then again, who else would have been in that MG but Gary Summers? He was last seen leaving his exhibition opening in a drunken, hyperanxious state ("A real attack of first-night nerves," I could hear Judy telling the investigating cop). His girlfriend checked his apartment, but found he wasn't home. The MG had vanished from the alley near the gallery where he'd parked it. The truck driver said he only saw one person in the MG (he should get his eyes checked out immediately). And in the matter of Rudy Warren, nobody would be looking for him, because he was supposed to be south of the border . . . and anyway, he had no one in his life who cared enough to question his whereabouts.

I was dead again.

I killed another glass of wine. I spun the dial of the radio, desperate for further news. But all I merited was a twenty-second item during the local news segment of NPR's *All Things Considered*, which essentially reiterated the facts of the incident.

I couldn't sleep that night. I couldn't get drunk either, even though I was starting on my third bottle of red by the time dawn had emerged. I kept pacing the cabin, trying to figure some way back to the land of the living. I can't be dead, I kept telling myself. Things were just starting to happen for me.

At seven, I turned on NPR and listened to *Weekend Edition* while making myself breakfast. There was nothing further about my death on the local news segment—but around an hour into the program, the *Weekend Edition* anchor in Washington made me spill my coffee when he began a new item:

> For an established artist, death in one's prime is the most romantic of finales—the premature swan song that makes those left behind mourn the loss of future great work. But there is something even more poignant about the death of an artist who—after years of struggle—passes away just as he is poised for a major breakthrough. As Lucy Champlain of member station KGPC in Mountain Falls, Montana, reports, the story of photographer Gary Summers is a tale of a major talent who died on the day he finally achieved something he'd struggled for years to attain: recognition.

Lucy Champlain came on the air. She sounded around thirty and had the sort of earnest voice that public radio stations favor.

> Up until a few weeks ago—when his first photograph appeared in *The Montanan*—nobody had ever heard of Gary Summers. He was a photographer in his late thirties from Connecticut who had recently settled in the town of Mountain Falls, Montana; a freelancer who had struggled for years to make a name for himself in New York, but who had only started to gain notice for his work when he came to Montana. According to Stuart Simmons, the editor of *The Montanan* . . .

Stu broke in here, his voice subdued.

I first met Gary after several of his pictures came to the attention of our photo editor, Anne Ames. And from the moment Anne and I saw these portraits of ordinary Montanans, we both knew that we had stumbled on a major talent.

Lucy Champlain picked up the narrative again.

Shortly after *The Montanan* began to publish Summers's portraits, he found himself caught up in the fire that devastated much of the Moose Lake Forest Reserve—one of the largest timberlands in the state. And his remarkable pictures of the firefighters in action—most notably, one showing a fire chief kneeling over the body of one of his colleagues—won him national recognition, including a prestigious spread in *Time*. Judy Wilmers—the owner of the New West Gallery in Mountain Falls and a personal friend of Summers—remembers how diffident the photographer was about his sudden success . . .

Judy was now being interviewed. She was unusually somber.

I think Gary had dwelt in obscurity for so long that, when he found himself in demand as a photographer, he found it all a bit overwhelming. And though he accepted two commissions from *National Geographic* and *Vanity Fair*, his real concern was his upcoming "Montana Faces" exhibition at my gallery . . .

Back to Lucy Champlain.

That exhibition opened two nights ago, to fantastic acclaim in a state where outsiders are often regarded with suspicion—especially those who dare to cast their own eye on things Montanan. But halfway through the opening party, Summers abruptly left . . .

Over again to Judy.

The party was packed and Gary—who was never the world's most sociable guy—must have found all the attention a little overwhelming, because he told a friend he was stepping out for some air. I wish to God he'd stayed put . . .

Back to Lucy Champlain.

Around an hour later, Summers was driving down Route 200—a notoriously treacherous road that snakes its way through the Rockies and across the Continental Divide. It was late, visibility was not good, and when he turned a corner, he found himself in the path of a large heavy-goods vehicle. Swerving to avoid it, he lost control of his own car and plunged off the road into the same heavily wooded valley where he'd taken some of his most memorable shots of firefighters at work. He did not survive the crash . . .

A final valedictory comment from Judy Wilmers. She sounded close to tears.

It's not just a senseless tragedy, it's also the most appalling loss. Because from the small body of work that he left behind, it's very clear that Gary Summers was on the verge of becoming one of the great American photographers of his generation. And now that promise will never be fulfilled . . .

I put my head in my hands. And thought: I really will be famous now. Posthumously.

There was no way out. Even if I did suddenly show up alive and well in Mountain Falls, the photographers would descend and my picture would be in every paper across the country.

I didn't know what to do. Except run. But where could I run to? And how would I finance my getaway? I checked my wallet. I only had eighty dollars in cash. Granted, I still had a bunch of bank and credit cards, and I had memorized all the ATM numbers. But from my knowledge of trusts and estates, I knew that Chemical Bank and assorted card companies would freeze Gary's assets as soon as they learned of his demise. Thankfully, today was Saturday—which meant that, even if someone in the bank had heard the story on NPR, they probably wouldn't place a stop order on the accounts until the start of business on Monday.

If I could somehow get out of here today—and make my way to a town—I'd be able to draw up to $2,000 on the four cards. I could make the same withdrawal on Sunday and then possibly snatch another $2,000 in the early hours of Monday—before the banks opened in New York. Six thousand bucks would give me enough cash to disappear and work up a new identity.

There was a problem, however. The nearest large town was Helena—at least seventy miles down some very vertiginous roads. My knee was still in bad shape. Even walking back to Route 200 would be an arduous task in my current hobbled state.

I stepped outside the cabin and tottered my way down to the edge of the lake, filling my lungs with fresh air, testing my bum knee to see if it might get me to the main road, whereupon I could thumb a ride to Helena.

Then I saw the campers. A young couple in their twenties, with one of those ancient VW microbuses that recalled my college days in the seventies. I noticed with relief that it had Washington plates. They were parked around a hundred yards from where I stood. They had a small tent pitched by the rear of the bus and were currently cooking breakfast on a little camper stove. As I approached them, I could see that they were well-scrubbed Eddie Bauer types—blonde, flannel-shirted, a little startled to see some scratched-up wreck of a guy limping toward them. They were both on their feet immediately. From their tense expressions, it was clear that they feared I might be the friendly local serial killer.

"Howdy," I shouted as I walked over. "Sorry to disturb you."

"That's all right," the guy said, but the expression on his face let it be known that I was anything but all right.

"Name's Dave Manning," I said. "Staying over at the cabin there. Friend of mine's place. Listen, I had a helluva bad accident yesterday evening on my mountain bike. Hit a real bad pothole on the road into here, threw me right into a tree."

"Ouch," the woman said. "You all right?"

"Better than the bike, which is now kind of bent out of shape. Where you guys from?"

"Seattle," the guy said.

"Vacationing?" I asked.

"Sort of," the guy said. "Just finished exams. We're grad students at U. Washington. Department of botany."

"You've come to the right place for that."

The woman said, "We're Howie and Peggy. You need a doctor or something?"

"Well, what I could eventually use is a ride back to Helena. My friend dropped me and my bike here on Thursday, but she's not due back to join me until Tuesday—and I really think I should get this knee checked out before then. You wouldn't have a mobile phone by any chance, would you?"

I gambled on them not possessing one. I gambled right.

"Not our style," Howie said. "But listen, we were kind of thinking of staying here until around two this afternoon, then we were planning to head down Bozeman way."

"Helena's on the way, if you wouldn't mind . . ."

They looked at each other, and I could see that they were weighing whether or not I might be an admirer of Jeffrey Dahmer. Eventually the guy shrugged and said: "Okay by us, if you don't mind sitting on the floor in the back."

"No sweat. You'll be doing me a big favor."

"We'll knock on your door at two, then," Peggy said.

"Can't thank you enough," I said and staggered back to the cabin.

My relief was huge. At least I'd found a way out of this nowhere hole. I would get to Helena by five. I'd hit the bank machines, buy some new clothes, then find the bus depot and grab the first Greyhound heading east. By midday tomorrow, I'd land somewhere like Bismarck, North Dakota—a midsized city with plenty of ATMs. Another quick run on my cards, a night in a hotel, a four A.M. wake-up call on Monday morning, a final series of withdrawals, then I'd dump the wallet and Greyhound it south to somewhere nice and large and anonymous. Dallas, perhaps. Or Houston. Six grand should buy me two months or so—and some clean documentation, with which to start . . .

What? A new life?

I didn't want to think about that. Or about the loss of my two former lives. Or the fact that I would never, ever see Anne Ames again. And how my death would bring her to grief yet again. And how—along with Adam and Josh—I would mourn her every hour of every day.

All I wanted to think about now was sleep. Something I hadn't experienced for two nights. Something I needed urgently if I were to remain lucid for the rest of the day. So, as soon as I reached the cabin, I wound up the old alarm clock by the bed and set it for one-thirty. Four hours of shut-eye wouldn't leave me feeling reborn, but it would have to do.

I stretched out on the bed and was comatose within seconds. I fell deep into a black netherland and stayed there for hours. Until I heard a vehicle pull up outside the cabin and footsteps approach the front door. Stirring awake, I squinted at the clock. Twelve-fifteen. The botanists must have decided to leave early. Fine by me. I sat up in bed, rubbed my eyes, and then heard a scream.

A loud, piercing scream—followed by silence.

Anne was at the door, her mouth opened in shock. She looked exhausted, gaunt, her eyes so red it was clear she had been crying for the past two days.

We stared at each other for a very long time.

And then I started to talk.

10

I TOLD HER EVERYTHING.

She remained standing while I talked, one foot in the door, as if ready to flee at any moment. When I got to the bit about killing Gary, I could actually feel her shudder—even though she was six feet from me. I spared her some of the more gruesome details, but she sucked in her breath as I explained about the fire aboard Bill's boat. And after telling her about Rudy's blackmail threats, she finally spoke.

"Did you kill him too?"

"No," I said. "The accident happened as reported. Only he was driving. And drunk. I managed to get out before . . ."

"Why should I believe that?" she said, her voice shaky. "Why should I believe any of this? Your whole life out here—*with me* —was a lie."

"Being with you was never a lie. Never."

"I don't believe you. I *can't* believe you."

I didn't know what to say. So I said nothing.

"The last two days . . ." she said, her voice barely audible, ". . . I really thought about killing myself. First Charlie, then you. You think you'll never survive the death of a baby. Finally you meet someone who makes you think there may be a way to live with the pain. And then . . ."

She broke off and started to sob. I was on my feet, approaching her.

"No!" she said, putting two hands up to ward me off.

I backed away and sat down on the bed again. Her sobbing subsided.

"You know, the only reason I came up here today," she said, "was because I couldn't stand all the sympathy . . . the pitying glances . . . because I had to get away from everyone in town . . . because it was here that I knew I loved . . ."

She shook her head violently, as if trying to expunge that last sentence.

"And now . . . now I wish to fuck I'd delayed a day. Because you would have been gone, wouldn't you? And I would never have known. You *are* going, aren't you?"

I nodded.

"How?"

"There's a couple camping a few hundred yards from here. They said they'd give me a lift to Helena."

"How did you explain away your injuries?"

"Biking accident."

"Another lie. And when you get to Helena?"

"I'll disappear."

"And that's what you want?"

"I don't have much choice. The cops . . ."

"You're dead, remember? How will they know?"

"You."

A long silence. I broke it.

"You are going to tell them, aren't you?"

She stared at the floor.

"I don't know."

Another silence. This time she ended it.

"I have to go," she said. "I can't stay here."

"Will you be back?" I asked.

"I'm not sure," she said. "Will you go today?"

"I don't want to."

She shrugged. "Your call, Gar—"

She cut herself off.

"I don't even know what to call you anymore."

She turned and left. A moment later, I heard her car door close, the engine turn over, the vehicle pull away. I lay back on the bed. I didn't move. A half hour passed. Then a knock came on the door. Howie poked his head in.

"Ready to roll?" he asked.

"My friend just showed up."

"Yeah, I saw the car."

"Anyway, she's coming back later—so I think I won't need that lift."

"That knee of yours going to be okay?"

"I'll live," I said. "Thanks anyway."

After I heard the botanists drive away, I got up. I boiled water for a bath. I had an hour-long soak. I hobbled down to the lake and watched the sun set. I lit the lamps in the cabin. I made a simple pasta with tomato sauce. I drank a bottle of wine. And though I fully expected this to be my last night ever of freedom, I felt an eerie calm. I had confessed. The secret was no longer mine. I would always live with the guilt, the shame. But at least the burden of the lie had lifted. And I slept well.

At ten the next morning, I heard a car rumble down the dirt track. I sat on the edge of the bed, awaiting the entrance of uniformed officers. But Anne walked in alone.

"You didn't leave," she said.

"No."

"Why?" she asked.

"You."

"I see."

"You didn't go to the police," I said.

"No."

"Why?"

She shrugged.

"You're being buried tomorrow," she said. "The coroner released the body. They didn't find any relatives back east, so you'll be staying in Montana."

"Will you be going to the funeral?"

"Of course. So will Beth. She's still in town."

"Who's looking after the kids?" I instantly asked.

Anne let out a sigh. "Her sister Lucy is looking after them. Beth showed me a picture of them. They're beautiful boys."

"Yes," I said, "they are."

"She's very upset, Beth. First Ben, then Gary. Or have I got that the wrong way around? Anyway, we had a drink last night at her hotel, after Elliot had gone to bed. She told me a little about her affair with Gary. And about her marriage to you. You know what I thought after she finished? I would never have gotten involved with that Gary . . . and I would never have married that Ben."

She shook her head, then looked me squarely in the eye.

"I'm pregnant. And I'm keeping it."

I tried to reach for her—to gather her in my arms—but she pushed me away.

"I'll repeat what I just said: I am pregnant. I am keeping it. But that doesn't mean I am also keeping you."

She moved toward the door.

"I'll be back in a few days. After your funeral. If you're still here, we'll talk again."

She returned on Tuesday evening. She brought me a pile of newspapers and magazines.

"You got great coverage," she said.

There was half a page of funeral photos in *The Montanan*, as well as an editorial signed by Stu, lamenting my loss. *The New York Times* ran a ten-paragraph story about Gary Summers in their "National News" section. So too did the *LA Times*, the *Chicago Tribune*, *The Boston Globe*, the *San Francisco Examiner*, and the *Seattle Post-Intelligencer*.

"According to Judy, the phone hasn't stopped ringing at the gallery," Anne said. "Judy told me some staff writer at *The New Yorker* has been assigned to write a lengthy piece. It looks like Random House is ready to pay $70,000 for the 'Montana Faces' book. And a bunch of Hollywood agents were on. They seem to think your life and tragic death would make a good movie. One of them actually called on behalf of Robert Redford. Guess he has this thing about Montana . . ."

I pushed the papers away. She knew what I was thinking.

"You never changed his will, did you?" Anne asked.

"No," I said. "I didn't."

"That's what you used to do—write wills?"

"Yes, that was my job."

"And who will benefit from his famous death?"

"Bard College."

"They'll get everything?"

"Yeah—the works. The house in New Croydon. The trust fund. All future royalties from his work—except, that is, what's due in commission to Judy. She'll do very well out of this too."

"Great," Anne said. "Just great."

"I didn't think I'd be dead so fast."

"Clearly."

She handed me a shopping bag. "Anyway . . . I stopped at the Kmart on the way out of town and picked you up some new clothes."

"Thanks."

"Meg Greenwood asked if I'd help clean out your apartment tomorrow. I'm going to give everything to Goodwill, if that's okay?"

"How about my pictures?"

"Judy seems to think she's legally entitled to all the negatives. Is she?"

"I suppose so. There was a contract . . ."

"So forget the pictures."

"Can you keep the laptop?"

"Don't see why not."

"Then, as soon as you've got it home, wipe the hard disc. It contains . . ."

"Evidence?"

"Yes."

"You're asking me to be an accomplice."

"You can still go to the cops."

"Yes," she said. "I can. Anything else you want from the apartment?"

"Rudy's typewriter. I'm pretty sure he left it there."

"Why do you need it?"

"Rudy has to send a letter of resignation to Stu. From Mexico."

"I don't know if I want to be a part of all this," she said.

"Then don't be. Turn me in."

She was gone for four days. When she arrived on Saturday, she was carrying Rudy's old portable Olivetti. And more magazines.

"How are you feeling?" I asked.

"I wake up every morning and get sick. Just like with Charlie."

She handed me the periodicals.

"You made the 'Milestones' column of *Time*," Anne said. "*Variety* ran a piece about the film interest in your story. And the guy from *The New Yorker*—Grey Godfrey, I think his name is—has hit town and is interviewing everyone."

"Will you talk to him?"

"No—but I know he's going to hassle me until I give in. So I'm going to disappear for a while."

"Where to?"

"L.A. I have old friends there. I'll probably be gone a week, ten days. You have enough to see you through here?"

"I'll be fine."

"That is—if you're still here when I get back."

"I'll be here," I said.

"We'll see," she said.

On the morning before she left for L.A., she said, "I don't know how you live with it."

"Like you live with any grief," I said. "You just do. I didn't mean to kill Gary."

"But you did."

"It was . . . a moment. One terrible moment."

"You can't excuse it away."

"I know. And I don't. And I should have gone to the police. But I panicked."

"You thought you could get away with it. And you did."

"And I met you."

She frowned.

"Big deal," she said.

Before she left, I handed her the letter I wrote on Rudy's typewriter—a rambling letter addressed to Stu Simmons, in which Rudy resigned from *The Montanan,* saying that he had now taken up residence in the Baja California city of Ensenada and saw no reason why he should return to eight-month winters and a newspaper where it was considered a capital offense to spit on the floor. I'd read enough of Rudy's columns to mimic his blowhard style. Anne studied it carefully and thought Stu would buy it. She also agreed to take a day trip to Tijuana and mail it from there.

She was gone eleven days. When she arrived back at the cabin, she looked rested.

"I've just given notice at *The Montanan,*" she said. "And I've just asked Meg to let my house."

This took me aback. "Why?"

"Because my friends in L.A. introduced me to some of their friends who introduced me to a guy named Joel Schmidt, who happens to run one of the biggest photo agencies in the country. And he offered me a job—as his number two. Seventy-five grand a year. I accepted."

"Oh."

"You sound surprised."

"I thought you loved it here."

"My child died here. You died here. I would not use the word 'love' when describing my relationship with Montana."

"You think you can live in L.A.?"

"Yes. I do. Could you?"

"You want me to come?"

"I'm still not sure. But . . ."

She touched her stomach.

". . . this child will need someone to look after him during the day while I'm at work. So . . ."

"That's the offer?"

"Yes," she said. "That's the offer."

I accepted it.

"We're going to have to find you a new name," she said.

I told her what to do. Within a week—after trawling through the death notices in the 1960 back editions of *The Montanan*—she found one for a four-year-old boy named Andrew Tarbell who drowned while on a family vacation in Mexico. After further checking, she discovered that, back then, death certificates of Montanans who died abroad were never lodged with the Montana Vital Records Office. Then she contacted the Alternative Post Office in Berkeley and said that she was calling on behalf of an Andrew Tarbell who wanted to avail himself of their mail-drop facilities. She also informed them that any mail they redirected should not contain his name on the envelope—only the number of the post office box that Anne had recently rented in Mountain Falls.

Then I drafted a letter to the vital records office, saying I was Andrew Tarbell, giving my date and place of birth, and requesting a replacement birth certificate. This letter was dispatched to those Alternative folk in Berkeley who, in turn, mailed it back to Montana. In due course, an official form arrived in Berkeley and was forwarded to Anne's post office box. The form required Andrew Tarbell's date of birth and the first names of his parents. That was no problem, as all this information was listed in his obituary in *The Montanan*. It also required a xeroxed copy of some sort of picture ID. At first, this looked like an insurmountable problem—until I suggested that Anne make another call to the Alternative Post Office in Berkeley. "Sure, we do fake ID," the guy at the post office told her, "for a price." Anne borrowed a Polaroid from the newspaper and bought a special film cartridge used for passport photos. Dropping by the cabin one evening, she shot my portrait, then sent the two-by-two-inch photo on to Berkeley and wired them the $300 fee they demanded (fake identification doesn't come cheap). Within a week, a laminated picture ID arrived in Anne's post office box—a very official-looking piece of documentation from a place called

Stockton Junior College. Beneath my mug shot were the words:

ANDREW TARBELL
FACULTY

The card also contained Tarbell's date of birth. Anne made a photocopy of the ID card and—enclosing it with the completed application form—rerouted it via California back to the vital records office in Helena. Around ten days later a replacement birth certificate for a thirty-nine-year-old white male named Andrew Tarbell ended up in my hands.

Anne made several trips to Los Angeles while I was awaiting the arrival of my new identity. She decided that—as I needed to maintain a nonexistent profile—it was best if we didn't live anywhere too beau monde–ish like West Hollywood or Santa Monica, as I might just stumble across some former Wall Street crony in such pleasanter parts of town. So she rented us a house in the Valley. Specifically, in Van Nuys.

"I have to warn you," she said on one of her infrequent visits to the cabin, "Van Nuys is a real suburban wasteland. And the house is your standard three-bed ranch job. But you'll adjust."

After her life was closed down in Mountain Falls—and her house was rented fully furnished—she arrived one evening at the cabin and announced: "Okay. We're off."

Before we left that night, she got me to fit a hinge and a padlock to the front door. And I cleaned out the stove and laid wood for the fire we'd light whenever we returned. But I knew that we'd never be seeing this cabin again.

And then, under cover of darkness, Anne smuggled me out of Montana. It took us four days to reach Los Angeles. On the second night—in a motel in Winnemucca, Nevada— she let me make love to her. Afterward, as I lay next to her, I lost it completely and started to cry. I didn't stop for ten minutes. She kept her back to me until I finally calmed down. Then she turned over and said:

"You'll live. We'll live. It will work out."

Anne was right: Van Nuys was the ultimate suburban night-mare. And the house was Early Nothing. But we lived. She started her job. I spent my days stripping floorboards and covering floral wallpaper with white emulsion. Though I had to give a skeptical civil servant some bullshit story about being taken overseas by my parents as a teenager and only recently returning to the States, I still managed to obtain an all necessary Social Security card. A driver's license followed. And after we got married at the Van Nuys registry office that November, Anne got used to calling me Andy. She didn't take my name.

On February 2, 1996, our son, Jack, was born. For both of us, it was love at first sight—though his presence in the house accentuated my longing for Adam and Josh. Around the same time, I read an announcement in *The New York Times* reporting the marriage of Elliot Burden and the former Beth Bradford. I lay awake for several nights, wondering if Adam and Josh would take his name, and were now calling Elliot "Daddy."

Jack was weaned within five weeks. Anne returned to work, and I assumed the duties of full-time househusband. Her job was exceedingly pressured—well, it was the third-largest photo agency in America—so I dealt with most of the night feeds, in addition to looking after him all day and running the domestic business of the home.

And meanwhile, the late Gary Summers lurked everywhere. The Random House edition of *Montana Faces* was well reviewed. The rights of the Grey Godfrey story in *The New Yorker*—"Death of an Emerging Lensman"—were sold to Robert Redford's production company in an undisclosed six-figure deal. According to Anne—who reads the trade papers at work—there was talk of George Clooney being interested in the role of Gary, but that was six months ago. Even if it does get made, I doubt if I'll see it. Just as I refused to read *The New Yorker* story. My name is Andrew Tarbell now. Why should I be interested in some dead photographer named Gary Summers?

Still, later that year, I did start taking pictures again. With her Christmas bonus, Anne treated me to a spiffy new Nikon.

And once we hired a baby-sitter to look after Jack in the afternoon, I began wandering the Valley, putting together a portfolio of suburban Angelino portraits. Anne thought them terribly accomplished—and technically more mature than my Montana work. But when I sent them out to the same photo editors who were chasing Gary, they all came back with rejection notes. In the professional photographic world, the name Andrew Tarbell meant nothing. He was a nobody, living in a nowhere corner of L.A.

Anne was even more upset than I was about this slew of rejections.

"You will get there again," she assured me. "You do have it. You'll always have it."

"I don't know anymore."

"It will work out," she said, stroking my hair. "Like we've worked out."

I suppose our life together really has worked out. Marriage is all about rhythm—and we have a nice one going. We love our son. We enjoy each other's company. We seem to avoid pettiness. We rarely bicker. We do get along. And though the Gary business is always there—hovering over us like a toxic cloud that could suddenly descend and poison everything—so far we've managed to keep it at bay.

Of course, there are many days when I stare out at the Valley and feel as if I am living in a ghastly cosmic joke. Just as there are nights when I replay that split second in Gary's basement and wonder where I would be now if I hadn't reached for that bottle.

At least, that old urge to run away—to flee domestic entrapment—has dissipated. Because when you've died twice and come back again, where can you run to anymore?

Still, urges never die, they simply lie dormant. And just last week—on the night that Adam was somewhere in Connecticut or New York, celebrating his birthday—I left the house around eight, telling Anne I was going to pick up a six-pack of beer at the local 7-Eleven. But as soon as I edged out of our cul-de-sac, I was bound for the highway. Numbers, numbers. The 101 brings you to the 10. The 10 to the 15. And before I had a chance to think about what I was doing, I was edging into the Mojave Desert, bypassing Barstow, heading across the Soda Mountains, making a beeline for the Nevada border.

I hit Vegas by two. With any luck I'd be in Salt Lake City by ten. And then? And then? I kept asking myself that question. But I couldn't come up with an answer. Maybe because the only real destination on the road is home.

A fast exit off the eastbound 15. A fast entrance onto the westbound 15. Dawn over the Mojave. Early morning traffic on the 10. A bad tailback on the 101. And I was back in Van Nuys just as the sun had reached full altitude. It was another perfect day in the Valley.

I pulled into the cul-de-sac. I parked in the driveway. Our front door opened. Anne stepped out into the sunshine, cradling Jack in her arms. She looked as if she hadn't slept. But she didn't glower; she didn't raise her voice. In fact, she didn't say a word. She just gave me a tired smile and a tired shrug, as if to say: *I know, I know . . . but this is it.*

And then Jack looked my way and waved his arms.

"Daddy, Daddy."

I was being called. This is it.